SYNTHESIZER EVOLUTION

FROM ANALOGUE TO DIGITAL (AND BACK)

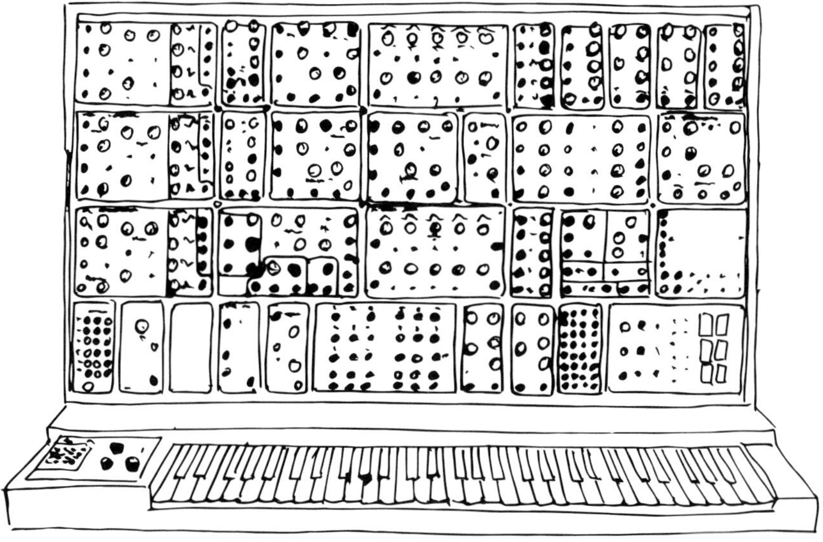

OLI FREKE

For:

M M
M F

BIOGRAPHY

Oli Freke is a London based musician, artist and author who has had a life-long passion for analogue synthesizers and electronic music. He has spent twenty years in the music industry, variously supporting the Human League on tour with his electro band Cassette Electrik, writing music for television and recently seeing success with a string of dance tracks. His Synth Evolution posters, launched in 2017, have become a popular product among synth fans and he was commissioned to produce a version for the London Design Museum's exhibition, *Electronic - from Kraftwerk to The Chemical Brothers* in 2020.

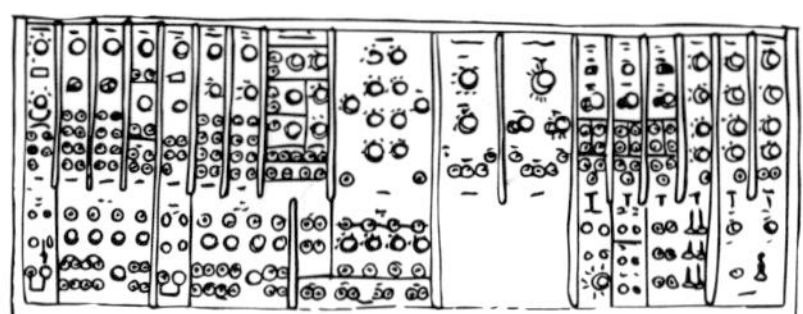

Moog System 35 1973
Analogue
Mono / 5 VCOs

First published by Velocity Press 2020

velocitypress.uk
synthevolution.net

All illustrations
Oli Freke

Cover design
Meg Mackintosh

Typesetting
Paul Baillie-Lane
pblpublishing.co.uk

ISBN: 9781913231064

CONTENTS

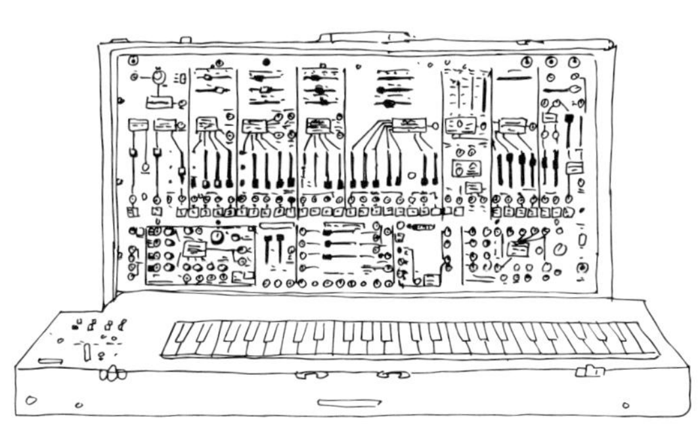

ARP 2600 1971
Analogue
Mono / 3 VCOs

PREFACE

A schoolboy, a school library and a book. The school was my secondary school, and the library book was Keyfax II by Julian Colbeck. For what seemed like every lunchtime, my friend Rafael and I would pore over the pages of Keyfax II and Keyfax III. Why? Because within its pages were the details of all the synthesizers of our dreams. Not having actual access to any of these instruments, all we could do was admire the futuristic designs and names of these machines, compare the technical specifications and absorb all the evocative and arcane terminology of ADSRs, filters, LFOs, VCOs and the rest.

And because we loved the electronic music of Jarre, Vangelis, Depeche Mode, Kraftwerk - and even hi-energy Polish space-disco - knowing that these were the machines responsible, gave them an impossible romance and mystique.

Synths that had 'real' names carried promise and mystery - Jupiter, Mirage, Odyssey, Quadra; those comprised of alphanumeric combinations were arcane and enigmatic - MKS-80, DX7, D-50, MS-20. Some were the size of fridges; some were the size of a mouse mat; all were beguiling, fascinating and compelling.

Catching glimpses of them on Top of the Pops was a thrill - what did those sliders do? How were the sounds carved out in real-time? How did they work when they weren't even plugged in??

In the (over) quarter-century since then, Rafael has gone on to be the head of sound design for a leading keyboard manufacturer and has worked on several Hollywood films. I've supported the Human League on tour, been a part of the London dance scene and composed music for television. And we've both been lucky enough to access and own some of those instruments that seemed so remote to us back in the 1980s.

Latterly, I found myself designing a poster featuring all those classic synthesizers. I became fascinated by the story of how synthesizers were once vast telephone exchanges of patch cables and knobs, but then became sleek digital slabs of plastic and modern electronics. I felt this needed to be represented by hand-drawn illustrations to focus the attention on the appearance and evolution of these machines. The project has been met with enthusiasm by those in the know, and also led to a commission from the Design Museum for their 2020 exhibition, 'Electronic - from Kraftwerk to The Chemical Brothers'.

And now I can close this particular loop by offering back to the world a new directory of 'all the synths', which is a tribute to the book I loved in my teens and a celebration of these magical machines that changed the face of music, and my life, forever.

Oli Freke

Buchla 400 1982
Analogue / FM
6 note polyphony

INTRODUCTION

The synthesizer has revolutionised music and culture over the last sixty years, and this book sets out to celebrate that impact. The modern transistor-based synthesizer arrived in the form of the analogue modular systems of Don Buchla and Robert Moog in the early 1960s. Since then, they've evolved dramatically with each new generation of technology, while also maintaining a direct connection and lineage to those earliest machines.

Synthesizers have had a futuristic appeal from the start - their appearance clearly expressing the latest technological advances of the time and their sound exploring sonic territory previously unimaginable. Once Wendy Carlos had demonstrated their validity as true musical instruments with *Switched-On Bach* in 1968, their influence on musical culture accelerated.

Pre-modern electronic instruments

Before the invention of the transistor, the evolution of electronic instruments was slow. Despite the technological advances of the 20th century, most of the early successful 'electrical' instruments were electromechanical rather than purely electronic. The electric piano was invented in the 1930s and amplified a vibrating tine via an electrostatic pick-up. The tone-wheel electric organ was invented by Laurens Hammond in 1935 and is based on rotating a disk within a magnetic field. These were obviously successful instruments, but are not purely electronic in the manner of the modern synthesizer.

Early electronic means of sound generation were the more authentic heirs of the modern synthesizer, and several different methods have been tried over the centuries. The very earliest date from the modern discovery of electricity in the 1600s. For example, the clavecin électrique (1759) was a simple bell ringing instrument, much like a set of tuned alarm-bells, and was driven by a capacitor-like Lieden jar. The Telharmonium of the 1890s was an extraordinary 200-ton device that could play its music down the new telephone lines to its New York subscribers. Its size and weight were due to the high voltages needed to generate audio tones from its primitive 'oscillators'.

Proto-synthesizers

Following these early experiments, the first really useable electronic instruments were made possible with the invention of the electronic valve in the 1900s - the vacuum-tube diodes, triodes, and thermionic tubes that enabled the construction of early electronic instruments. These often exploited the 'heterodyne effect' of small frequency differences between two very high-frequency sources. (The output of a tube with a radio frequency of 500kHz combined with another at 498kHz will produce a resulting beat-frequency in the audio range of 2kHz.)

The audion piano (1915), Theremin (1922), and ondes Martenot (1928) all used this technique. Whilst not entirely changing the face of music, they had their adherents - the ondes Martenot was used by Oliver Messiaen, Maurice Ravel and Edgard Varèse in several works, and the Theremin found a niche in sci-fi films and special effects, after its initial 'sensation' phase captured people's attention with its futuristic non-touch control mechanism.

It was the Hammond Novachord (1939) that can be considered the first true synthesizer. Its 160 vacuum-tubes and 1,000 capacitors comprised actual audio oscillators, and the instrument had full polyphony. It even offered some basic tone control and an envelope generator.

However, to build an electronic circuit to do anything more complicated than generating a simple tone, a large number of these early electronic components was required. Thus the expense and complexity meant this first generation of synthesizers were the exclusive preserve of large corporations, institutions and universities. Only they could afford the components to build them, and the engineers to run and program them. Examples include the RCA MkI and MkII synthesizers at the Columbia-Princeton Electronic Music Center (1951), the BBC Radiophonic Workshop (1958), Bell Labs 'Alles' synthesizer (1970s), and the IRCAM research institute in Paris (1977). The RCA machine was the first to be referred to by the new word 'synthesizer'.

A problematic limitation of these large machines was that they tended not to be playable in 'real-time' and needed laborious programming to extract sounds and music from them. The RCA MkII, for example, was only programmable by punchcard. This limited the performance options and replaying recordings on tape (and sometimes vinyl) was the only way for an audience to experience these works.

Although these appealed to the sound researcher and the academic musician, the resulting music was too experimental and too limited in its dispersal to make much impression on the prevailing musical culture of the time.

A notable exception to this, however, was to be found in national broadcasters with their well-funded R&D departments. These institutions experimented with the nascent synthesizers and tape-manipulation techniques in their in-house music production studios.

In this way, electronic music started to be heard more widely by the public, through such programmes as the BBC's Dr Who in the 1960s (thanks to their Radiophonic Workshop), and in the advertisement music of Raymond Scott in the United States, who had set up Manhattan Research Inc. in the 1950s. Germany also had the Studio for Electronic Music (WDR) and Italy the Studio di Fonologia Musicale (Studio of Musical Phonology), both associated with their respective national broadcasters.

Electronic music then, during the 1950s and 1960s was having some effect on the culture, but it was either fairly superficial or, by contrast, too esoteric. There were the novelty records such as The Tornados' 'TelStar' (1962) which used the clavioline, a proto-synthesizer; and academic researchers working on their laboratory machines - such as Charles Wuorinen at RCA who won the 1970 Pulitzer Prize for Music for his composition, 'Time's Encomium'. But this was not a piece of music many of the public would have heard.

A more significant niche for electronic music was found in the science-fiction soundtracks of the 1950s and 1960s, due to its literally alien sounds. This led to the now clichéd sound of the Theremin to indicate other-worldliness, as famously utilised by Bernard Herman for the soundtrack of 'The Day the Earth Stood Still' in 1951.

The invention of the modern synthesizer

This all changed with the increasing availability of the transistor in the early 1960s. Don Buchla and Robert Moog used these transistors to invent their breakthrough 'modular' synthesizers. Instead of taking up an entire room, the much smaller modular components could be combined to make a functional instrument that was now merely the size of a large cabinet. These first synthesizers comprised individual modules whose circuits were dedicated to one task each - an oscillator, a filter, etc. Thus multiple modules could be patched together to create a huge range of sounds in a newly powerful way.

Although nothing like as miniaturised as today's technology, the benefits over the room-sized devices were numerous: they could be played in real-time, they had a compellingly flexible sound, they were *relatively* affordable - and they weren't the size of entire laboratories.

Don Buchla had built his system for the San Francisco Tape Center in 1964 for use by Morton Subotnick and Ramon Sender and it was paid for by a grant from the Rockefeller Institute. Robert Moog had been building and selling Theremin kits in his teens. He was inspired to build his first modular synthesizer by working with composer Herb Deutsch and by an influential paper of Harold Bode on the possibilities afforded by the transistor and a possible modular synthesizer.

These first modular systems of Moog and Buchla set the basic signal-flow template for the analogue synthesizers to follow. The core modules of which included the following:

- Voltage Controlled Oscillator (VCO) - sound generation.
- Voltage Controlled Filter (VCF) - change the timbre.
- Low Frequency Oscillator (LFO) - modulators to alter pitch, timbre and volume.
- Voltage Controlled Amplifier (VCA) - dynamically change a sound's volume over time.
- Mixer to balance relative volumes of oscillators.

Once this pattern had been set - and was seen to be successful - the golden age of synths was launched, with a now-famous roll-call of innovative companies that got their start in the 1960s and 1970s: ARP, E-mu, Elka, EMS, Korg, Oberheim, Roland, Sequential Circuits, Yamaha, and many more, who constructed synths along these lines.

Like the organic evolution of life, the evolution of synthesizers had to be driven by something that would select for success. This something, in the capitalist context, was the need to sell synths to make money to then invest in new models. And selling 'synth product' could only be done by meeting the needs of musicians and the music industry.

An early evolutionary choice was almost immediately presented to the buying public in those first synthesizers of Moog and Buchla, who had taken somewhat different philosophical approaches. Buchla, representing experimentalism, chose not to provide 'standard' piano keyboards. Instead, he favoured capacitance touch-plates and provided novel (aka complex) tone generation options. Meanwhile Moog, more conventionally, supplied his machines with piano-type keyboards and used the simpler form of subtractive synthesis.

Musicians who were used to playing keyboards in rock bands, and composers who were classically trained, made a choice - it was to be piano-style keyboards and standard tunings that would form the first major branch of the synth family tree, whilst the experimental approach would become a niche.

Modular, semi-modular and fully hardwired synths became a familiar sight in progressive rock bands throughout the 1970s. Rick Wakeman of Yes and Keith Emerson of ELP being particularly prominent. This new synth sound also appeared on an increasingly broad range of records. The Beatles and Stevie Wonder were early adopters, and even the Rolling Stones dabbled in this new world with '2000 Light Years From Home' (1967).

Not only this, of course, but new genres of electronic synthesizer music were now possible and became popular. One style was exemplified by artists such as Jean-Michel Jarre, Vangelis, Tomita, Tangerine Dream and Kraftwerk throughout the 1970s, introducing the world to brand new sounds and the music it inspired. A synthpop style more based on existing pop music formats was pioneered by Gary Numan, The Human League and the Yellow Magic Orchestra, bringing the synthesizer to prominence via the UK's Top of the Pops, new wave gigs and into the general consciousness of the public.

Evolving beyond analogue

Once established, however, it wasn't long before the demanding musicians of the late 1970s started to express some dissatisfactions, and their requirements helped drive the next phase of synth evolution. For example, tuning was a long-standing problem with analogue oscillators - so digitally controlled oscillators (DCOs) were introduced for better tuning stability. Being limited by monophonic playing was another frustration, so manufacturers started to build polyphonic synths, despite the problems of the increased cost, complexity and weight of the resulting machines.

Realism was another issue. Although a great number of musicians and composers delighted in the sound of analogue, there was also demand for better mimicry of acoustic instruments. Strings and bold brass sounds aside, analogue synths weren't really about realism - it wasn't really the point. 'Realistic sounds' had previously been provided by the Chamberlin, Mellotron and Vako Orchestron in the preceding decades, but those tape-based behemoths were lo-fi and limited in sound sculpture options.

Digital synthesis & FM

So the industry turned to digital methods enabled by the new wave of microprocessors becoming available. An early technique was additive synthesis, but it hadn't gained much traction. Additive synthesizers construct a tone from individually selected harmonics (a kind of digital pipe organ) and can sound great - but the earliest attempts were also laborious and unpredictable to use in practice. Synthesizers that first offered additive synthesis, such as the NED Synclavier (1977), soon added sampling to their arsenal, a much more useful function.

The revolutionary digital synthesis technology was to be frequency modulation (FM). Licenced from Stanford University in the mid-1970s, Yamaha's breakthrough use of FM in their DX7 synthesizer (1983) was capable of unheard of realism, especially in its electric pianos and bells, and offered a whole new palette of complex and compelling tones. Another key feature was the ability to recall a great number of different sounds instantly. Compared to the laborious knob-twiddling of the increasingly 'dinosaur' analogue synthesizers, this was a miracle.

Digital samplers

Another digital technology that actually preceded the DX7, but became affordable around the same time, was that of sampling - the ability to record real-world sounds, store them digitally and then play them back at the desired pitch.

The Fairlight CMI, Synclavier II and Computer Music Melodian were the first commercial samplers available from the mid-1970s. But they cost tens of thousands of pounds and were completely out of reach of the average musician. Expensive as they were though, it was clear that a whole new sound world was opening up.

Those musicians and producers who had access to them were already changing the sound of popular music with their use. Stevie Wonder was perhaps the earliest to use a sampler on a commercial recording in 1979, using a Computer Music Melodian on 'Journey Through the Secret Lives of Plants'. Producers like Trevor Horn also pioneered their use in brash, excitingly modern pop productions such as Frankie Goes to Hollywood's 'Relax' (1983). Peter Gabriel (who set up a company to import the Fairlight CMI) and Kate Bush were also notable early users.

As the cost of digital technology dropped, a new generation of samplers became affordable. Early successes were the E-mu Emulator (1981) and Ensoniq Mirage (1984). Lo-fi and with limited storage (two seconds) maybe, but it was enough to usher in a new world of sound.

Once sampling reached the general musician, one path music culture could have taken might have been a revival of the musique concrète of the 1950s. The means to process those real-world sounds was now far easier than the old tape-based methods of cutting, splicing and re-recording. And indeed, some pop bands experimented like this, such as Depeche Mode's song 'Pipeline' (1982) which was constructed from samples they made themselves by tapping things around their studio.

But what actually happened in the majority of cases was the realisation that any piece of *previously recorded* music could now be sampled and re-used in new productions.

This meant that hip-hop producers could now directly sample the vinyl funk and soul drum breaks they'd previously used for rapping over. House producers could sample the classic disco tracks they wished to rework with the new four-to-the-floor electronic beat. Producers of mainstream music now had access to vast catalogues of sample libraries containing high-quality recordings of acoustic instruments.

Sample & synthesis

With increasingly affordable Read-Only Memory chips (ROM) and seeing the demand for this realism, synthesizer companies responded by making new digital synths that were essentially sample playback machines. They made it so that musicians didn't have to go out and record their own instruments or practise creative sampling - or even time-consumingly load libraries up from a floppy disk drive. The sounds would come pre-loaded in ROM and could, again, be recalled in an instant.

The Roland D-50 (1987) wasn't the first of these 'sample & synthesis' (S&S) keyboards, but it *was* the first to be affordable enough to sell in the tens of thousands. After the success of the DX7, the D-50 became the next best-selling-synth of the decade, to be beaten only in 1988 by the Korg M1, another S&S synth.

And it's safe to say that all these realistic and glossy sounds from the DX7, D-50, M1, and many more besides, are the synths that gave mid-late 1980s pop and rock music its gloss and its sheen. Polished pop productions from Madonna, George Michael, Prince and Whitney Houston were all making use of these new sounds in favour of real-world orchestral ensembles or full rock and R&B bands of the previous eras.

MIDI

Another important step had been taken back in 1981 - the introduction of the MIDI standard. The 'Musical Instrument Digital Interface' had been instigated by Ikaturo Kakehashi of Roland and Dave Smith of Sequential Circuits, and then ratified by all the major manufacturers of the time. This enabled synthesizers, drum machines, samplers and sequencers to be connected together in a way that the previous proprietary methods had not permitted.

This gave ultimate flexibility to musicians to select and connect together instruments from any manufacturer. The Sequential Circuits Prophet 600 (1982) was the first synth to sport the new MIDI ports. And the inclusion of built-in MIDI ports in the Atari 520 ST home computer in 1985 made it the choice of musicians until well into the 1990s. Musically, MIDI enabled musicians to create multi-track compositions that could be played back in real-time rather than having to record one part at a time onto multi-track tape which had been the necessary practice before this.

The 1990s

Going into the 1990s, the sample and synthesis machines continued to evolve - but were mainly just refined with more memory, more polyphony, more sequencer capacity, more effects, and so on. They were very successful and they were meeting the needs of the musicians of the time.

By the mid-1990s, after a decade of increasingly sophisticated, but arguably increasingly indistinguishable ROMpler workstations ('ROMpler' becoming the somewhat derisive name for S&S synths), there came a new demand from the musical underground which had been evolving in parallel to the mainstream.

While mainstream pop and rock had been coasting along in the mid-80s and early-90s becoming ever more polished, there had been a dance music revolution going on in Chicago, Detroit, New York, the UK and across Europe. The post-disco need to dance and provide social commentary had catalysed hip-hop, house and techno in America. In the UK, acid house, rave and jungle were the new expressions of dance-music based youth culture. Breakbeat hardcore and trance were the European counterparts. All of which drove new sounds and demanded new features from the technology used to create it.

These hip-hop, house, techno and jungle artists had been going on a sampling spree following the sampling revolution of the mid-80s, and were grabbing all manner of drum breaks, synth stabs, and vocals from the previous decades of recorded music. In doing so, they were generating new music styles and driving youth culture, which was ultimately to challenge the pre-eminence that pop, rock and R&B had enjoyed up to that point.

This creative sampling led manufacturers to provide hybrid machines combining the sampler, drum machine and sequencer in one box, which were geared towards the creation of this new music. The Akai MPC60 (1988) kick-started this new wave of grooveboxes, as they became known.

Resurgence of analogue

Alongside the explosion in sampling, the dance music scene had developed a fetish for the Roland TB-303, a basic analogue bassline machine from 1982. Humble it may have been, it nonetheless spawned the entire genres of acid house, acid techno and acid-anything-else following the release of Phuture's 'Acid Trax' in 1986. This record introduced the world to its unique ability to create a certain kind of psychedelic squelching bassline, which cast a hypnotic techno-spell over the dancefloor, in a way that nothing else could.

By the early 1990s, there was soaring demand for the TB-303 and other, previously unfashionable analogue synthesizers, driving prices for desirable models sky-high. (At the time of writing, it is still all but impossible to buy an original TB-303). This resurgence of interest in analogue synths coincided with the increasingly undifferentiated ROMpler synths, which were now perceived as less-than-exciting, and a rash of hardware TB-303 clones appeared in the market to take advantage.

Analogue and physical modelling

At the same time, the last revolution in hardware synthesizers was also about to emerge - the ability to model analogue circuits and acoustic instruments in software. It was now actually possible to emulate the behaviour of the electronic components of analogue synthesizers and acoustic instruments using numbers in a computer.

The first 'physical modelling' synth was the Yamaha VL-1 (1993) which modelled acoustic instrument 'drivers' and 'resonators' such as the plucked or hammered string, the blown pipe, etc. This was a remarkable technical achievement, but it didn't become the new 'must-have' technology. Perhaps it wasn't the sound producers were looking for, or simply that the rise of computers trumped their appeal.

The Korg Prophecy (1995) and Nord Lead (1995) were the first to model actual analogue circuitry in a hardware synth. Like the VL-1 these also made an impact on their arrival - but also like the VL-1, these machines didn't cause analogue modelling to drive a new synth revolution. However, the Novation Supernova and Access Virus were very successful examples of the genre in the late-90s.

The rise of computers

The lack of a real revolution featuring analogue modelling can be attributed to a couple of factors. The first being a resurgence of interest in actual vintage analogue synths (originating from the TB-303 fashion), and, secondly the rise of the personal computer in music-making.

As well as using MIDI to control external synthesizers, drum machines and samplers, computers were now able to record and manipulate audio directly. In the first place this rendered hardware samplers redundant overnight, thanks to their high quality recording capability and abundant memory.

Another advantage computers had was the ability to offer this new analogue modelling magic as well. An early program by Propellerhead Software called 'ReBirth' (1997) was an emulation of the TB-303 in computer code. Not only that, the program also provided *two* TB-303s *and* a TR-808 *and* a TR-909 drum machine - all in one interface. Despite the rash of TB-303 hardware clones (there are six direct clones of the TB-303 in this book!), this clearly pointed to a future of virtualising synthesizers and drum-machines 'in the box'.

And an industry has indeed since sprung up offering accurate software replications (known as plugins) of classic synths and drum machines, as well as many other analogue and digital type synthesizers. Using these in the environment of a computer Digital Audio Workstation (DAW) is still the model for the vast majority of modern electronic music-makers and producers today. However, despite the convenience and apparent sound-quality of these emulations, there has always been a lingering doubt that a computer can *truly* replicate the real-world complexity of electricity coursing through real diodes, capacitors and transistors.

Summary

So there we have it: the analogue synthesizer was conjured into existence in the early 1960s, only to make way for the more reliable and wider sound palettes of the digital FM and ROMpler synths twenty years later. Sampling then swiftly became the de facto method for making dance music, and the TB-303 drove the resurgence of analogue synths in the 1990s as people also tired of the sound-alike ROMplers. All of which was swept away by the computer that could do it all digitally, once and for all…

But what of the synthesizer now, twenty years after the computer revolution rendered external synths, samplers and drum machines all but obsolete?

Well, some musicians have grown tired of staring at computer screens and their grids of notes that look more and more like an Excel spreadsheet every day, and of clicking around on tiny pixelated representations of synths. They have rediscovered the joys of real analogue synthesis. The sense that turning a knob is adjusting the actual electricity flowing through real components. And a return to a physical interface of knobs and sliders which is simply more intuitive and less 'right-brain' than the computer screen.

And it's not just analogue synthesizers that are back in favour, but also the original modular concepts of Bode, Moog and Buchla, with now an estimated 5,000 different modules available in the Eurorack format. This range of modules offer authentic analogue synthesis, sophisticated digital synthesis and every other type of audio signal processing and control in-between.

This, in turn, has led to a renaissance of electronic music-making; whether in 'conventional' mainstream electronic music, pop music, cutting edge dance styles or in truly experimental forms of music.

Not only this, but the latest evolutionary phase has seen the actual re-construction and sale of some of the most revered synthesizers of the 1970s. Brand new Minimoogs, ARP Odysseys, Korg MS-20s, Roland TB-303s, and more, can be bought once again, fifty years since they first appeared.

Truly from analogue to digital - and back again!

Korg Prophecy 1995
Analogue modelling / Mono

SYNTHESIZERS

What is a synthesizer?

Without a working definition of 'synthesizer', it would be hard to justify what's included in this chapter. And despite there having been many various types of electrical, electro-mechanical and electronic instruments over the last two hundred years, I believe there is both a concrete definition of a modern synthesizer and a watershed moment which marked the beginning of the modern synthesizer age.

The basic definition, as far as this book is concerned, is that a synthesizer's sound generation method must be *purely electronic.* It's not an electro-mechanical system (which rules out electric tonewheel organs and electric pianos) - and it's certainly not an acoustic one (which rules out pipe-organs, despite claims that their ability to mix timbres makes them early synthesizers).

Furthermore, to qualify as a *modern* synthesizer it should be based on transistors, voltage control and modern electronics - not the vacuum-tubes of yore. There were indeed some very interesting proto-synthesizers that used vacuum tubes, such as the Givelet (1930) and Novachord (1939). However, they were not particularly practical and could not offer the ease of sound-sculpture afforded by the new transistor-based synthesizers of the 1960s.

The watershed moment, then, was the independent invention of the transistor-based voltage-controlled modular synthesizer by Robert Moog and Don Buchla in the early 1960s, and the subsequent successful commercialization of those instruments. Before this, there had been machines approaching my definition of a synthesizer, but they were either too large, too inaccessible or too inflexible for satisfactory music composition. The modular synthesizers were a magnitude better on all three counts.

Once the modular synthesizer was invented, and then replicated and improved upon, it became an instrument that musicians of the day could actually use, and whose sounds were then heard by an increasing proportion of the public.

The record that brought the name Moog to the public's full attention was Wendy Carlos' 'Switched-On Bach' in 1968, famously making sole use of the new Moog modular synthesizer. This demonstrated that synthesizers could make real music, and could be appreciated for what they were - instruments that were both accessible and musical.

Following this, the Moog began to show up on some high profile artists' recordings during the 1960s and 1970s; for example, The Doors - 'Strange Days' (1967), The Beatles - 'Here Comes the Sun' (1969) and Stevie Wonder - 'Music of My Mind' (1972). As the size and cost of the machines reduced, their use increased and drove the electronic music styles of the 1970s. Namely the 'orchestral' use of synths by Jean-Michel Jarre, Vangelis and Tomita and the futurism of Kraftwerk, Tangerine Dream and Yellow Magic Orchestra.

This chapter follows the evolution of synthesizers from early, large modular systems to smaller, more portable versions during the 1970s. Then to the digital revolutions of the late 1970s with sampling and additive synthesis, and which evolved further in the 1980s with the use of digitally stored waveforms and samples. Finally, the invention in the mid-90s of 'analogue modelling' synthesis completes the journey.

So, what is an 'analogue synthesizer' and how does it generate sound?

All analogue synths have an oscillator - the component that produces an oscillating electric signal in the audio frequency range. This is then output to a loudspeaker which converts that oscillating electric signal to acoustic waves in the air that we can then hear.

The oscillators used in analogue synths are known as 'Voltage Controlled Oscillators' (VCOs), and they were first built with the new technology of transistors in the early 1960s. VCOs typically generate a signal by causing an electric charge to build within a capacitor to a certain level, at which point it is allowed to decay again. Once fully discharged the cycle repeats, and the rate - or frequency - of this cycling process is determined by an external control voltage. In this way the oscillator's pitch can be varied in a musical way.

The charge and discharge cycle of the capacitor is essentially what generates the waveforms we associate with analogue synthesis: the triangle, sawtooth, and square waves. Further signal shaping can derive pulse and sine waves from these too. ('Noise' is created by the amplification of the thermal noise of a resistor or semiconductor).

Worth noting is that a Digitally Controlled Oscillator (DCO) still outputs an analogue waveform, but the input control voltage is first generated by a digital source and sent in via a digital-to-analogue converter. The digital signal is a code representing the frequency of the required control voltage. This approach can give better tuning stability. (And is not to be confused with the later fully digital oscillators which would store and output digital representations of waveforms).

The concept of voltage control of the pitch led to the use of voltage control for the other elements of a synthesizer - the envelope, filter and more. Once this innovation was secured, all the other components of the analogue synthesizer fell into place very quickly and were the principle of most analogue synthesizers to follow:

- Voltage Controlled Oscillator (VCO) - generates the basic sound, and outputs one or more of the following waveforms: sinewave, triangle, saw, square/pulse, each having its own distinctive harmonic properties.
- Voltage Controlled Filter (VCF) - the raw output of a VCO contains the full harmonic spectrum of the waveform; removing bands of frequencies enabled a more subtle tone to be achieved - a *low-pass* filter removes the high frequencies for a 'warmer', rounder tone; a *high-pass* filter removes the lower frequencies for a thinner, more piercing sound. *Band-pass/band-reject* filters remove notches for a variety of effects. A further refinement is to create a feedback loop at the cut-off frequency, which is called resonance and creates tonal intensity. The use of filters to subtract frequencies from an initial richly harmonic source is the reason that analogue synthesis is also referred to as 'subtractive synthesis'.
- Low Frequency Oscillator (LFO) - the need to vary the otherwise static audio tone led to the development of the LFO which is usually used to modulate the pitch (for vibrato), volume (for tremolo), or the filter cut-off frequency (wah-wah).
- Hard-sync and ring-modulation - new harmonics can be generated by synchronising two or more oscillators in various ways.
- Voltage Controlled Amplifier (VCA) (also commonly referred to as an 'ADSR' - standing for Attack, Decay, Sustain and Release). Changing the volume or filter cut-off level after note onset adds interest and character to a sound; and is a way to help mimic acoustic instruments - fast volume onset and short decay times for percussive sounds; slow-swell volume onset and long 'sustain' phase for organs and strings.
- Control of the pitch (playing the synth!) - the majority of synthesizers soon followed the Moog example and used a piano-type keyboard as a controller, but there has always been a proportion of users who preferred Don Buchla's philosophy of using less conventional non-piano-like trigger-switches or pads. There is also the automatic generation of notes using arpeggiators, sequencers, and algorithmic note generators which were there right from the start.

The basic signal flow using these elements is illustrated below in a very simple synthesizer plan:

The bold lines indicate audio signal flow. The dotted lines are the voltage control signals and which act on the audio signal. Pressing a key generates a frequency signal that causes the VCOs to play the appropriate pitch using the selected waveform. The key press also triggers a Gate On signal that allows the audio through the VCF and VCA so the mixed VCO signal can be heard. Both the VCA and VCF (in this diagram) have envelope generators to dynamically change the sound over time; these are also triggered by the Gate On/Off signal. An LFO can be used to further modulate the volume or pitch.

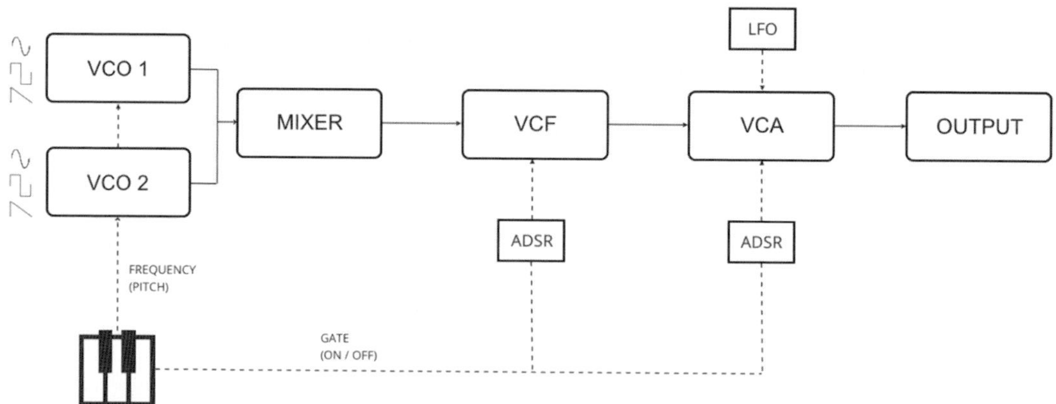

Digital synthesis

Analogue synthesis is not the end of the story, of course, and research into other forms of audio signal generation was also taking place throughout the 1960s and 1970s. If the electrical current flowing within an 'analogue' synth can be thought of as *the actual soundwave in electrical form* (to which it is 'analogous'), then 'digital' is the set of numbers in a computer's memory that *represents the sound but is not the sound itself*.

The early digital sound synthesizers were often inventive and interesting, but they suffered the limitations of the processing power available at the time. The resulting machines were too complicated, too hard to work with - or just too outlandish. For example, Marvin Minksy, the legendary artificial intelligence researcher, was involved in designing an algorithmic sound generator called the Triadex Muse in 1972; the idea being that a semi-random series of sine wave tones could replace the radio!

Additive synthesis

Arguably, the first really successful digital instruments were samplers - the subject of another chapter - but many early samplers also offered 'additive harmonic synthesis'. Actually quite similar to the drawbars of a Hammond organ, these made sound by adding sine waves to create a new, coherent, tone. This was usually a painstaking task, in complete contrast with the immediacy of an analogue synth with knobs. However, there have been some noble attempts to commercialise this method of synthesis - the RMI Harmonic Explorer (used by Jean-Michel Jarre on Oxygene), the NED Synclavier I (the Synclavier II added sampling), and the Kawai K5 and K5000. Despite these efforts, it's never really caught on as a mainstream synthesis method.

FM

The breakthrough digital technology was 'frequency modulation' (FM), and it was delivered by Yamaha in the form of the DX7 in 1983. Having secured the patents to this technology from John Chowning of Stanford University, it had taken nearly a decade to commercialise the technology. But when it was finally released it took the world by storm. Goodbye unreliable analogue synths with dodgy tuning and which could weigh a ton, and hello to a lightweight unit with a massive 16-note polyphony and a range of sounds that were both impressive in realism and accessed a part of the sonic spectrum most analogue synths couldn't reach. (Analogue and digital frequency modulation had featured on some synths before, but it had been limited and didn't also provide 32 named and recallable patches in the way the DX7 did).

FM works in a similar way to ring-modulation or the hard-sync found on some analogue synths, but takes it to a new level. In the DX7 there are six 'operators' which can manipulate each other in various algorithmic configurations. One operator's frequency could modulate another's. But that first operator could also be modulated in turn by yet another operator, and so on. This quickly leads to a high degree of complexity - and a rich source of harmonics too. FM became known for the quality of its electric pianos and its percussive, metallic sounds, but it could also produce rich pads and complex evolving tones. After a while, the complexity of programming the unpredictable operator/carrier algorithms caused many users to rely just on presets, and it was felt that some of the creativity of sound design had been lost.

Other manufacturers adopted similar concepts to FM - the Phase Modulation of Casio being one - but they had to tread carefully around Yamaha's patents. Another branch of the digital synthesis family tree was the use of digitally stored waveforms. The Korg DW-6000 and DW-8000 (both 1985) used this method; the 'DW' standing for 'Digital Waveforms', using stored numbers representing the waveforms to generate sound, rather than actually varying real voltages in analogue circuitry.

A more exciting use of digital waveforms was called wave-sequencing, in which multiple stored single-cycle digital waveforms could be played back in sequence. This could create smoothly evolving tones, if the different waves were similar, or could make excitingly abrupt changes in tone if they were completely different. Wave sequencing was pioneered by PPG in their Wave synthesizers of the early 1980s, and whose evolution was taken further by the Korg Wavestation (1990).

Sample and synthesis

The most significant digital synthesis method used in keyboards of the 1980s was derived from the invention of sampling. In theory, sampling could provide 'perfect' reproduction of acoustic instruments - and of any other real-world sound - but in reality (at that time), the results weren't terribly realistic due to the low-resolution 8-bit chips and the low sampling rates used. (Lower resolution recordings 'cost' less microchip silicon to store and process, so were favoured due to the then high cost of computer chips).

Nevertheless, samples were beginning to be built into synths as the raw sonic material, as opposed to the basic waveforms generated by analogue or digital oscillators. These stored samples were then processed using the standard synthesizer techniques of VCF, LFO, ADSR, etc. This method, therefore, is generally known as 'Sample & Synthesis' (S&S).

There were some well regarded 'sample playback' synths early on - the 360 Systems Digital Keyboard (1982) and the Kurzweil K150 (1986) being notable - but these were expensive and did not break through into the general market.

It wasn't until the arrival of the Roland D-50 in 1987 that the world got their hands on this technology. The D-50 combined a short transient sample for the onset of a sound (the distinctive 'chiff' of a flute or percussive thump of a piano) and a looped sample for the main duration of the sound. Up to four of these sounds ('partials') could be combined in the D-50, and like the DX7 before, it ushered in a new world of digital sound. The D-50 gave rise to successive generations of this type of instrument, also known later (somewhat derisively) as ROMplers - the Korg M1, the Kawai K1, the Yamaha SY-77 (also with FM) and others. Roland referred to their version of sample and synthesis as Linear Arithmetic, for reasons that remain unclear!

Around this point, in the early 1990s, the synth world became a less romantic place. Out were the magnificent analogue beasts of the 70s - derided as 'dinosaurs' at the time - and in were increasingly indistinguishable ranges of ROMpler workstations from the big manufacturers. All of which kind of looked the same - a basic piano keyboard with a panel above featuring a two-line LCD and a couple of rows of buttons. Perhaps this is harsh - they afforded the musician an unheard-of range of quality sounds at an affordable price. They had sophisticated sequencers with which entire musical arrangements could be composed, not to mention the onboard effects to spice it all up. They were a complete instrument... but it's still hard to get excited about a mid-90s ROMpler workstation - perhaps that's just me!

Analogue and physical modelling

There was one last synth evolution of the 20th century waiting to happen - and is the reason for the 'and back' of this book's title. And it was actually a digital and an analogue revolution. Just as the world was indeed tiring of the unending ranges of keyboard 'workstations', several manufacturers released physical modelling synthesizers. Yamaha launched the Yamaha VL-1 in 1993, mathematically modelling the 'drivers' and 'resonators' of acoustic instruments. Then Korg and Nord launched their respective Prophecy and Lead synths in 1995, which modelled the circuitry of analogue synths in software. Novation also launched an analogue modelling drum machine, the Drum Station in 1996, which emulated the TR-808 and TR-909 drum machines.

Analogue modelling promised the rich, inspiring tones of analogue synths, but in the form of small, easily portable synths with recallable presets. However, it didn't lead to a revolution of hardware synthesizers as the world was beginning to replace external hardware with computers which could (begin to) do it all.

So instead of driving a new range of keyboards with this new modelling technology, it all went into computers in the form of software plugins that could run on what became known as 'Digital Audio Workstations' (DAWs). And indeed, in the decades that have followed a vast number of plugins have been created that faithfully model nearly every vintage synthesizer ever made, as well as brand new synth plugins of all types, and every other kind of audio processor imaginable.

Of course, since 1995, more and more is possible within a computer, and we've also now seen a huge renaissance in the interest in real analogue synths and new modular systems. But 1995 seems like the right place to stop, at least as far as this book is concerned. It means we cover all the glories of the analogue and digital revolutions of the 1960s, 70s and 80s, and it takes us right up to the invention of the Korg Prophecy and Nord Lead, where the digital emulates the analogue and closes the loop.

Notes on the instruments included (and not included) in this chapter

I have tried to include all the major, commercially available synthesizers since the Moog and Buchla modular synthesizers of 1963 up until the invention of the analogue modelling synthesizer of 1995.

I have not attempted to capture each and every one of the mid-90s ROMplers; too numerous and too visually undifferentiated.

Similarly missing are most of the one-offs, novelties, prototypes or barely commercial synthesizers released from one-man bands, garage inventors or tiny companies who never made it beyond one synthesizer or prototype.

I have not attempted to cover the large number of Soviet synthesizers... perhaps a further volume for those!

Not included are the following :

- Electric pianos
- Electric and electronic organs
- Home keyboards (excepting notable ones)
- Novelties and toys
- A number of string synthesizers are included, but there are many more that aren't. They occupy an interesting half-way house between true synthesizers and basic 'preset' type machines with full polyphony that don't offer the sound shaping of true synthesizers.

Finally - inevitably - with an undertaking of this sort, there may be the occasional omission or error in the entries. I welcome corrections and requests for additions for any future editions.

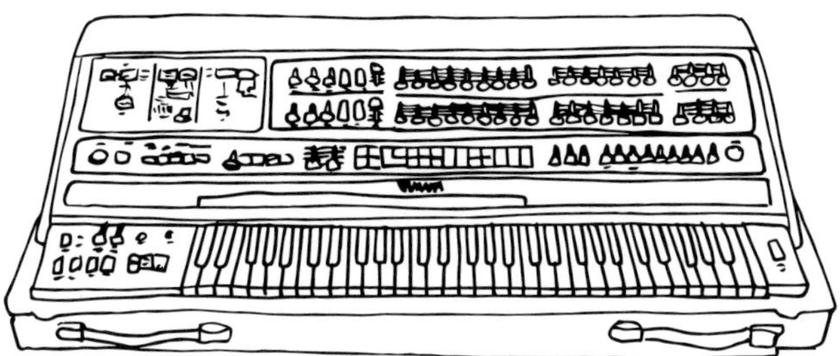

Yamaha CS-80 1977
Analogue / 8 note polyphony
2 VCOs per voice

ABBREVIATIONS & KEY

Additive Synthesis
Waveforms constructed from individual sine waves (harmonics) to create a tone. Can be digital or analogue.

Analogue Modelling
Digital modelling of analogue circuitry in software.

Consonant Vowel Synthesis
Combination of digital waves and processing with dynamic filters; used by Casio.

DCO (Digitally Controlled Oscillator)
An analogue oscillator whose frequency is controlled digitally.

Divide Down
This method to create full polyphony is usually found in organs, string synths and ensemble synths. An oscillator is fixed to the top octave and its voltage is 'divided down' to create lower frequencies.

DO (Digital Oscillator)
Waveforms generated using a digital source. These can be simple one cycle analogue-like sine, square and sawtooth waves, or can be much more numerous and complex as found in later wavetable synths.

Ensemble Synths
Usually limited to presets with little or no sound editing, they often featured emulations of acoustic instruments such as brass, reeds, piano and clavichord. They typically have full polyphony using divide-down technology.

FM (Frequency Modulation)
The synchronization and modulation of two or more digital oscillators to create harmonically rich waveforms. Patented by John Chowning of Stanford University in 1973 and subsequently licenced by Yamaha.

Linear Arithmetic
Roland's name for Sample & Synthesis. Also 'Super LA'.

MIDI (Musical Instrument Digital Interface)
A technical standard from 1981 enabling different manufacturers' equipment to control each other. It also enabled full computer control of note playback and a further 128 digital parameters over 16 channels. The connectors were originally 5-pin DIN sockets, but have been superseded by USB in recent years.

Modular Synthesizers
Synths that are comprised of separate modules that can be patched together using cables or pin matrices to create flexible audio and signal control paths.

Paraphonic
Full polyphony achieved by divide-down technology and all notes also sharing one envelope generator (and filter envelope if present).

Phase Distortion
Similar to FM; used by Casio, Con Brio, and others.

Physical Modelling
Digital modelling of acoustic instruments in software.

Polyphony
The number of sounds that can be played simultaneously.

Sample & Synthesis
Digital waveforms, often samples, that are used for the source sound, and are then processed using conventional synth techniques such as filtering, envelopes and LFOs. Known also as PCM (Pulse Code Modulation) and by Yamaha as AWM (Advanced Wave Memory).

Semi-Modular
Synths that are partially hardwired, but which also can be patched in other ways using cables or matrix buttons.

Spectrum Dynamic Synthesis
Digital waves whose harmonic content evolves over time, unlike the static digital waves of more conventional digital oscillators. Used by Casio in their late 80s digital synths.

String Synths
Like ensemble synths, string synths are typically preset only but specialise in the emulation of string sounds and string sections using additional vibrato and chorusing for a fuller sound. Usually fully polyphonic due to use of divide-down technology.

VCO (Voltage Controlled Oscillator)
Fully analogue audio waveform generator.

Vector Synthesis.
Blending multiple oscillators using a joystick, envelope generators, LFOs or other methods. Pioneered by Sequential Circuits in their Prophet VS synth.

Wavetable
Digital waveforms that can be sequenced by a digital oscillator for smooth evolving tones or dramatic tonal shifts depending on the waves and sequencing used.

Waveform Plotting
The ability to draw waveforms graphically.

SYNTHESIZERS

360 SYSTEMS (USA)

360 Systems hold the distinction of creating the world's first keyboard to use digital samples of real instruments. Bob Easton, the CEO, was inspired by the Mellotron and Chamberlin but wanted to achieve better realism. 360 Systems also worked closely with Oberheim releasing an innovative guitar-to-synthesizer converter called the 'Slavedriver' for which Oberheim produced a customised SEM in 1978.

360 SYSTEMS DIGITAL KEYBOARD *1982*

Sample & Synthesis
8 note polyphony / 1 waveform per voice
World's first commercial synth to use samples. Used one chipset per sound, each of which could be swapped out for new voices or could have more voice cards added.

ACCESS MUSIC (GERMANY)

Access originally wrote software editors for synths whose complicated menus were hard to 'access' and therefore program. However, they pivoted to create one of the first analogue modelling synths, the Virus, in 1997. It was the first of a long series of 'Virus' synths, running from models A to C, the Indigo and T-series.

ACCESS VIRUS *1997*

Analogue modelling / FM
12 note polyphony
2 modelled VCOs per voice + sub
One of the first analogue modelling synthesizers.

ACE ELECTRONIC INDUSTRIES (AKA ACE TONE) (JAPAN)

Founded by Ikutaro Kakehashi in 1960 the company made a range of musical products including electronic organs, drum machines, amplifiers and effects pedals. Whilst much better known for these, they also made the PS-1000 synthesizer.

The Hammond Organ Company also distributed Ace Tone 'Rhythm Ace' drum machines under the Hammond brand, and apparently made engineering improvements to them as well.

Ikutaro Kakehashi left Ace Tone in 1972 to found Roland.

ACE TONE PS-1000 *1975*

Analogue
Mono / 1 VCO
Very reminiscent of the Roland SH-3a (1974).

AKAI (JAPAN)

The Akai Electric Company was founded by Masukichi Akai and his son Saburo in 1946. By the 1970s they were making products such as reel-to-reel tape machines, radio tuners, cassette decks, amplifiers and record decks. The word 'Akai' means 'red' in Japanese so was used for their logo colour.

In 1984, Akai Professional started manufacturing professional music audio equipment such as multitrack recorders, synthesizers, samplers and drum machines.

Despite their prominence during the 1980s - thanks mainly to their samplers - Akai left the audio industry in 1991 and filed for insolvency in the year 2000, after which the brand name has passed to other companies.

AKAI AX73 *1986*

Analogue
6 note polyphony / 1 VCO per voice
An external sampler could introduce a sound for further editing. The VX90 is the rackmount version.

AKAI AX80 *1984*

Analogue
8 note polyphony / 2 VCOs per voice
Akai's first professional synthesizer.

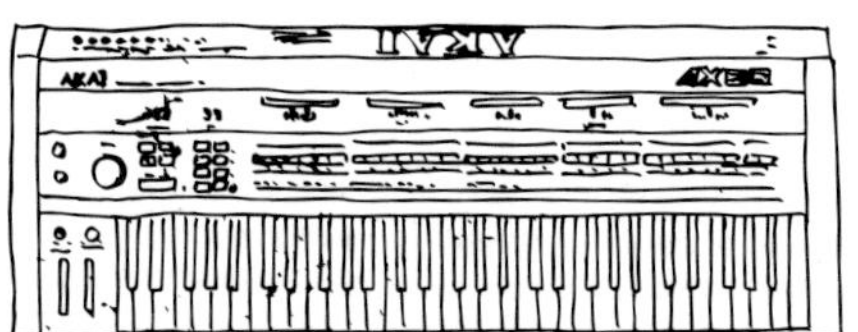

AKAI VX600 *1986*

Analogue
6 note polyphony / 2 VCOs per voice

AKAI AX60 *1985*

Analogue
6 note polyphony / 1 VCO per voice
Not available in the UK.

ALTAIR ESTRADIN 231 *1983*

Analogue
Mono / 3 VCOs
A Minimoog clone from Russia.

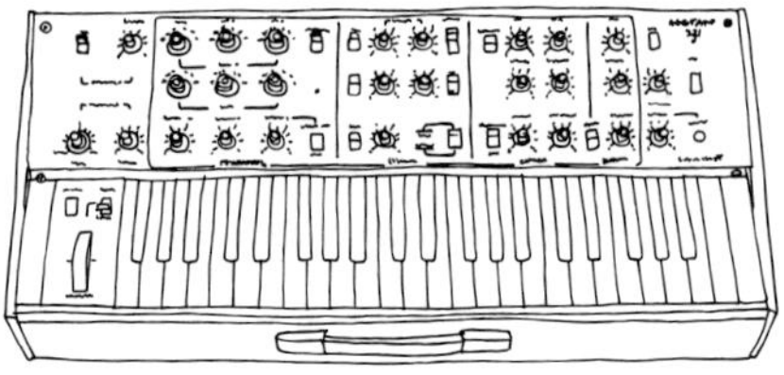

ARIES 300 MUSIC SYSTEM *1970*

Analogue
Modular / Mono
Aries was based in Massachusetts, USA, and sold a variety of modules and kits. Denis Collin, who designed the 300, also contributed to the ARP 2600.

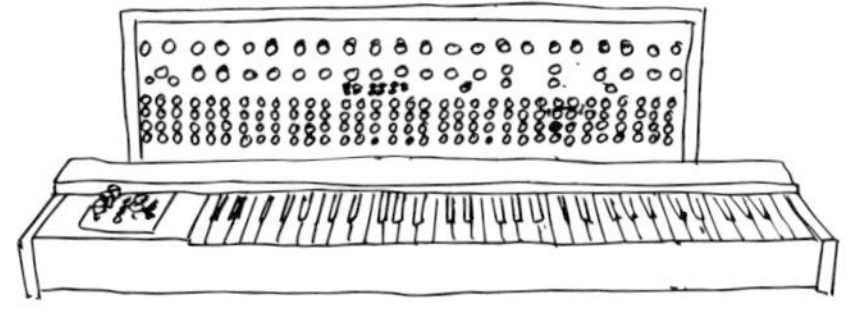

ARIES SYSTEM III *1979*

Analogue
Mono / 2 VCOs
Included a 16 step sequencer.

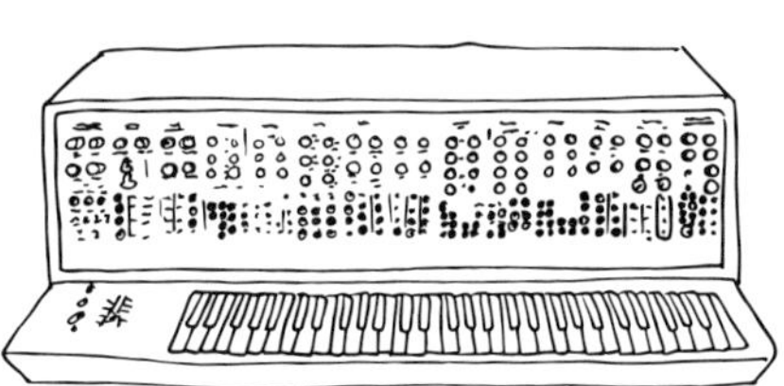

ARP INSTRUMENTS (USA)

ARP was founded by Alan R Pearlman and David Friend in 1969, and they found almost immediate success when the ARP 2500 (1970) was featured in Steven Spielberg's *Close Encounters of the Third Kind*. The musician playing the famous five-note motif in the film was Philip Dodds, ARP's vice-president of engineering.

The ARP 2600 was one of their most influential synthesizers and it went through three versions with the first known as the 'Blue Marvin', before the second and third versions updated the components (to avoid a Moog patent infringement on the filter) and the livery also changed to grey and grey/orange.

Despite their success – outselling Moog for most of the 1970s - the company ran into financial difficulties in the early 1980s. The development of a guitar-controlled synthesizer, the Avatar, was hugely expensive and the 4-Voice Piano was rushed to market with flaws. Declaring bankruptcy in 1981, the firm's assets were acquired by CBS Musical Instruments who released the Rhodes Chroma (based on ARP designs) in 1982 - which ironically become a huge success.

After a long-dormant period, the recent interest in analogue synthesizers has led to the relaunch of the Odyssey and the 2600 in 2015 (built by Korg in collaboration with David Friend). Imitation being the sincerest form of flattery, Behringer has also released clones of the Odyssey and the 2600.

ARP 2002 *1969*

Analogue / Modular / Mono
ARP's very first production synth, but very few were made.

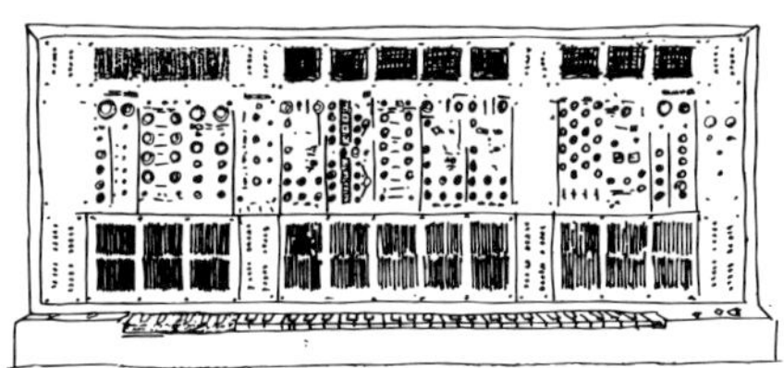

ARP 2500 *1970*

Analogue
Duophonic / 5 VCOs
Used for the famous end sequence of *Close Encounters of the Third Kind* (1977).

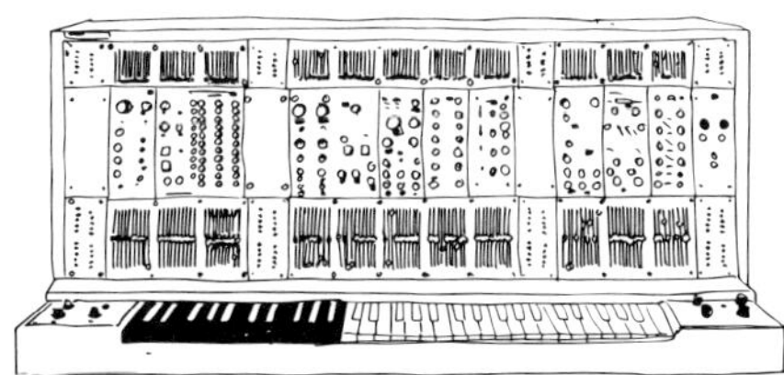

ARP SOLOIST *1970*

Analogue
Mono / 1 VCO
Simple mono-synth with 18 presets and some performance parameters.

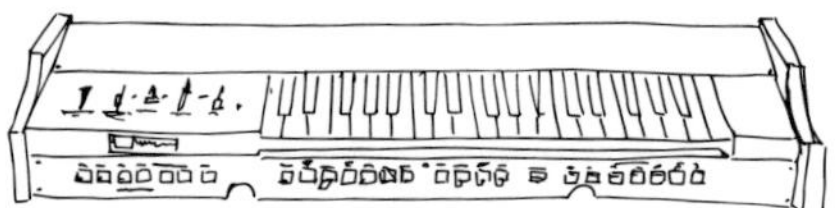

ARP PRO-SOLOIST *1972*

Analogue
Mono / 1 VCO
An updated Soloist, with more presets and more stable tuning. Gary Numan played an ARP Pro-Soloist on the album 'Telekon'.

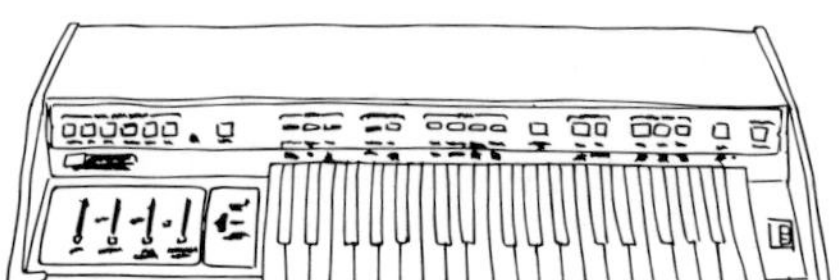

ARP 2600 *1971*

Analogue / Mono / 3 VCOs
This influential and famous synth gained ARP the reputation they still enjoy. Was used by Ben Burtt to perform R2D2's voice in *Star Wars* (1977).

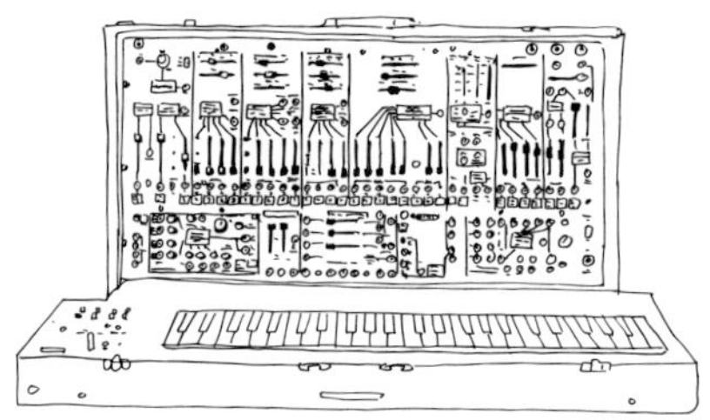

ARP EXPLORER *1974*

Analogue
Mono / 1 VCO
The circuits of the Explorer were incorporated by Solina into their String Machine, which itself was then re-badged as the ARP String Machine.

ARP ODYSSEY (2800) *1972*

Analogue
Mono/Duo / 2 VCOs
Peter Howell, 'Doctor Who Theme' (1980) (lead). Revived by Korg in 2015.

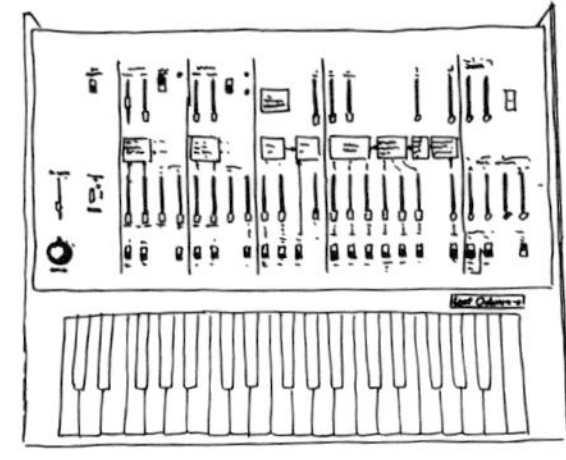

ARP STRING ENSEMBLE *1974*

Analogue
Full polyphony (divide-down)
A rebadged Solina String Ensemble, derived from the Eminent 310 Unique.

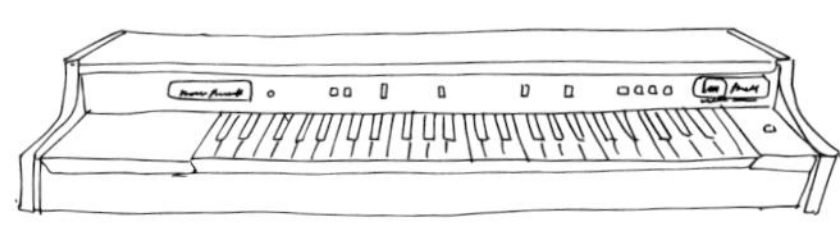

ARP AXXE *1975*

Analogue
Mono / 1 VCO
A simplified Odyssey with just one oscillator.

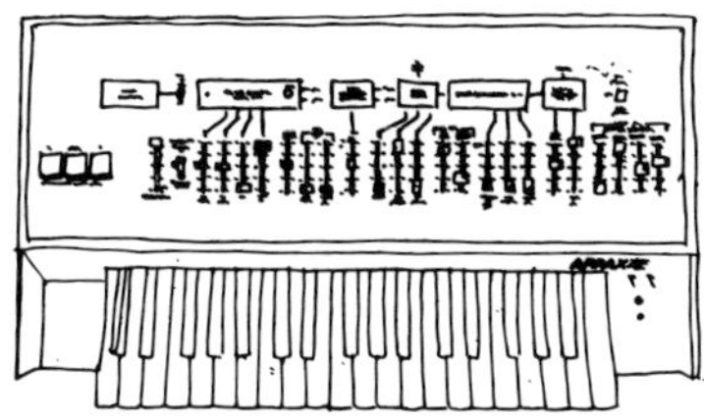

ARP OMNI *1975*

Analogue / 4 presets
Full polyphony (divide-down)
The Omni was ARP's best selling synthesizer. It had polyphonic ensemble and synth sections (divide-down) and a bass synth (mono), which could all be played simultaneously.

ARP MODULAR SYNTHESIZER LAB *1975*

Analogue / Mono / Modular
ARP's separates system.

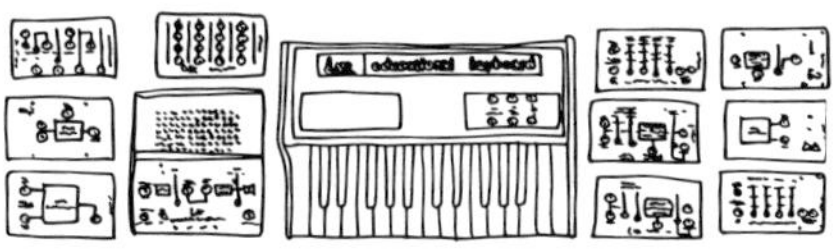

ARP LITTLE BROTHER *1975*

Analogue
Mono / 1 VCO + sub
A simple expander module.

ARP ODYSSEY MK2 (2810) *1975*

Analogue
Mono/Duo / 2 VCOs
The Odyssey Mk1 was re-released as the Mk2 due to claims of infringing Moog filter patents. The Mk3 (2820) was released in 1978.

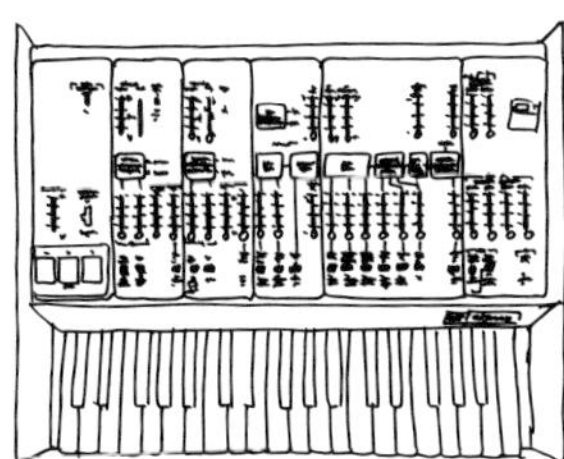

ARP PRO/DGX *1977*

Analogue
Mono / 1 VCO
A further update to the Soloist series, but remains a simple preset monosynth.

ARP AVATAR *1977*

Analogue
Mono / 2 VCOs per voice
One of the several guitar synthesizers attempted during the 1970s. The concept never really caught on, and the cost of developing the Avatar contributed to the demise of ARP.

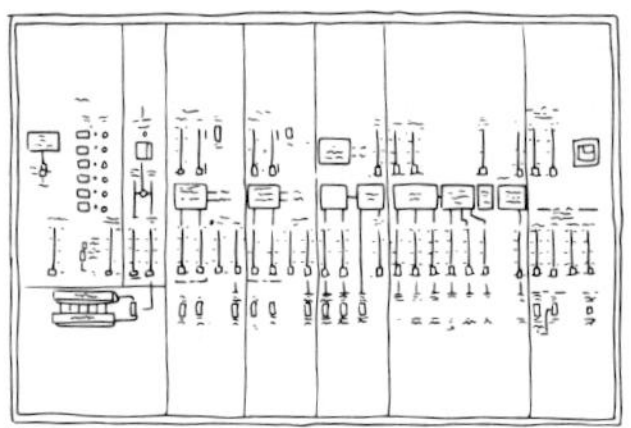

ARP QUARTET *1979*

Ensemble / 4 presets: brass, piano, reeds, strings
Full polyphony (divide-down)
Two presets could be played together. The Arp Quartet is a rebadged Siel Orchestra.

ARP OMNI MK2 *1978*

Analogue / 4 presets
Full polyphony
Stephen Morris (Joy Division/New Order) played an Omni Mk2 and Quadra.

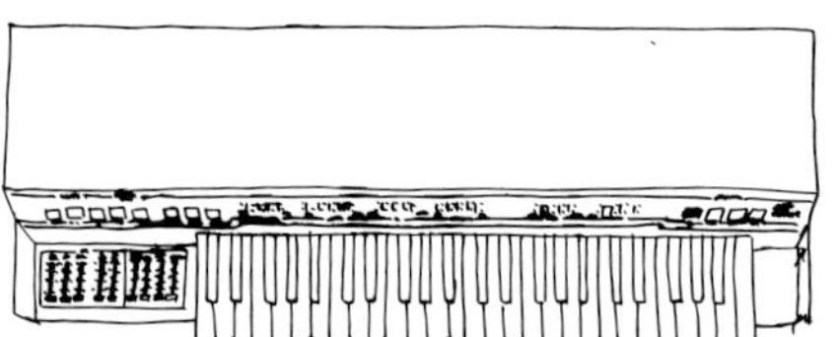

ARP SOLUS *1980*

Analogue
Mono / 2 VCOs

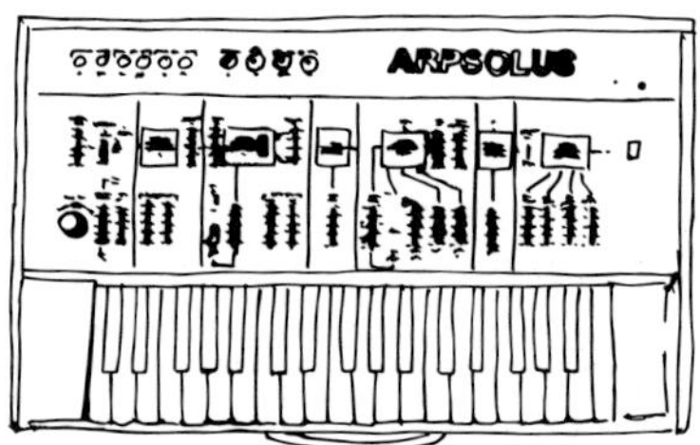

ARP QUADRA *1978*

Analogue
Bass Synth & Lead Synth: 2 VCOs - Mono/Duo
Poly Synth & String Synth: Full polyphony (divide-down)
The Quadra combined four different sections.

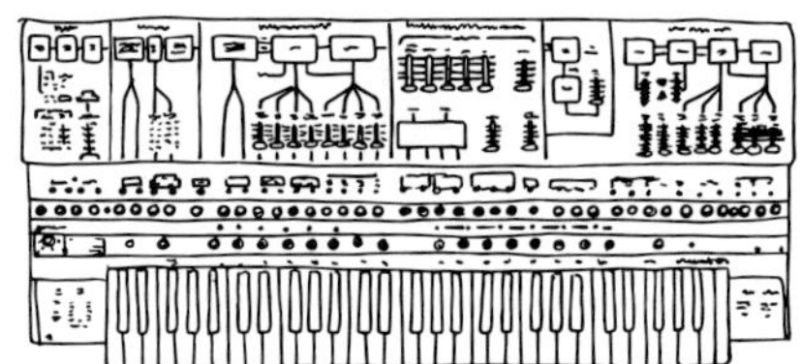

AUDIO SYSTEMS ELECTRONICS MCS-70 *1977*

Analogue
Mono / 3 VCOs
Advanced for its use of 64 digitally stored patches.

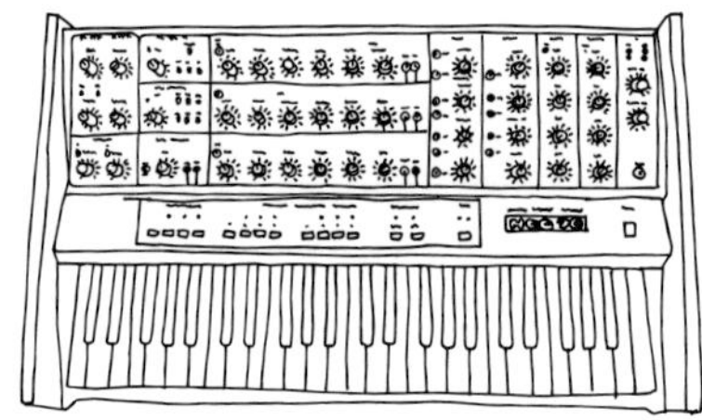

BEHRINGER (GERMANY)

Behinger are well known for their clones of classic synths - the Minimoog, Korg MS-20, Roland TR-808 and more, but they became successful over the last twenty years making affordable mixing desks and other recording equipment.

The company was originally set up by Uli Behringer as a result of his building electrical audio equipment for his fellow students.

BEHRINGER UB-1 *1977*

Analogue
Mono / 2 VCOs
Before the company became successful as a manufacturer of affordable mixers and effects, Uli Behringer built a synth at the age of 16.

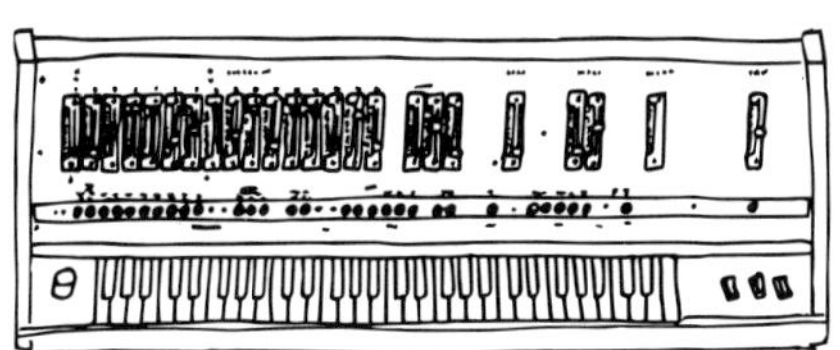

BRAINTEC TRANSISTOR BASS 3 *1994*

Analogue
Mono / 2 VCOs
Braintec (Germany) became 'MAM', another company to release a TB-303 clone.

BUCHLA ELECTRONIC MUSICAL INSTRUMENTS (USA)

Don Buchla was responsible for one of the earliest synthesizers commercially available - the Series 100 modular synthesizer in 1963. It was commissioned by the San Francisco Tape Center for Morton Subotnick and Ramon Sender who wanted a voltage controlled synthesizer for their compositions.

Buchla's philosophy was one of experimentalism and his synthesizers often took an unconventional route: instead of a piano-type keyboard he favoured touch-sensitive plates, and he frequently shunned the conventional 'analogue oscillator and filter' combination in favour of FM, AM and ring modulation which generate more complex harmonics. Buchla's instruments are also amongst the earliest of the analogue/digital hybrids, making use of the nascent microcomputer technology of the late 1970s.

Buchla stopped creating new synthesizers in the late 1980s, instead developing a range of MIDI controllers. He returned to synthesizer design in 2004, with a digital-analogue hybrid, the 200e.

BUCHLA MUSIC BOX SERIES 100 *1963*

Analogue / Mono / Modular
One of the first ever modular synthesizers, it even had a sequencer. Morton Subotnick, 'Silver Apples of the Moon' (1967).

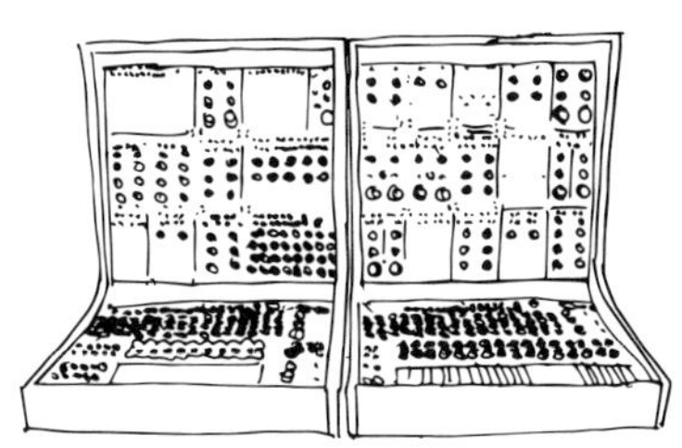

BUCHLA SYSTEM 101 *1970*

Analogue
Mono / 2 VCOs
Unusually for Buchla, this simplified version had a piano-style keyboard.

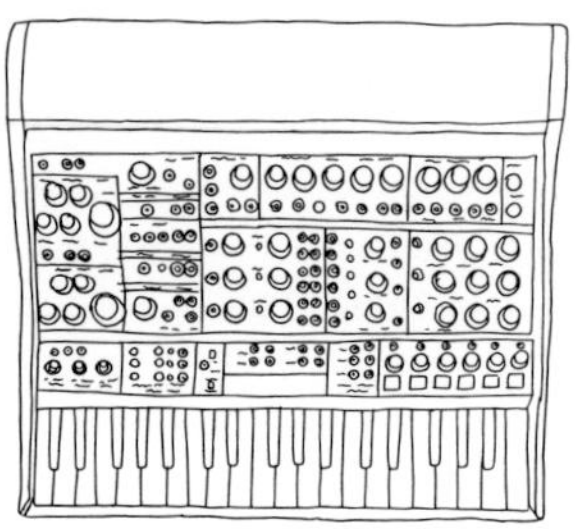

BUCHLA MUSIC EASEL *1972*

Analogue / FM / Additive
Duophonic / 2 Oscillators

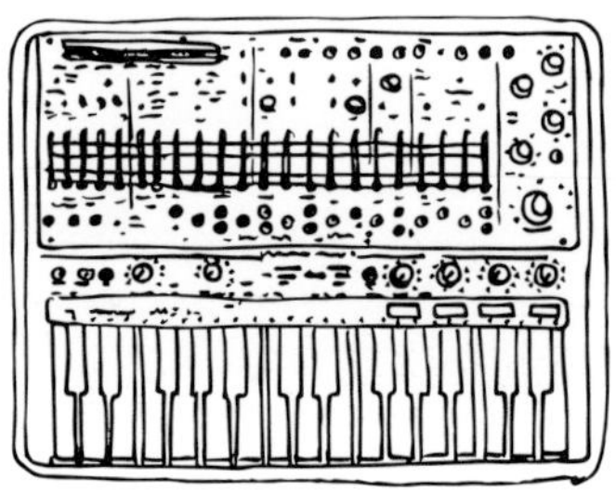

BUCHLA 200 (THE ELECTRIC MUSIC BOX) *1970*

Analogue / Mono / Modular
A system with a large range of modules. The Sili-Con Cello was also comprised of 200 series modules.

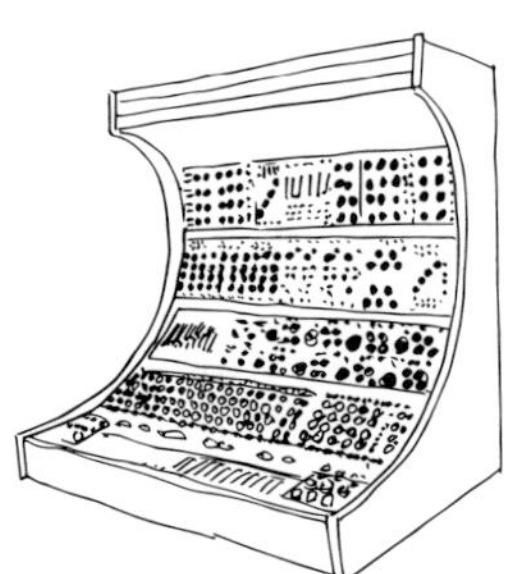

BUCHLA 300 *1973*

Analogue / FM / Additive
4 note polyphony / 4 oscillators
Most commercial synths used analogue subtractive synthesis in the 1970s, but Buchla preferred to start with the more complex tones generated by FM and AM, though standard analogue waveforms were possible. The 300 also incorporated 200 series modules as well.

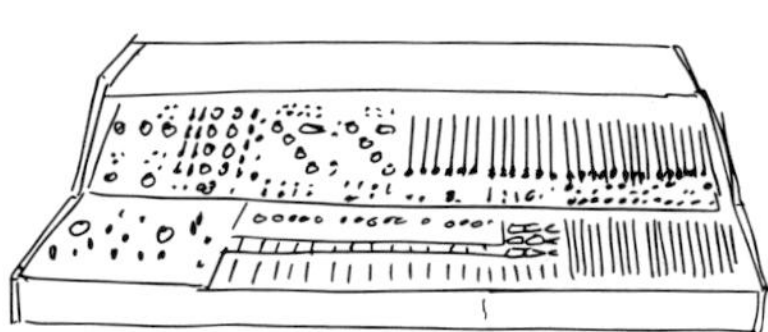

BUCHLA 500 *1971*

Analogue / FM
4 note polyphony / 4 oscillators
The 500 and 300 series were digitally controlled versions of the 200 series.

BUCHLA TOUCHÉ *1978*

Analogue
8 note polyphony / 3 VCOs per voice
Very few of these were ever made; the Touché could also repeat phrases using its proto-loop sequencer.

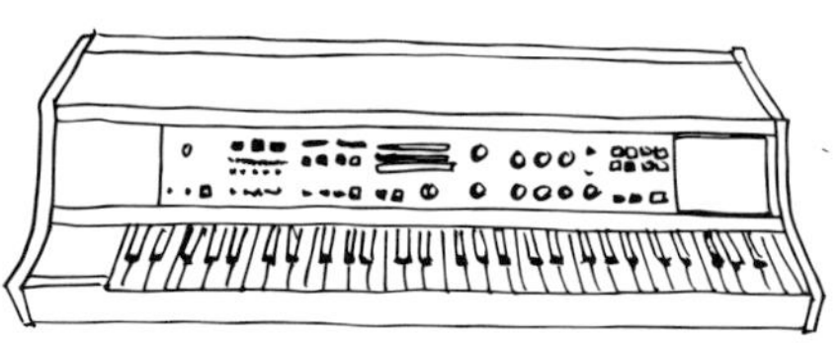

BUCHLA 400 *1982*

Analogue / FM
6 note polyphony
Microcomputer oscillators and control. Could be used with the 200 series modules.

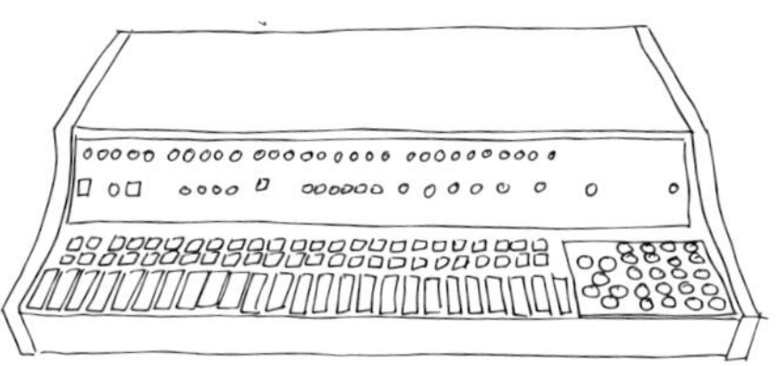

BUCHLA 700 *1987*

Analogue / FM
12 note polyphony / 4 DOs per voice
A powerful digital synth with MIDI and multiple sound sources.

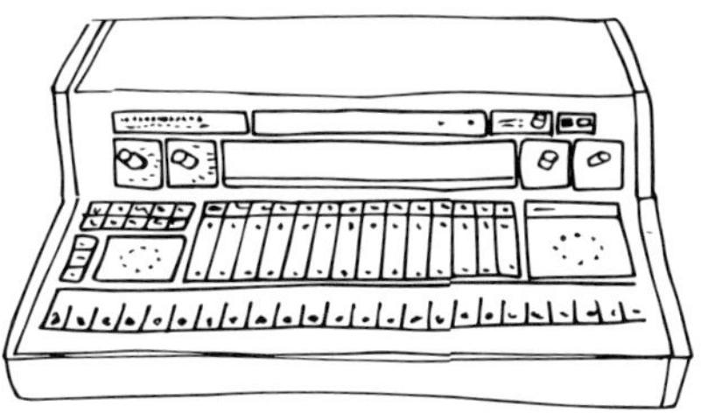

CASIO (JAPAN)

Casio was established in 1946 as Kashio Seisakujo by Tadao Kashio. The company's first products were cheap consumer gadgets, but by 1957 they had launched the world's first electronic calculator (initially using electromechanical relays, later transistors). Having met with success, Casio extended their range of electronic products to include watches, cameras and home keyboards.

The world's first digital home keyboard was the Casiotone VL-1, launched in 1980, and used simple buttons in place of a real keyboard. Casio went on to introduce the joys (or curse!) of auto-accompaniment with the CT-401 in 1981.

Subsequently, Casio launched a professional range of 'CZ' synthesizers from 1984 which used a type of frequency modulation called 'Phase Distortion Synthesis'. Though similar to Yamaha's FM technology, it was different enough to avoid patent infringement. During this phase, Casio even introduced a sampling keyboard, the SK-1 in 1985. Though barely more than a toy, it was an achievement considering the cost of professional samplers at the time.

The culmination of Casio's music synthesizer ambitions were realised in the form of the Cosmo ZZ-1 which was demoed by electronic musician Isao Tomita in 1984 and featured all the types of synthesis and sampling available to the company at the time. Some of these technologies made their way into their range of professional synthesizers. Casio's last synth aimed at the professional, the HZ-600, was released in 1987 after which they reverted to the home keyboard market.

CASIO CASIOTONE VL-1 *1980*

Digital
Mono / 1 digital oscillator
The world's first commercial digital synthesizer, immortalised by Trio's 'Da Da Da' (1982). Generates sound using 'Walsh functions', algorithms that can describe complex waveforms.

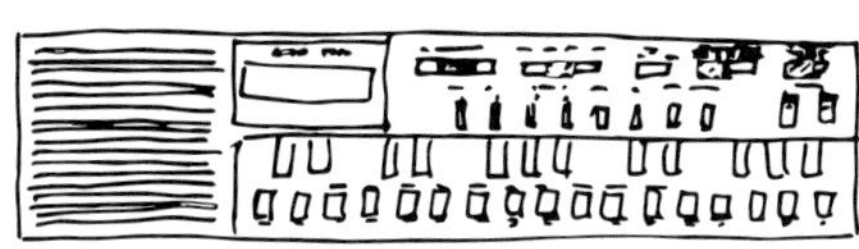

CASIO CASIOTONE 201 *1980*

Consonant Vowel Synthesis
8 note polyphony / 2 DOs per voice
Consonant Vowel Synthesis mixes two digital waves and uses filter formants to mimic instruments and the human voice. The 301 was also released in 1980.

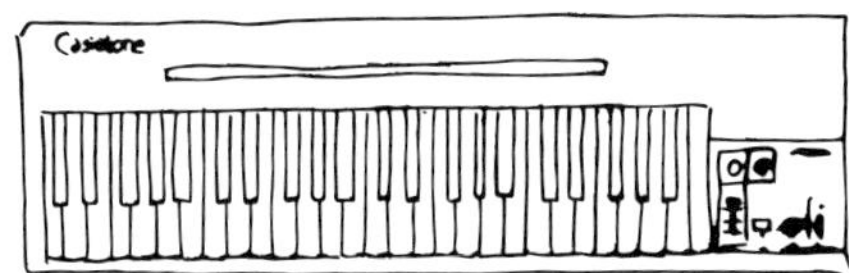

CASIO CASIOTONE 101 *1981*

Consonant Vowel Synthesis
8 note polyphony / 2 DOs per voice.

CASIO CASIOTONE 701 *1981*

Consonant Vowel Synthesis
8 note polyphony / 2 DOs per voice

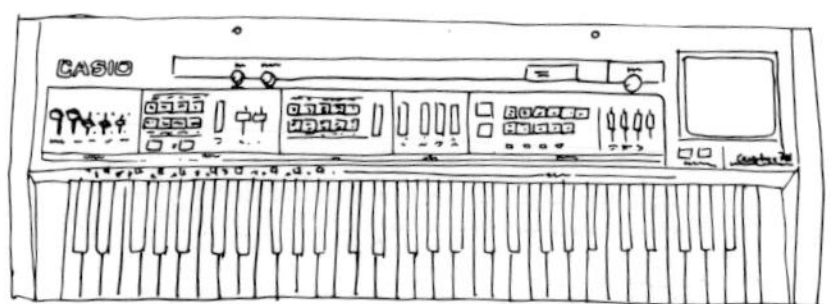

CASIO CASIOTONE 401 *1981*

Consonant Vowel Synthesis
8 note polyphony / 2 DOs per voice
First of the (in)famous Casio auto-accompaniment keyboards.

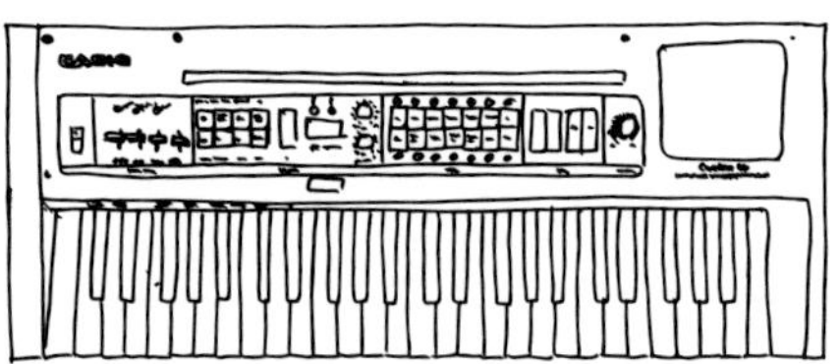

CASIO CASIOTONE 501 *1983*

Consonant Vowel Synthesis
8 note polyphony / 2 DOs per voice

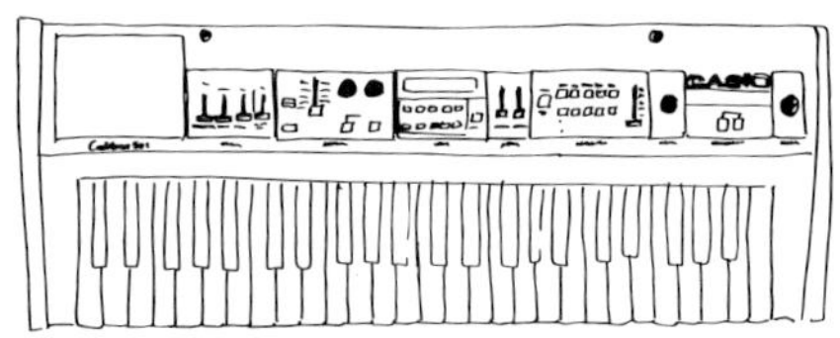

CASIO CASIOTONE 601 *1981*

Consonant Vowel Synthesis
8 note polyphony / 2 DOs per voice
The 610 was a variant.

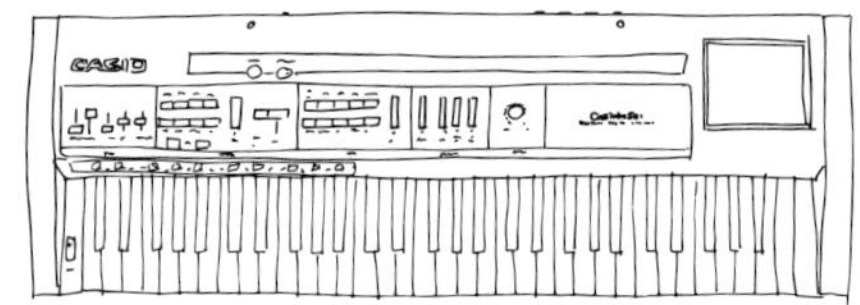

CASIO COSMO *1984*

Phase Distortion / Sampling / Subtractive synthesis
Designed for Tomita as a concept system, it had six-phase distortion units (PDUs), wave-drawing synthesis, a sample playback unit/sampler (SPU / ZZ-1) and a sequencer.

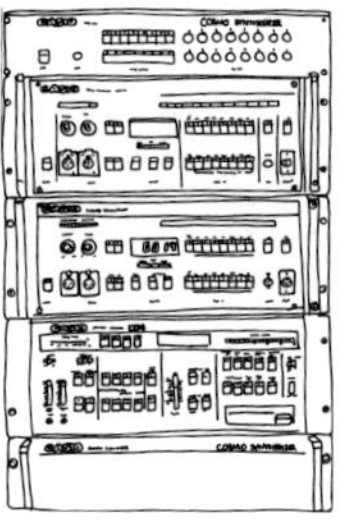

CASIO CZ-101 *1984*

Phase Distortion
8 note polyphony / 1 DO per voice
First of Casio's professional CZ synthesizers derived from the Cosmo concept system, the CZ-101 had mini-keys, affordable polyphony and fully recallable patches. Doubling the number of oscillators for half the polyphony was possible on all CZ synths.

CASIO CZ-230S *1986*

Phase Distortion
8 note polyphony / 1 DO per voice
A simplified preset version of the CZ-101.

CASIO CZ-1000 *1985*

Phase Distortion
8 note polyphony / 1 DO per voice
Identical to the CZ-101, but with full size keys.

CASIO CZ-3000 *1986*

Phase Distortion
16 note polyphony / 1 DO per voice
A CZ-5000 without the sequencer. (There was also a CZ-2000S and a CZ-2600S).

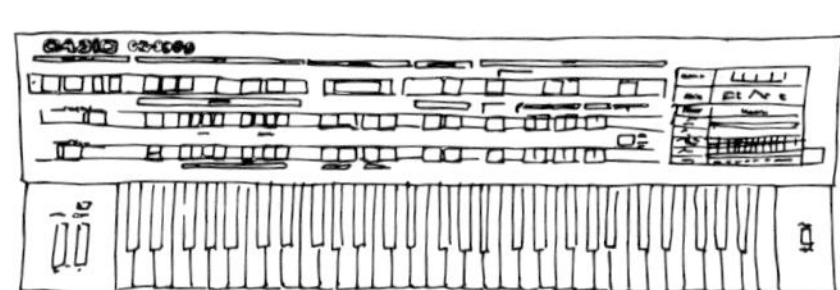

CASIO CZ-5000 *1985*

Phase Distortion
16 note polyphony / 1 DO per voice
The power of two CZ-1000s in one machine.

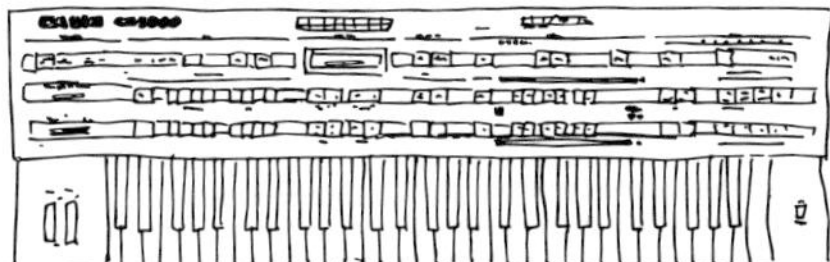

CASIO CZ-1 *1986*

Phase Distortion
16 note polyphony / 1 DO per voice
Last and best of the CZ range.

CASIO HZ-600 *1987*

Spectrum Dynamic Synthesis
8 note polyphony / 1 DO per voice
The oscillators have 32 stored digital waveforms and just one analogue filter. Based on presets, this was much more of a home keyboard than a full synthesizer.

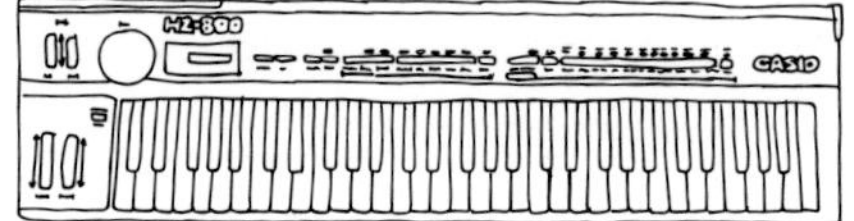

CASIO HT-3000 *1987*

Spectrum Dynamic Synthesis
8 note polyphony / 1 DO per voice
The HT-6000 was the top of the range version and had four digital oscillators per voice.

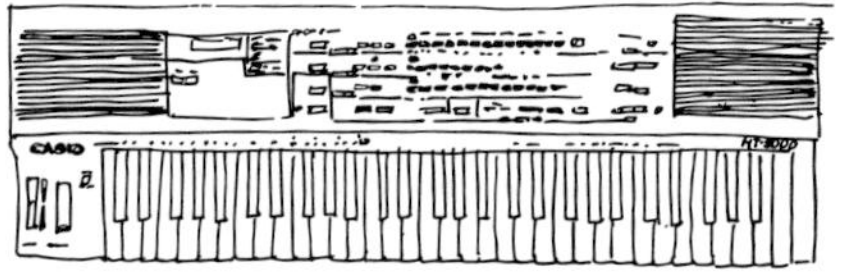

CASIO VZ-1 *1988*

Phase Distortion / FM
16 note polyphony / 8 Operators per voice
The VZ-10M and VZ-8M were rackmount variants.

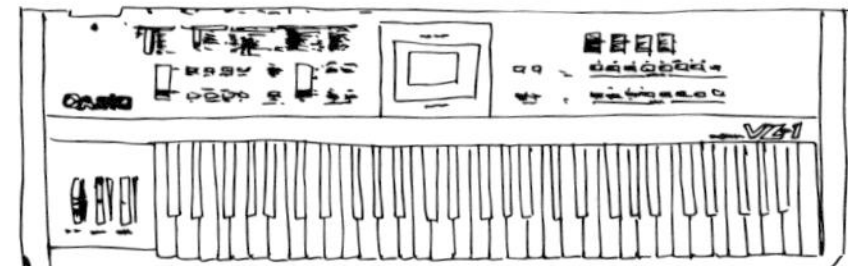

CEM (CURTIS ELECTROMUSIC SPECIALTIES) (USA)

CEM was founded by Doug Curtis in 1979 and produced microchips for audio signal processing. A brief list of some of the many synths to use CEM chips include: Akai AX synths, Crumar Trilogy, Stratus & Composer, Digisound 80, Ensoniq, Fairlight CMI, LinnDrum, MemoryMoog, Oberheim OB and Matrix, Roland SH-101, Jupiter 6, Sequential Circuits Prophet, and Waldorf Wave.

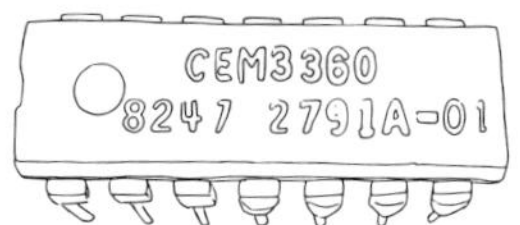

CHEETAH MS6 *1988*

Analogue
6 note polyphony / 2 DCOs per voice
Cheetah were a Welsh company of the late 1980s who found a niche for affordable digital synthesizers which could be used with home computers.

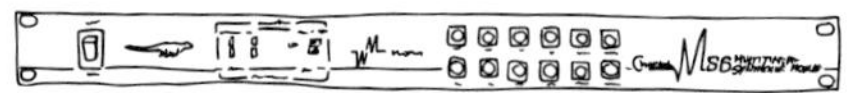

CHEETAH MS800 *1989*

Wavetable
15 note polyphony / 1 DO per voice (or layered up to 14)
'Annoying' and 'terrible' are some of the words used to describe programming this synth.
Aphex Twin named an EP in its honour.

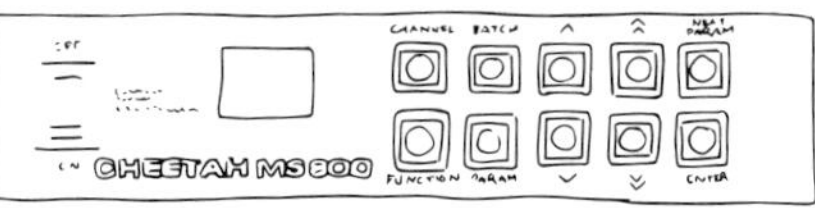

CLAVIA DIGITAL MUSICAL INSTRUMENTS (SWEDEN)

Clavia was formed in 1984 by Hans Nordelius and Mikael Carlsson. Their first product was the Digital Percussion Plate One which was followed by the Ddrum series. In 1995 Clavia released their first analogue modelling synthesizer, the Nord Lead, which immediately gained success due to the quality of its sound and its novel use of rotary LED encoders for easier programming. Since then, there have been many updates to, and variants of, the original Nord Lead.

CLAVIA NORD LEAD *1995*

Analogue Modelling
4 note polyphony
2 modelling oscillators per voice
Breakthrough virtual analogue synthesizer.

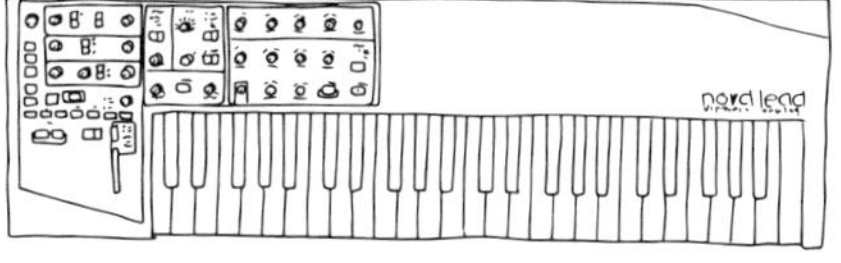

CLEF MICROSYNTHESIZER B30 *1982*

Analogue
Mono / 2 VCOs + 2 subs
UK-based Clef Products (Electronics) licensed the B30 from Allan Bradford who went on to design for Drawmer, WEM, Joe Meek, and others. This synth kit was supplied with Practical Electronics magazine. Clef also made the 'Master Rhythm' drum machine.

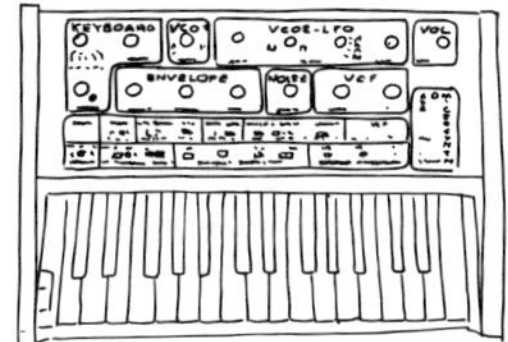

CON BRIO (USA)

Con brio is the musical term for 'with vigour' and this short-lived, but influential company certainly expressed that. Formed in 1978, their first instrument, the ADS 100, was used to create the sound effects for *Star Trek: The Motion Picture* (1979) and *Star Trek II: The Wrath of Khan* (1982).

It was a digital workstation that supported FM, additive synthesis and phase modulation synthesis. By the time Con Brio created their third instrument, the ADS 200-R, they had attracted the legal attention of Yamaha who owned the patents for FM - though no legal action was taken. One member of the company, Tim Ryan, went on to found the company that became M-Audio.

CON BRIO ADS 200 *1980*

Additive / FM / Phase Modulation
16 note polyphony / 64 DOs per voice (as partials or operators)
The Advanced Digital Synthesizer 200 was based on the prototype ADS 100 and the subsequent ADS-200R only saw one model built, which was never sold.

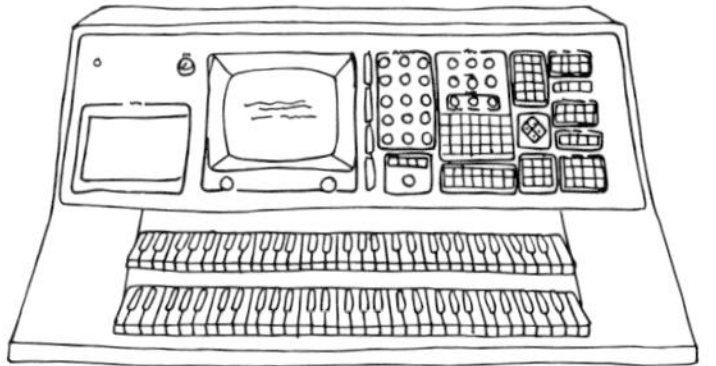

CONTROL SYNTHESIS DEEP BASS NINE *1994*

Analogue
Mono / 1 VCO
Control Synthesis was a music shop based in Stoke-on-Trent, UK, who commissioned this TB-303 clone.

CRUMAR (ITALY)

The Crucianelli company was founded in 1888 as an accordion manufacturer. The Crumar brand itself was formed in the late 1960s by Marco Crucianelli and business partner Marchetti. Initially making tone-wheel organs and ensemble synths during the 1970s, they started making analogue synthesizers later that decade. Notably, the Crumar Spirit (1983) was designed by Bob Moog, and they also licenced Bell Labs' 'Digital Synthesizer' technology to make the General Development System prototype in 1980. From this was derived the Digital Keyboards Synergy (1981) which featured additive synthesis and phase modulation. The 'Bit' brand saw the release of more conventional digital synthesizers from 1985. However, they ceased trading in 1987. The Crumar brand-name was resurrected in 2008 for a new range of electric organs.

CRUMAR ORCHESTRATOR *1975*

Ensemble Synth / Analogue
Full polyphony (divide-down)
Presets: brass, piano, clavichord, cello, violin
Other Crumar ensemble synths were the Performer, Composer, T1, and T2.

CRUMAR DS-1 *1978*

Analogue
Mono / 2 DCOs
Crumar's first true synthesizer, following the ensemble synthesizers.

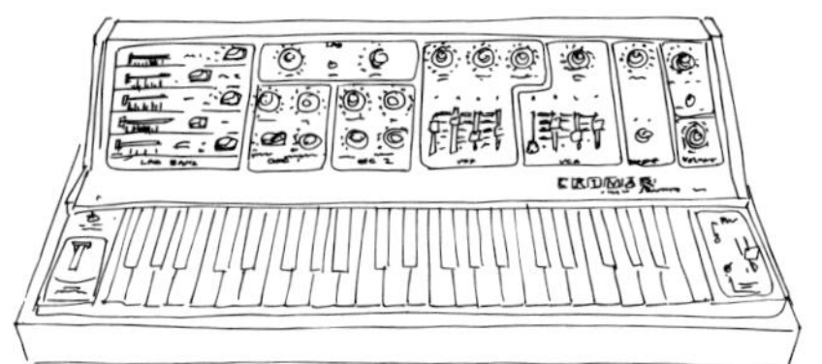

CRUMAR DS-2 *1978*

Analogue Synth: Mono / 2 DCOs
String Synth: Full polyphony (divide-down)
Combining a mono synth with a preset string synth.

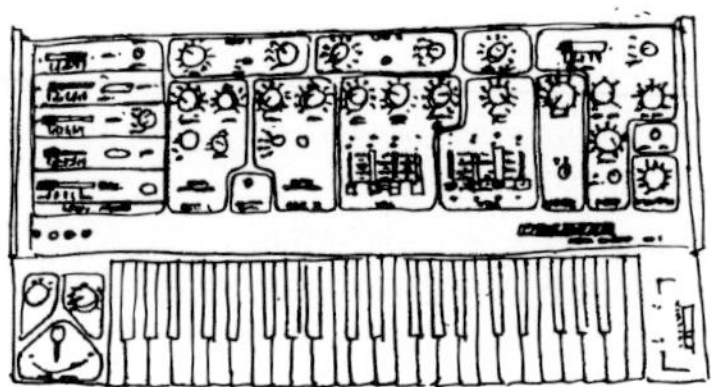

CRUMAR GDS (GENERAL DEVELOPMENT SYSTEM) *1980*

Additive / 32 partials
Based on the Bell Labs Digital Synthesizer, the GDS was the productionised version and made use of the Z80 chip. Wendy Carlos used a GDS for the *TRON* (1982) soundtrack.

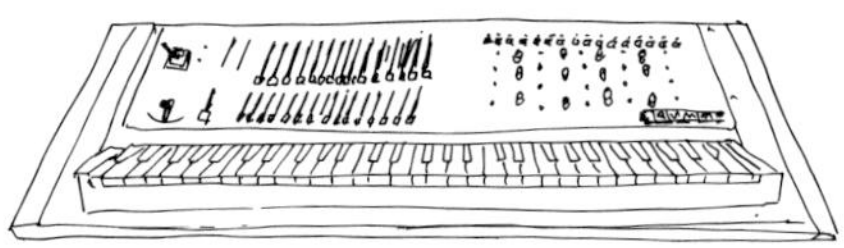

CRUMAR TRILOGY *1981*

Analogue section: Mono / 2 DCOs
String section: Full polyphony (divide-down) / 2 DCOs
Organ section: Full polyphony (divide-down)

CRUMAR STRATUS *1982*

Analogue
6 note polyphony / 2 DCOs
Comprises synth and organ generators.

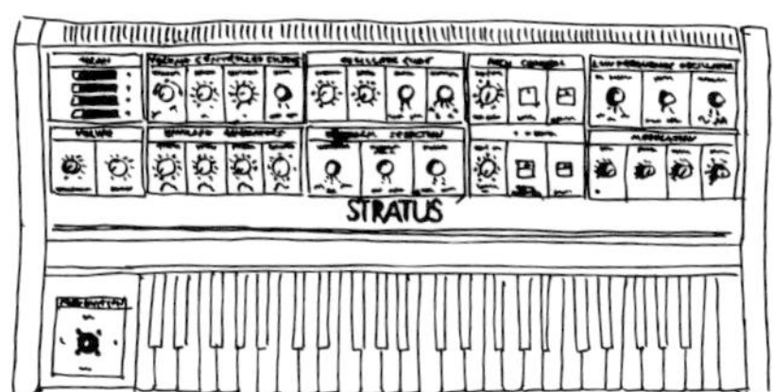

CRUMAR BIT 99 *1985*

Analogue
6 note polyphony / 2 DCOs per voice
The Bit 01 Expander was the rackmount version.

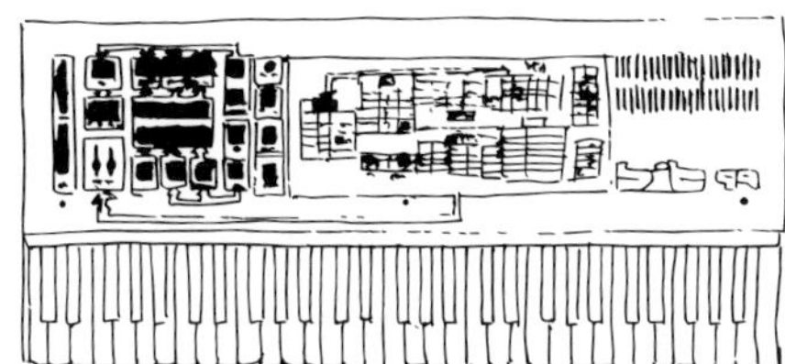

CRUMAR SPIRIT *1983*

Analogue
Mono / 2 VCOs
The Spirit was co-designed by Robert Moog.

DAVOLI DAVOLISINT *1972*

Analogue
Mono / 2 VCOs
Davoli Krundaal Musical SRL (Italy) released Italy's first analogue synth in 1972. Lacking filters, it was a basic lead synth for use with an organ.

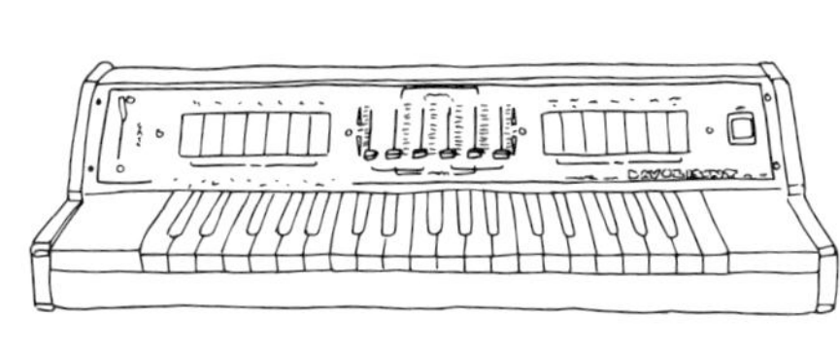

CRUMAR BIT ONE *1984*

Analogue
6 note polyphony / 2 DCOs per voice
808 State owned a Bit One.

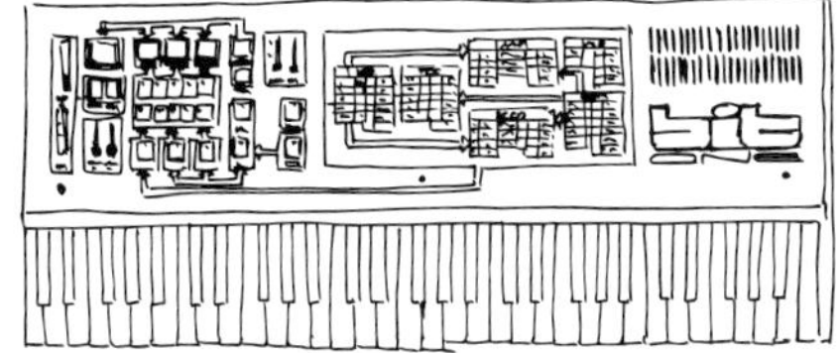

DEWTRON APOLLO *1973*

Analogue
Mono/Duo / 2 VCOs
This Dorset-based UK company made several synths, sold modular kits and a set of bass pedals.

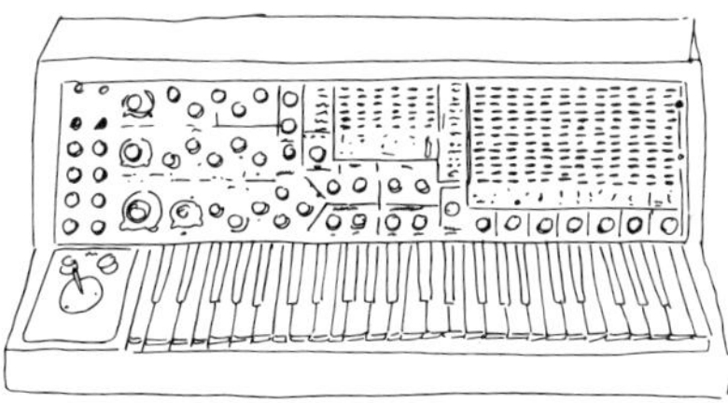

DGS (DIGITAL SOUND) (HOLLAND)

DGS was a Dutch distributor of Sequential Circuits, Crumar, PPG and RSF in the early 1980s. They also produced two monosynths designed by a company called Syntrance - the Scorpion and the Spider. (The Scorpion not to be confused with the KMI Scorpion Stage Synthesizer.) There were also plans for a range of modular systems - the 1,2 and 3, but it's not clear if they came to market in 1982 as planned. The brochure also makes it clear that the Spider (in their opinion) was better than the ARP 2600, Korg MS-20 and 'Roland', and invited potential customers to come to their showroom in Hilversum to try them all side-by-side. A Synton modular was available to compare with their DGS modular.

DIGISOUND 80 *1980*

Analogue / Mono / Modular
Digisound was launched in 1980 by Charles Blakey, who was a synth kit designer based in Blackpool, UK. His company sent kits out by mail-order and the system eventually comprised over 20 modules with VCOs, LFOs and even digital oscillators by 1985.

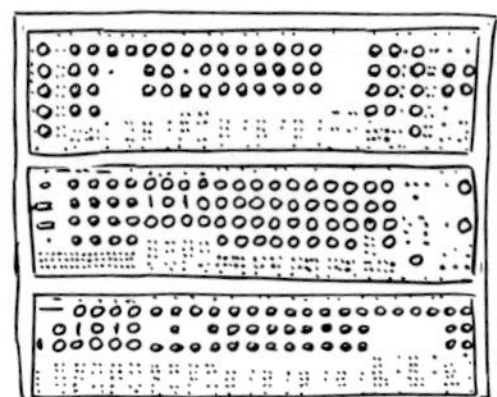

DGS SCORPION *1982*

Analogue
Mono / 2 VCOs
A rebadged E-Pro Spirit; the DGS logo bore an uncanny resemblance to the ARP logo.

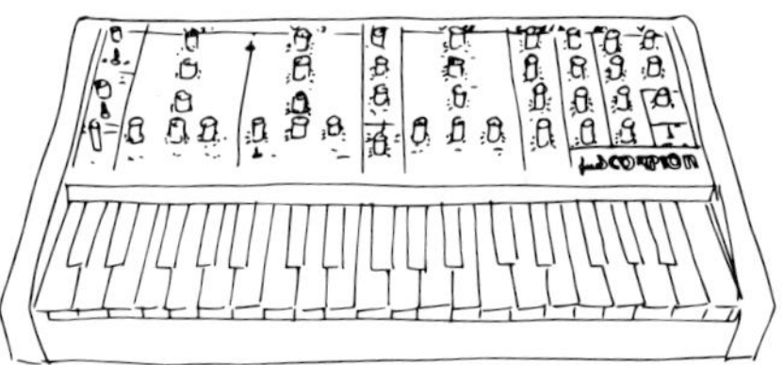

DIGITAL KEYBOARDS SYNERGY *1982*

Additive
16 note polyphony / 2 DOs per voice
Digital Keyboards (Italy) was a subsidiary of Crumar. The Synergy was derived from the Crumar GDS, which itself was derived from the Bell Labs Digital Synthesizer.

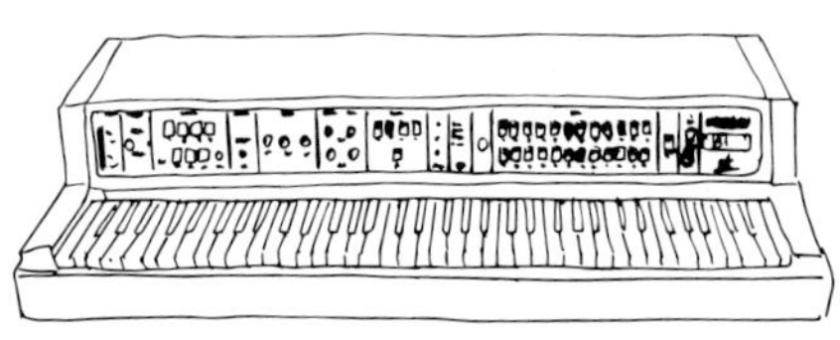

DGS SPIDER *1982*

Analogue
Mono / 3 VCOs
'The world's best monosynth' apparently...

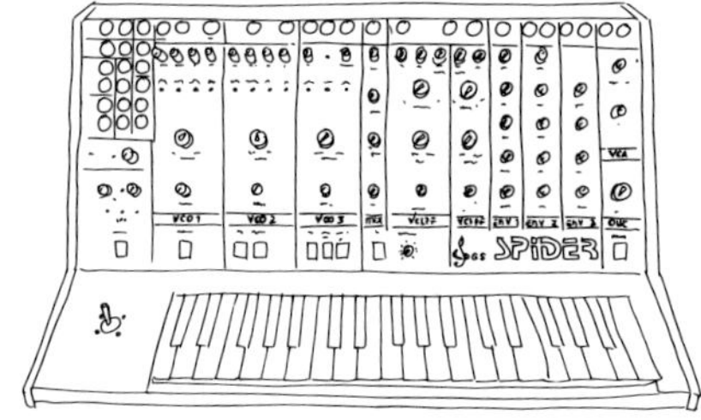

DOEPFER (GERMANY)

Founded in 1979 by Dieter Döpfer, Doepfer has a long history of building analogue synthesizers and MIDI controllers. They also launched a sequencer co-designed with Kraftwerk in 1992. They have long been a byword for modular systems since their 'Eurorack' format was introduced in the A-100 modular system in 1996. Eurorack has since been adopted as the 21st century modular standard and it's estimated that over 5,000 different modules have been designed since the resurgence in interest in modular systems in recent years.

DOEPFER MS-404 *1994*

Analogue
Mono / 1 VCO
A TB-303 type monosynth, though includes LFOs.

DOEPFER A100 *1995*

Analogue / Modular
Keeping the modular synthesis flame alive in the 1990s with a powerful and flexible system. This led to the adoption of the Eurorack format for the 21st century modular renaissance.

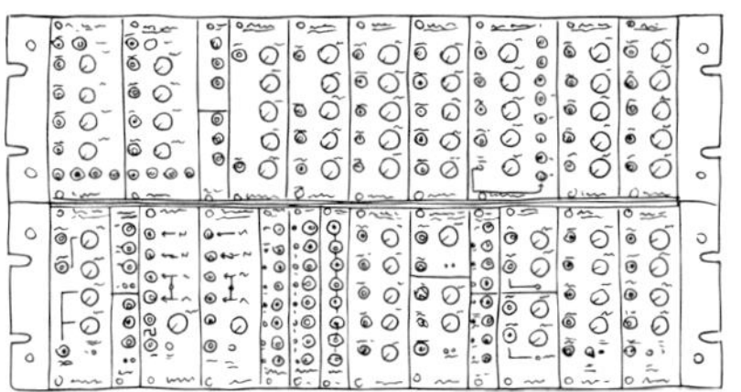

E-MU (USA)

E-mu was formed in 1971 by Dave Rossum, Steve Gabriel, Jim Ketcham, and were joined later by Scott Wedge. Initially called Eμ, they changed their name to 'E-mu' for the release of their first product, the E-mu modular synthesizer (1973). During the 1970s they developed and licenced a digital keyboard scanning technology to Oberheim, which was used in the Oberheim Four Voice and Eight Voice, and to Dave Smith for the Sequential Circuits Prophet 5. Royalties for these were an important income source for E-mu through the leaner years of the late 1970s.

After the vastly expensive and unsuccessful Audity synthesizer in 1980, which was made untenable when Sequential stopped payment of those royalties, E-mu made a name for themselves in the world of sampling. Making use of the new Z80 chips and collaborating on the design of the SSM chip, E-mu was able to release the relatively affordable Emulator in 1981 and built upon that early success with a series of updated versions and sampling drum machines throughout the 1980s. In the 1990s, E-mu was bought by Creative Technology and continued to release the series of Proteus ROMpler instruments. Creative Technology then attempted an ill-fated merger of E-mu and Ensoniq which ended both companies.

E-MU 25 *1971*

Analogue
Mono / 3 VCOs
The prototype for the later modular system, only two were made.

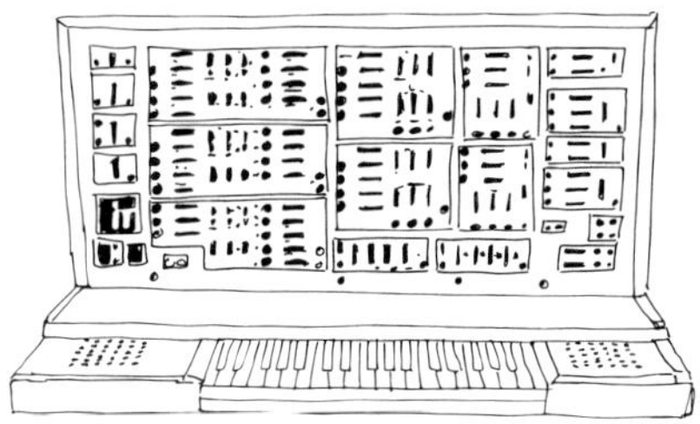

E-MU MODULAR *1973*

Analogue
Mono/Duo / Modular
E-mu's first products were modular synths, though they became better known for samplers in the 1980s.

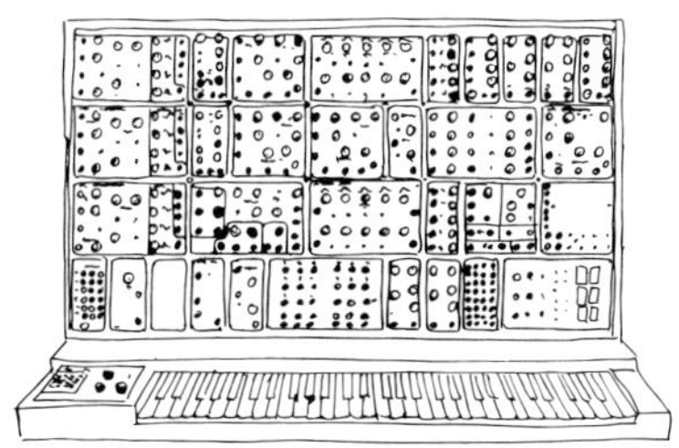

E-MU AUDITY *1980*

Digital Waveforms
16 note polyphony / 1 voice card per note
Was commissioned by Peter Baumann of Tangerine Dream, and the prototype was shown at the 1980 AES convention. However, it was never productionised.

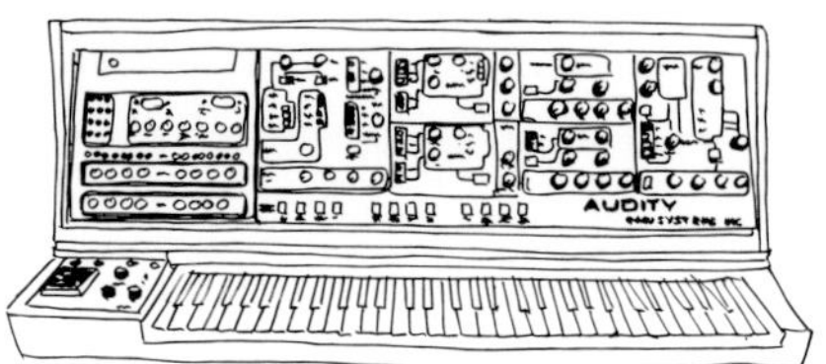

E-PRO MINI SYNTH *1983*

Analogue
Mono / 1 VCO
Simple synth from Holland.

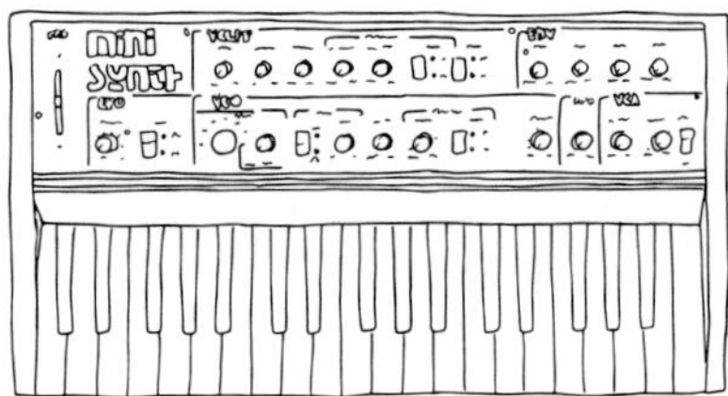

E-MU PROTEUS *1989*

Sample & Synthesis
32 note polyphony / 2 Samples per voice
Sample playback machine leveraging E-mu's expertise in sampling. Subsequent versions included the Proteus 2 & 3.

EDP (ELECTRONIC DREAM PLANT) (UK)

EDP was founded by Chris Huggett and Adrian Wagner (great-great-grandson of composer Richard Wagner). A distinctive insect range of synthesizers and sequencers followed - the Wasp, Gnat and Spider. Huggett went on to design other British synth classics such as the OSCar and Novation Bass Station. Wagner left in 1981 and set up Wasp Synthesizers, which lasted only a year but produced the Special versions of the Wasp and Gnat.

E-PRO SPIRIT *1982*

Analogue
Mono / 2 VCOs
Which came first, the E-Pro Spirit or the DGS Scorpion?

EDP WASP *1978*

Analogue
Mono / 2 DCOs
Very popular and affordable synth used by many musicians of the era. The Wasp Special (1981) had an upgraded case but retained the membrane keys. The Stranglers - 'Just Like Nothing on Earth' (1981).

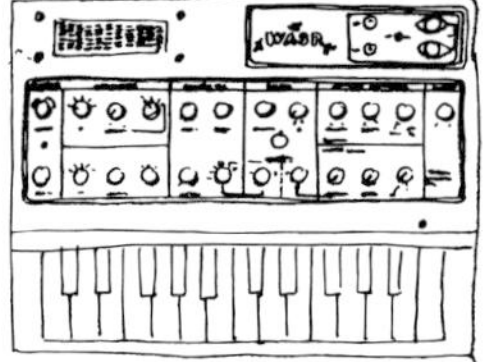

EDP WASP DELUXE *1979*

Analogue
Mono / 2 DCOs
The 'deluxe' upgraded the membrane keyboard to a standard physical keyboard.

EDP GNAT *1980*

Analogue
Mono / 1 DCO
One oscillator version of the Wasp; the Gnat Special (1982) had a wooden case. Designed by Anthony Harrison-Griffin, who also designed the OSCar.

EEH BANANA *1983*

Analogue / 6 note polyphony / 2 VCOs per voice
Electronic Engineering Hoffman (EEH), Germany, worked with Synthesizer Studio Bonn (SSB) to design the somewhat bizarrely named Banana synth. It's rumoured they were also planning a Coconut drum machine. SSB also created two sequencers for Ralf Hütter and Florian Schneider in the early 1980s.

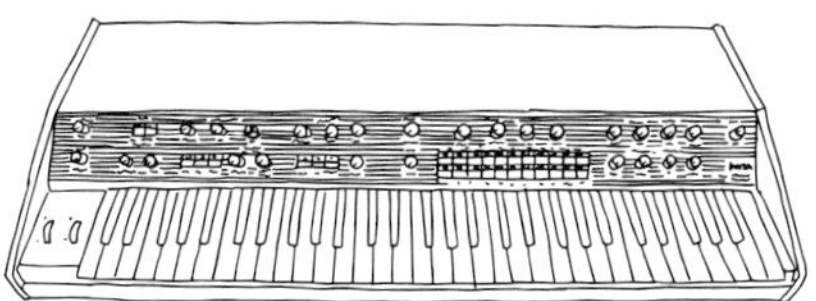

EKO (ITALY)

EKO were an electric guitar company set up in 1959, but who diversified into combo-organs in the 1960s. They also produced a drum machine (the ComputeRhythm) and a preset synth. The ComputeRhythm was notable for its 16 step sequencer, a revolution at the time, and which was used by both Jean-Michel Jarre and Manuel Göttsching.

EKO EKOSYNTH P15 *1979*

Analogue
Mono / 1 VCO
Simple monosynth, named for the number of presets it had. It was possible to mix two presets for slightly more complex results.

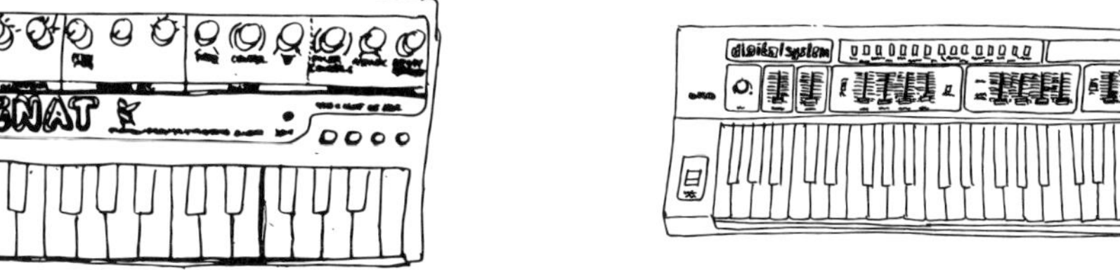

ELECTRO-HARMONIX (USA)

Founded in 1967 by Mike Matthews, Electro-Harmonix became well known for their guitar pedals and stomp-boxes. Famous among them are the 'Big Muff Pi' fuzz-box and 'Memory Man' series of delay pedals. More recently re-introducing vacuum tubes for the desirable quality of non-linear distortion they provide. In addition, they created the MicroSynth for the processing of guitar tones and the stand-alone MiniSynth.

ELECTRO HARMONIX MICRO-SYNTHESIZER *1979*

Analogue
Mono / 1 VCO
A guitar synthesizer with filter and envelope generator.

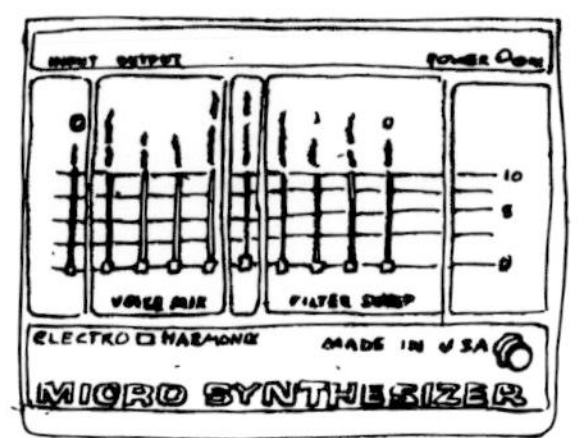

ELECTRO HARMONIX MINI-SYNTHESIZER *1980*

Analogue
Mono / 1 VCO
Very basic synth with membrane keys.

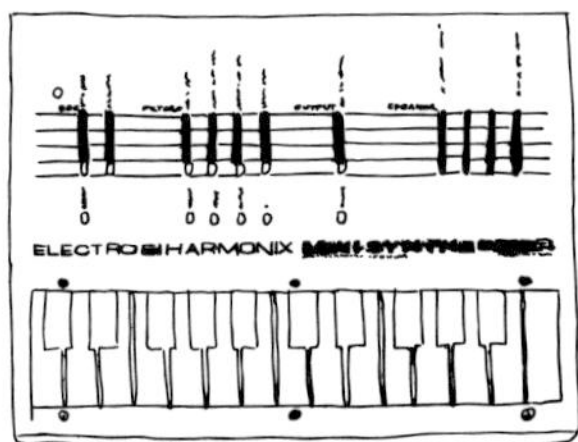

ELEKTOR FORMANT *1977*

Analogue / Mono / 3 VCOs
Dutch Elektor magazine published this DIY modular synthesizer, designed by C. Chapman. Doepfer designed a voltage controlled phaser module for it.

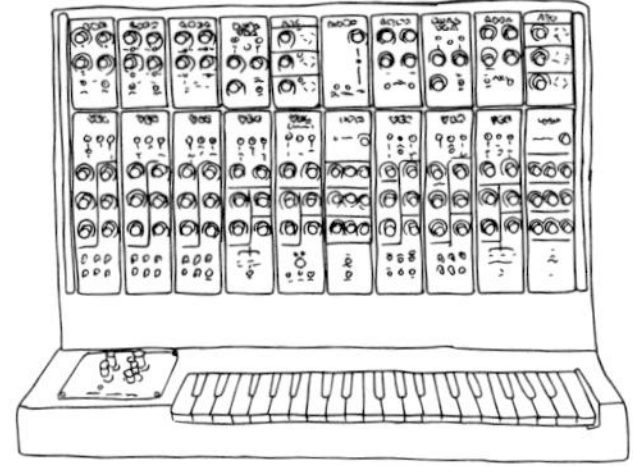

ELKA (ITALY)

Another Italian home organ manufacturer, Elka made the successful Rhapsody string machine before moving into the synthesizer market with the 505 Solist in 1978. By 1986 they had created the Synthex, an instrument made famous as the sound of Jarre's 'laser harp'. Pietro Crucianelli was president of Elka in the 1980s - the Crucianelli family company having built instruments throughout the 20th century, and another member of the family founding Crumar in the late 1960s.

ELKA RHAPSODY 610 *1975*

Analogue
Full polyphony (divide-down)
A well regarded string synthesizer used by Jarre, Tangerine Dream and Klaus Schulze. Other models of Rhapsody included the 490 (1975).

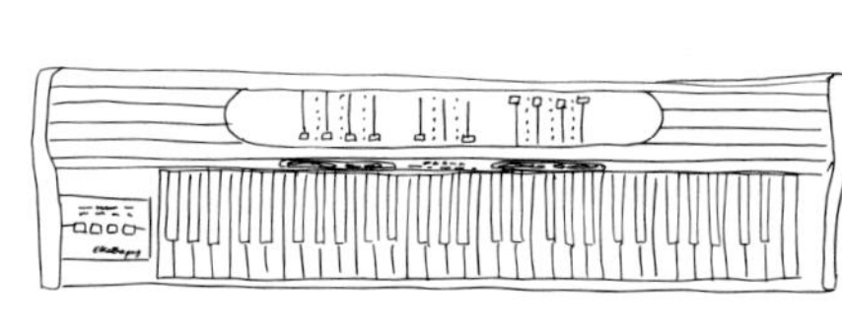

ELKA SOLIST 505 *1978*

Analogue / 11 Presets
Mono / 1 VCO
An organ-top monosynth.

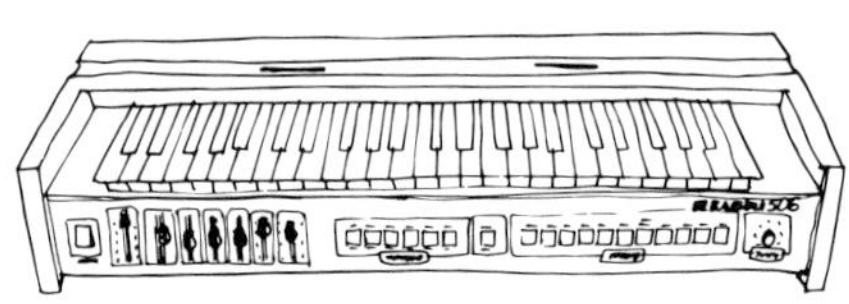

ELKA SYNTHEX *1981*

Analogue
8 note polyphony / 2 DCOs per voice
The sound of Jarre's Laser Harp (Third Rendez-Vous, 1986).

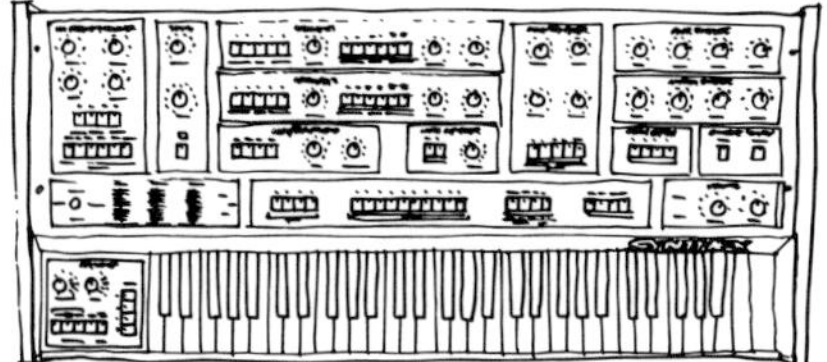

ELKA EK-22 *1986*

Analogue
6 note polyphony / 2 DCOs per voice
The EM22 was the tabletop version.

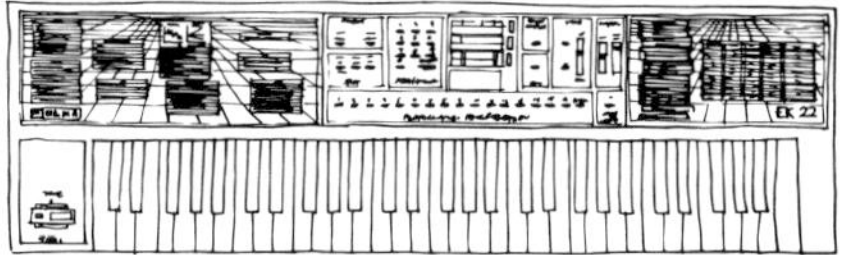

ELKA EK-44 *1986*

FM ('Digital Control Generator')
9 note polyphony / 4-operator / 2 DCGs per voice
The EK44 used Yamaha FM chips. The EM44 is the tabletop version; the rackmounts are the ER44 & ER33 (1x DCG per voice).

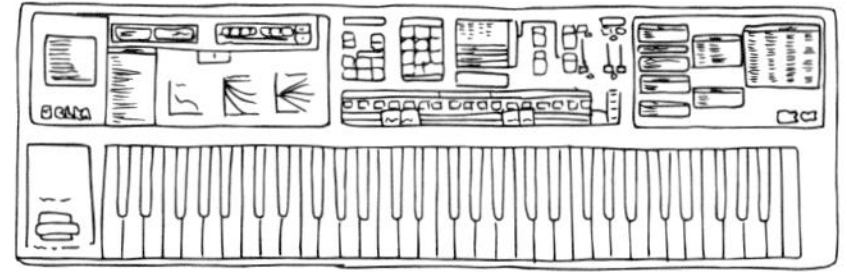

EMINENT ORGELBOUW (HOLLAND)

Eminent Organs are a Dutch organ maker founded in 1929. They are famous in the synth world for the Eminent 310 Unique organ which incorporated the world's first polyphonic 'divide-down' string synthesizer. It is also the sound of Equinoxe I. The string synthesizer in the Eminent 310 Unique was sold separately as the Solina String Synthesizer - and also rebadged as the ARP String Ensemble. Eminent patented the ensemble effect, though both Eminent and ARP continued to evolve the technology in their respective organs and string synthesizers.

EMINENT 310 UNIQUE *1972*

Analogue / 12 oscillators
Full polyphony (divide down)
First commercially available string machine; used by Jean-Michel Jarre - 'Equinoxe I' (1978).

EML (ELECTRONIC MUSIC LABORATORIES) (USA)

EML were founded in 1969 and their first synth, the ElectroComp 100 was aimed at the education market before they were sold more widely. Employee David Van Koevrering also worked for Moog before - and after - some years with EML.

EML ELECTROCOMP MODEL 100 *1969*

Analogue
Mono/Duo / 4 VCOs
One of the earliest polyphonic synths.

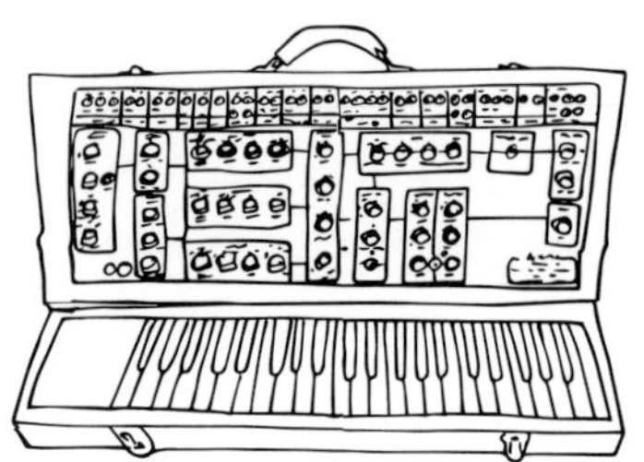

EML ELECTROCOMP MODEL 400/401 *1972*

Analogue
Mono / 2 VCOs
The 400 was the step sequencer designed for the 401 synthesizer.

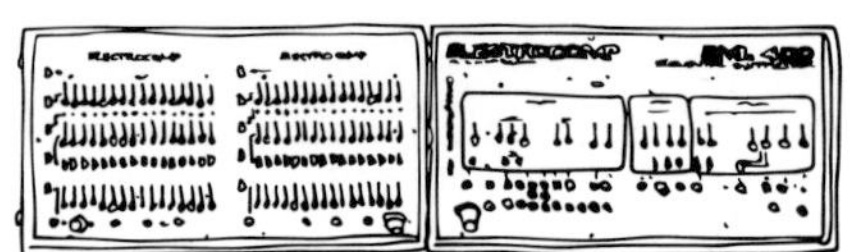

EML ELECTROCOMP MODEL 200 *1969*

Analogue
Mono / 2 VCOs
Also used as an expander for the Model 100.

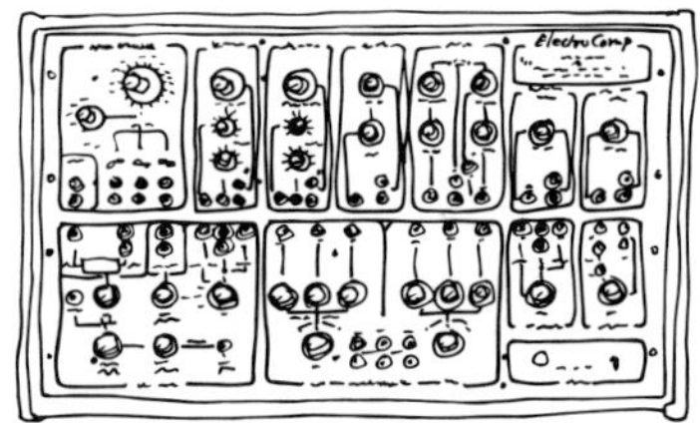

EML ELECTROCOMP MODEL 101 *1972*

Analogue
Mono/Duo / 4 VCOs
An updated 100, with op-amp oscillators for better tuning stability.

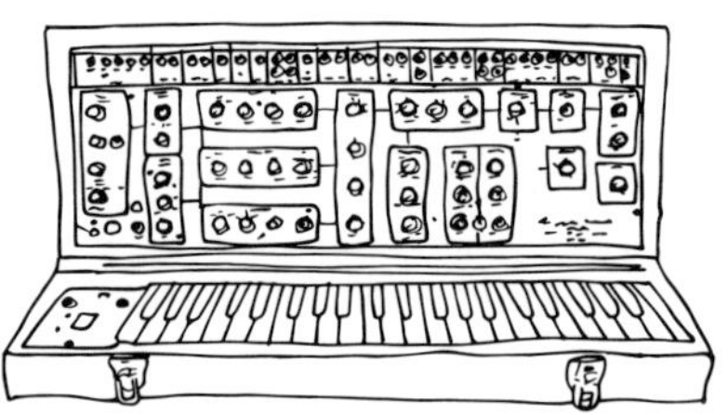

EML ELECTROCOMP MODEL 300 *1970*

Analogue
Mono / 2 VCOs
A controller, sequencer and expander for other EML modules.

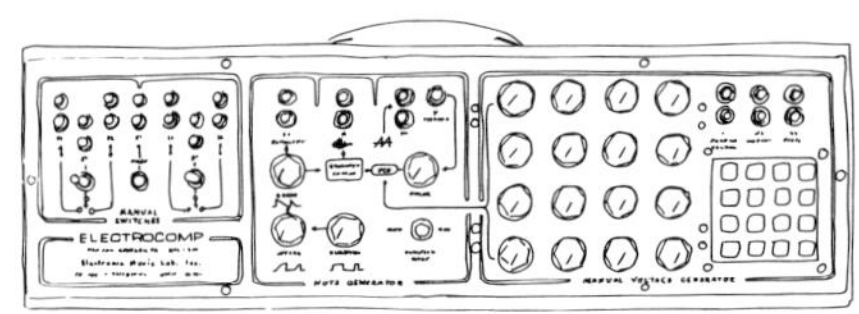

EML ELECTROCOMP MODEL 500 *1973*

Analogue
Mono / 2 VCOs
DEVO - the "Whip-it" sound.

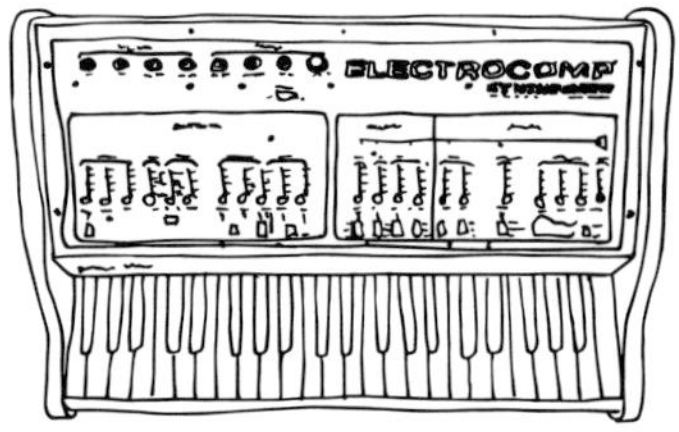

EML SYNKEY 1500 *1976*

Analogue
Mono / 13 VCOs
The 13 VCOs are tuned to each note of the 12 tone scale so that chords can be constructed by selecting the desired intervals. The SynKey 2001 could be programmed by punchcard.

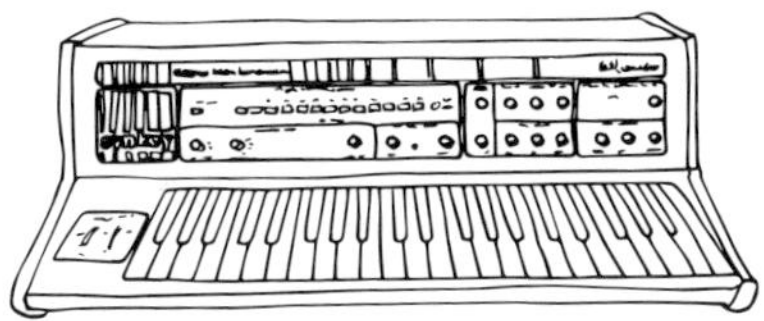

EML POLY-BOX *1977*

Analogue
13 x 2 pitch banks / 13 note polyphony
No internal VCOs - generates chords from a mono input.

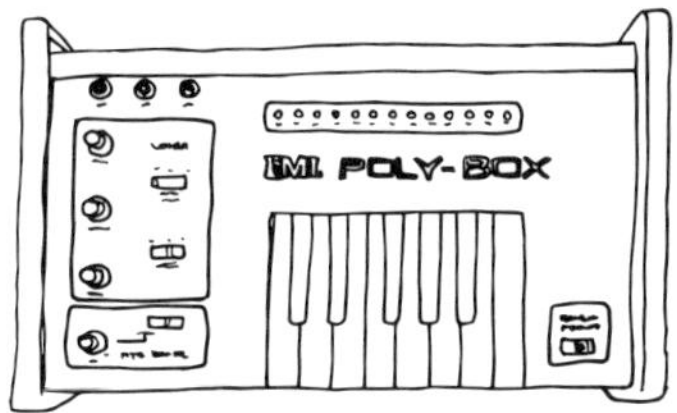

EMS (ELECTRONIC MUSIC STUDIOS LTD) (UK)

EMS is one of the legendary synthesizer companies of the 1970s. Formed in 1969 by Peter Zinovieff, Tristram Cary and David Cockerell, it came about after Zinovieff had already built an extraordinarily futuristic electronic system called the MUSYS. Two DEC PDP8 minicomputers controlled a room-sized synthesizer - hugely advanced technology for the time, but not a practical or commercial success. So EMS was set up to sell more manageable electronic instruments and to fund the MUSYS. Striking sonic gold almost immediately with the VCS3 in 1969, they went on to create a variety of influential instruments which were widely used by high profile acts such as Pink Floyd, The Who and Tangerine Dream.

David Cockerell left EMS in 1972 and after working for Electro-Harmonix joined Akai in the 1980s to design the influential S-series samplers. Unfortunately for EMS, the failed products and prototypes began to mount up during the 1970s - there was an ill-advised guitar synth (called the Sound Freak), an expensive vocoder called the '5000' (and costing £5000), and an even more expensive controller for the already vastly expensive Synthi 100. This wasn't sustainable and EMS effectively ceased to exist in 1979 when it was sold to Datanomics.

Robin Wood, an early employee, acquired the rights to EMS designs in 1985 and built VSC3s and Synthi As to order. Their legacy and influence remain undimmed.

EMS VCS 3 ('THE PUTNEY') *1969*

Analogue
Mono / 3 VCOs
A significant synthesizer, the 'Voltage Controlled Studio, attempt #3' was used widely, including in the BBC Radiophonic Workshop, and was one of the earliest portable synths.

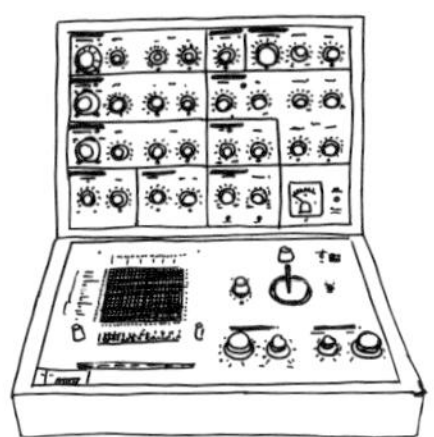

EMS SYNTHI KB-1 *1970*

Analogue
Mono / 3 VCOs
Never commercially released; the prototype was sold to Yes.

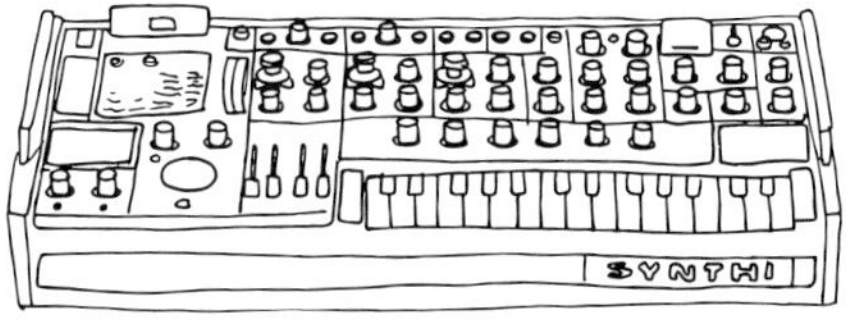

EMS SYNTHI 100 *1971*

Analogue
4 note polyphony / 3 VCOs per voice
The BBC Radiophonic workshop owned one (called 'The Delaware'). It was used for 'Dr Who' (1972-4) and 'The Hitchhiker's Guide to the Galaxy' radio series (1978).

EMS SYNTHI A ('THE PORTABELLA') *1971*

Analogue
Mono / 3 VCOs
Like a VCS3 and often found in universities and schools. The Synthi P was to be an improved version but was only ever a prototype.

EMS SYNTHI AKS *1972*

Analogue
Mono / 3 VCOs
Synth and sequencer used for Pink Floyd's 'On The Run' (1973).

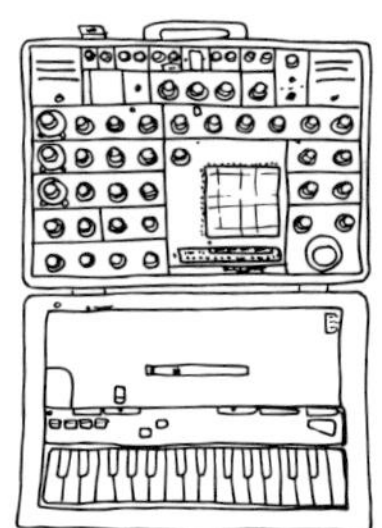

EMS SYNTHI E *1975*

Analogue
Mono / 1 VCO
An 'educational' and simplified version of the VCS3.

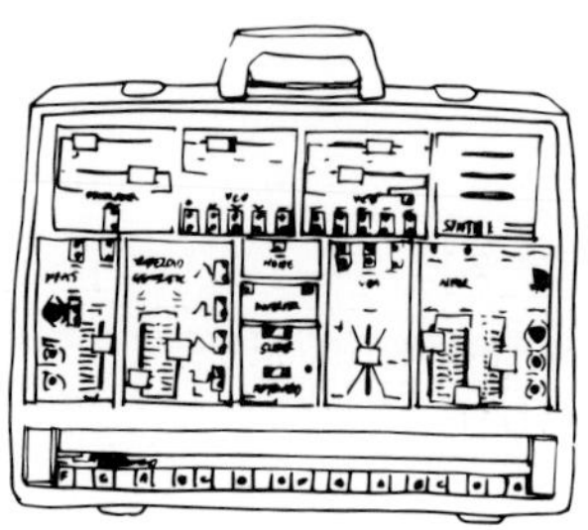

EMS POLYSYNTHI *1978*

Analogue
Full polyphony (divide-down)

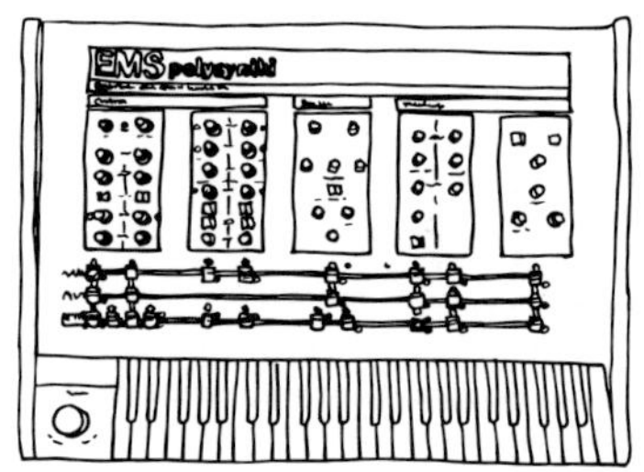

ENSONIQ (USA)

First there was a company called 'Peripheral Visions' that designed the Commodore 64. Then that company was engaged to build a keyboard for the Atari 2600, but the videogame crash of 1983 put an end to the project. So they did what anyone would do - changed the company name to 'Ensoniq' and designed an influential range of synthesizers and samplers. Until that is, they were acquired in 1998 by Creative Technology who merged them in a failed pairing with E-mu which saw both companies wound up in the early 2000s.

ENSONIQ ESQ-1 *1986*

Digital Waveforms
8 note polyphony / 3 DOs per voice
The ESQ-1 had 32 sampled waves and digital waveforms, and analogue filters. The ESQ-M was the rackmount.

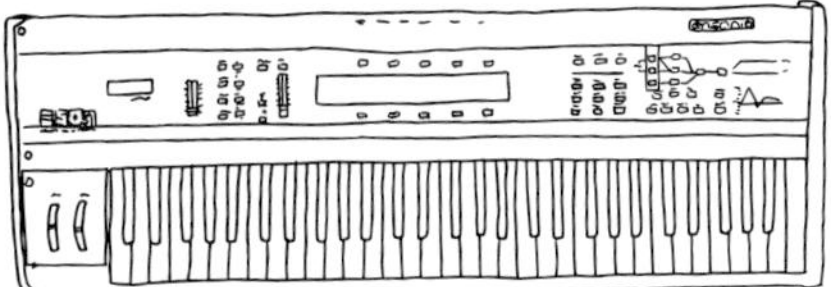

ENSONIQ SQ-80 *1988*

Digital Waveforms
8 note polyphony / 3 DOs per voice
An updated ESQ-1 with more waveforms.

ENSONIQ VFX *1989*

Transwave
21 note polyphony / 3 DOs per voice
Transwave synthesis is Ensoniq's term for wavetable synthesis; it was also possible to sample waveforms directly.

ENSONIQ SD-1 *1990*

Transwave
21 note polyphony / 3 DOs per voice
Similar to the VFX, but with a disk drive. The SD-1/32 increased polyphony to 32.

ENSONIQ SQ-1 *1990*

Digital Waveforms
21 note polyphony / 3 DOs per voice
A simpler VFX with many subsequent variants: SQ1+, SQ-R+, SQ-2, SQ-1+32, SQ-R+32, SQ2 32, KS-32.

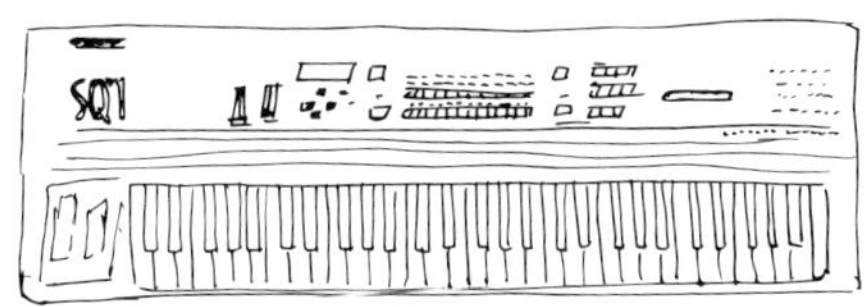

ENSONIQ TS-10 *1993*

Digital Waveforms / Transwave
32 note polyphony / 3 DOs per voice
An updated VFX with more features and waves.

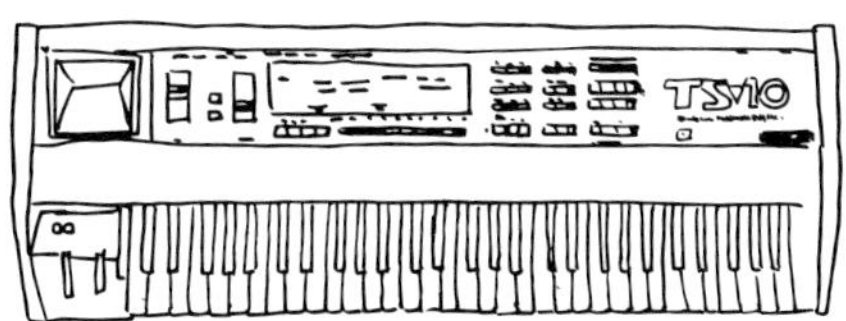

ENSONIQ TS-12 *1993*

Digital Waveforms / Transwave
32 note polyphony / 3 DOs per voice
Like the TS-10 but with a longer 76 note keyboard.

ENSONIQ FIZMO *1998*

Transwave
48 note polyphony / 2 DOs per voice
Transwaves are wavetables that can be manipulated in real-time for evolving harmonics and tones.

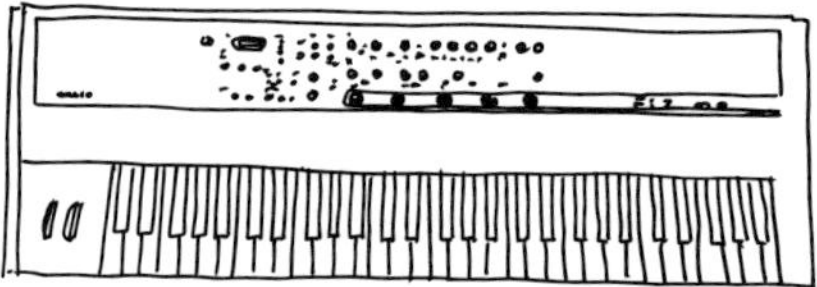

FBT ELECTRONICA SYNTHER-2000 *1973*

Analogue / Mono / 3 VCOs
Like many Italian synth companies, FBT was not originally a synthesizer company but a manufacturer (in this case) of amplifiers and mixing desks. It seems that the Synther-2000 was their only synthesizer - a Minimoog clone without filter resonance.

FORMANTA (RUSSIA)

Manufactured from the mid-1970s, the Formanta synths were commissioned according to Soviet quotas and made in the Katchkanar factory, which also made military and radio equipment. The Formanta Polivoks was actually a very innovative machine and was largely unknown to the west until Glasnost in the late 1980s. After that, instruments were able to flow in both directions across the iron curtain and a large number of previously unknown Russian synthesizers came to light.

FORMANTA POLIVOKS *1982*

Analogue
Mono/Duo / 4 VCOs
Unruly, but mighty Russian synthesizer classic.

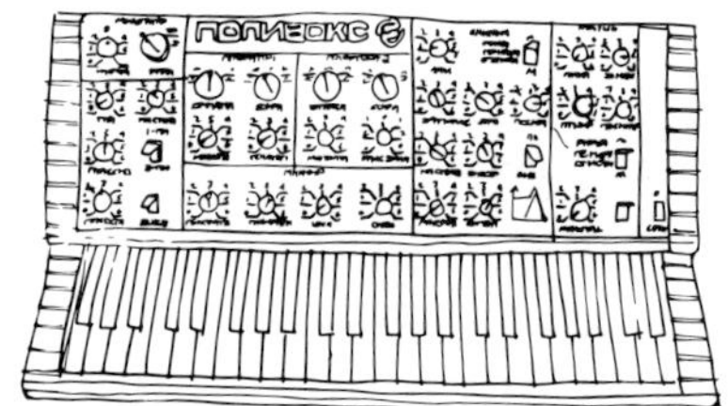

FORMANTA EMS-01 *1985*

Analogue
Synth section: Mono / 2 VCOs
Organ section: Full polyphony (divide-down)
Impressive dual-mode synth with stereo phaser effect.

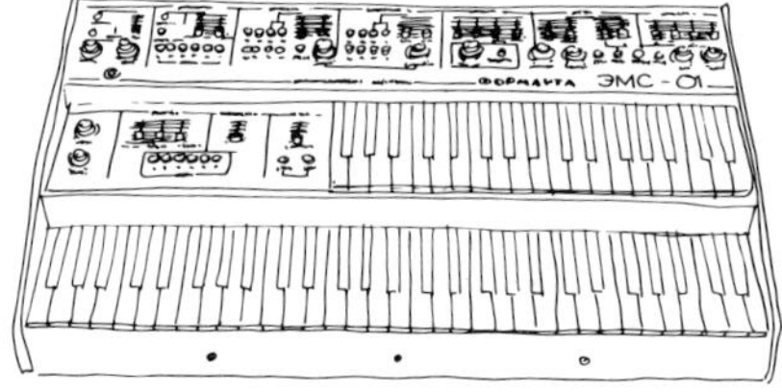

FREEMAN (USA)

As a keyboard player in a band, Ken Freeman wanted a better string sound than was available at the time. So he invented the divide-down architecture required for full polyphony (which he based on existing organ technology). He combined this full polyphony with oscillators that had independent rates of vibrato, thus mimicking a string section.

Unfortunately for Freeman, the Solina String Ensemble and the Crumar Stringman got to market first (and to some sounded better). Freeman subsequently left the audio industry and went on to compose the theme tunes to the UK television medical dramas Casualty and Holby City, amongst other things.

FREEMAN SYMPHONIZER *1973*

Preset String Synth
Full polyphony / 2 VCOs (divide-down)
One of the first string synthesizers.

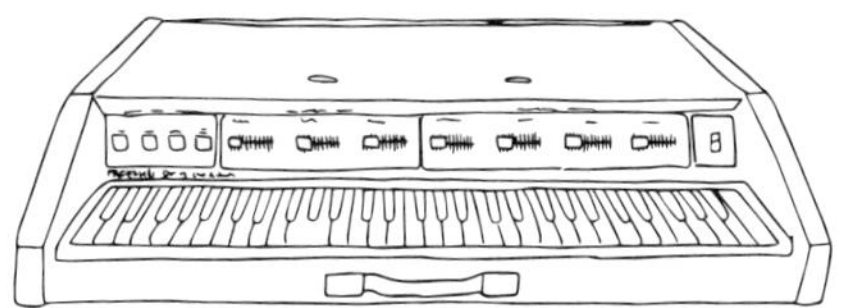

GLEEMAN PENTAPHONIC *1982*

Analogue
5 note polyphony / 3 VCOs per voice
Bob and Al Gleeman designed the Pentaphonic in 1982, their only synth (though it was also released as a 'Clear' variant with see-through casing).

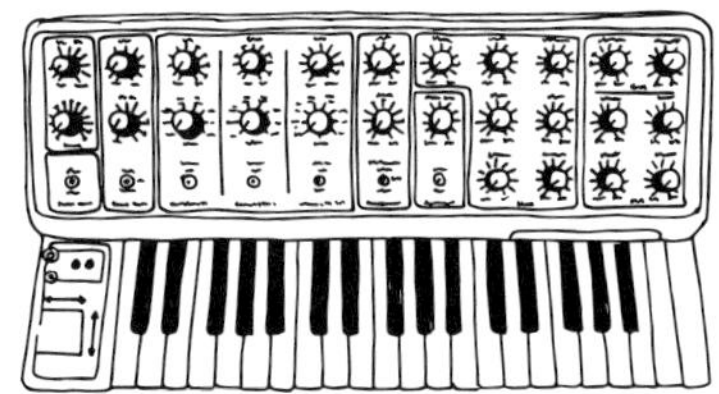

GROOVE ELECTRONICS STINGER *1989*

Analogue
2 note polyphony / 2 DCOs per voice
UK firm Groove Electronics' only synth product was the 'Stinger', equivalent to two Wasp synths. They also produced MIDI interfaces and retrofits for pre-MIDI instruments.

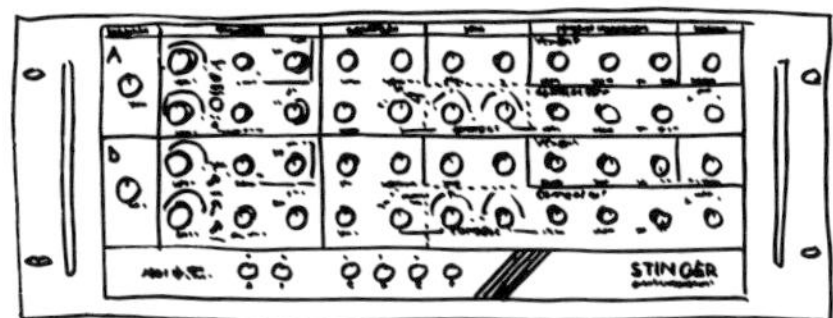

HILLWOOD BLUE COMETS 73 *1973*

Analogue
Mono / 1 VCO
Hillwood was a Japanese company who licenced synths and designs to Multivox, as well as releasing own-brand machines.

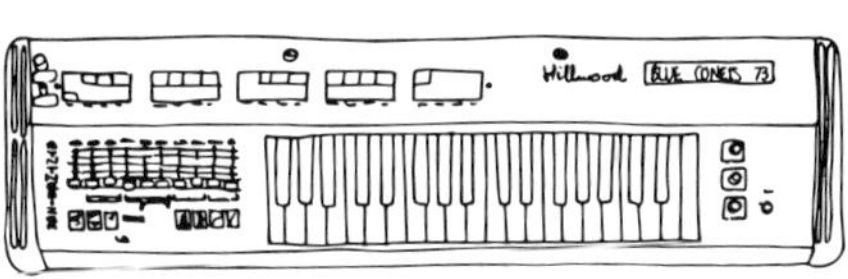

HITACHI (JAPAN)

Hitachi is a multinational conglomerate with interests ranging from aircraft engines and power systems to domestic electrical appliances and mining equipment. In the audio space, they are more known for their hi-fi and home audio systems - but they also made an analogue synthesizer range, of which the below is an example.

HITACHI LO-D HMS-30 *1978*

Analogue
Mono / 2 VCOs
The Lo-D includes drum machine and sequencer.

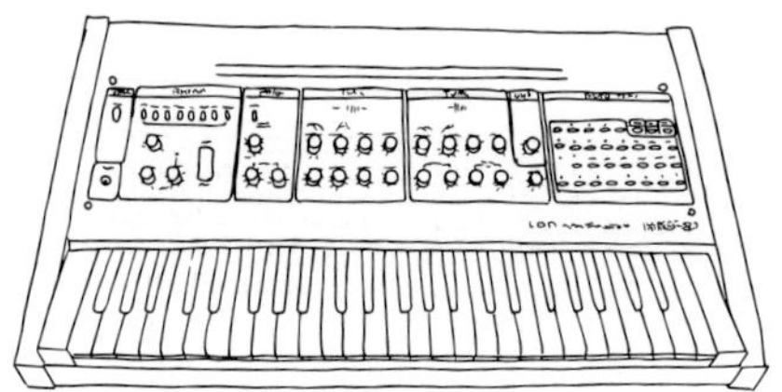

IONIC INDUSTRIES PERFORMER *1973*

Analogue
Mono / 3 VCOs
Ionic Industries, based in America, made only one machine, the Performer, which was a clone of the EMS VCS3. It replaces the pin matrix with a push-button system, presumably for increased reliability, and included an effects section.

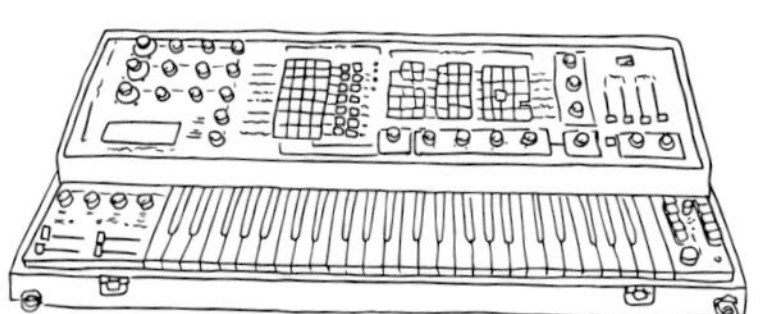

JEN ELETTRONICA (ITALY)

Jen is an Italian brand better known for their guitar equipment such as the Cry-Baby wah-wah pedal. Nevertheless, they also produced a line of synthesizers in the mid-70s, including the 3 VCO Syntar guitar synthesizer in 1978, pictured below.

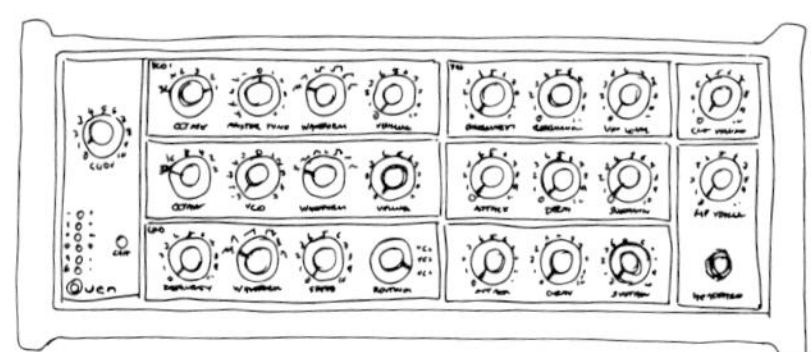

JEN STRING MACHINE SM-2007 *1976*

Preset String Synth: cello, viola, violins
Full polyphony (paraphonic)
Rebranded as the VOX String Thing and then acquired by Crumar.

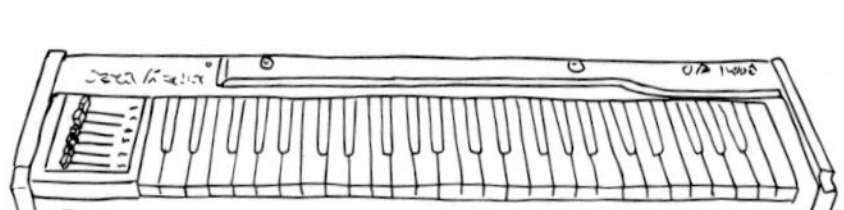

JEN SYNTHETONE SX1000 *1978*

Analogue
Mono / 1 VCO
The VCO is a square wave generating organ chip which is then passed through a waveshaper to form the sawtooth and pulse-width modulation.

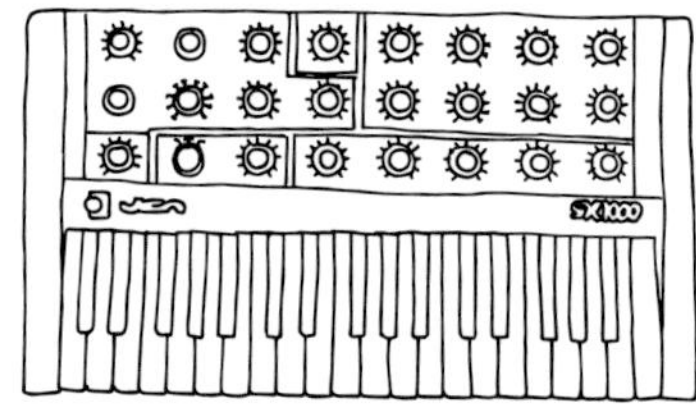

JEN SYNTHETONE SX2000 *1978*

Analogue
Mono / 1 VCO

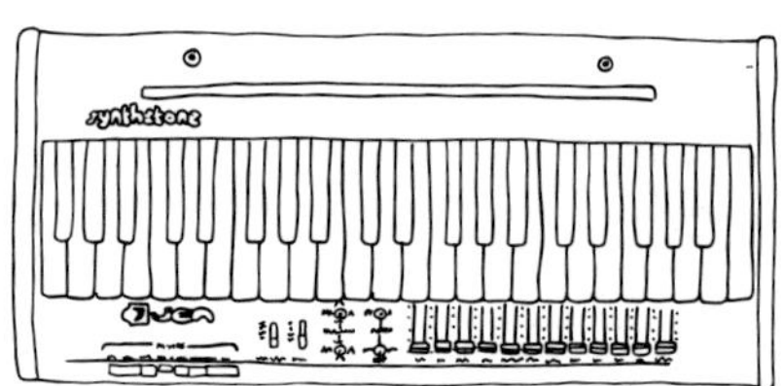

JEN SYNX 508 *1983*

Analogue
5 note polyphony / 1 VCO per voice

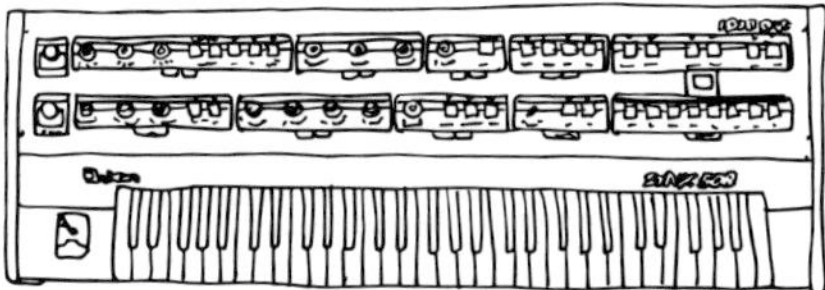

JEREMY LORD SYNTHESISERS (UK)

Jeremy Lord was a synthesizer manufacturer in the 1970s, but he was not able to compete with the larger companies of the time to sustain the effort. His son, Simon Lord, was a founding member of Simian (who went on to become Simian Mobile Disco), and sometimes goes by the moniker Lord Skywave, which was the name of the Lord synthesizer.

JEREMY LORD SYNTHESISERS SKYWAVE *1977*

Analogue
Mono / 2 VCOs
The Skywave not being a commercial success Jeremy Lord later turned to making medical equipment instead.

JWM ELECTRONICS (UK)

Known only for the Thunderchild SZ3540 synthesizer (1977), it was claimed by its advertising material to have been used on Jeff Wayne's War of the Worlds. It was available 'exclusively' from Chappell's of London - but it's thought only two models were ever made.

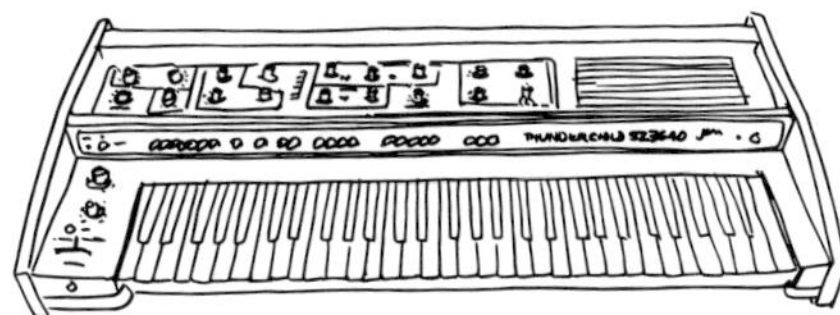

KAWAI MUSICAL INSTRUMENTS (JAPAN)

Koichi Kawai was born in 1886 and around the turn of the 19th century he became an apprentice of his neighbour, Torakasu Yamaha, who owned a reed-organ repair company. By the 1920s Kawai was working in Yahama's piano department, but once new management started to diversify beyond musical instruments, Kawai left to set up his own piano company. Since then, the Kawai Musical Instruments Company have become known for their high quality grand pianos.

In the 1980s Kawai started making synthesizers under the brand name Teisco. These instruments were solid, if not exceptional. The digital synths - the K1 and K4 especially, were much more successful, being affordable alternatives to the then dominant Korg M1. The K5 and K5000 are notable for being rare examples of mainstream additive synthesizers. In an interesting footnote, Kawai now own Lowrey (organs) who manufactured one of the first string synthesizers, the Freeman Symphonizer.

KAWAI K3 *1986*

Digital Wavetable / Additive
6 note polyphony / 2 DOs per voice
The K3 included the ability to build custom waves using additive synthesis. The K3M is the module.

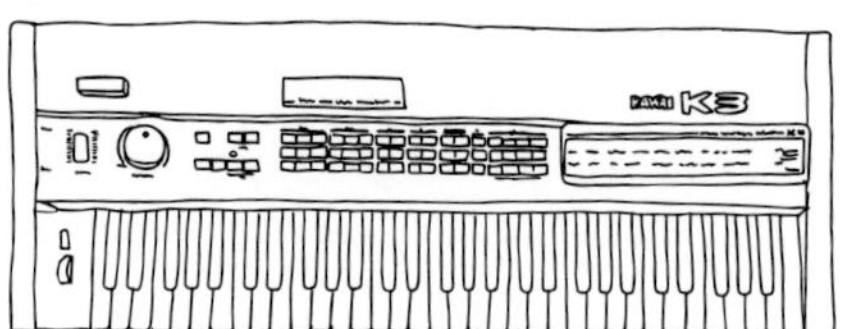

KAWAI K4 *1989*

Sample & Synthesis
16 note polyphony / 2 DOs per voice
Same as the K1, but with resonant filters and effects. The next Kawai ROMplers were the Spectra KC10 (1991) and K11 (1993).

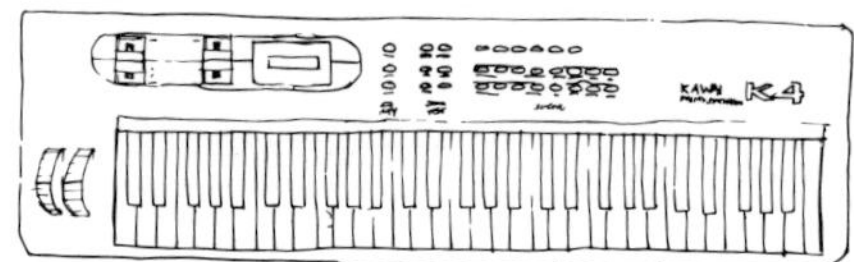

KAWAI K5 *1987*

Additive
16 note polyphony / 2 DOs per voice
One of only a few successful additive synthesizers ever made; up to 126 harmonics per oscillator.

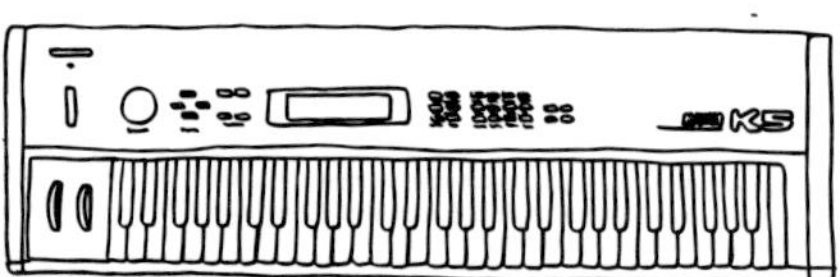

KAWAI K5000 *1996*

Additive
6 note polyphony / 2 DOs per voice
Workstation building on the K5's additive synthesis. Variants were the K5000S, K5000R (rackmount), and K5000W (which added ROMpler sounds).

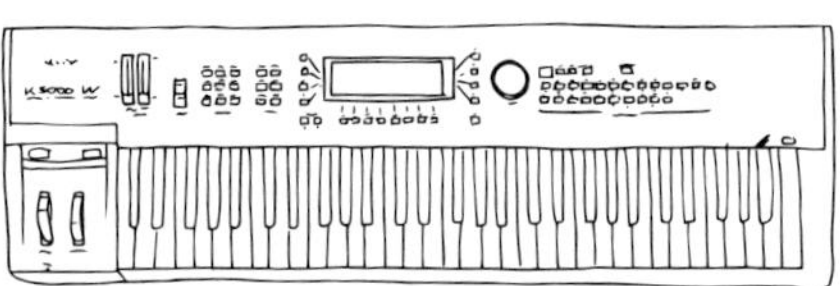

KAWAI K1 *1988*

Sample & Synthesis
16 note polyphony / 2 DOs per voice
Affordable M1-style ROMpler, though lacking filters. The K1ii (1989) added a ring modulator, effects and updated the PCM sounds.

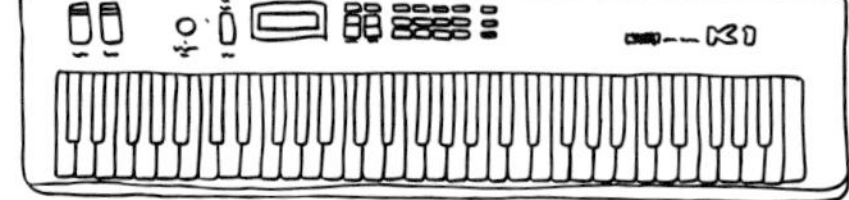

KMI SCORPION STAGE SYNTHESIZER *1977*

Analogue / Mono/Duo / 2 VCOs
Keynote Musical Instruments were a small UK synth manufacturer who never broke through with their 'Scorpion Stage Synthesizer'. There seems to be some evidence that they were first to the Keytar concept, but weren't able to capitalise on it.

KINETIC SOUND PRISM *1979*

FM / Additive / Waveform plotting
24 note polyphony / 6 oscillators per voice
A highly experimental American synthesizer which claimed six different types of synthesis including wave-shaping, wave blending and FM. It wasn't to be a success given its cost of $45,000 and only two ever were ever made.

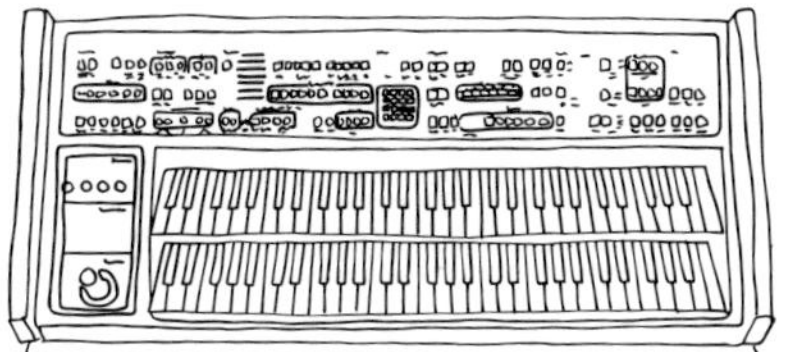

KORG (JAPAN)

Tsutomu Kato and Tadashi Osanai founded Keio Gijutsu Kenkyujo in 1962. Their intention was to build a better drum machine because Osanai was dissatisfied with the accompaniment offerings of the time such as the Wurlitzer Sideman.

Having launched the company with the electro-mechanical Doncamatic DA-20 in 1963, they then diversified into organs. As they did so, they changed the company name to Korg, taking the K and O from their initials, and the 'oRG' from organ.

From the 1970s, Korg released a series of successful and influential analogue synthesizers, including the famous MS-20. In 1988 Korg released the M1 which is one of the best selling synths of all time. Korg continued to innovate into the 1990s with the release of the Korg Prophecy in 1995, which was one of the first to model analogue circuitry in software. Korg continues as one of the leading companies in the synth and professional audio market, most recently re-releasing their classic MS-20, and pairing with ARP to re-release the ARP Odyssey (2015) and ARP 2600 (2020).

KORG MINI-KORG 700 *1972*

Analogue
Mono / 1 VCO
Korg's first synthesizer, designed for use on top of a home organ.

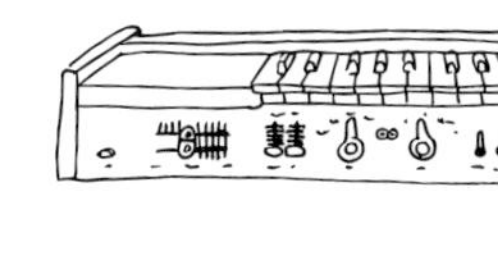

KORG MINI-KORG 700S *1974*

Analogue
Mono / 2 VCOs
Double the oscillators of the 700 and included an effects section. The Normal - 'Warm Leatherette' (1978); also Mute Record's first release.

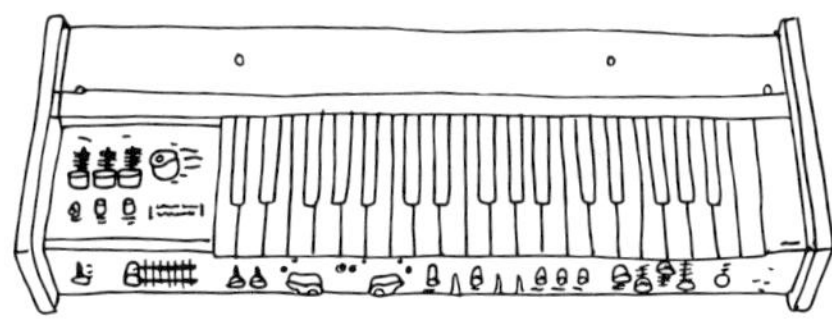

KORG MAXI-KORG 800DV *1974*

Analogue
Mono/Duo / 2 VCOs with sub oscillators
DV - Dual Voice. Was essentially two 700S's in one box, with a longer keyboard and more waveforms.

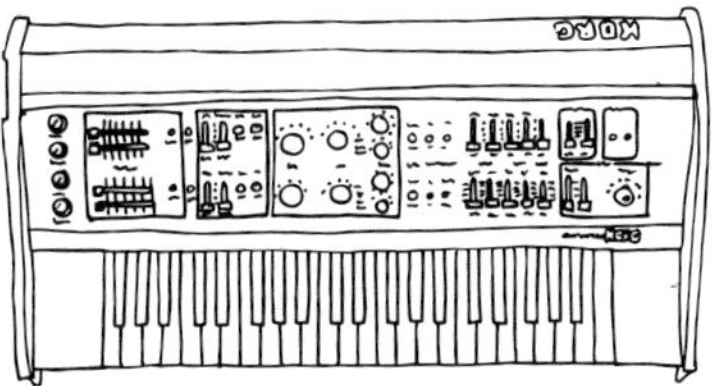

KORG 900PS *1975*

Analogue
Mono / 29 presets

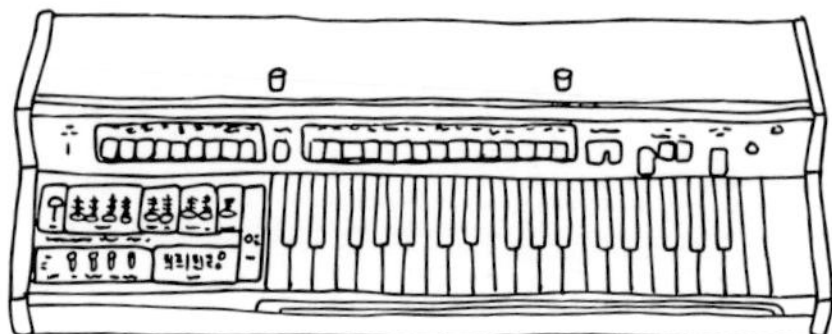

KORG PE-1000 *1976*

Ensemble / 7 presets
Full polyphony (divide-down)
'PE' standing for 'Polyphonic Ensemble'. Also available was the PE-2000, which had an alternative set of presets.

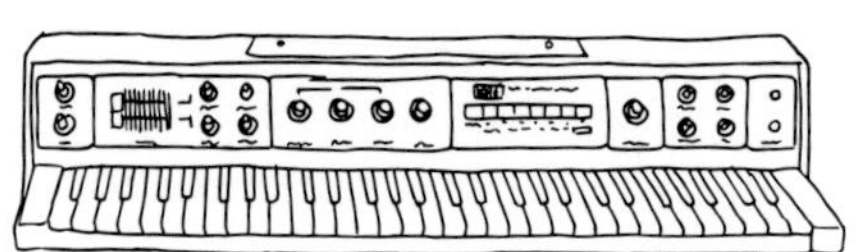

KORG SB-100 SYNTHE-BASS *1975*

Analogue
Mono / 1 VCO
Soft Cell - 'Tainted Love' (1981) (bassline).

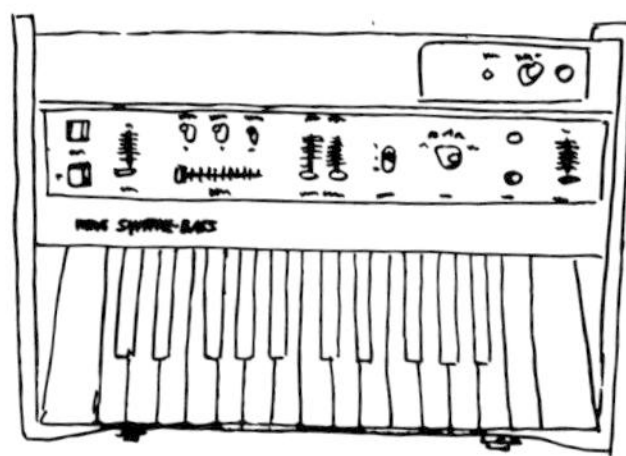

KORG M500 MICRO-PRESET *1977*

Analogue
Mono / 6 presets
OMD used the very recognisable presets on their early singles.

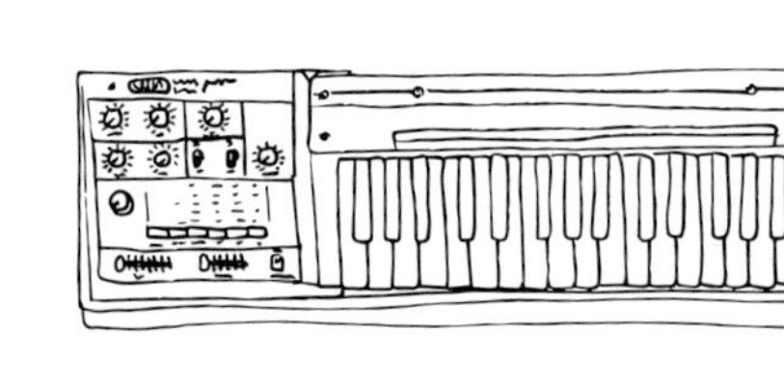

KORG 770 *1976*

Analogue
Mono / 2 VCOs
Human League - 'Dare' album (1981) (basslines).

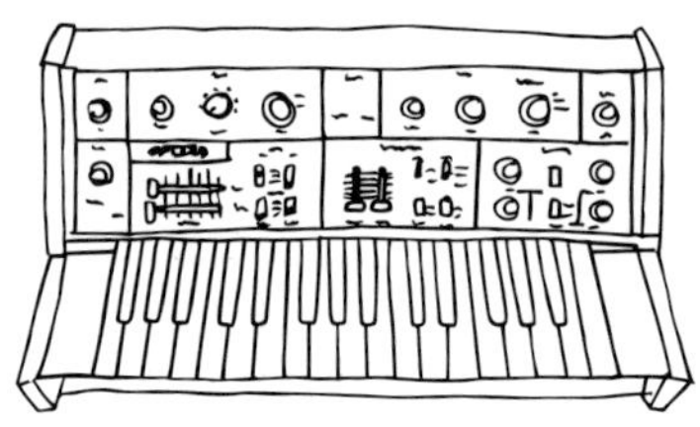

KORG PS-3300 *1977*

Analogue / 48 note polyphony / 3 VCOs per voice
A mighty synthesizer with full 48 note polyphony, 'PS' standing for 'Polyphonic Synthesizer'. Used on Space - 'Magic Fly' (1977).

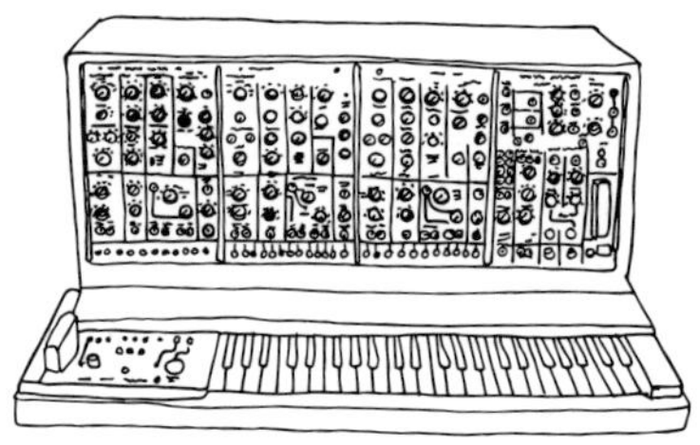

KORG PS-3100 *1977*

Analogue
48 note polyphony / 1 VCO per voice
Another of the PS polyphonic range. Yellow Magic Orchestra - 'Rydeen' (1979).

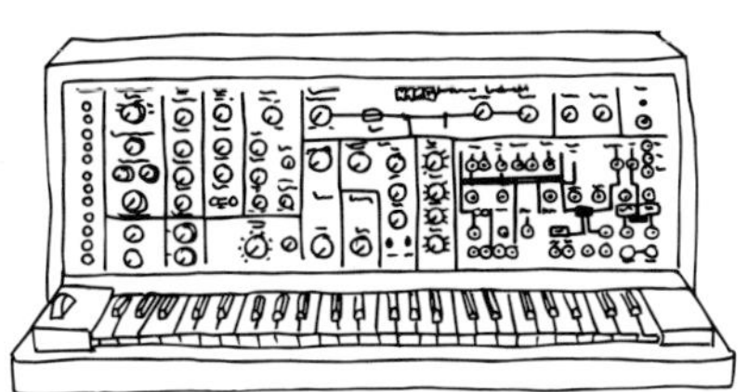

KORG MS-50 *1978*

Analogue
Mono / 1 VCO
A fully patchable version of the MS10.

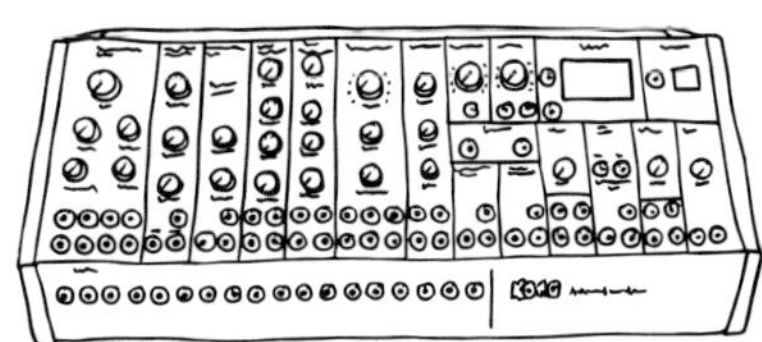

KORG MS-10 *1978*

Analogue
Mono / 1 VCO
The MS-10 has one VCO; the MS-20 has two.

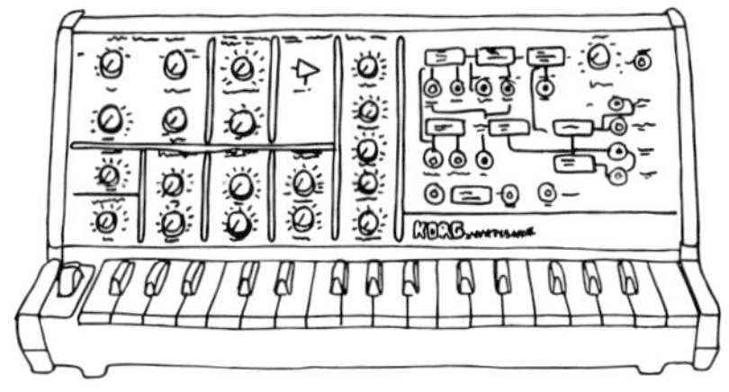

KORG PS-3200 *1978*

Analogue
48 note polyphony / 2 VCOs per voice
Another of the 'mighty' PS range of semi-modulars with their extraordinary full analogue polyphony.

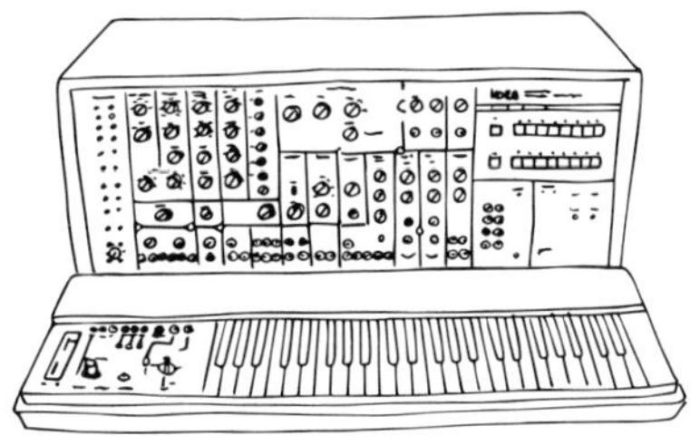

KORG MS-20 *1978*

Analogue
Mono / 2 VCOs
Korg's classic semi-modular. Daft Punk - 'Da Funk' (1995) and Mr Oizo - 'Flat Beat' (1999).

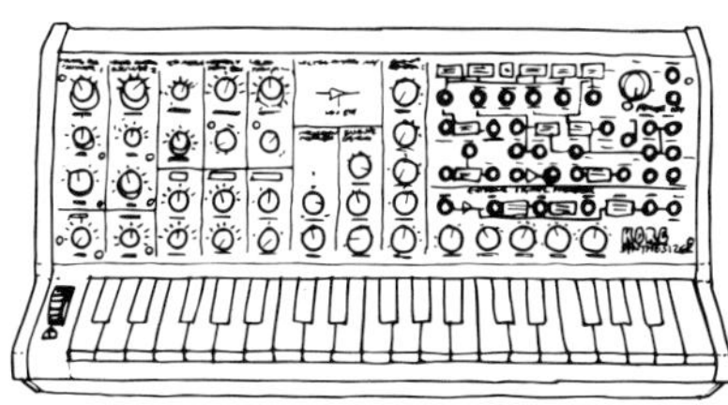

KORG DELTA *1979*

Analogue section: Mono / 1 VCO
String synthesizer section: Full polyphony (divide-down).

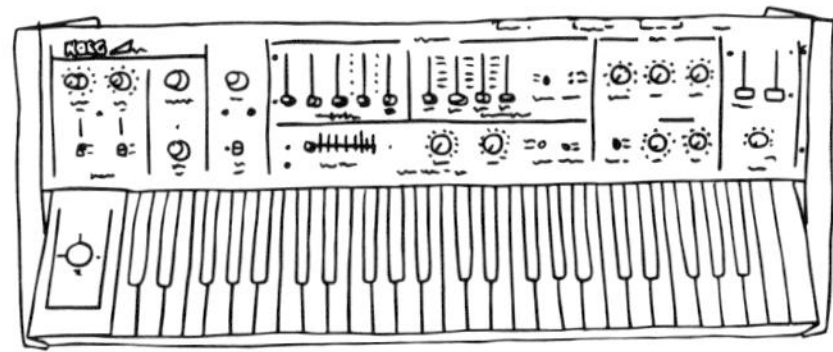

KORG SIGMA (KP-30) *1979*

Analogue section: Mono / 1 VCO
Presets section: Mono / 1 VCO
Preset duophonic synth; combine the 'analogue' and the 'instruments' presets for a variety of sounds.

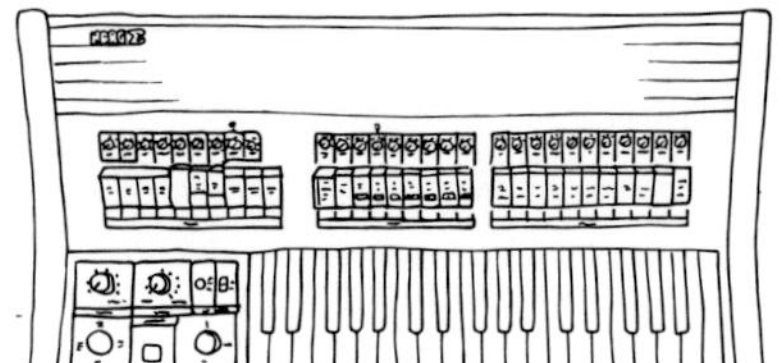

KORG POLYSIX *1981*

Analogue
6 note polyphony / 1 VCO

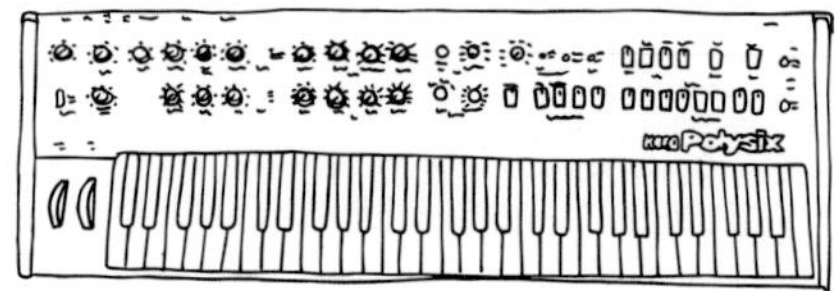

KORG LAMBDA ES50 *1979*

Analogue / 3 VCOs
Full polyphony (divide-down)
There were 9 presets which combined 'percussive' and 'ensemble' sounds, with only limited editing.

KORG MONO/POLY *1981*

Analogue
Mono/Poly / 4 VCOs
Four VCOs which could be used for four-note polyphony or one fat unison lead. Also had an arpeggiator.

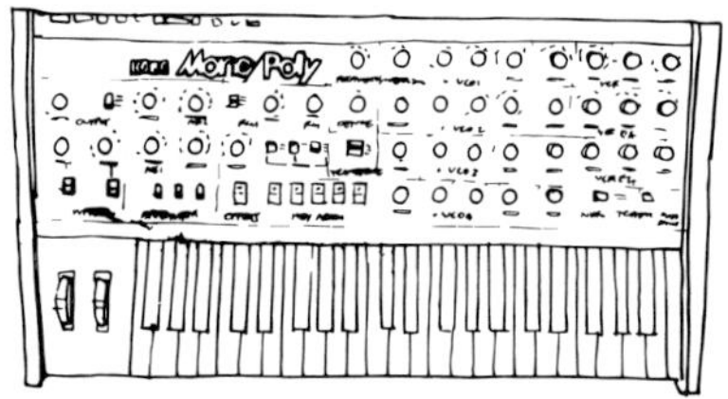

KORG TRIDENT *1980*

Analogue section: 8 note polyphony / 2 VCOs per voice
Brass section: Mono / 1 VCO
String section: Full polyphony (divide-down)
The Trident MkII added a tape interface, more memory and other features.

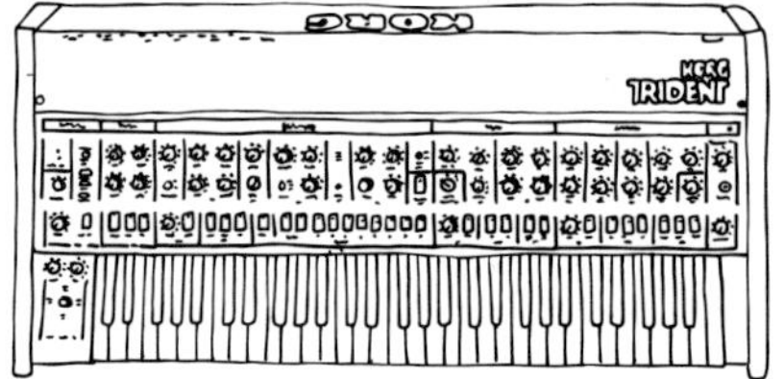

KORG POLY-61 *1982*

Analogue
6 note polyphony / 2 DCOs per voice
The Poly-61M added MIDI in 1984.

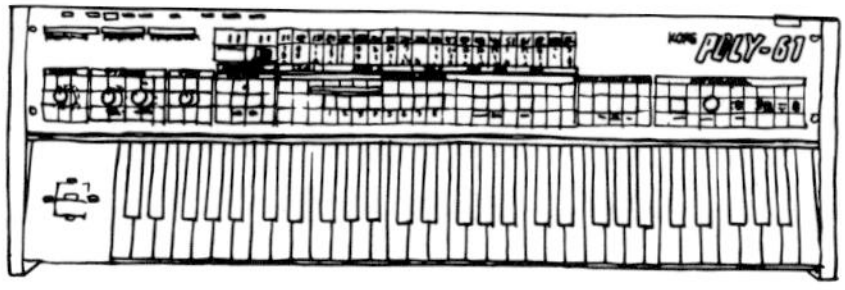

KORG POLY-800 *1983*

Analogue
8 note polyphony / 1 DCO per voice
Filter was not polyphonic. The rackmount was the EX-800; the Poly-800II added MIDI in 1985.

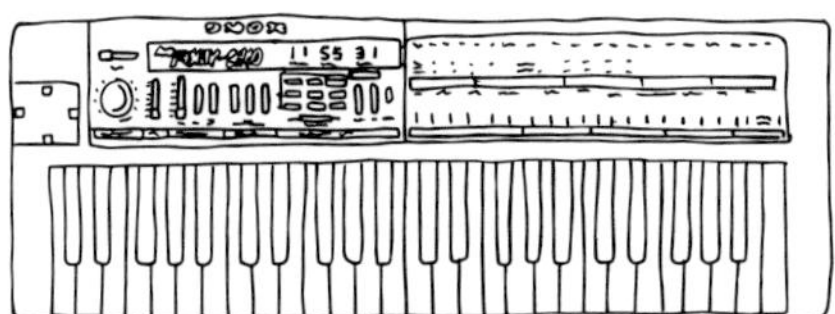

KORG DS-8 *1986*

FM
8 note polyphony / 4-operator
'DS' stands for 'Digital Synthesizer'. The Prodigy - 'No Good' (1994) (synth stab).

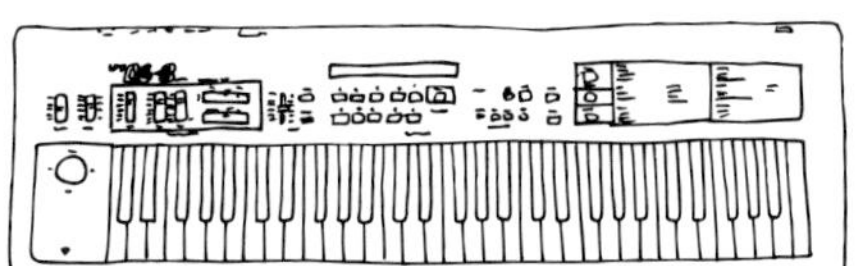

KORG DW-6000 *1985*

8 Digital Waveforms
6 note polyphony / 2 DOs per voice
'DW' stands for 'Digital Waveform' - the DOs had eight stored waveforms.

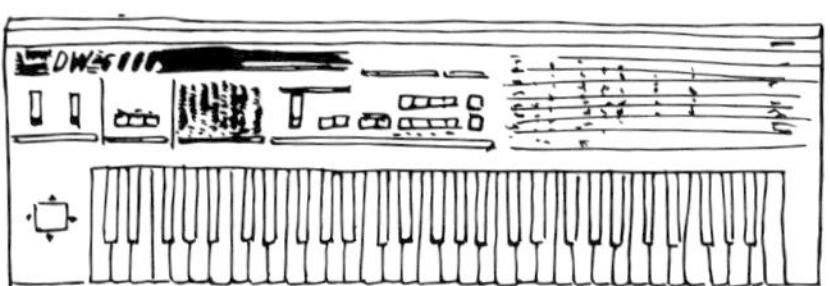

KORG 707 *1987*

FM
8 note polyphony / 4-operator
A simpler DS-8.

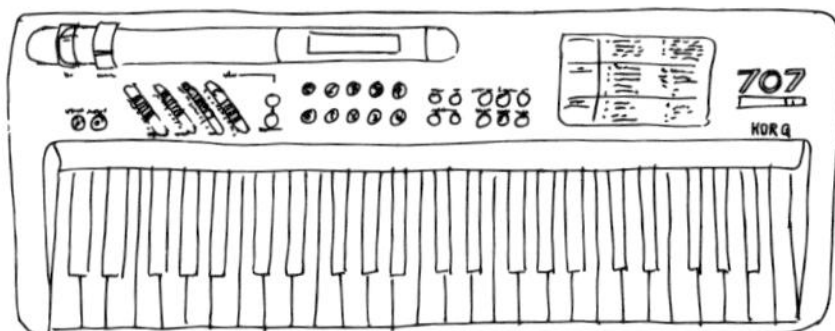

KORG DW-8000 *1985*

16 Digital Waveforms
8 note polyphony / 2 DOs per voice
The EX-8000 was the rackmount.

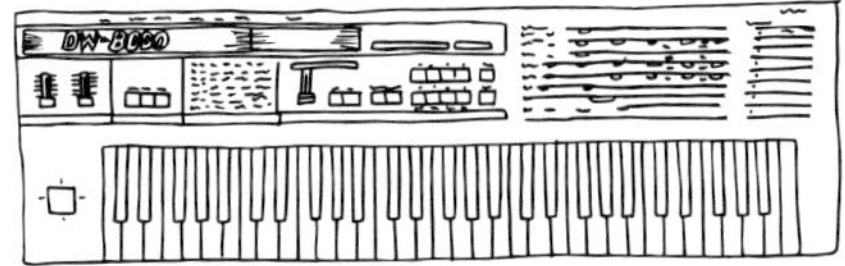

KORG M1 *1988*

Sample & Synthesis
16 note polyphony / 2 DOs per voice
One of the best selling synths of all time; its 16-bit sounds, multi-timbrality, and onboard effects guaranteed its success. The famous organ sound can be heard prominently on dance tracks such as Robin S - 'Show Me Love' (1993) and Crystal Waters - 'Gypsy Woman' (1991).

KORG T1 *1989*

Sample & Synthesis
16 note polyphony / 2 DOs per voice
Building on the success of the M1, the T1 had a weighted keyboard and there were many variants - the T2, T2 EX, T3, and T3 EX.

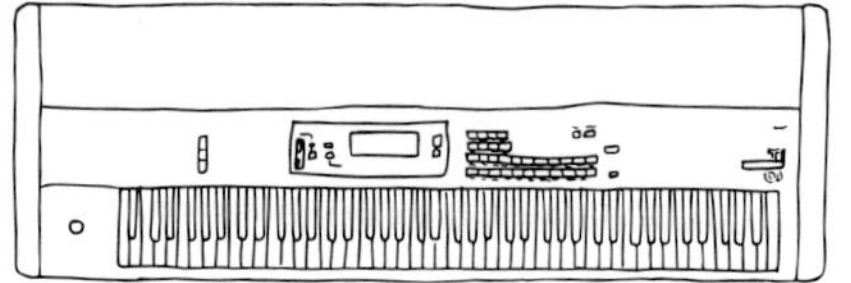

KORG WAVESTATION *1990*

Vector Synthesis / Wave Sequencing
32 note polyphony / 4 DOs per voice
Designed by Dave Smith, vector synthesis was first seen on the Prophet VS. Wave sequencing is the cross-fading and sequencing of oscillator waveforms. The Wavestation A/D (1993) added audio in. Ozric Tentacles - 'Strangitude' (1991) (middle-eight).

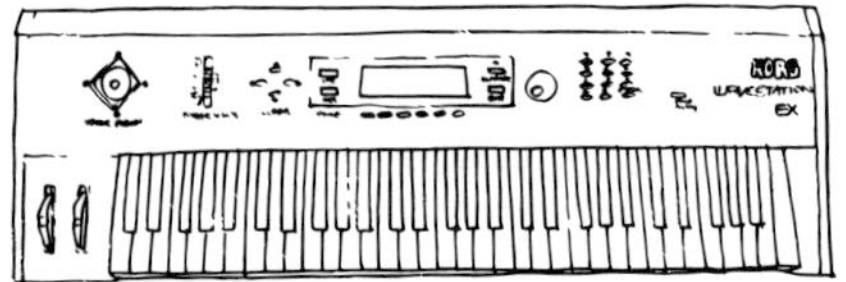

KORG 01/W *1991*

AI² (Sample & Synthesis)
32 note polyphony / 2 DOs per voice
Moving into full workstation mode, Korg released the 03R/W, 05R/W, X2, X3, X5, X5D and later the Triton and OASYS series during the 1990s.

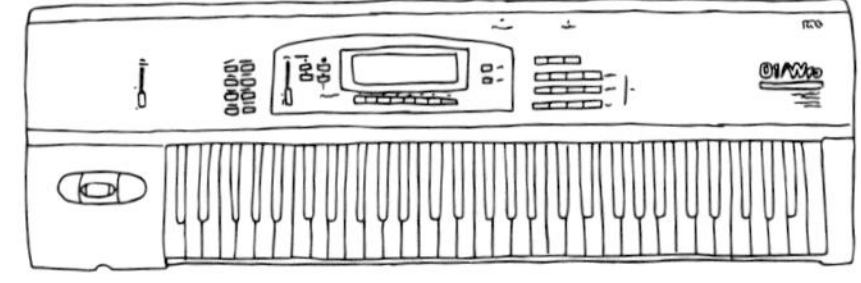

KORG PROPHECY *1995*

Analogue Modelling / Mono
Early analogue modelling synth based on Korg's Open Architecture SYnthesis Studio (OASYS), which was to be a computer-based system offering multiple modelled synthesis techniques. The Prophecy used the analogue modelling part of that OASYS technology. The Korg Z1 (1997) was the 12-note polyphonic equivalent of the Prophecy.

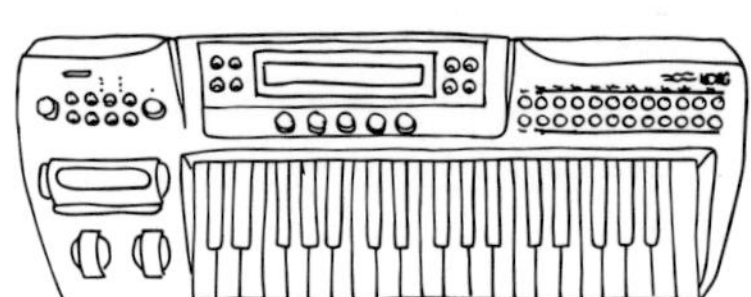

KURZWEIL MUSIC SYSTEMS (USA)

Kurzweil Music Systems was a joint venture between Stevie Wonder and Ray Kurzweil. This came about following Kurzweil demonstrating his Reading Machine for blind people on US television. Stevie Wonder challenged Kurzweil to make a musical instrument that combined the sonic possibilities of electronic instruments with the playability of acoustic instruments. Thus the K250 sampler was born in 1984, with one of the earliest and best digital reproductions so far of a grand piano. Subsequent products built upon this sampling expertise to create high quality studio instruments such as the K2000. (See the Sampler chapter for the details of the K250.)

KURZWEIL K150 *1986*

Additive
16 note polyphony / 15 harmonic partials per voice

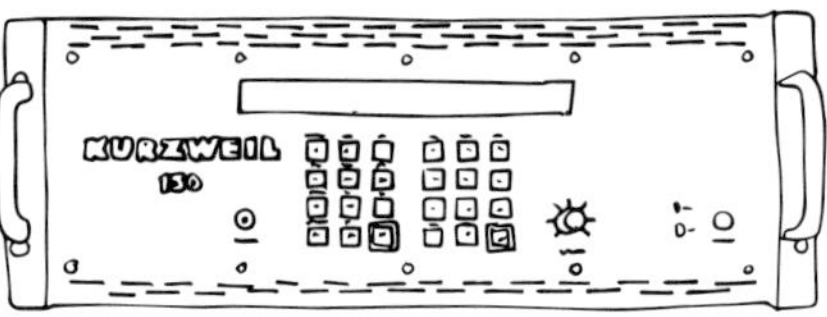

KURZWEIL K1000 *1988*

Sample & Synthesis
24 note polyphony / 2 DOs per voice
The sounds are derived from the K250 sample libraries.

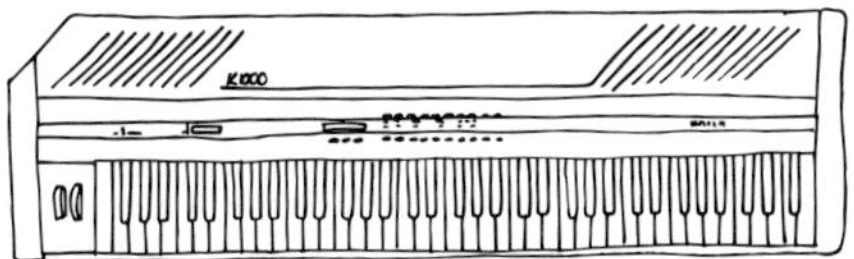

KURZWEIL K2000 *1991*

Sample & Synthesis
24 note polyphony / 2 DOs per voice
Well respected and high quality studio instrument, it also had the ability to sample directly at 16-bit / 44.1kHz.

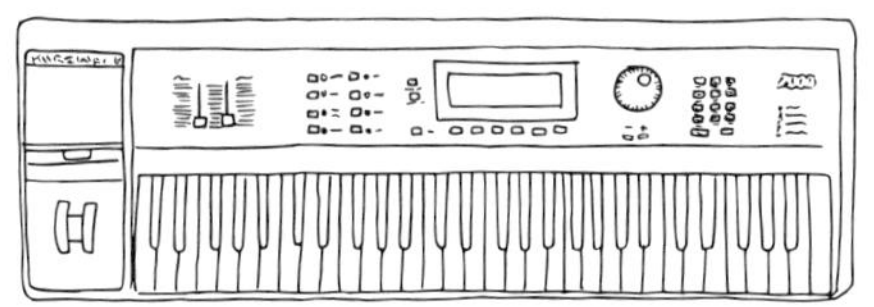

MAM FREEBASS FB-383 *1996*

Analogue / Mono / 1 VCO
A TB-303 clone which was made by Music And More (MAM), a German-based company which sold through Turnkey, Charing Cross Road, under the 'Freeform Analogue Technologies' brand.

MAPLIN 4600 *1976*

Analogue / Mono / 4 VCOs
Maplin were a UK-based electronics shop who sold synthesizer kits throughout the 1970s. Models included the 3800 and 5600, and some kits were also available through Electronics Today International magazine.

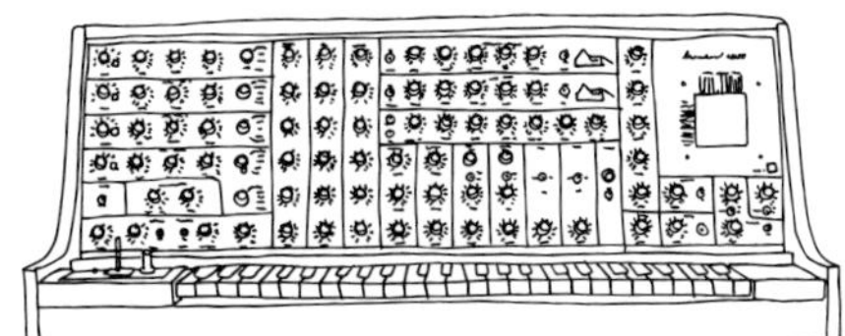

MOOG MUSIC INC. (USA)

There probably isn't a more famous synthesizer make than Moog and no more famous synthesizer model than the Moog Minimoog Model D (1970). The reputation is justified - Moog was the first company to produce a reduced-sized synth at a price musicians could actually afford. Prior to the Minimoog, the company were famed for their modular systems played by virtuosos such as Rick Wakeman, Keith Emerson and Wendy Carlos. Reducing that complexity to a portable and playable instrument was a triumph.

Robert Moog founded the R.A. Moog Company with his father in 1953 in order to sell Theremins, but was encouraged to make his first analogue (and modular) synthesizer by composer Herbert Deutsch.

Despite the success of the Minimoog, and the brand recognition of the company, Moog only ever made a profit in one year - 1969. And despite making a comprehensive range of instruments over the following decades, they only ever racked up more debt and were passed from company to company, first muSonics in 1971 and then Norlin in 1973. This enabled ARP to dominate the 1970s analogue synth market.

By 1977 Robert Moog had left the company to set up Big Briar, and only had the Moog Music trademark returned to him in 2002. The company has since then released a number of new analogue synths including a re-issue of the Minimoog Model D in 2016.

MOOG MODULAR *1964*

Analogue / Mono / Modular

Herb Deutsch worked with Bob Moog to help specify the functionality of his first synthesizer and used it on pieces such as 'Jazz Images - A Worksong and Blues' (1964), which is also the first composition to use a Moog synthesizer.

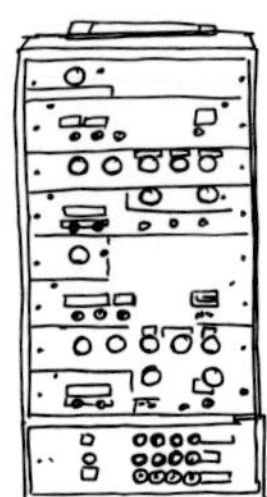

MOOG SYNTHESIZER 1C *1967*

Analogue / Mono/Duo / 3 VCOs

The 1c was the simplest of the C series. Used the 900 series of modules, of which there are over 50 (covering VCO, VCA, VCF, LFO, spring reverb, 8-step sequencer, controllers, and more.) This and other modules were used by Wendy Carlos for her seminal 'Switched-On Bach' (1968).

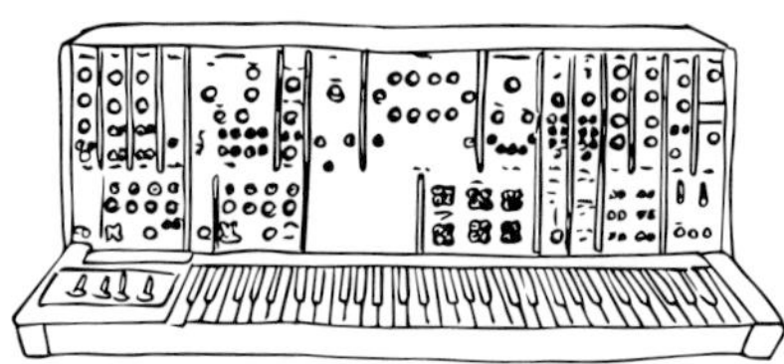

MOOG SYNTHESIZER 2C *1967*

Analogue / Mono/Duo / 6 VCOs

Like all modular systems, the number and combination of modules can vary. A mono or duophonic keyboard could be used with these early Moog modulars.

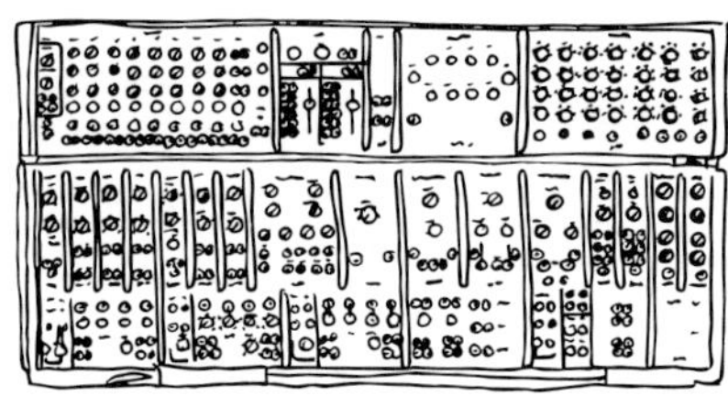

MOOG SYNTHESIZER 3C *1967*

Analogue / Mono/Duo / 9 VCOs

The most complex of the C series. Foundation of The Original New Timbral Orchestra ('TONTO'), the largest modular rig in the world at the time. Stevie Wonder - 'Talking Book' (1972).

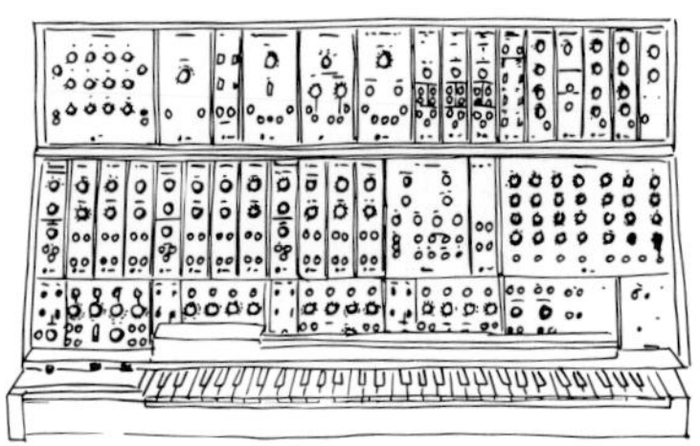

MOOG SYNTHESIZER IP/IIP/IIIP *1967*

Analogue / Mono/Duo / 3, 6, or 9 VCOs

The 'P' series are the portable versions of the 'C' series. Donna Summer - 'I Feel Love' (1977); Tomita - 'Snowflakes are Dancing' (1974).

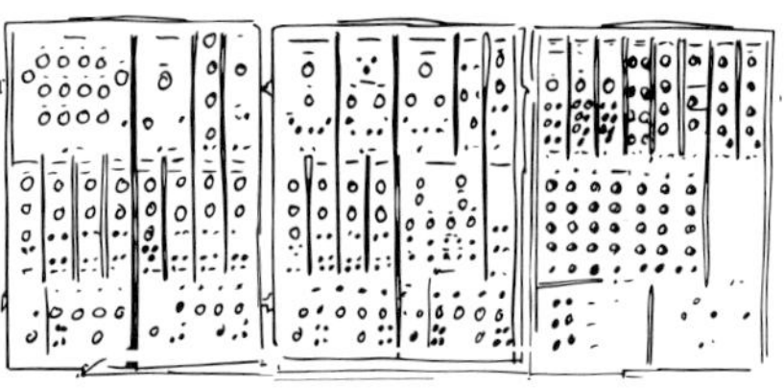

MOOG MINIMOOG MODEL D *1970*

Analogue / Mono / 3 VCOs

One of the most iconic synths ever made; offering the essence of Moog's modular synths in a 'mini' hardwired form. Parliament - 'Flashlight' (1978).

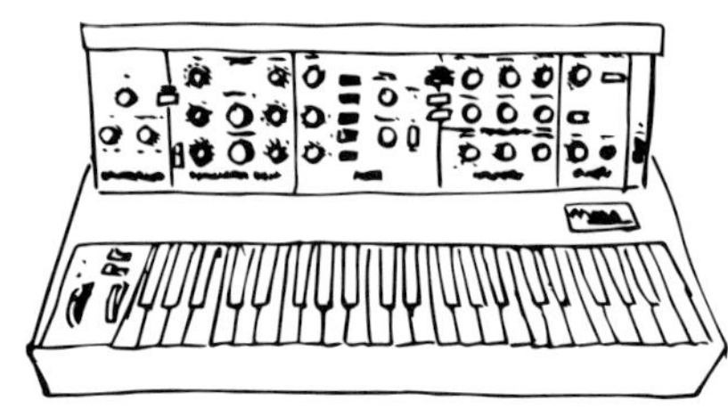

MOOG SYSTEM 10/12 *1971*

Analogue / Mono / 3 VCOs
The 10 and 12 were very similar looking modular systems based on the 900 series; the 12 had an updated and more stable VCO.

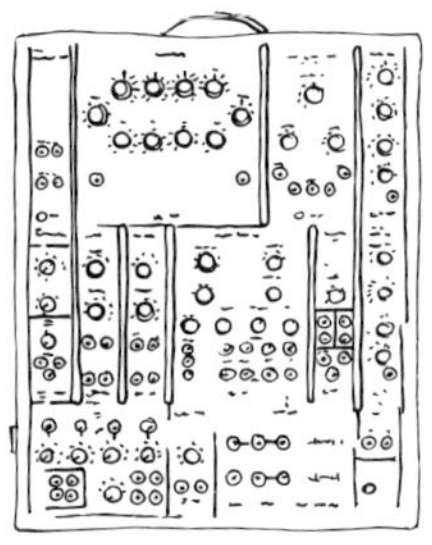

MOOG SONIC SIX *1972*

Analogue / Mono/Duo / 2 VCOs

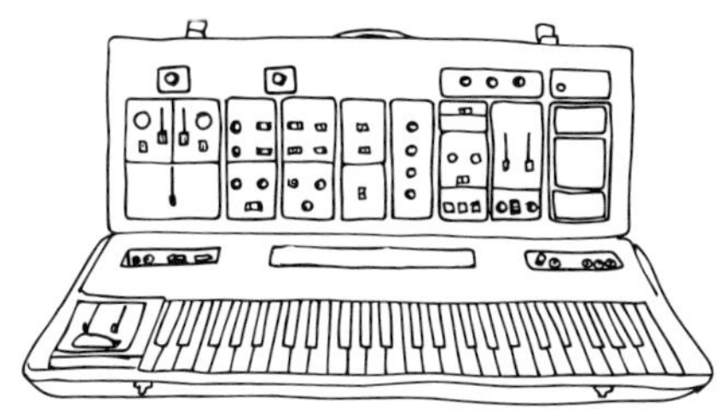

MOOG SATELLITE *1972*

Analogue
Mono / 1 VCO
Designed for use with home organs and built into some Cordovox organs.

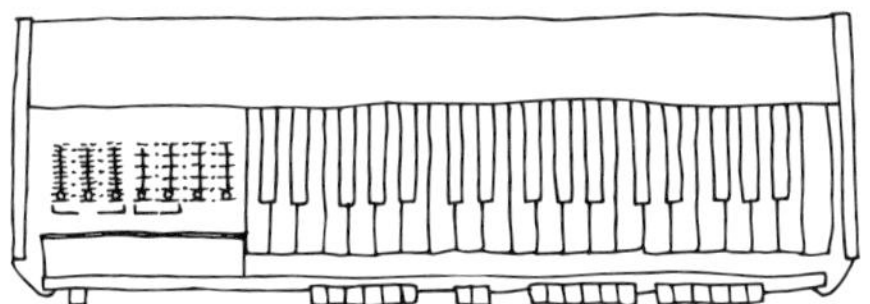

MOOG SYNTHESIZER 15 *1973*

Analogue / Mono/Duo / 3 VCOs

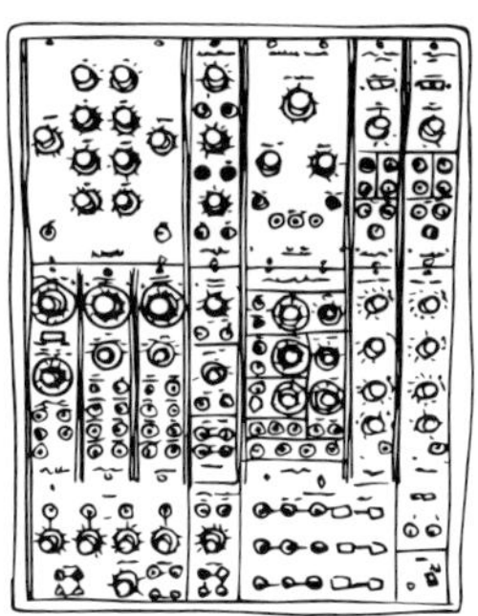

MOOG (MUSONICS) SONIC V SYNTHESIZER *1972*

Analogue
Mono/Duo / 2 VCOs
Not put into production - and actually designed by Gene Zumchak at muSonics. It became the Sonic Six after muSonics merged with R.A.Moog Inc. in 1971.

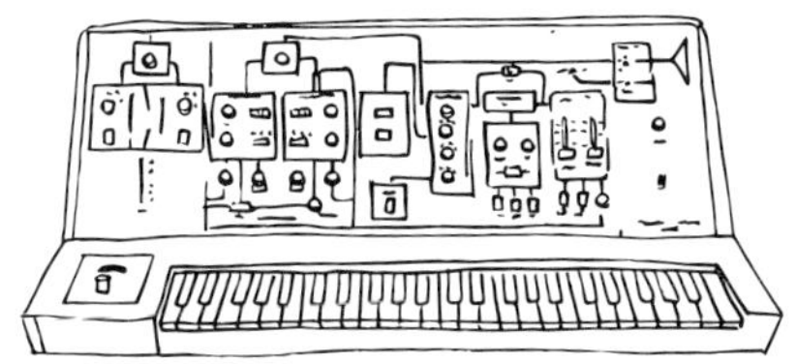

MOOG SYNTHESIZER 35 *1973*

Analogue / Mono/Duo / 5 VCOs

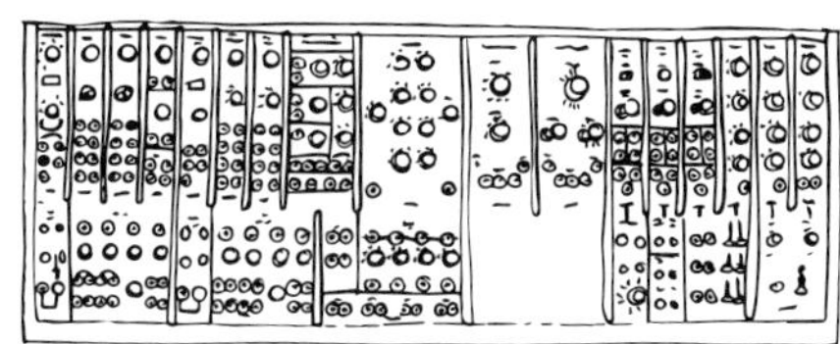

MOOG SYNTHESIZER 55 *1973*

Analogue / Mono/Duo / 7 VCOs

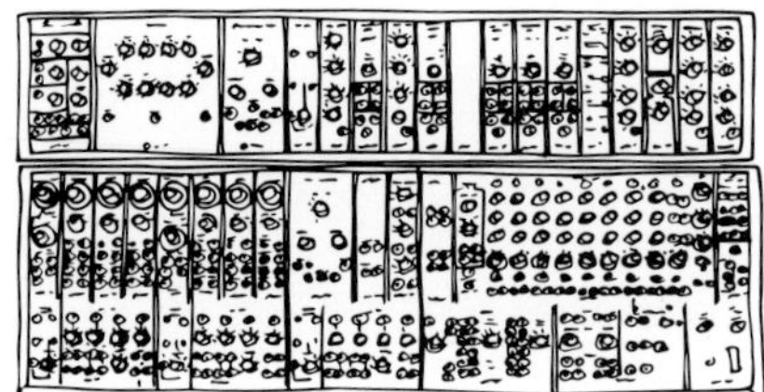

MOOG MICROMOOG *1975*

Analogue
Mono / 1 VCO + sub

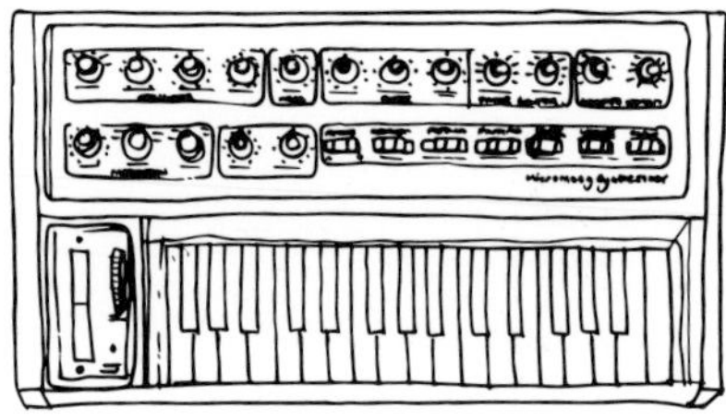

MOOG CONSTELLATION (PROTOTYPE) *1973*

A system that was to have comprised the Apollo (polyphonic synth), Lyra (mono synth) and Taurus (bass mono synth). The Apollo and Lyra were released separately as the Multimoog and Polymoog.

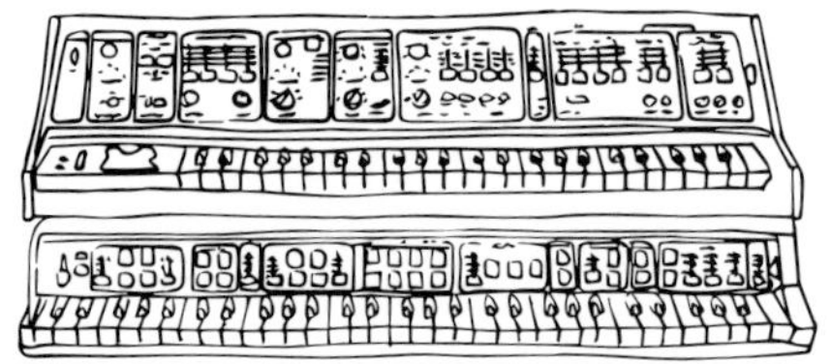

MOOG MINITMOOG *1975*

Analogue / 6 presets
Mono / 2 VCOs
Like the Satellite, designed for home organ use but updated to two oscillators.

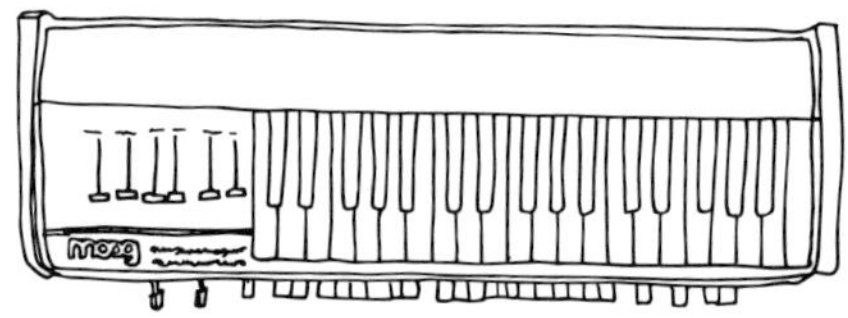

MOOG CDX *1975*

Analogue synth section: Mono / 1 VCO
Organ section: Full polyphony
This was a hybrid of a Cordovox Organ and a Moog Satellite.

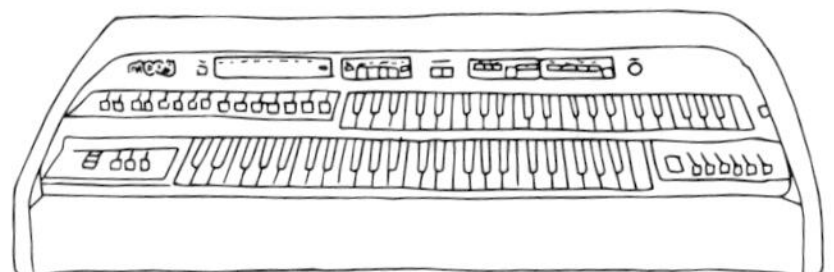

MOOG POLYMOOG 203A *1975*

Ensemble synth: 8 Presets (strings, piano, organ, harpsichord, funk, clavi, vibes, brass)
Full polyphony (divide-down)
The later Polymoog Keyboard (280a) increased the number of presets to fourteen. Gary Numan - 'Cars' (1979) (vox humana preset).

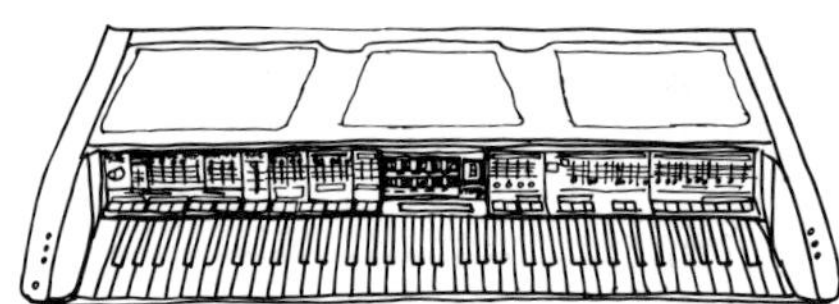

MOOG TAURUS *1975*

Analogue
Mono / 2 VCOs
A bass unit to be operated by the feet; it was to be part of the Moog Constellation.

MOOG LIBERATION *1980*

Analogue synth section: Mono / 2 VCOs
Organ section: 10 note polyphony
Moog's 'Keytar' instrument.

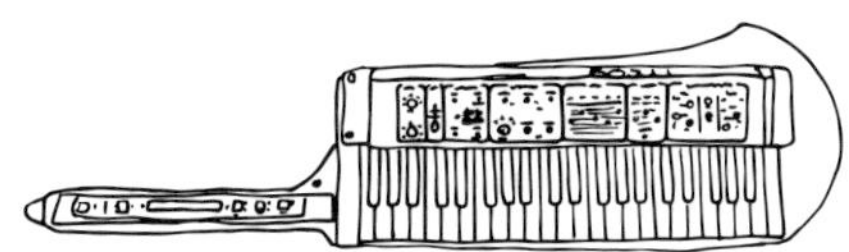

MOOG MULTIMOOG *1978*

Analogue
Mono / 2 VCOs
An updated Micromoog.

MOOG OPUS 3 *1980*

Presets: string / brass / organ
Full polyphony (divide-down)

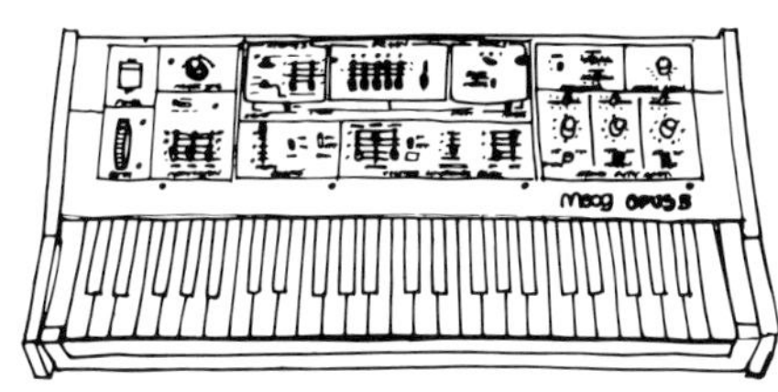

MOOG PRODIGY *1979*

Analogue
Mono / 2 VCOs
A simpler two-oscillator Moog with dramatic oscillator sync. Cassette Electrik - 'The Smartest Bomb'. Also one of Depeche Mode's first synths.

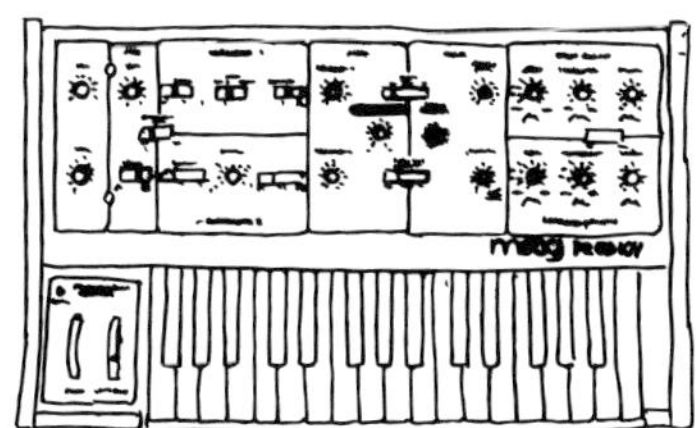

MOOG REALISTIC CONCERTMATE MG-1 *1981*

Analogue synth section: Mono / 2 VCOs
Organ section: Full polyphony (divide-down)
Manufactured by Moog and sold in the US under the Realistic brand.

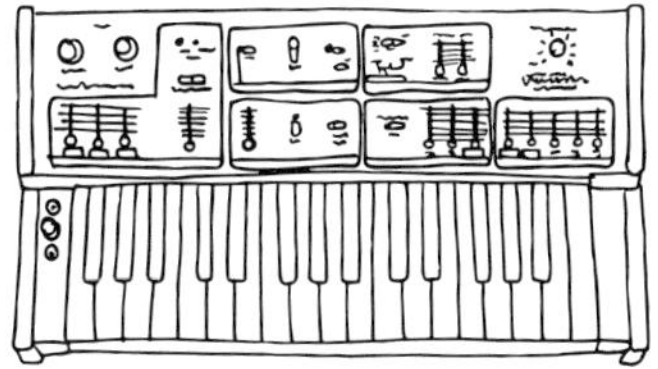

MOOG ROGUE *1981*

Analogue
Mono / 2 VCOs
A very simple synth whose two oscillators had to use the same waveform. It's name, however, does give the clue to the correct pronunciation of 'Moog'!

MOOG THE SOURCE *1981*

Analogue
Mono / 2 VCOs
The first Moog to offer patch memory and a built-in sequencer. New Order - 'Blue Monday' (1983) (bassline).

MOOG TAURUS II *1981*

Analogue
Mono / 2 VCOs

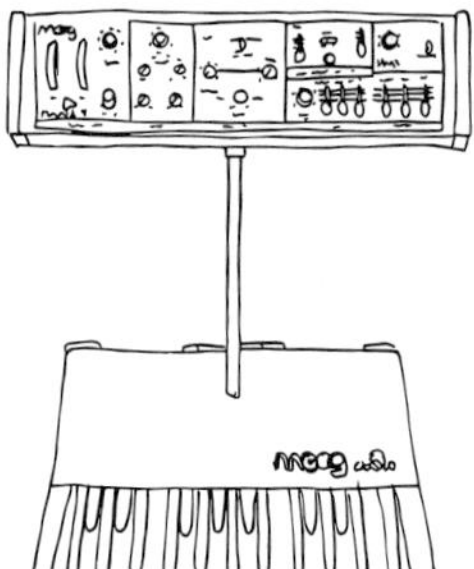

MOOG MEMORYMOOG *1982*

Analogue
6 note polyphony / 3 VCOs per voice
The last Moog to be made before Moog Music went out of business in 1987. The Memorymoog Plus added MIDI, a sequencer and autotuning.

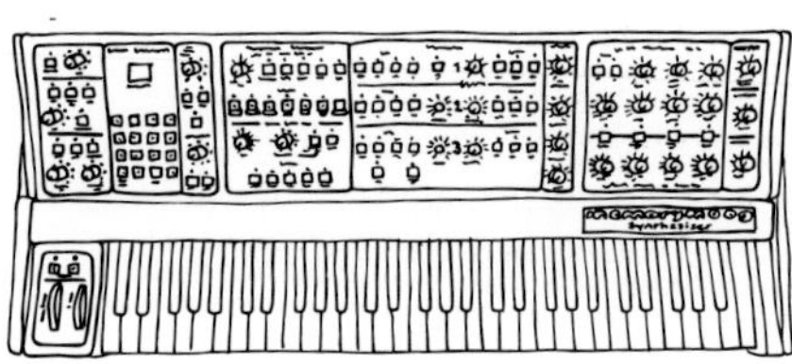

MULTIVOX (USA)

Multivox released a series of string and ensemble synths during the 1970s and 1980s. Often licenced from Japanese companies such as Hillwood they released a lot of instruments, but were never considered members of the pantheon of classic synthesizer manufacturers.

MULTIVOX MX-3000 *1978*

Analogue bass & lead sections: Mono
String section: full polyphony (divide-down)
The MX-3000 was the top of the range; other ensemble/string synths included the MX-20, MX-2000 duo, MX-30, MX-51, MX-61, MX-65, MX-202.

NOVATION DIGITAL MUSIC SYSTEMS (UK)

Novation was founded in 1992 and their first product was the MM10, a MIDI controller for the Yamaha QY10. They broke through with the analogue Bass Station in 1993 which was modelled on the TB-303, but with double the oscillators. Following this success, the Drum Station launched in 1995 which used analogue modelling to recreate classic drum-machine sounds. The Supernova in 1998 was a cutting edge and successful analogue-modelling polyphonic synth. Novation's technical director is Chris Huggett, previously of EDP Wasp and the Oxford Synthesiser Company (OSC).

NOVATION BASS STATION *1993*

Analogue
Mono / 2 DCOs
Also available as the Bass Station Rack.

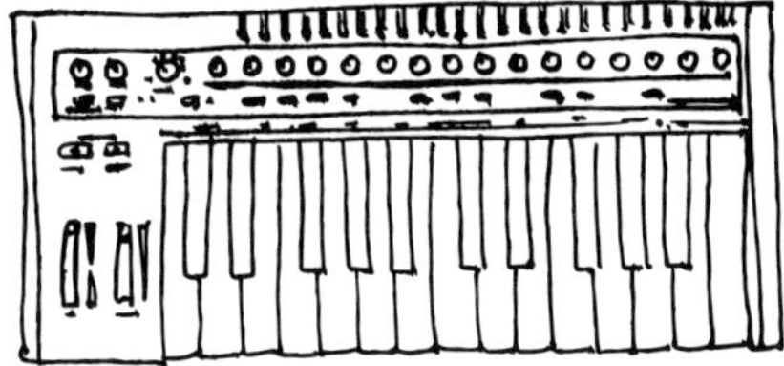

NOVATION SUPERNOVA *1998*

Analogue Modelling
16 note polyphony / 3 modelling oscillators per voice
Popular analogue modelling synth of the 1990s.

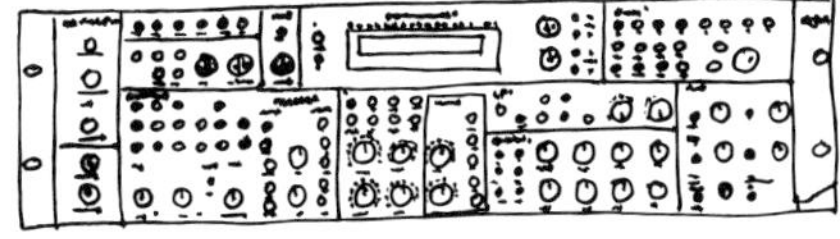

OBERHEIM (USA)

Tom Oberheim founded the company in 1969 and it went on to become a giant of the synthesizer industry. Oberheim Electronics was initially an ARP dealer, but when customers wanted a sequencer Oberheim designed the DS-2 to meet the demand. Customers then wanted an expander synth to add to their set-up so the Synthesizer Expander Module (SEM) was born. It had a multi-mode filter - including high-pass - as it was thought that customers would already have a synth with a low-pass filter, thus providing a complementary sound.

Their early synthesizers continued to be based on the SEM, which was combined in increasingly unwieldy combinations to generate polyphony. Following this, the OB series of synths used the Z80 microchip for storing patches. This series of synths became well-known for their brass-type sounds and were extensively used by Prince. The company went bankrupt in 1986 and Tom Oberheim got the rights back to his brand-name in 2019.

OBERHEIM SEM *1974*

Analogue
Mono / 2 VCOs
Multiples of the 'Synthesizer Expander Module' were used in subsequent synthesizers.

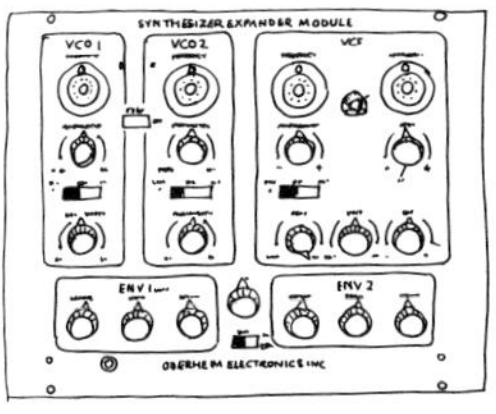

OBERHEIM TWO VOICE *1975*

Analogue
2 note polyphony / 2 VCOs per voice
Two SEMs combined to create a two-voice synthesizer.

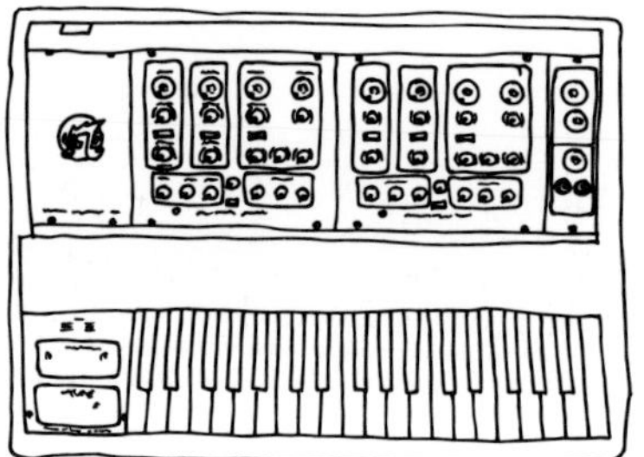

OBERHEIM OB-1 *1978*

Analogue
Mono / 2 VCOs
A simplified SEM with 8 recallable patch memories - the first analogue synth to offer these.

OBERHEIM FOUR VOICE *1975*

Analogue
4 note polyphony / 2 VCOs per voice
Four SEMs combined to create a four-voice synthesizer.

OBERHEIM OB-X *1979*

Analogue
4, 6 or 8 note polyphony / 2 VCOs per voice
Queen - 'Flash Gordon' (1980); Prince - '1999' (1982).

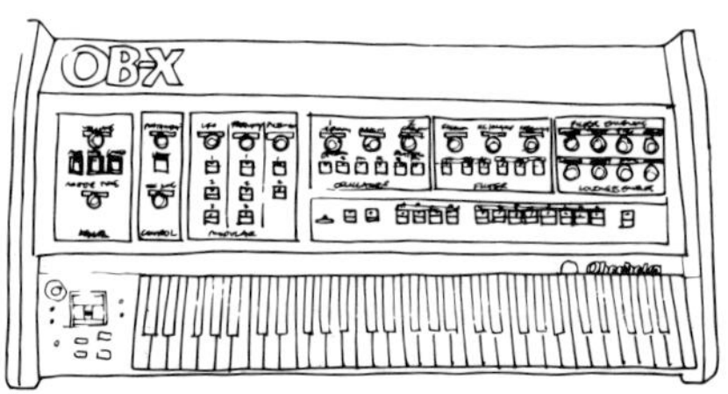

OBERHEIM EIGHT VOICE *1977*

Analogue
8 note polyphony / 2 VCOs per voice
Eight SEMS combined to create a beast of an eight-voice synthesizer.

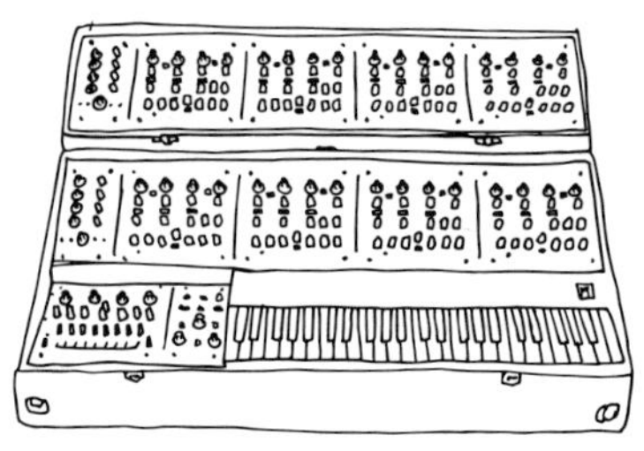

OBERHEIM OB-SX *1980*

Analogue
4, 5 or 6 note polyphony / 2 VCOs per voice
Essentially a preset synth.

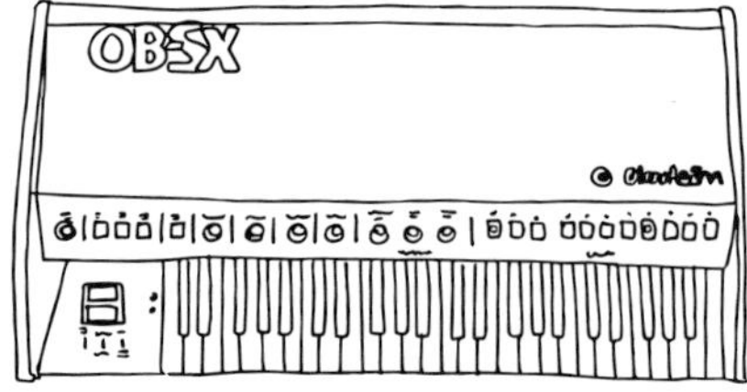

OBERHEIM OB-XA *1981*

Analogue
4, 6 or 8 note polyphony / 2 VCOs per voice
Van Halen - 'Jump' (1983); Depeche Mode - 'Love In Itself' (1983) (chords).

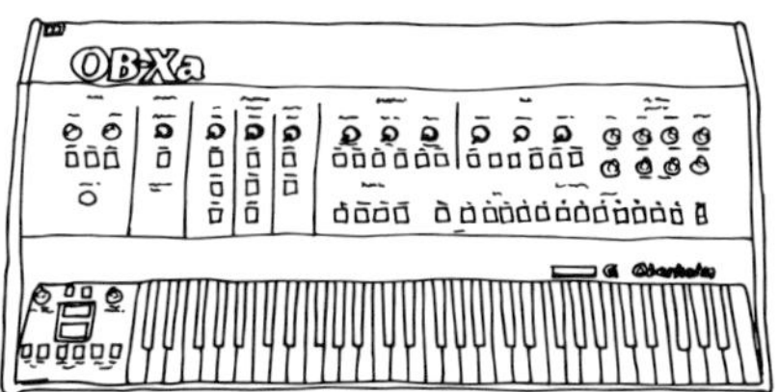

OBERHEIM OB-8 *1983*

Analogue
8 note polyphony / 2 VCOs per voice

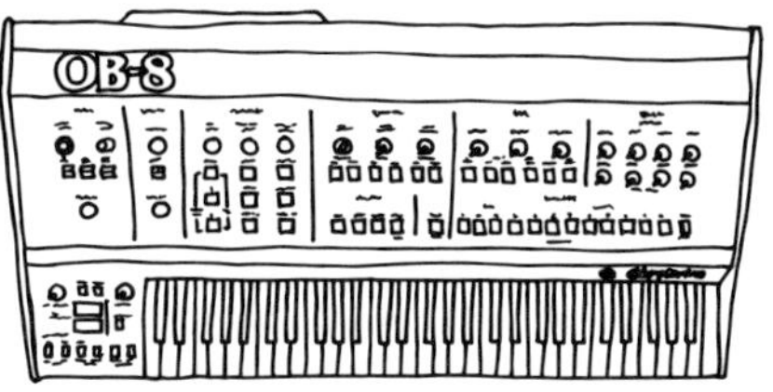

OBERHEIM MATRIX 12 *1985*

Analogue
12 note polyphony / 2 DCOs per voice
The equivalent module is the Xpander with six-voice polyphony.

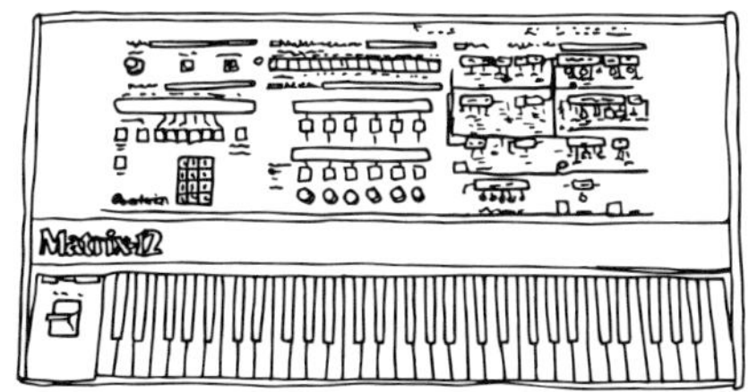

OBERHEIM MATRIX 6 *1986*

Analogue
6 note polyphony / 2 DCOs per voice
The Matrix 6R is the rackmount, as is the Matrix-1000, but a mostly preset version.

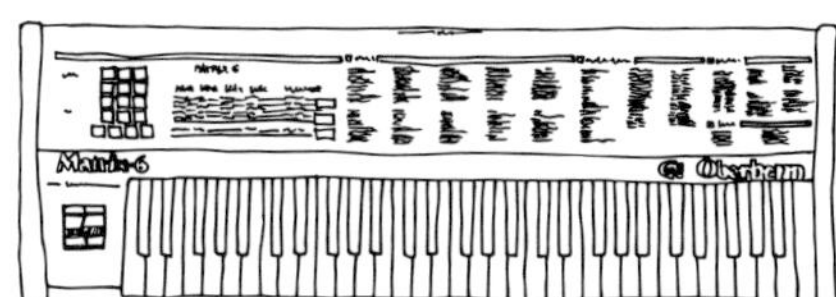

OBERHEIM OB-MX *1994*

Analogue
12 note polyphony / 2 VCOs per voice
Remarkably, this was designed by Don Buchla.

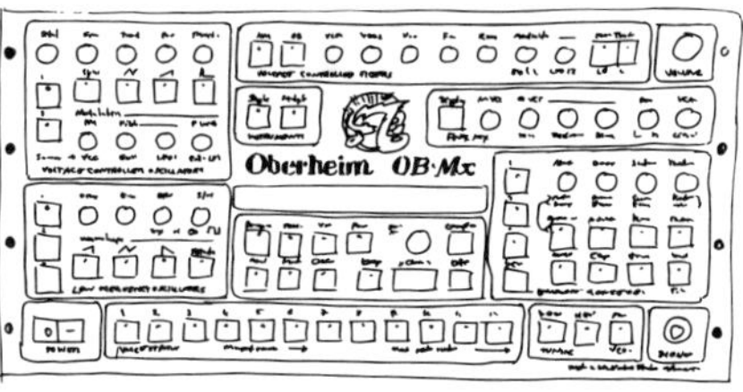

OCTAVE ELECTRONICS (USA)

Octave formed in 1975 and are famous for their two feline named synths - the Cat and the Kitten. Along the way Octave got embroiled in a copyright dispute with ARP who attempted to sue, causing a revision to the Cat. Octave then formed a joint venture with Plateau Electronics in 1979 and went on to release a powerful, but hard to program polyphonic synth called the Voyetra Eight in 1983. Leaving the synth business in the late 1980s, the company became 'Voyetra Technologies' to make MIDI interfaces and subsequently merged with Turtle Beach to make computer and gaming peripherals.

OCTAVE THE CAT *1976*

Analogue
Mono/Duo / 2 VCOs + subs
Octave was nearly sued by ARP for cloning their designs. ARP in their turn was sued by Moog for cloning their filters. The Cat Series Revision Model (SRM) was designed to avoid any further trouble.

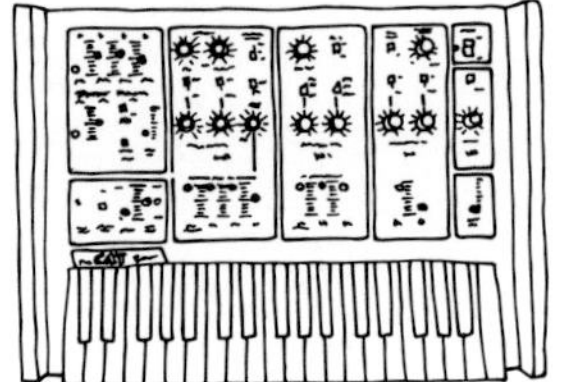

OCTAVE THE KITTEN *1977*

Analogue
Mono / 1 VCO + 2 subs
A simpler Cat. The Kitten II was released in 1981.

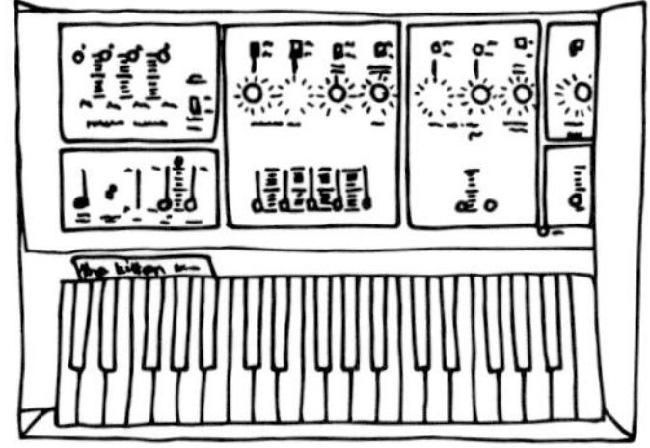

OCTAVE-PLATEAU VOYETRA EIGHT *1983*

Analogue
8 note polyphony / 2 VCOs per voice
Innovative for the time, but never enjoyed great success partly due to needing the Voyetra One or a computer to edit it easily.

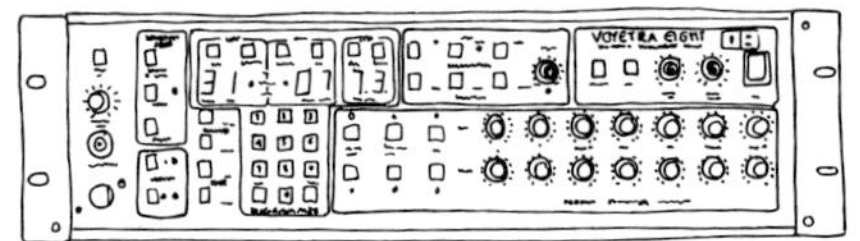

OCTAVE-PLATEAU VOYETRA ONE *1983*

Analogue
Mono / 2 VCOs
Also served as a (necessary) programming front panel for the Voyetra Eight.

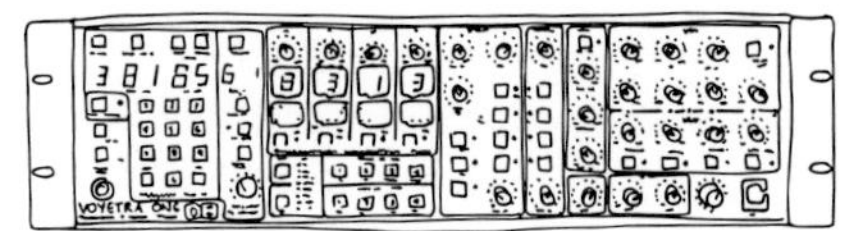

OSC (OXFORD SYNTHESISER COMPANY) (UK)

The Oxford Synthesiser Company evolved from Electronic Dream Plant which had recently folded. Paul Wiffen and Chris Huggett formed the company to continue synthesizer design and production, and to build on the success of the Wasp synthesizer. The OSCar's uniquely rugged design was courtesy of Anthony Harrison-Griffin and is considered something of a classic.

OSC OSCAR *1983*

Analogue / Additive
Mono/Duo / 2 DCOs
Classic and unique looking British synth of the early 1980s. It included a sequencer, dual filters, PWM and built in distortion. Stevie Wonder - 'Skeletons' (bassline).

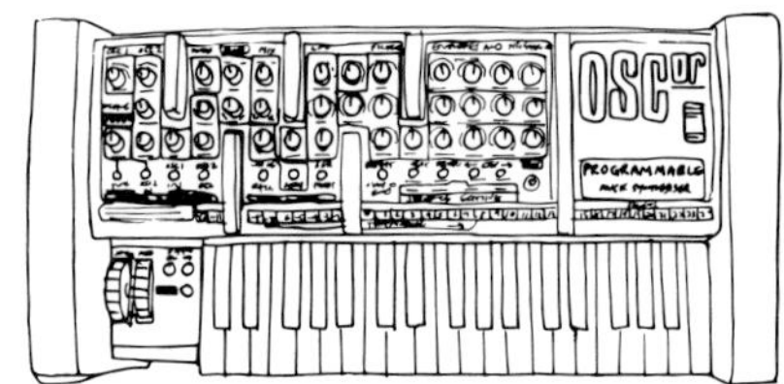

PAIA ELECTRONICS (USA)

PAiA are well known for their synth kits which were a real alternative to the large modular systems of Moog and others at the time. They were founded by John Simonton in the 1960s, and the name comes from a town on the island of Maui (in Hawaii). PAiA's first synth was the successful 2700 line, and PAiA introduced the first programmable electronic drum machine, the PAiA Programmable Drum Set, in 1975.

PAIA MODULAR 2700 *1972*

Analogue / Mono / Modular

PAIA MODULAR 4700 *1974*

Analogue / Mono / Modular

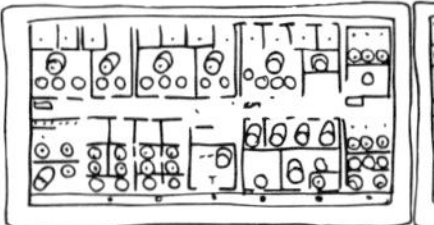
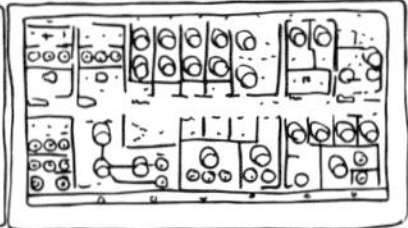

PAIA OZ 3760 *1976*

Analogue / 1 VCO
18 note polyphony (divide-down)
Fully polyphonic portable synth with built-in speaker (the circle on the top). Came with a touchpad pitch bend on the end of a wire.

PAIA PROTEUS 1 *1978*

Analogue
Mono / 2 VCOs

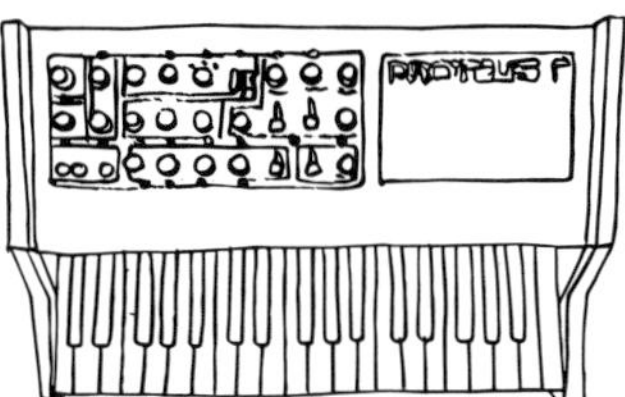

PEAVEY ELECTRONICS (USA)

Peavey are much better known for their association with rock music and their guitar amplifiers, but they made a series of sample-playback synths in the late 1980s and early 1990s. At a time when many synth manufacturers were producing so-called ROMplers, there was not much to distinguish Peavey's contribution to the genre.

PEAVEY SP *1989*

Sample & Synthesis
16 note polyphony / 1 DO per voice
A sample playback range that included the SP+, SX, and SX+.

PEAVEY DPM 3 *1989*

Sample & Synthesis
16 note polyphony / 2 DOs per voice
A range of 'DPM' ROMplers were released throughout the 1990s.

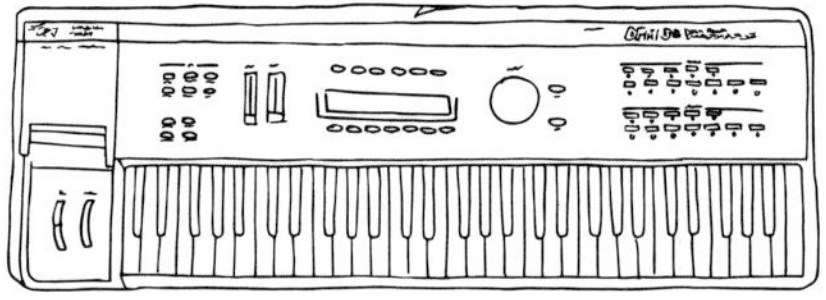

POLYFUSION SYSTEM 2000 *1977*

Analogue / Mono / Modular
Polyfusion was set up by ex-Moog employees Alan Pearce and Ron Folkman, and were well known for modular synthesizers in the 1970s. Ron Folkman relaunched the Polyfusion brand at Knobcon 2018.

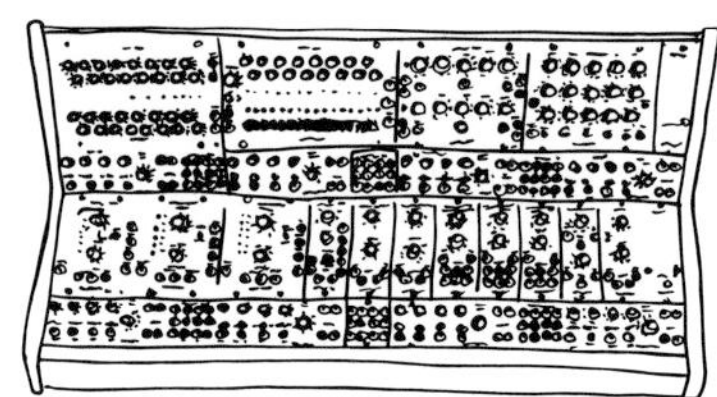

POWERTRAN (UK)

Powertran synthesizer kits were sold through the magazine Electronics today in the late 1970s and early 1980s. Tim Orr, the designer of the Transcendent 2000 synthesizer, had previously designed EMS synthesizers. New Order used a Powertran sequencer for 'Blue Monday' (1983).

POWERTRAN TRANSCENDENT 2000 *1978*

Analogue
Mono / 1 VCO

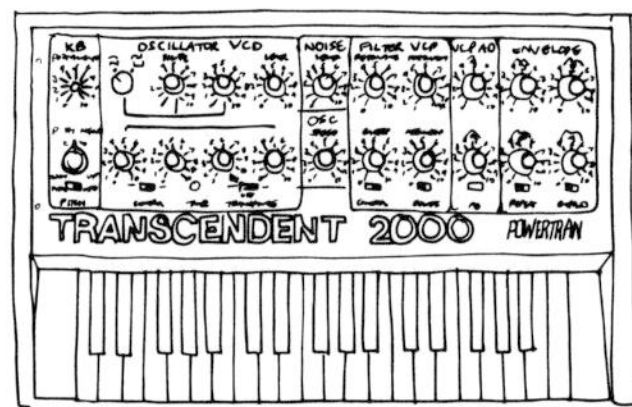

PALM PRODUCTS GMBH (PPG) (GERMANY)

Founded by Wolfgang Palm in 1975, PPG are best known for their innovative wavetable synthesizers, the Wave 2.2 and Wave 2.3, with their distinctive and evolving tones. Always innovating, PPG attempted to build a studio computer in 1986 called the Realizer, which was to have modelled analogue and digital synthesis. This was never to reach production and the company folded in 1987. Waldorf Music, founded in 1988, made use of the PPG wavetable concept in instruments such as the MicroWave. Wavetable synthesis also lived on in other machines such as the Korg Wavestation.

PPG SYSTEM 100 *1975*

Analogue / Mono / Modular
PPG's first synthesizer.

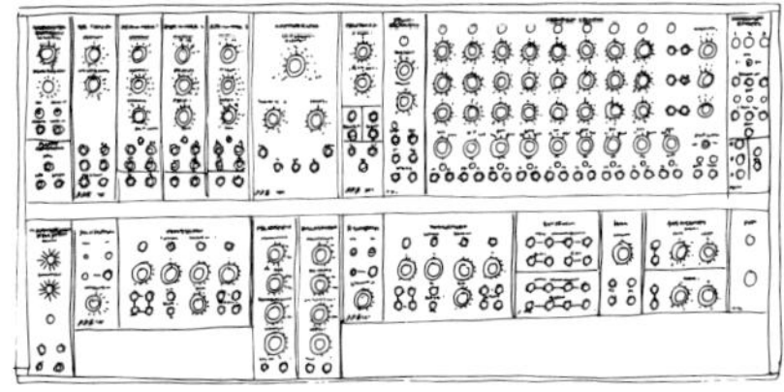

PPG 1003 SONIC CARRIER *1976*

Analogue
Mono/Duo / 2 DCOs
One of the earliest synths to feature digitally recallable presets.

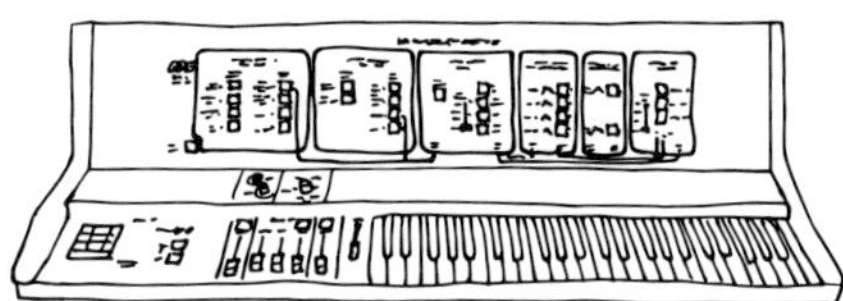

PPG 300 *1975*

Analogue / Mono / Modular

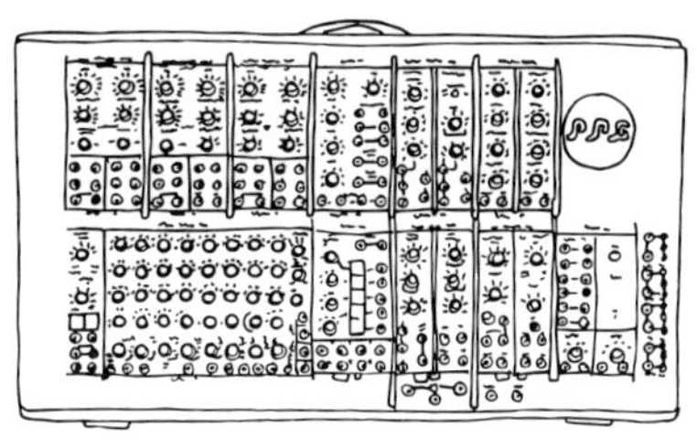

PPG 340 WAVE COMPUTER *1978*
PPG 380 EVENT GENERATOR *1978*

8 digital waves / 8 note polyphony
The first digital synthesizer from PPG also came with a computer terminal for control and visualisation, and a keyboard.

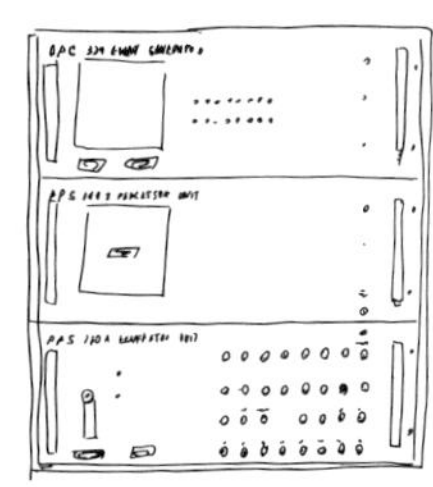

PPG 1020 *1976*

Analogue
Mono / 2 DCOs
The 1020 updated the earlier model 1002's VCOs with DCOs.

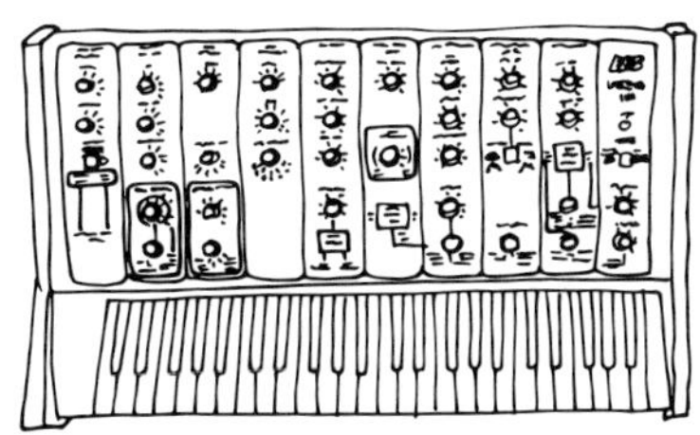

PPG 360 WAVECOMPUTER *1978*

Wavetable
4 or 8 note polyphony / 2 or 4 voice boards
PPG's first wavetable synthesizer.

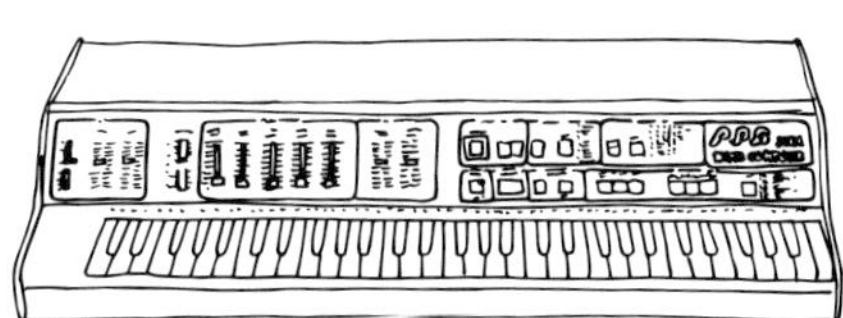

PPG WAVE 2.0 *1981*

Wavetable (Wave 2.3 added sample playback)
8 note polyphony / 2 DOs per voice
The Wave 2.0 and 2.2 had 8-bit waveforms; the 2.3 was upgraded to 12-bit. Depeche Mode, 'See You' (bells, vocal tones). The EVU was the rackmounted Wave 2.3.

PPG PRK (PROCESSOR KEYBOARD) *1983*

Wavetable
Up to eight voice cards / 4 wavetables per card
Primarily a controller keyboard with no internal sound generation. It could, however, load voice cards which would play back through a Wave 2.

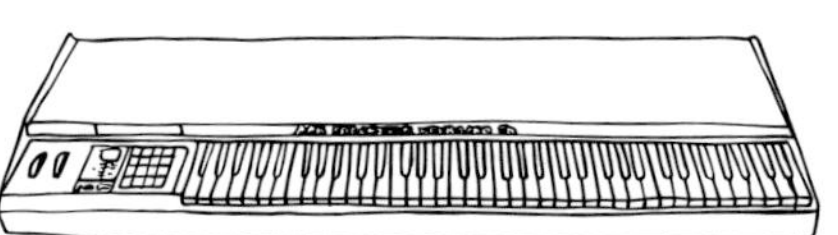

PPG WAVETERM A & WAVETERM B *1983*

A computer paired with the Wave 2 series for programming and sampling (Waveterm A was 8-bit and the B was 12-bit).

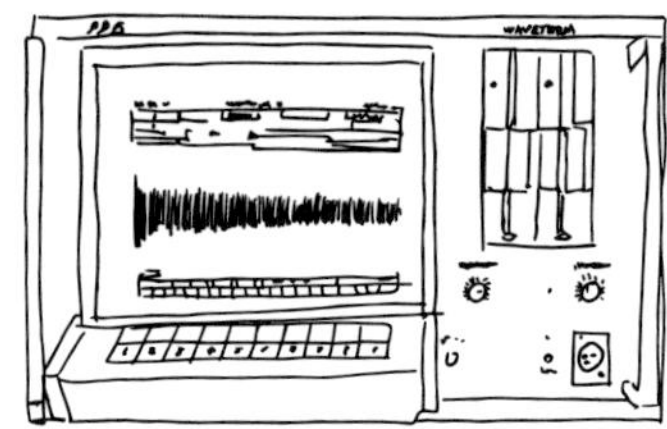

PPG REALIZER *1986*

Analogue / FM / Wavetable / Sampler
Way ahead of its time, the Realizer attempted to be a digital studio that could model analogue circuits and other digital synthesis methods. It was never released.

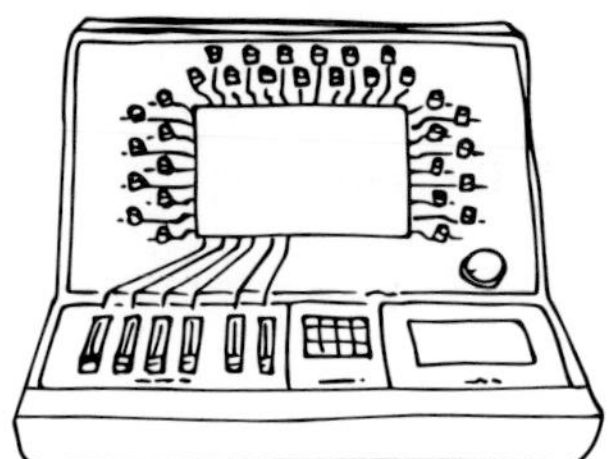

RHODES (USA)

Much more famous for their eponymous electric pianos, Rhodes also released two synthesizers in the early 1980s. Their parent company CBS Musical Instruments acquired the designs for the Chroma from ARP who had gone into administration. The Chroma was an early microprocessor instrument and could be synchronised with an Apple IIe.

RHODES CHROMA *1982*

Analogue
16 note polyphony / 1 DCO per voice
Was to have been the ARP Chroma; it featured digital control of oscillators, wave-shaping and filtering using the Intel 80186 chip. The Expander was the rackmount.

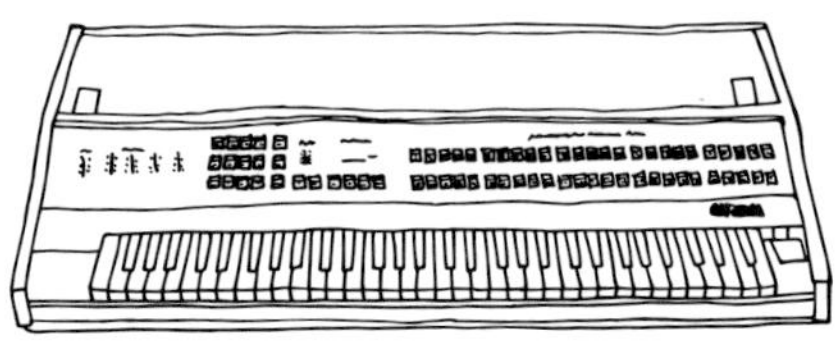

RHODES CHROMA POLARIS *1984*

Analogue
6 note polyphony / 2 DCOs per voice
A simplified Chroma.

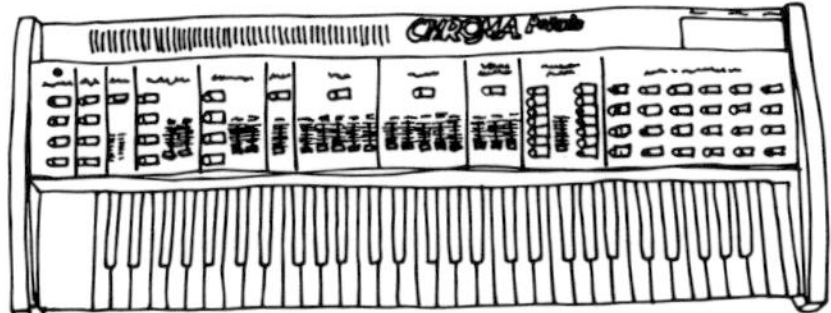

RMI KEYBOARD COMPUTER (KC-1) *1974*

Digital Wavetable
Full polyphony (divide-down)
Very early, but preset, digital synth using Allen Organs' digital oscillators. The KC-II was released in 1975.

ROCKY MOUNT INSTRUMENTS (RMI) (USA)

Founded in 1966, RMI was a subsidiary of the Allen Organ Company, and their first instruments were electric pianos and combo-organs such as the Explorer made in the late 1960s. Their innovative Harmonic Synthesizer was used by Jean-Michel Jarre for the lead sound of 'Oxygene IV', one of the most iconic electronic music tracks of all time. Allen Organ themselves installed the first electronic church organ in 1939.

RMI HARMONIC SYNTHESIZER *1974*

Additive / FM / AM
Duo / 16 harmonics per voice
Early use of digital oscillators and basic FM synthesis.

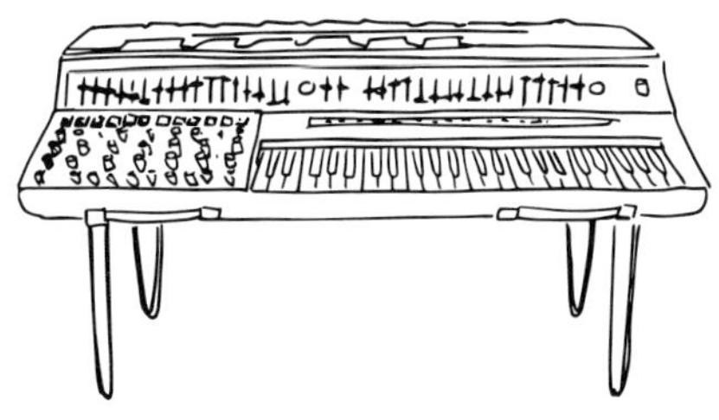

ROLAND CORPORATION (JAPAN)

Ikutaro Kakehashi founded Roland in 1972, having already released a large range of guitar amps, electric organs and drum machines with his former company Ace Tone. Since then Roland have produced a huge number of synthesizers, drum machines and samplers, several of which have had a lasting and significant impact on music and culture.

Not many individual synthesizers and drum machines have single-handedly inspired entire genres, but the TB-303, the TR-808, and TR-909 have achieved exactly that. Hip-hop, Chicago house, acid-house, and techno were all underground dance scenes built on these instruments - and which went on to dominate the commercial music landscape.

Other significant instruments include the Jupiter 8, which is one of the finest of the polyphonic analogue synthesizers. The D-50 introduced the affordable realism of 'sample and synthesis'. Many other of their machines are either highly desirable or highly influential - the SH-101, the Alpha-Juno, and the System 100 semi-modular, to name just a few.

Roland also owned the rights to the Rhodes name until 2000, and also own the Boss guitar-pedal brand.

ROLAND SH-1000 *1973*

Analogue
Mono / 1 VCO
Roland - and Japan's - first synthesizer, featuring presets with limited editing.

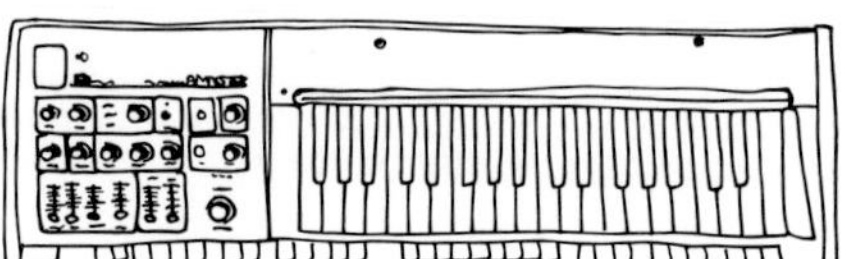

ROLAND SH-2000 *1973*

Analogue
Mono / 1 VCO

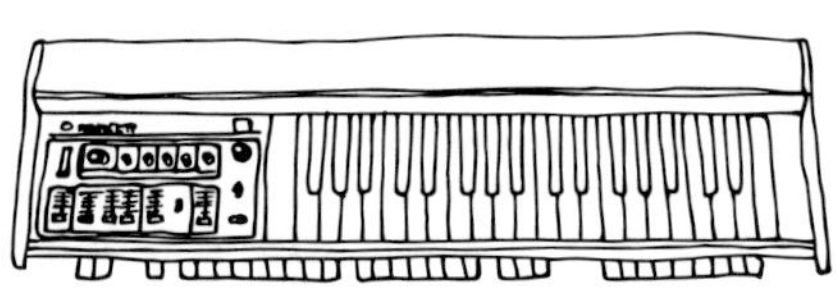

ROLAND SH-3A *1974*

Analogue / Additive
Mono / 1 VCO
The SH-3a is a variant of the initial SH-3 which may have infringed copyrights.

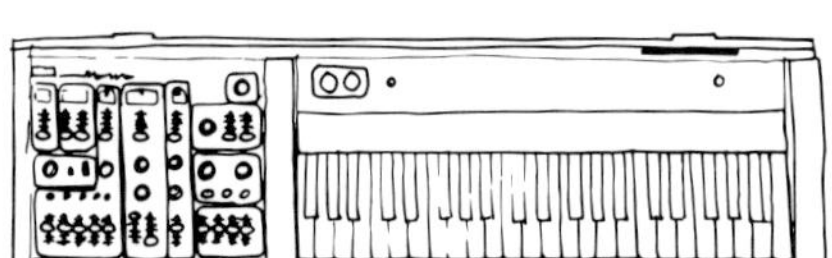

ROLAND RS-101 *1975*

Preset synth: brass and strings
Full polyphony (divide-down)
The RS-202 added the famous ensemble effect. The RS-505 introduced the term 'paraphonic'. The RS-09 had strings and organ; the SA-09 just had the organ section.

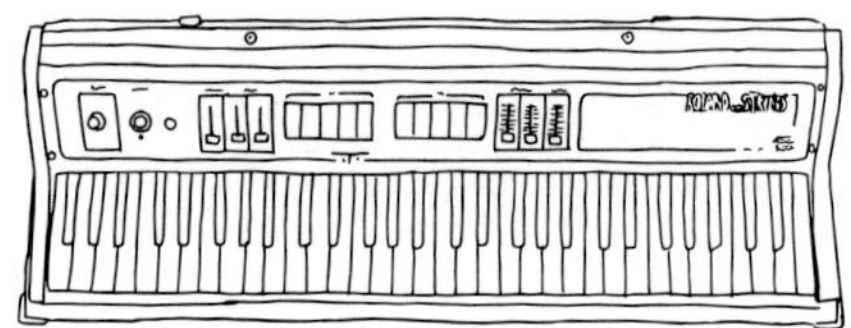
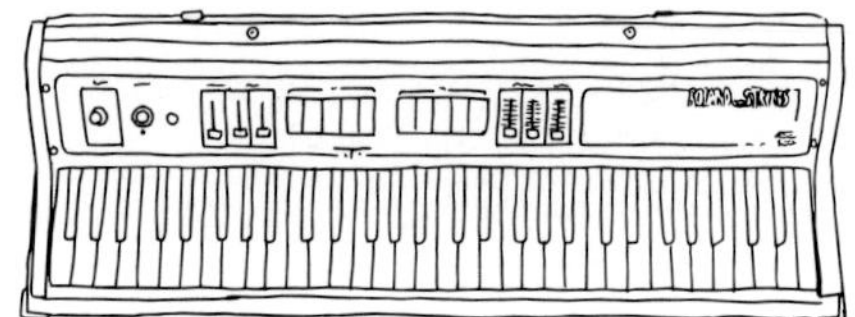

ROLAND SYSTEM 100 *1975*

Analogue / Mono / Semi-modular

ROLAND SH-5 *1976*

Analogue
Mono / 2 VCOs

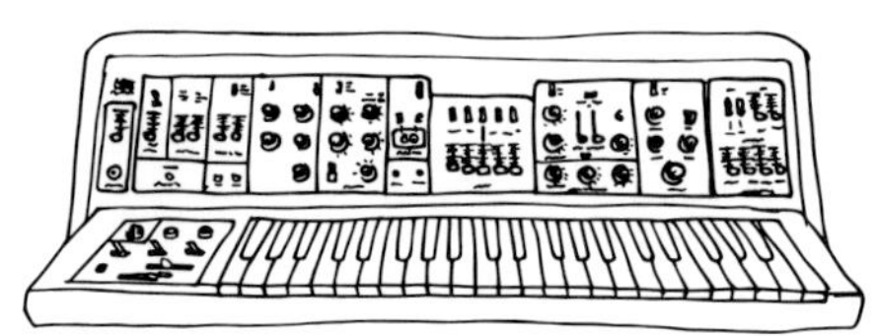

ROLAND SYSTEM 700 *1976*

Analogue
Mono / 3 VCOs

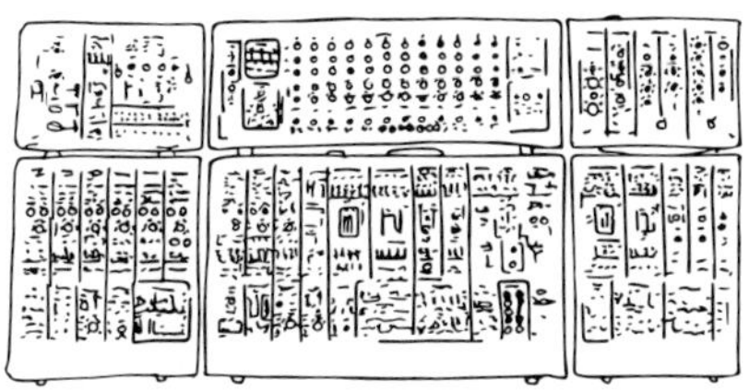

ROLAND GR-500 *1977*

Analogue / 6 note polyphonic
A guitar synth that came with a modified guitar and worked in various modes: guitar EQ, ensemble chords, bass or lead synth, and could even control an external synth.

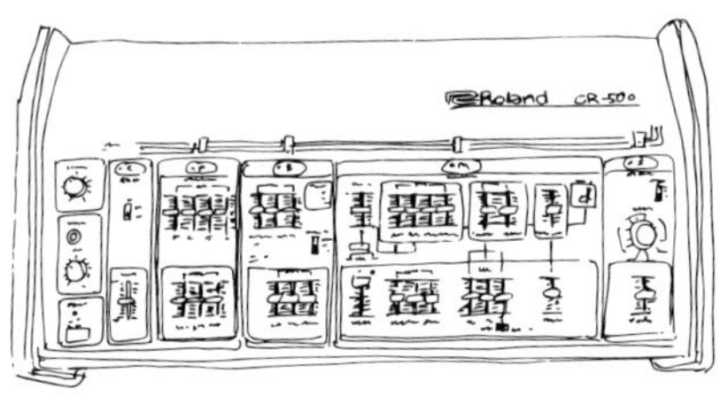

ROLAND JUPITER 4 *1978*

Analogue
4 note polyphony / 1 VCO per voice
Duran Duran - 'Hungry Like The Wolf' (1982) (arpeggio).

ROLAND SH-1 *1978*

Analogue
Mono / 1 VCO

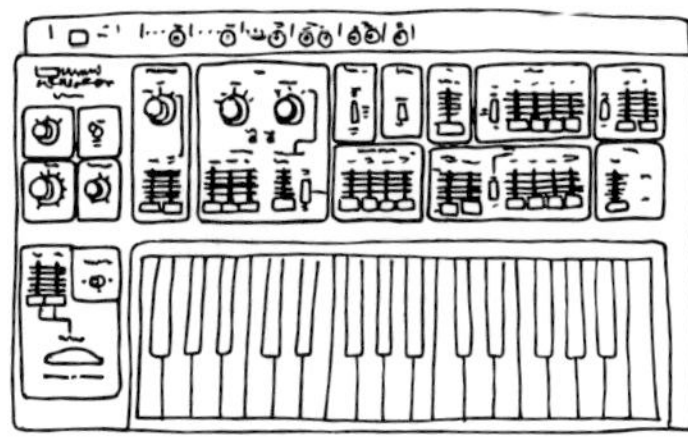

ROLAND SH-7 *1978*

Analogue
Mono/Duo / 2 VCOs

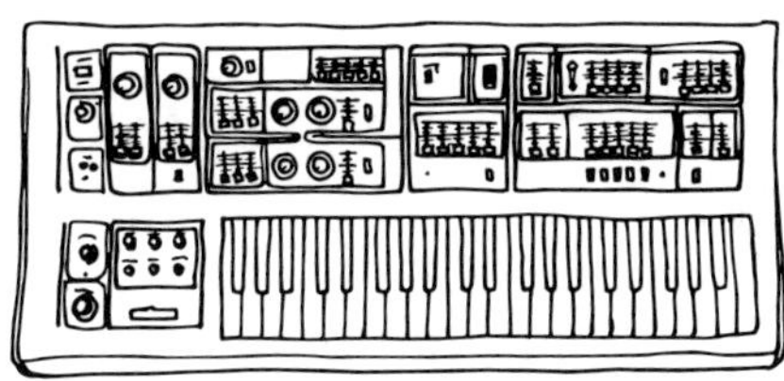

ROLAND SH-2 *1979*

Analogue
Mono / 2 VCOs
An SH-1 with two VCOs.

ROLAND SYSTEM 100M *1979*

Analogue / Mono / Modular
Powerful and flexible system with over 20 modules.

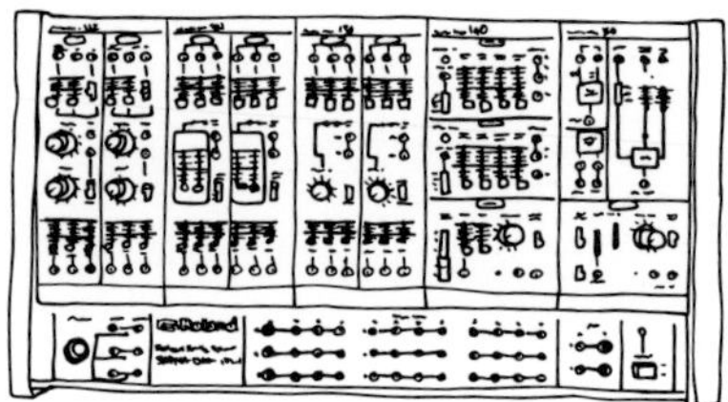

ROLAND PROMARS MRS-2 *1979*

Analogue / 10 presets
Mono / 2 VCOs
Also known as the Compuphonic. Designed to be paired with the Jupiter 4.

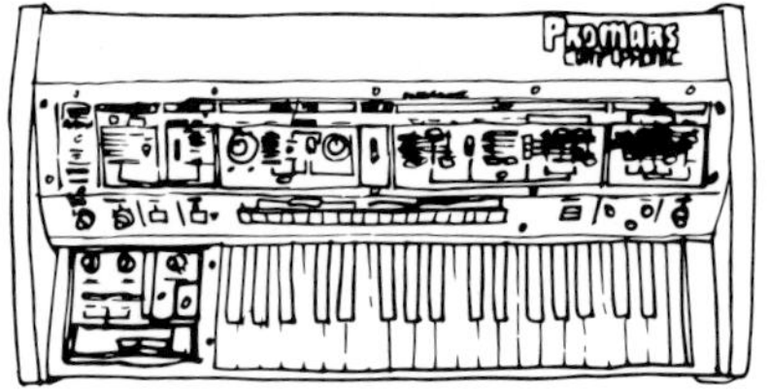

ROLAND VP-330 *1979*

Preset synth / Vocoder
Full polyphony (divide-down)
The classic 1970s vocoder effect. Vangelis - 'Chariots of Fire' (1981).

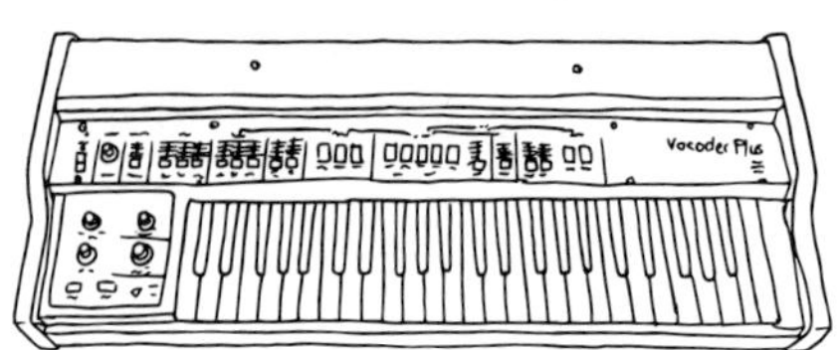

ROLAND SH-09 *1980*

Analogue
Mono / 1 VCO

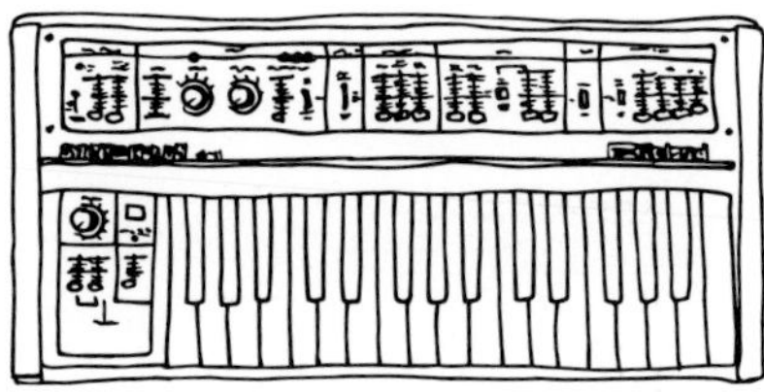

ROLAND JUPITER 8 *1981*

Analogue
8 note polyphony / 2 VCOs per voice
One of the classic polysynths of the analogue era.
Queen - 'Radio Ga Ga' (bassline, pads); Jan Hammer - 'Crockett's Theme' (bassline).

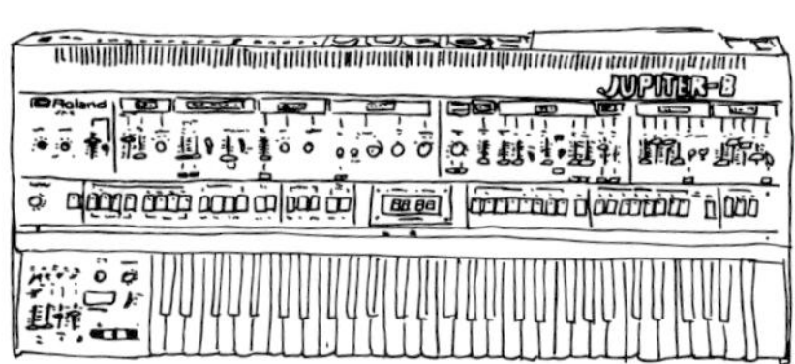

ROLAND JUNO 6 *1982*

Analogue
6 note polyphony / 1 DCO per voice

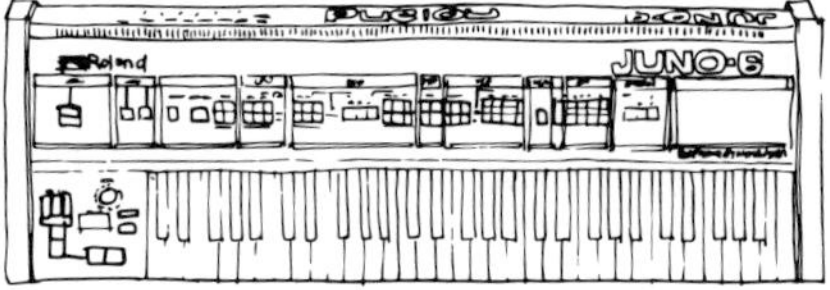

ROLAND JUNO 60 *1982*

Analogue
6 note polyphony / 1 DCO per voice
A Juno 6 with 56 patch memories and a Digital Control Bus (DCB), the precursor to MIDI. Cabaret Voltaire – 'Just Fascination' (1983).

ROLAND CMU810 *1982*

Analogue
Mono / 1 VCO
Similar to the SH-101 & MC-202.

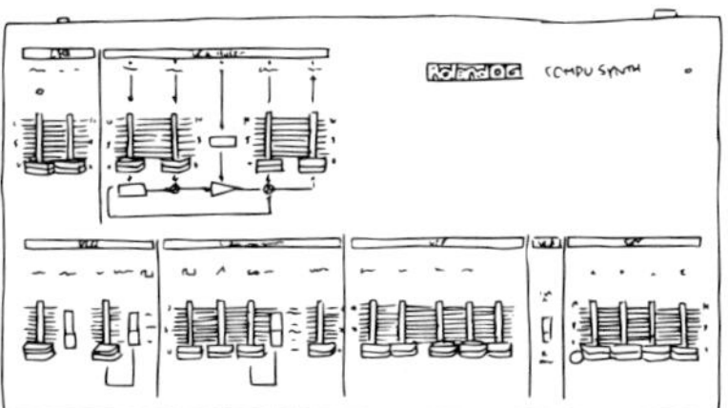

ROLAND SH-101 *1982*

Analogue
Mono / 2 VCOs + sub
Extremely popular monosynth, then and now. A Guy Called Gerald - 'Voodoo Ray' (1988).

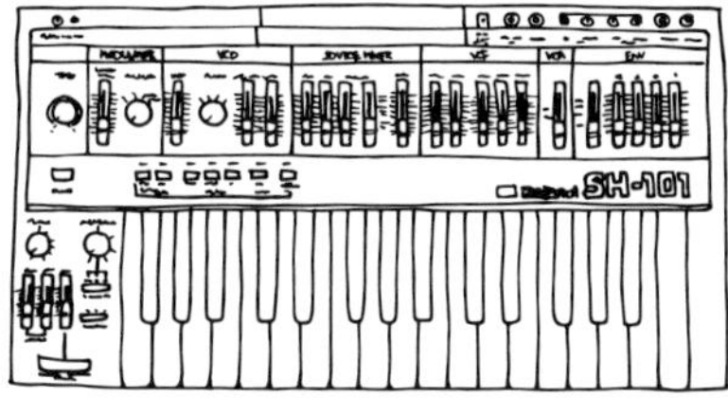

ROLAND JUPITER 6 *1983*

Analogue
6 note polyphony / 2 VCOs per voice
Ray Parker Junior - 'Ghostbusters' (1984) (bassline).

ROLAND TB-303 *1982*

Analogue
Mono / 1 VCO
The machine that kick-started the acid house revolution in 1986 with Phuture's 'Acid Trax' debuted by DJ Ron Hardy at The Music Box, Chicago.

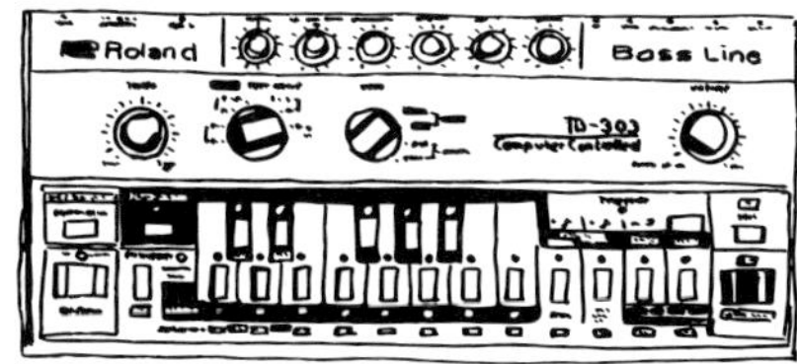

ROLAND JX-3P *1983*

Analogue
6 note polyphony / 2 DCOs per voice
The MKS-30 is the rackmount version.

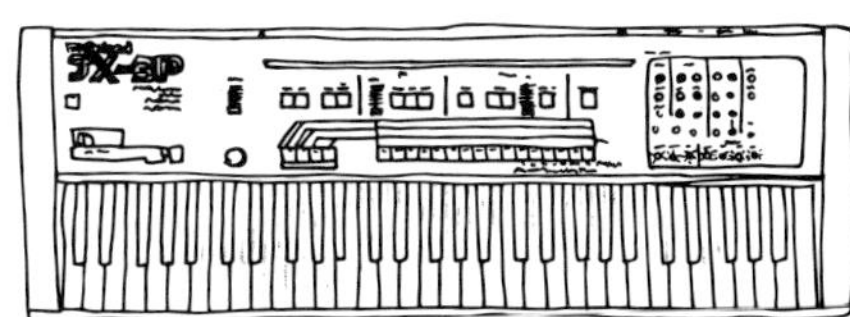

ROLAND MC-202 *1983*

Analogue
Mono / 1 VCO
The MicroComposer 202 was a follow up to the TB-303.

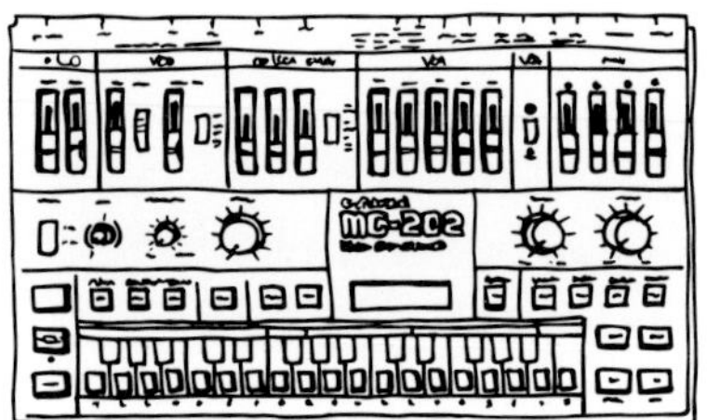

ROLAND MKS-7 SUPER QUARTET *1985*

Analogue
There are four separate sections: 'melody', 'chord', 'bass' (based on the Juno 106) and 'rhythm' (using TR-707 sounds).

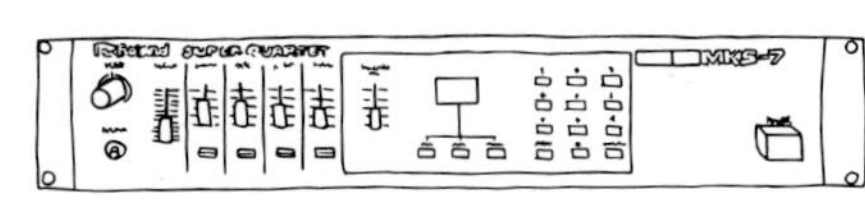

ROLAND MKS-80 SUPER JUPITER *1984*

Analogue
8 note polyphony / 2 VCOs per voice
A rackmounted, and updated, Jupiter 8. The MPG-80 is the optional programmer.

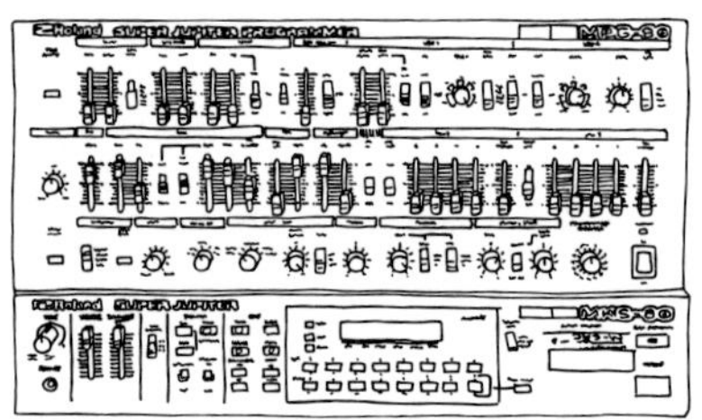

ROLAND JX-8P *1985*

Analogue
6 note polyphony / 2 DCOs per voice

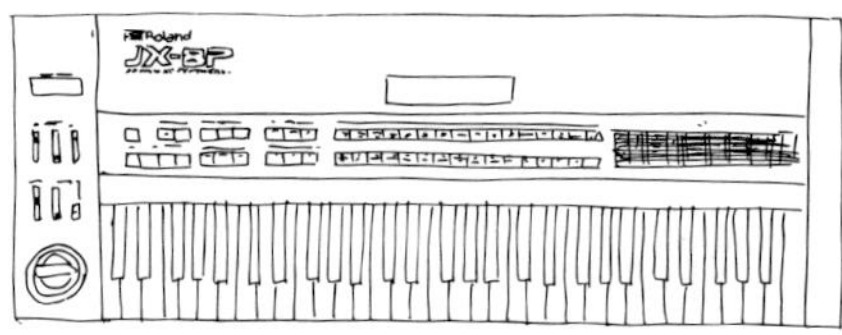

ROLAND JUNO 106 *1984*

Analogue
6 note polyphony / 1 DCO per voice
The Juno 106S was a version with speakers, as was the HS-60.

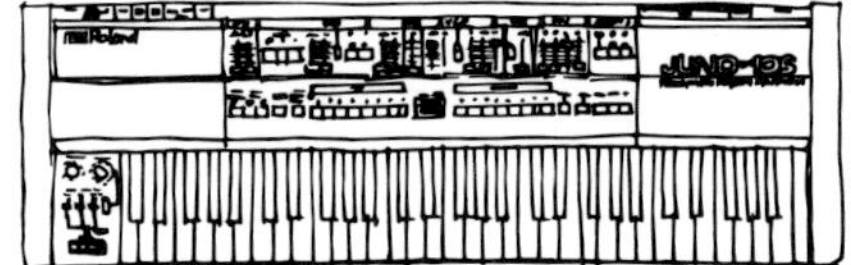

ROLAND ALPHA-JUNO 1 *1985*

Analogue / 6 note polyphony / 1 DCO + sub per voice
Preset 69: What the…? is the 'sound of the hoover', used extensively in breakbeat hardcore, rave, jungle and techno. First used in Second Phase - 'Mentasm' (1991). The MKS-50 is the rackmount; the HS-10 has built-in speakers.

ROLAND ALPHA-JUNO 2 *1986*

Analogue

6 note polyphony / 1 DCO + sub per voice

This updated Alpha Juno had a longer keyboard and aftertouch. The HS-80 has built-in speakers. The PG-300 programmer offered one-slider-per-function control for both Alpha-Junos.

ROLAND MT-32 *1987*

Sample & Synthesis

8-32 note polyphony / 1-4 partials per voice

Simple ROMpler. One partial per voice gave 32 note polyphony and four partials per voice gave 8 note polyphony. Designed for use with the PR-100 sequencer (or computer).

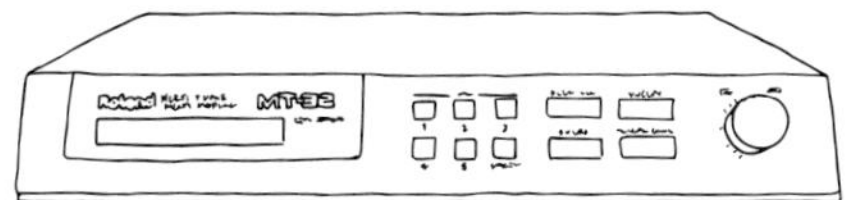

ROLAND JX-10 (SUPER JX) *1986*

Analogue

12 note polyphony / 2 DCOs per voice

The MKS-70 is the rackmount version. The PG-800 programmer was available.

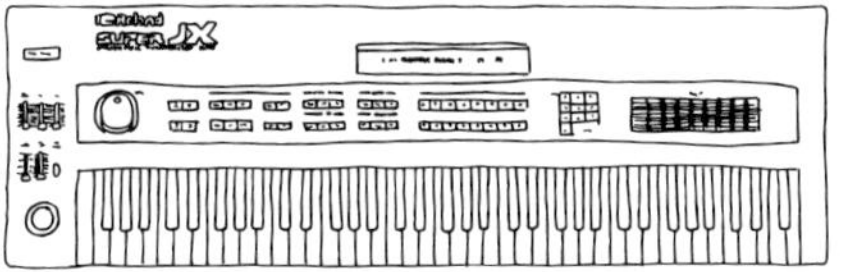

ROLAND D-10 *1988*

Linear Arithmetic (Sample & Synthesis)

8-32 note polyphony / 1-4 partials per voice

Based on an MT-32. The D-110 was the rackmount.

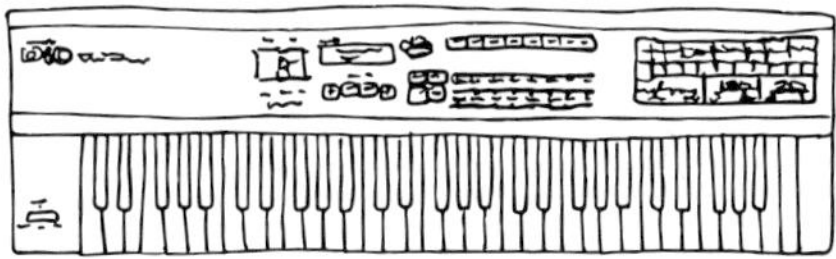

ROLAND D-50 *1987*

Linear Arithmetic (Sample & Synthesis)

16 note polyphony / 4 partials per voice

Roland nails the ROMpler. Heard everywhere in the 1980s. The D-550 was the rackmount equivalent. Enya - 'Orinoco Flow' (1988); Miles Davis - 'Cantembe' (1989).

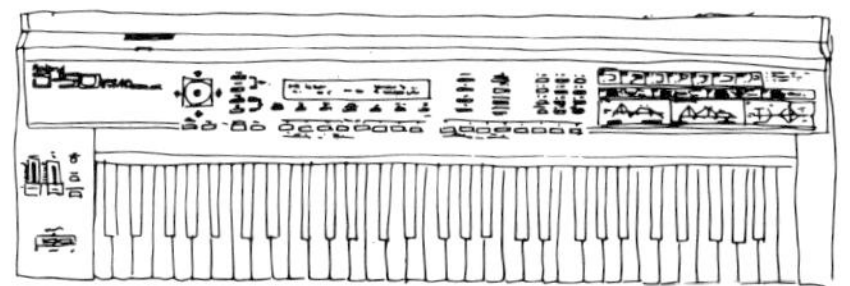

ROLAND D-20 *1988*

Linear Arithmetic (Sample & Synthesis)

8-32 note polyphony / 1-4 partials per voice

A D-10 with a sequencer.

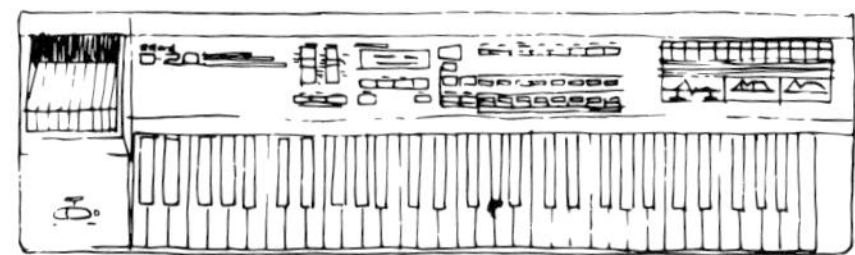

ROLAND U-110 *1988*

Sample & Synthesis
31 note polyphony / 1-2 tones per voice
A simple preset ROMpler with six part multi-timbrality and six audio outs. Using 2 tones per voice gave 15 note polyphony.

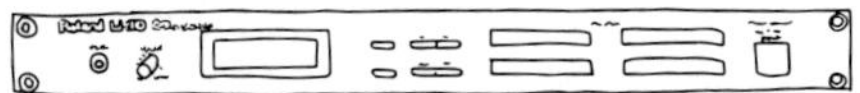

ROLAND D-70 *1990*

Super LA (Sample & Synthesis)
30 note polyphony / 4 Partials per sound
A culmination of the U-series and, disappointingly, not a top-of-the-range D-50 as the name suggests.

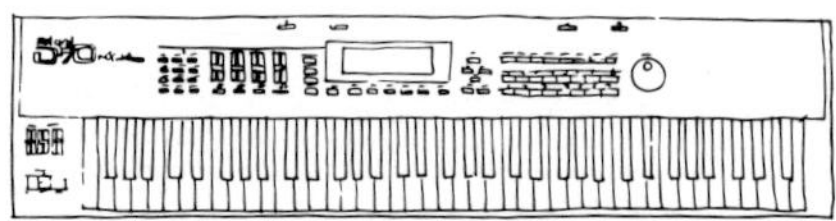

ROLAND U-20 *1989*

Sample & Synthesis
30 note polyphony / 1-2 tones per voice
Using 2 tones per voice halved the polyphony to 15. Six part multi-timbral.

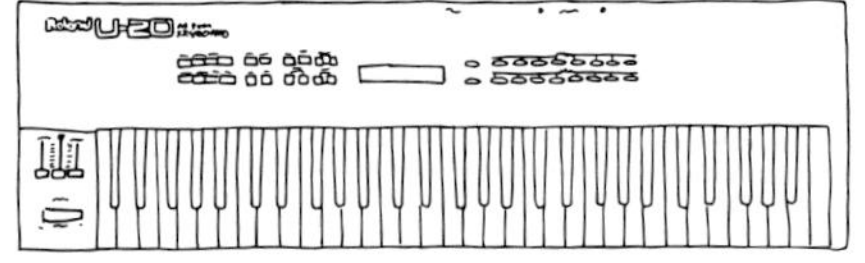

ROLAND JD-800 *1991*

Sample & Synthesis
24 note polyphony / 4 Partials
A return to switches and sliders following a decade of 2 line LCDs. The JD-990 was the rackmount.

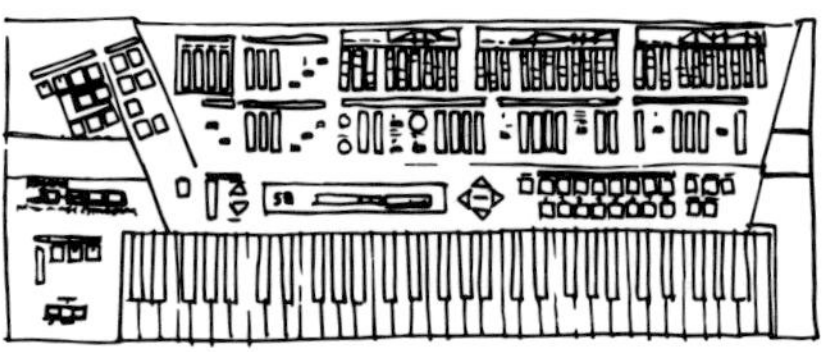

ROLAND D-5 *1989*

Linear Arithmetic (Sample & Synthesis)
8-32 note polyphony / 1-4 partials per voice
Like the D-10 only included a drum-sounds channel.

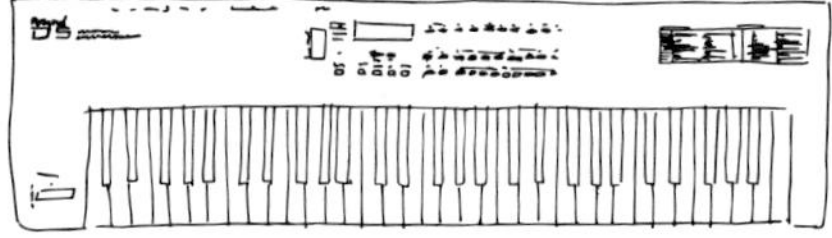

ROLAND JV-80 *1991*

Sample & Synthesis
28 note polyphony / 1-4 tones per voice
The first of the JV series of ROMplers: JV-880, JV-50, JV-30, JV-35, JV-50, JV-90, JV-1000, JV-1080, JV-2080…

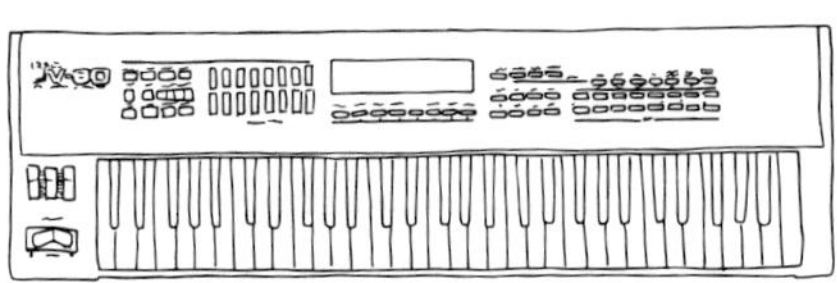

ROLAND SC-55 *1991*

Sample & Synthesis
24 note polyphony / 2 DOs per voice
The first of the 'Sound Canvas' series, a straight-forward 'General MIDI' compliant synthesizer. Variants and updates include the SC-55ST, SC-88V, and SC-88.

ROLAND JP-8000 *1997*

Analogue Modelling
8 note polyphony / two modelled oscillators per voice
Roland's entry into the virtual analogue world and famous for its 'supersaw' sound. Darude - 'Sandstorm' (1999) ('Sandstorm' was the name of the supersaw preset used!).

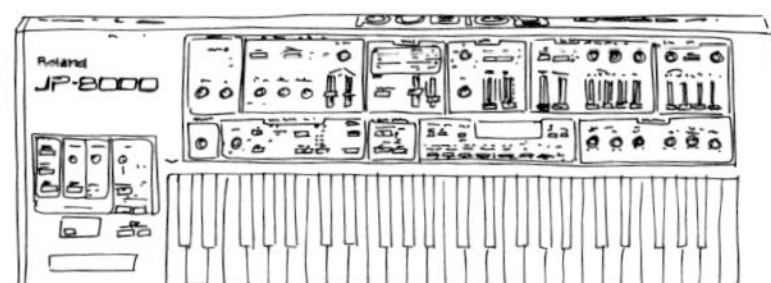

ROLAND JX-1 *1991*

Sample & Synthesis
24 note polyphony / 2 DOs per voice
A basic synth along the lines of the SC-55 General MIDI device. Variants and updates: MT-120S, MT-20.

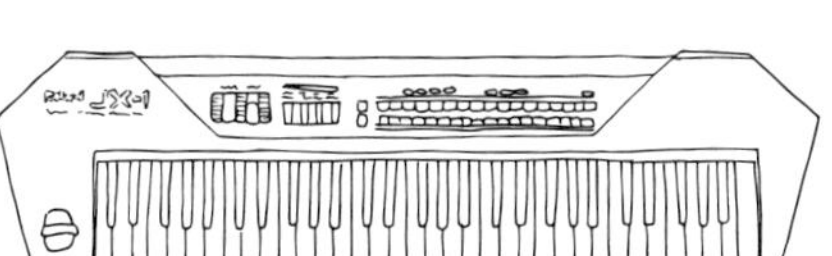

ROLAND MC-303 *1996*

Sample & Synthesis
28 note polyphony / 2 DOs per voice
Roland's first recognition of the enduring popularity of the TB-303. A synth/drum machine aimed at the growing dance and DJ market. Updates included the MC-505 (1998).

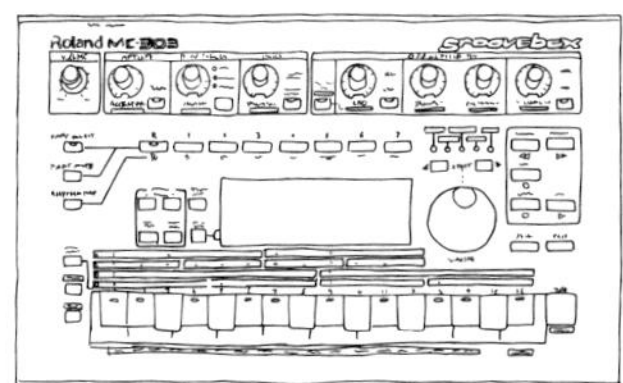

RSF (FRANCE)

R.S.F. stands for Ruben and Serge Fernandez, the brothers who started the company in the 1970s. They made a number of monophonic and polyphonic instruments between the mid-70s and early 80s.

RSF MODULAR MODEL 11 *1976*

Analogue
Mono / 3 VCOs

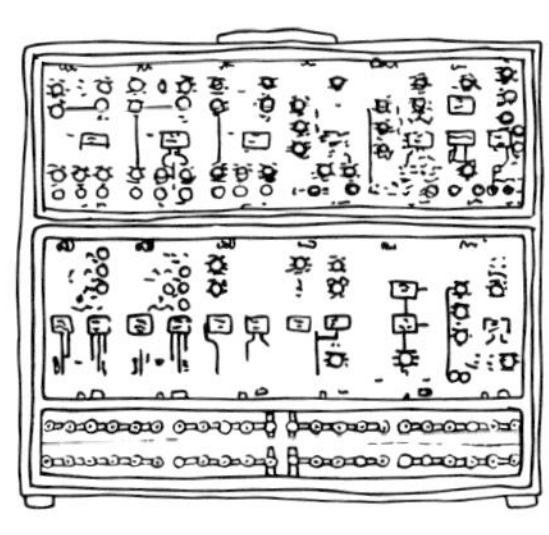

RSF KOBOL *1978*

Analogue
Mono / 2 VCOs
Also available were the Kobol Expander and Expander II.

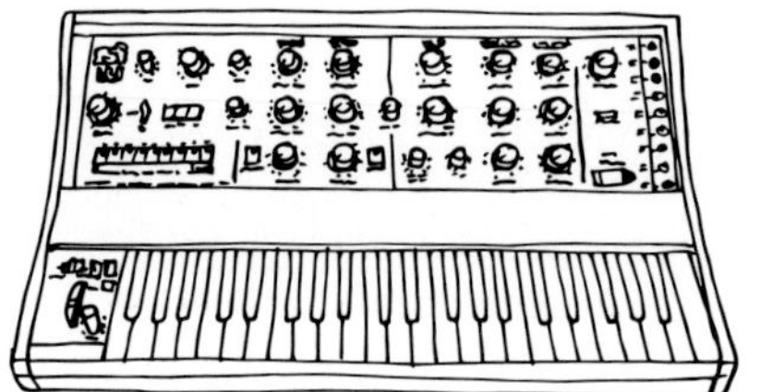

RSF BLACKBOX *1982*

Analogue
13 note polyphony / 1 VCO
Similar to the earlier EML Polybox (1977).

RSF POLYKOBOL II *1983*

Analogue
8 note polyphony / 2 VCOs per voice
Extremely rare polyphonic synth from RSF, rumoured to have suffered severe maintenance issues. The first version was released in 1980.

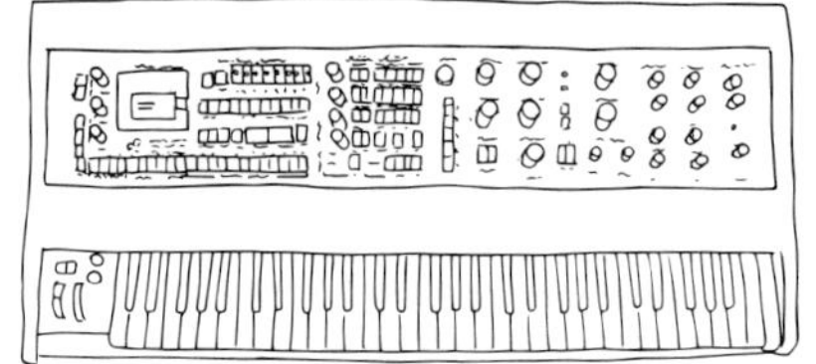

SAIC WALDECK SOUND SYNTHESIZER *1978*

Analogue
Mono / 3 VCOs
Built by Steve Waldeck at the School of the Art Institute of Chicago, the 'Waldeck Sound Synthesizer' was modelled on an EMS VCS3.

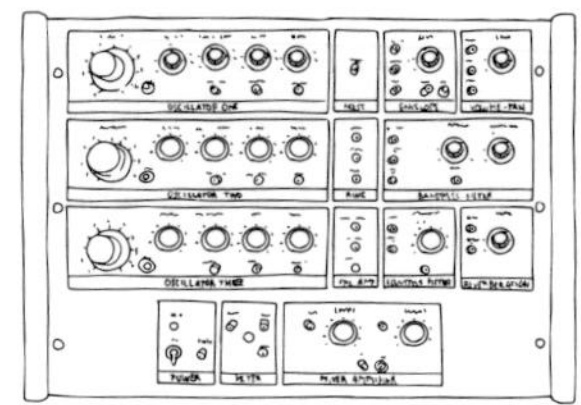

SEIKO DS-202 *1983*

Additive
8 note polyphony / 16 partials per tone
Unusually for a home keyboard, the DS-202 was an additive synth.

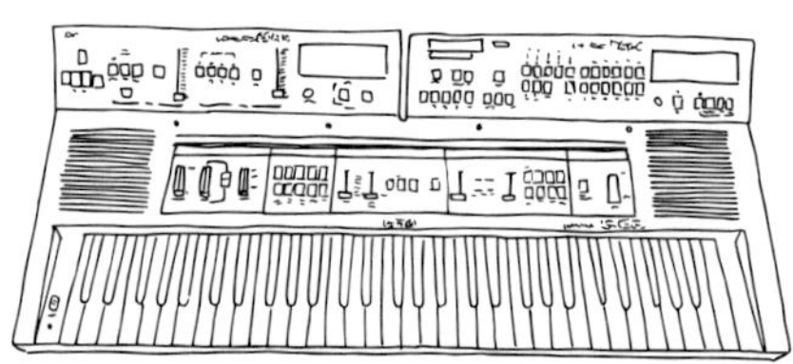

SEQUENTIAL CIRCUITS (USA)

Dave Smith is one of the legends of the synth industry, founding Sequential Circuits in 1978. He found immediate success with the microprocessor-controlled Prophet 5 which offered recallable patches in a more practical form-factor than the competing Yamaha CS-80. It was used by many artists and film-composers of the time, such as Quincy Jones, Madonna and John Carpenter. Several versions followed - the Prophet-10 and the Pro-One, the latter also meeting with success.

SEQUENTIAL CIRCUITS CONT...

Dave Smith and Ikutaro Kakehashi of Roland worked together on the MIDI standard in the early 1980s, which earned them a Technical Grammy Award in 2013. The Prophet 600 was the first synthesizer to sport MIDI ports.

Sequential Circuits ceased trading in 1987 and Dave Smith set up Dave Smith Instruments in 2002, before returning to Sequential in 2015 after Yamaha returned the brand name to him in a gesture of goodwill.

SEQUENTIAL CIRCUITS PRO-ONE
1981

Analogue
Mono / 2 VCOs
Very popular monosynth, it included an arpeggiator and sequencer.

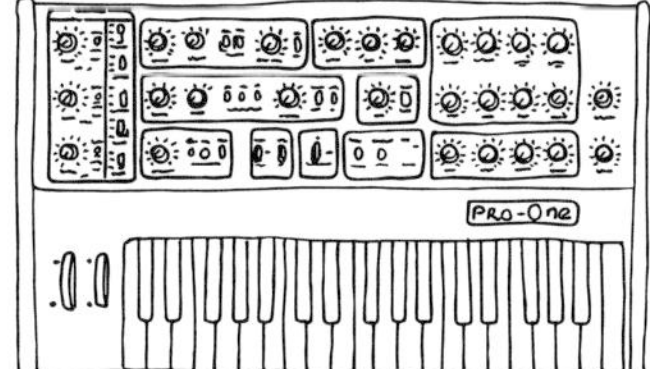

SEQUENTIAL CIRCUITS PROPHET 5
1978

Analogue
5 note polyphony / 2 VCOs per voice
The first polyphonic synth with full patch memory. The first two versions used SSM chips, the third used Curtis chips which were much more stable. The Cars - 'Let's Go' (1979) (synth lead).

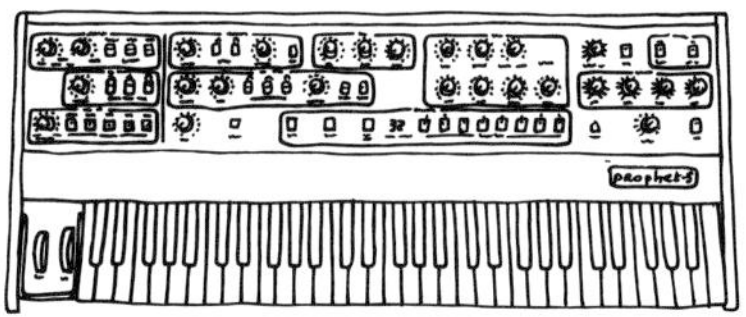

SEQUENTIAL CIRCUITS FUGUE *1981*

Analogue section: Mono / 1 DCO
String section: Full polyphony (divide-down)
Sold in Europe as the Siel Cruise.

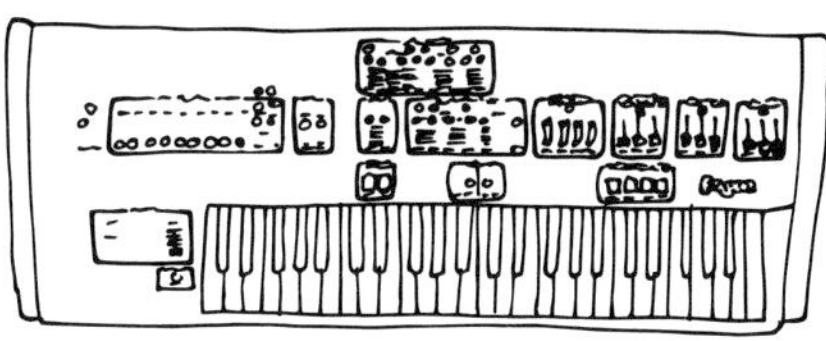

SEQUENTIAL CIRCUITS PROPHET 10
1980

Analogue
10 note polyphony / 2 VCOs per voice
Essentially two Prophet 5's for double the polyphony, it too only became stable with a third revision.

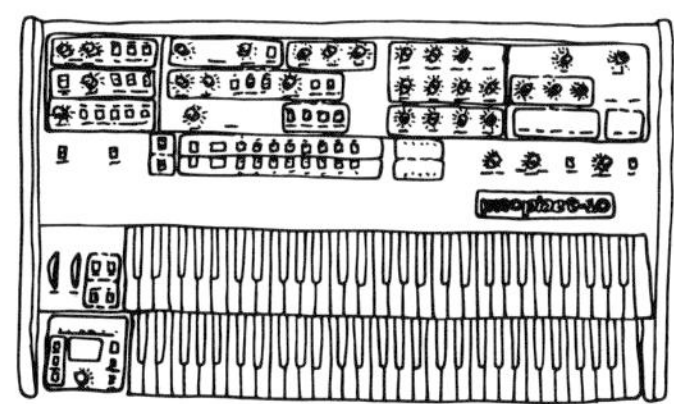

SEQUENTIAL CIRCUITS PROPHET 600
1982

Analogue
6 note polyphony / 2 VCOs per voice
First synth to support the newly agreed MIDI standard.

SEQUENTIAL CIRCUITS PRELUDE *1982*

Ensemble presets: brass, strings, reed, piano
Full polyphony (divide-down)
Sold in Europe as the Siel Orchestra 2.

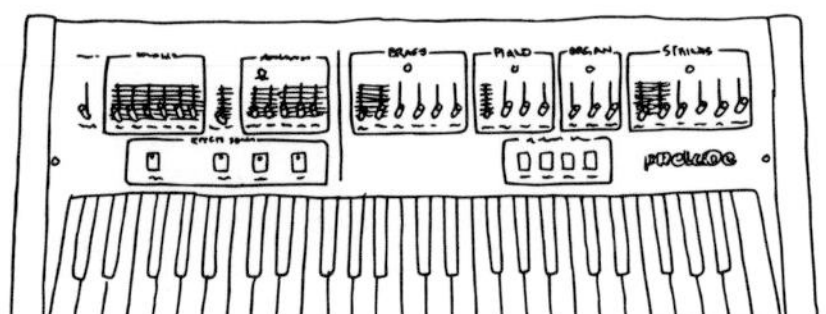

SEQUENTIAL CIRCUITS SIXTRAK *1984*

Analogue
6 note polyphony / 1 VCO per voice
The first multi-timbral MIDI synth.

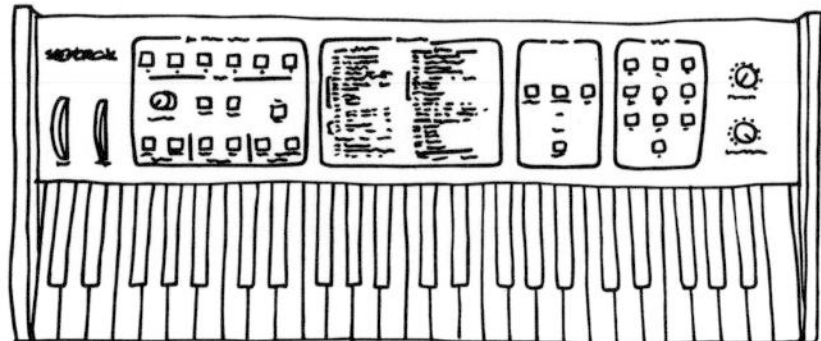

SEQUENTIAL CIRCUITS PROPHET T8 *1983*

Analogue
8 note polyphony / 2 VCOs per voice
The culmination, and best, of the Prophet line.

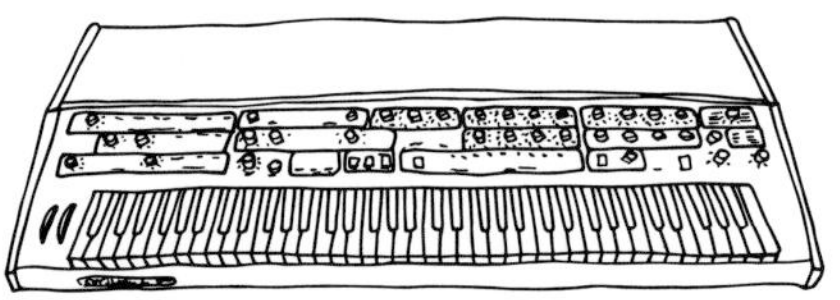

SEQUENTIAL CIRCUITS MULTITRAK *1985*

Analogue
6 note polyphony / 1 VCO per voice
The Max, SixTrak, MultiTrak (an updated SixTrak) and Split-8 were built around a CEM 3394 chip.

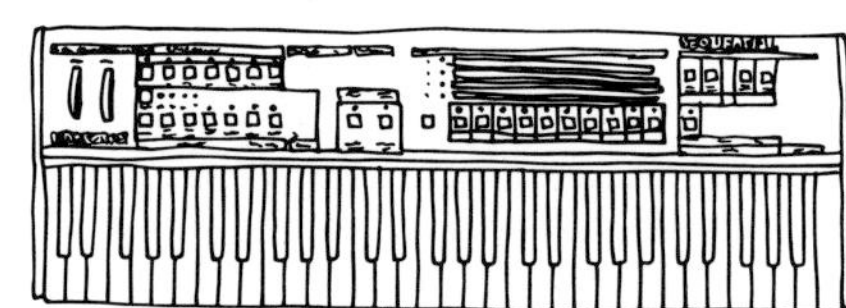

SEQUENTIAL CIRCUITS MAX *1984*

Analogue
6 note polyphony / 1 VCO per voice
A preset synth, only editable via computer (Commodore 64 or Mac/PC).

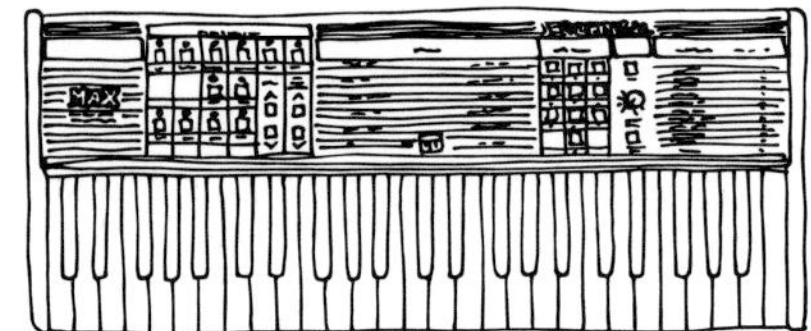

SEQUENTIAL CIRCUITS SPLIT-8 *1985*

Analogue
8 note polyphony / 1 VCO per voice
Built in Japan and marketed there as the Pro-8.

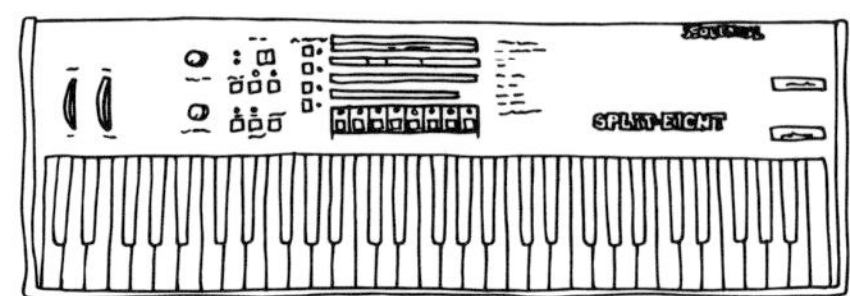

SEQUENTIAL CIRCUITS PROPHET VS
1986

Vector Synthesis
8 note polyphony / 4 DOs per voice
The four digital waveforms that comprised a sound could be blended in varying proportions with the joystick. The Prophet VS Rack is the rackmount equivalent.

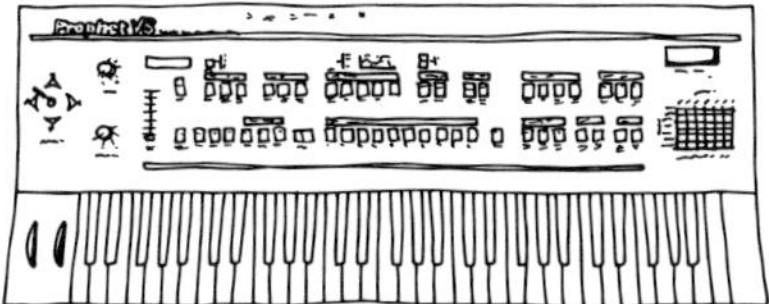

SERGE SYNTHESIZER (USA)

Serge Tcherepnin was a professor at the California Institute of the Arts (CalArts) in the early 1970s and wanted to build a modular synthesizer that was as powerful as competing systems, but at a more affordable cost. He left CalArts to develop the business further with fellow founders Rich Gold and Randy Cohen.

Serge Synthesizers are held in high regard and were used by many musicians, including Stevie Wonder and John Adams. Several modules were also incorporated into Malcolm Cecil's 'TONTO' system.

SERGE TCHEREPNIN MODULAR SYNTHESIZER *1973*

Analogue / Mono / Modular

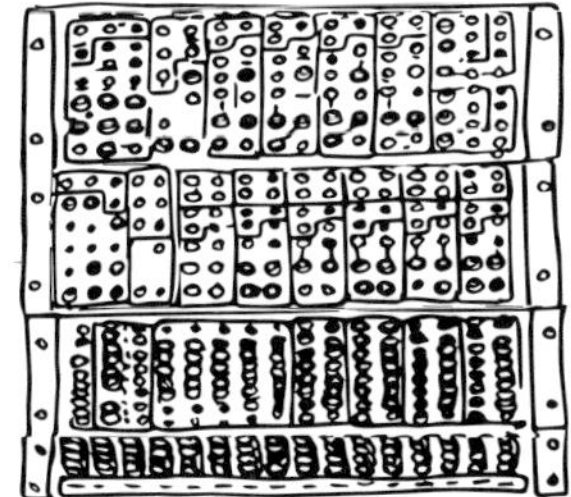

SIEL (SOCIETA INDUSTRIE ELETTRONICHE) (ITALY)

SIEL were better known for organs before they entered the synth market in the 1970s. They designed string machines for ARP and Sequential Circuits and released a number of own-brand synthesizers between 1980 and 1983 before being acquired by Roland in 1987.

SIEL ORCHESTRA *1979*

Analogue
4 presets: brass, organ, piano, strings
Full polyphony (divide-down)
Sold in the US as the ARP Quartet.

SIEL MONO *1980*

Analogue
Mono / 1 DCO
Ten presets with synth parameters for editing.

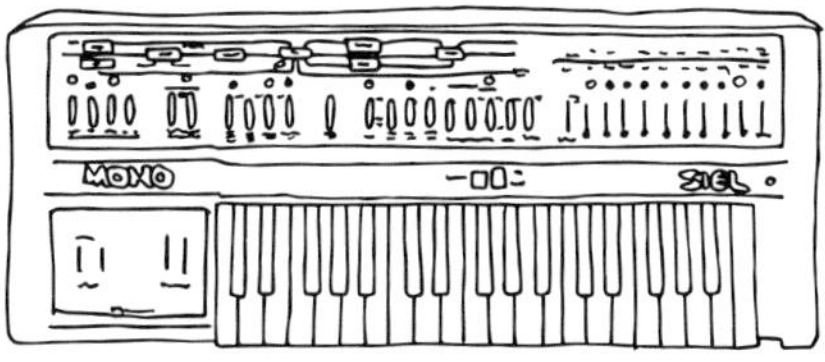

SIEL CRUISE *1981*

Analogue preset section: Mono / 1 DCO
String section: Full polyphony (divide down)
A Siel Mono combined with the Siel Orchestra. Sold in the US as the Sequential Circuits Fugue (same controls, different front panel design).

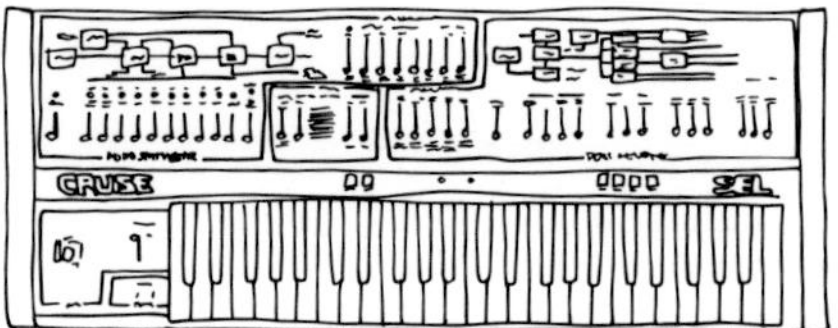

SIEL KIWI *1985*

Analogue
6 note polyphony / 2 DCOs per voice
Improved MIDI spec version of the DK-600.

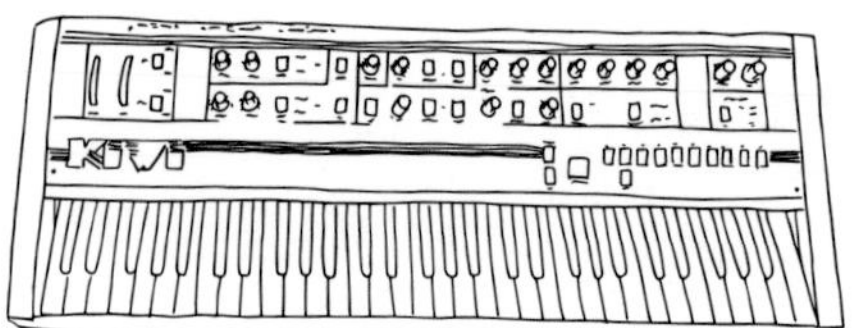

SIEL OPERA 6 *1983*

Analogue
6 note polyphony / 2 DCOs per voice
Very similar to the DK-600; there were two subsequent versions with added features.

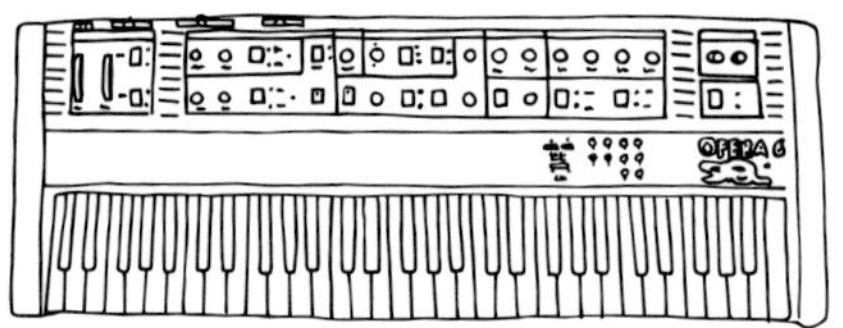

SIEL DK-80 *1985*

Analogue
12 note polyphony / 2 DCOs per voice

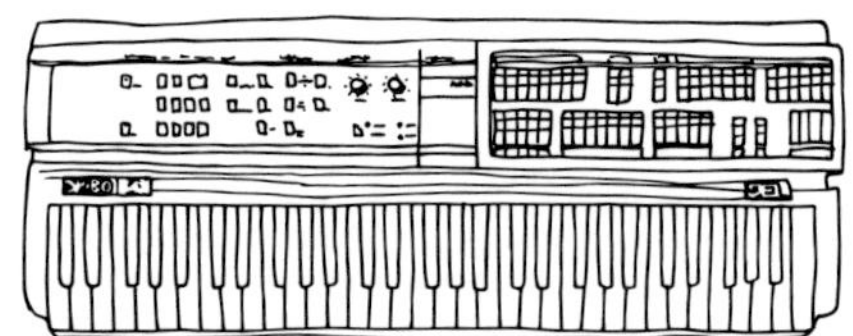

SIEL DK-600 *1984*

Analogue
6 note polyphony / 2 DCOs per voice
The EK-600 Expander was the rackmount.

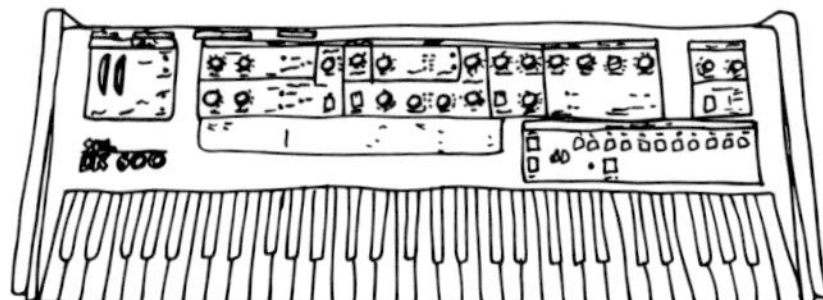

SIEL DK-70 *1986*

Analogue
8 note polyphony / 1 DCO per voice
A battery powered portable synth.

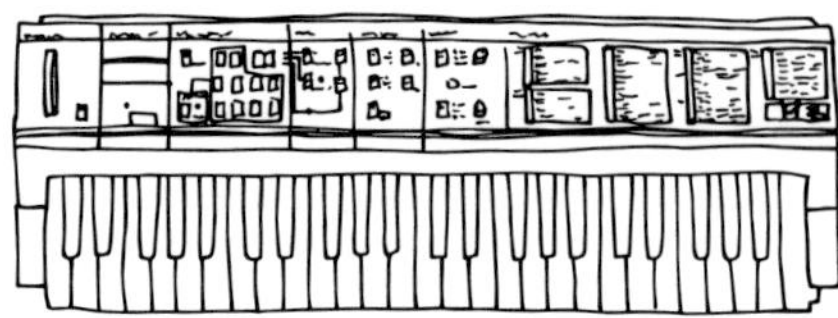

SIEL DK-700 *1986*

Analogue
6 note polyphony / 2 DCOs per voice

SSM (SOLID STATE MICRO TECHNOLOGY FOR MUSIC) (USA)

Microchips of the early 1980s created in partnership with E-mu and used in many synthesizers and samplers: Akai AX series, Aries Modular, Cheetah MS6, Doepfer, E-mu drum machines and samplers, Elka Synthex, Ensoniq, Kawai K3, Oberheim, Sequential Circuits, Siel and Waldorf.

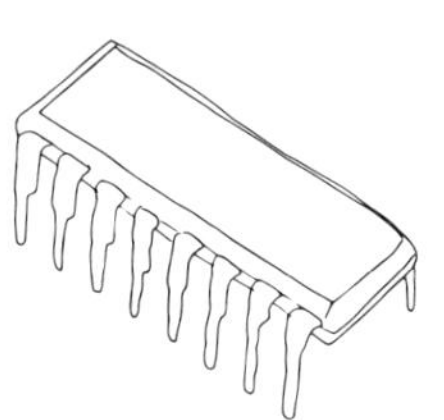

SOLINA STRING ENSEMBLE *1974*

Analogue string synth
Full polyphony (divide-down)
The Solina String Ensemble was derived from the Eminent 310 Unique organ's string synth. It was sold in the US as the ARP String Ensemble.

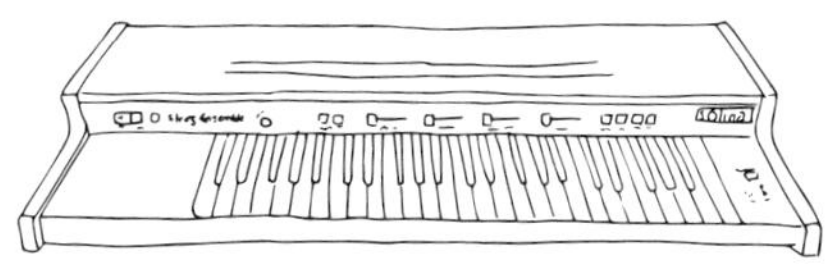

SOLINA STRING SYNTHESIZER *1975*

Analogue section: 1 VCO
String synth: Full polyphony (divide-down)
This was an ARP Explorer 1 combined with a Solina String Ensemble, a rare beast.

SOLTON PROJECT 100 *1985*

Digital Waveforms
6 note polyphony / 2 DOs per voice
Solton was an Italian brand; the MS100 was the rack-mount with 12 note polyphony.

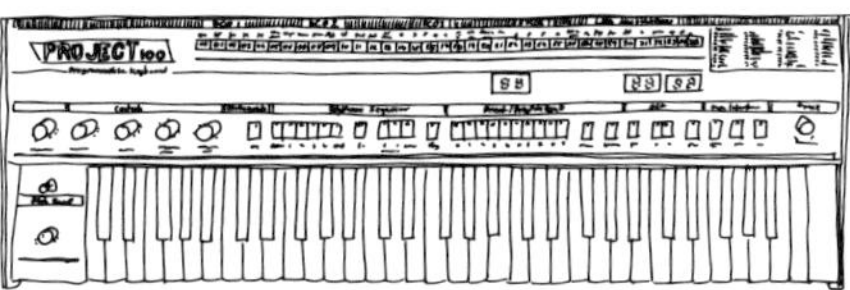

STEELPHON S900 *1970*

Analogue
Mono / 2 VCOs
Steelphon were principally an Italian manufacturer of electric guitars, but they also made the preset S900 synthesizer too.

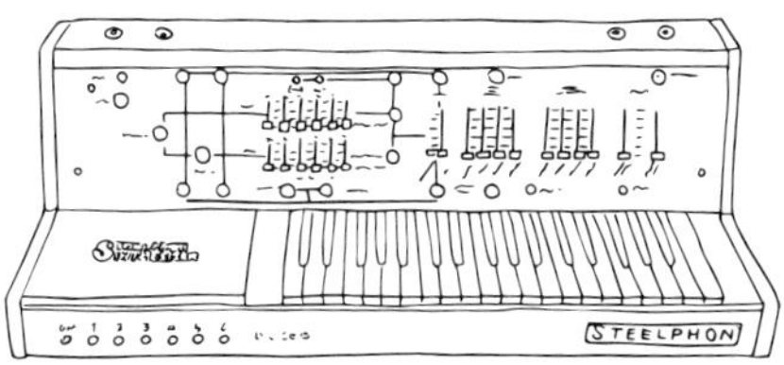

STEINER PARKER SYNTHACON *1975*

Analogue
Mono / 3 VCOs
Steiner-Parker (USA) made a small but influential range of analogue synthesizers. The filters from the Synthacon, designed by Nyle Steiner, can currently be heard in modern Arturia synthesizers such as the MiniBrute.

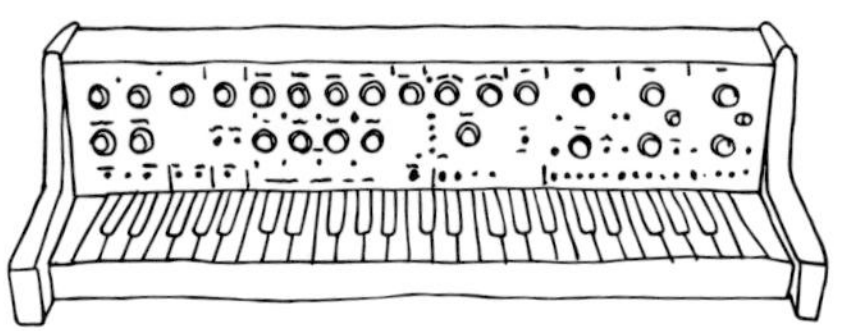

STEINER PARKER SYNTHASYSTEM *1975*

Analogue
Mono/Duo / 3 VCOs

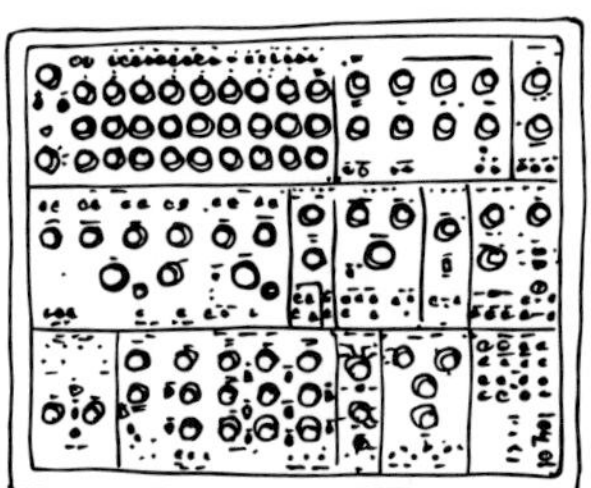

STEINER PARKER MINICON *1977*

Analogue
Mono / 1 VCO

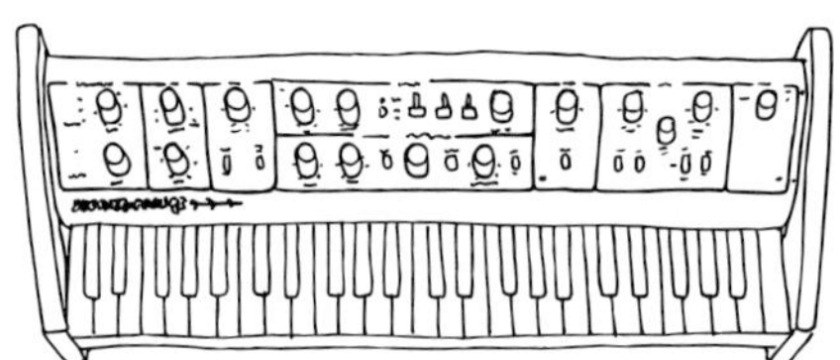

STEINER PARKER MICRON *1977*

Analogue
Mono / 1 VCO
A very compact oscillator with basic LFO and volume envelope generator.

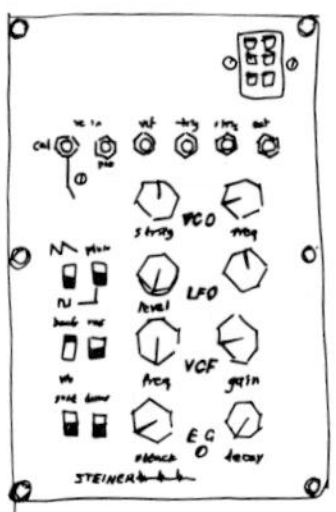

STRAMP SYNCHANGER II 4000 *1976*

Analogue
Mono / 1 VCO
Stramp (Germany) was named for Peter Strueven Amplification. PPG's Wolfgang Palm designed the Synchanger, a guitar synthesizer / synth expander.

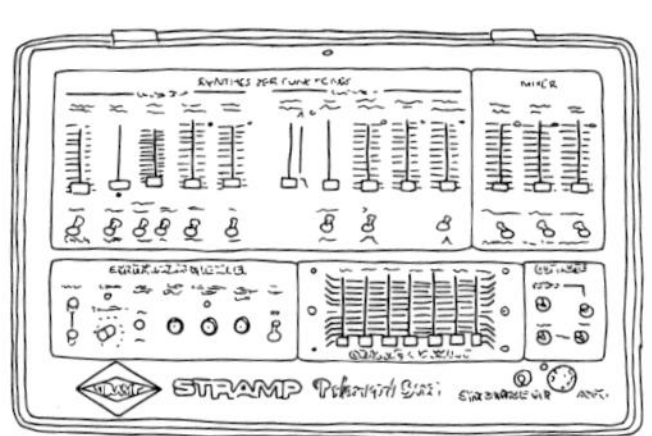

STRIDER DCS *1976*

Digital
12 note polyphony / 1 DO per voice
Advanced digital synthesis for the time with ten programmable patch slots; the DCS II was released in 1979.

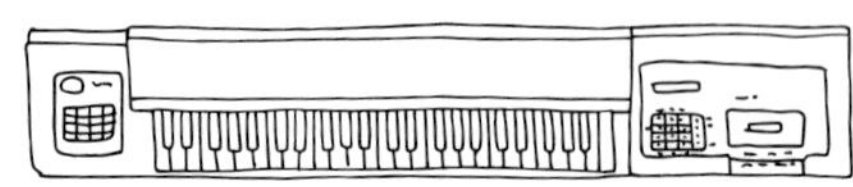

SYNTAURI ALPHA *1979*

Additive

The Syntauri Corporation's alphaSyntauri Digital Synthesizer ran on Apple II computers and featured additive synthesis and FFT resynthesis. Despite undercutting systems like the NED Synclavier and Fairlight CMI, they appear to have ceased trading by 1988.

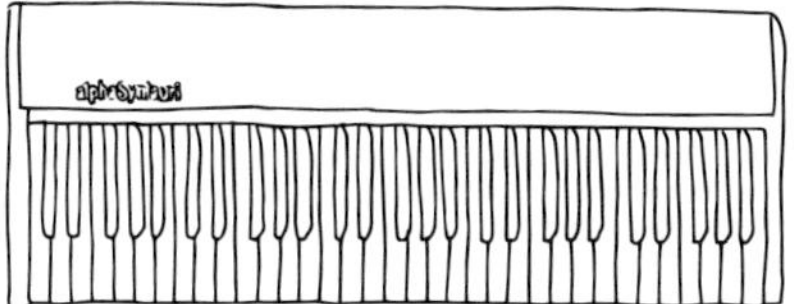

SYNTECNO TEEBEE *1997*

Analogue

Mono / 1 VCO

Dutch firm SynTechno's only product was this TB-303 clone; though by the third version it included a ring-mod source inspired by the Korg MS-20.

SYNTON (HOLLAND)

Synton was formed in the 1970s and were initially manufacturers of vocoders. Discovering the limited market for vocoders, they moved into the distribution of electronic instruments from Fairlight, E-mu and Ensoniq. They then started the manufacture of synthesizers during the 1970s and Bob Moog represented Synton whilst running Big Briar (having left Moog Music in 1978). Synton went bust in 1989 but was re-started by Marc Paping and Bert Vermeulen in order to create the Fenix modular synths in the late 1990s.

SYNTON COLLEGE MULTI LEVEL INSTRUCTIONAL SYNTHESIZER *1970*

Analogue

Mono / 2 VCOs

Like several companies in this era, the educational establishment was identified as a target market.

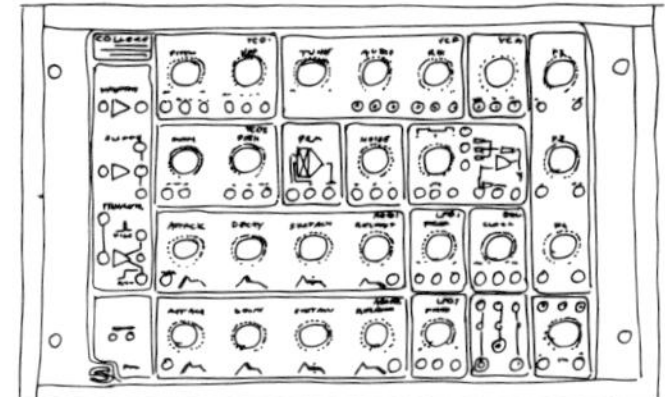

SYNTON MODULAR SERIES 2000/3000 *1970s*

Analogue / Modular

A powerful modular system that was used by Karlheinz Stockhausen.

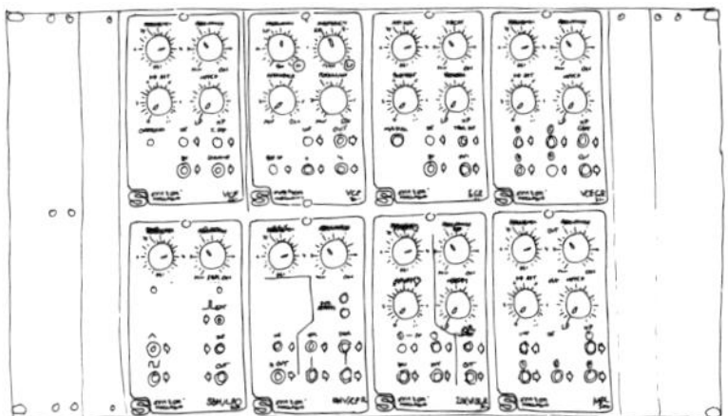

SYNTON SYRINX *1983*

Analogue

Mono / 2 VCOs

Featured an unusual formant filter due to their previous experience of manufacturing vocoders.

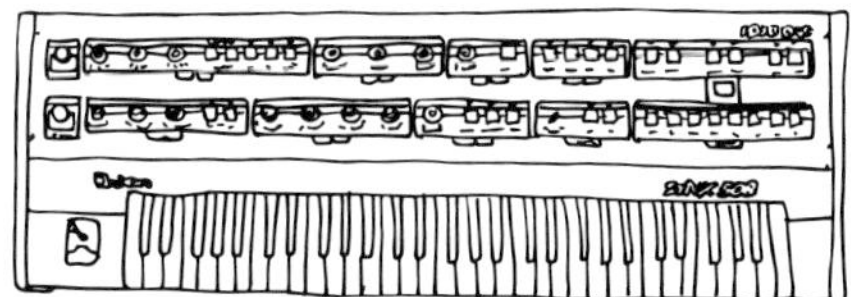

SYNTON FÉNIX *1997*

Analogue / Modular
Mono / 3 VCOs
One of the few companies making new modular systems in the 1990s.

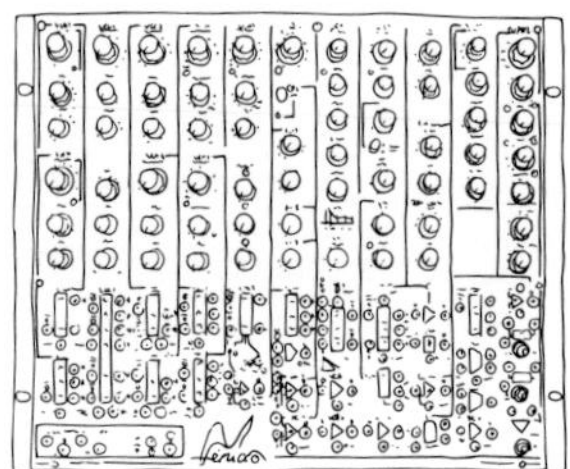

TECHNOS 16π *1980*

Additive / 64 harmonics
The Canadian firm Technos experimented with innovative digital synthesis in the early 1980s. This prototype of the 16π was never productionised, but it paved the way for the AXCEL.

TECHNICS SY-1010 *1979*

Analogue
Mono / 1 VCO
The one VCO had only one waveform (sawtooth).

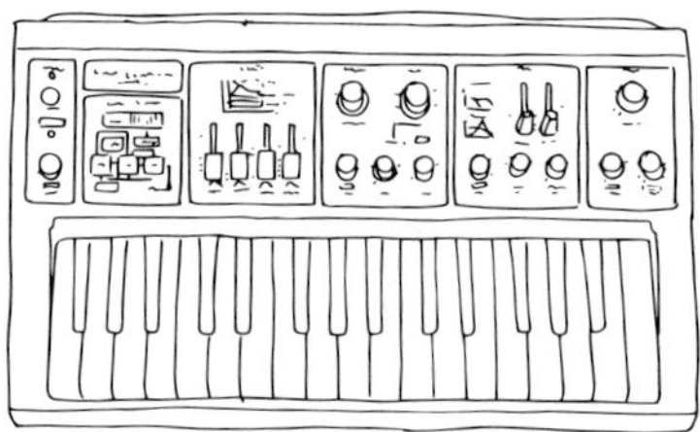

TECHNOS AXCEL *1987*

Additive / Resampling
32 note polyphony / 1024 harmonics
An innovative resampling synth using Fast Fourier Transform (FFT) and a bank of 1024 harmonic oscillators, but the 'ACoustic piXEL' never caught on.

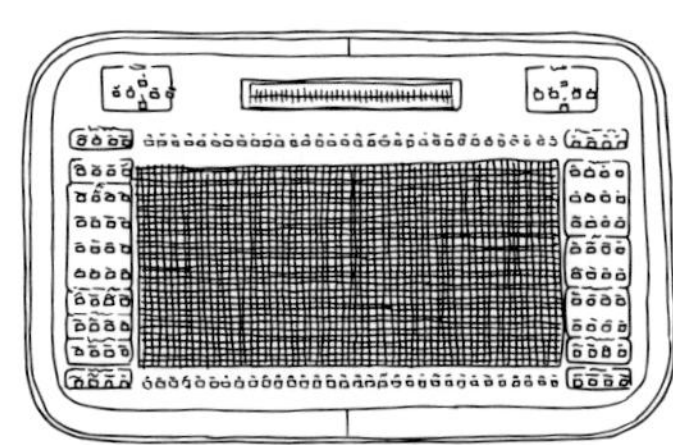

TECHNICS SX-WSA1 *1995*

Acoustic Modelling
64 note polyphony / 4 oscillators per voice
Acoustic instrument modelling using the principles of 'drivers', 'resonators' and 'modifiers'. A powerful and novel synthesizer, but which didn't catch on.

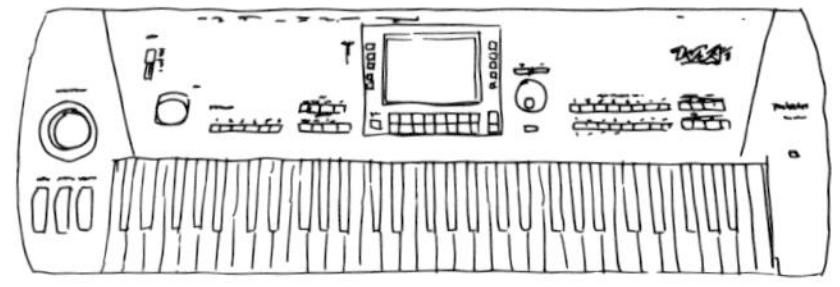

TEISCO (JAPAN)

Teisco was a subsidiary of Kawai and was the brand name for their early analogue synthesizers. Some models can be found branded with either name, but they are the same synth.

TEISCO/KAWAI 100F *1977*

Analogue
Mono / 1 VCO
Vince Clarke's first synth as one of the founding members of Depeche Mode. The variant 100P was preset-only.

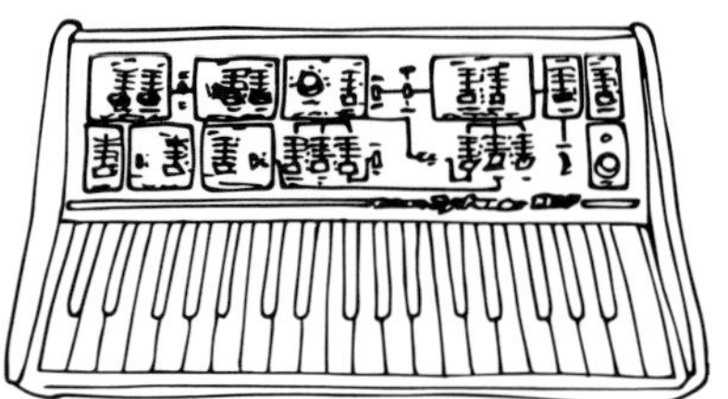

TEISCO/KAWAI SYNTHESIZER 60F *1980*

Analogue
Mono / 1 VCO
The preset-only version was the S60P.

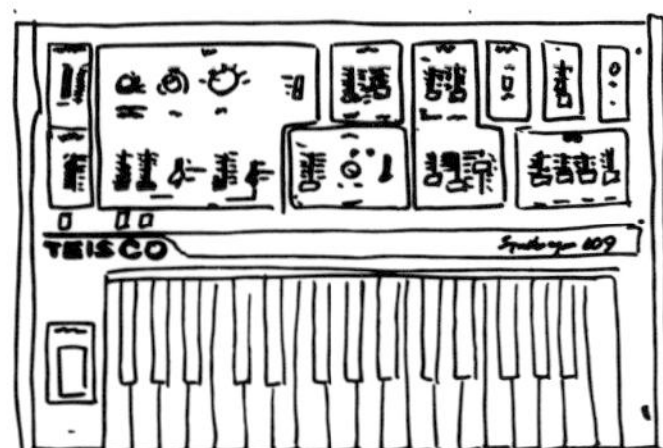

TEISCO/KAWAI S100P *1979*

32 Presets / Analogue
Mono / 1 VCO

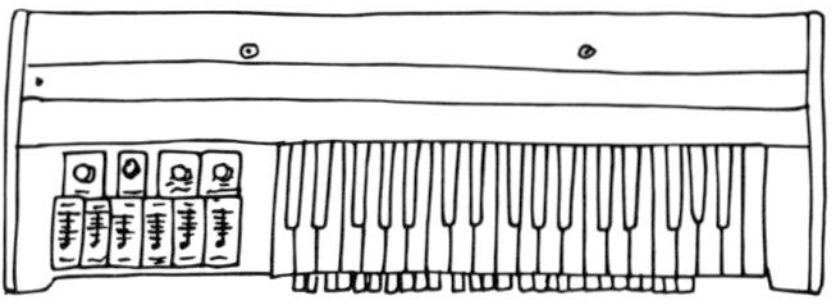

TEISCO/KAWAI SX-400 *1981*

Analogue
Mono/Duo/Quad / 4 VCOs
All four oscillators had to use the same waveform.

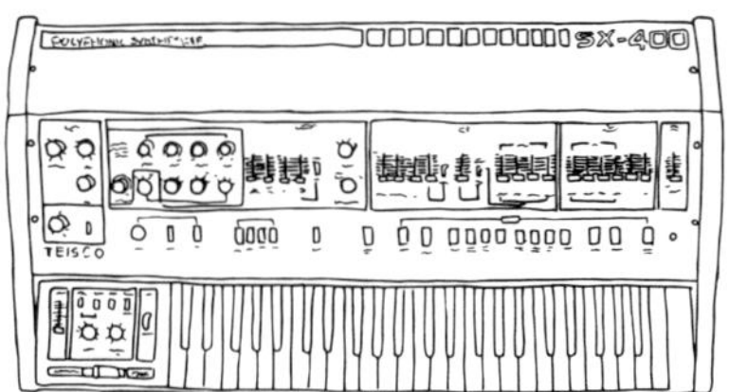

TEISCO/KAWAI 110F *1980*

Analogue
Mono/Duo / 2 VCOs

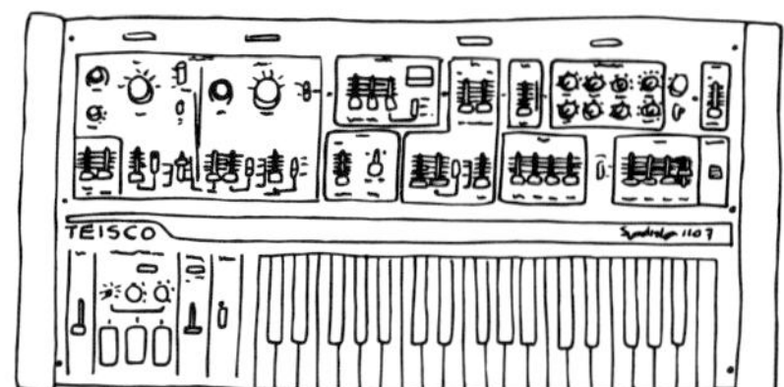

TEISCO/KAWAI SX-210 *1983*

Analogue
8 note polyphony / 1 DCO (+ sub) per voice

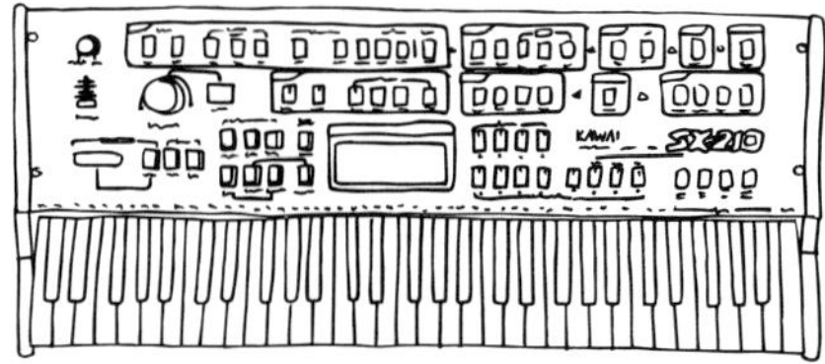

TEISCO/KAWAI SX-240 *1984*

Analogue
8 note polyphony / 2 DCOs per voice

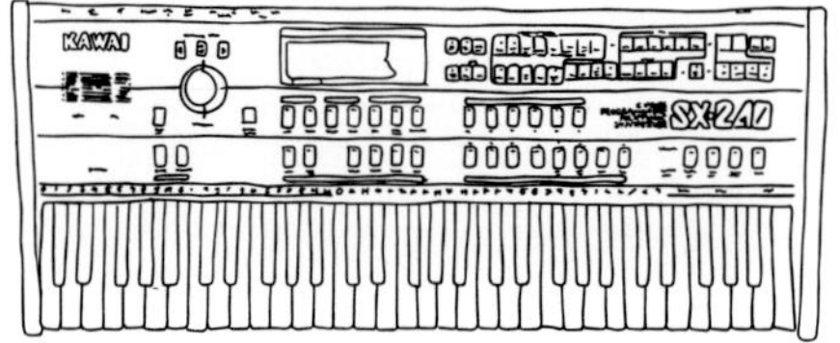

VEB TIRACON *1987*

Analogue
6 note polyphony / 1 VCO (+ sub) per voice
The Tiracon offered digital control over its analogue sounds. The company was based in the former East Germany and their full name was 'VEB Automatisierungsanlagen Cottbus', which translates as 'The Cottbus Automation and Engineering Plant'.

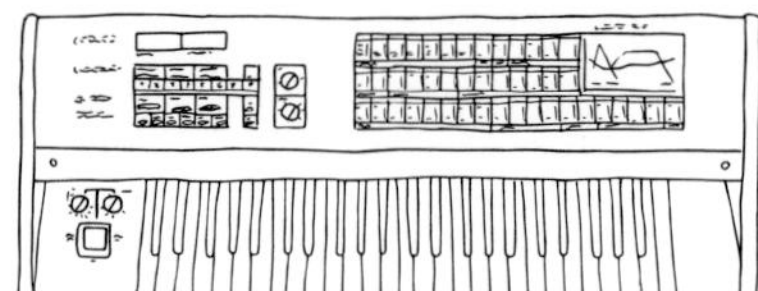

TONTO (UK) LATE 1960s

The Original New Timbral Orchestra was the largest modular system in the world and comprised units from Serge, Moog, Roland and more. Malcolm Cecil and Robert Margouleff used it on Tonto's Exploding Head Band albums 'Zero Time' (1971) and 'It's About Time' (1974).

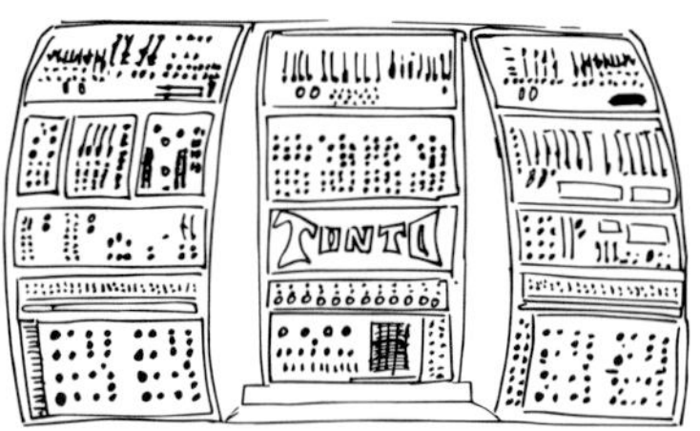

VERMONA SYNTHESIZER *1980*

Analogue / Mono / 2 VCOs
East German synthesizer of the 1980s.

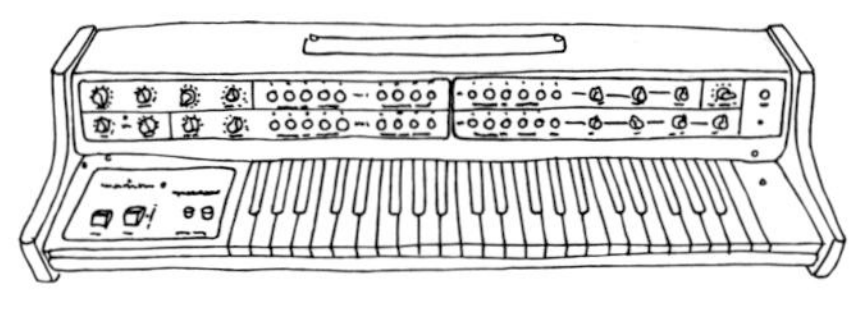

TRIADEX MUSE *1972*

Analogue / Mono / 1 VCO
A rather extraordinary instrument that used algorithms to produce ever-changing music. It was designed by Edward Fredkin and the legendary MIT professor and AI researcher Marvin Minksy. Apparently intended to replace the radio, it was perhaps a little ahead of its time.

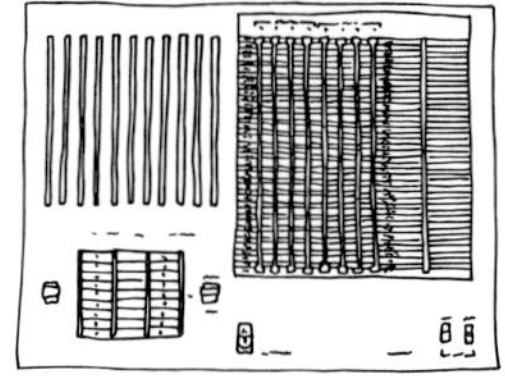

WALDORF MUSIC (GERMANY)

Named for the German town of Waldorf, the company was set up by Wolfgang Düren in 1988. Düren was a distributor of PPG products, and Waldorf continued developing wavetable synthesis following PPG's demise in 1987.

WALDORF MICROWAVE *1989*

Wavetable
8 note polyphony / 2 DOs per voice
PPG employees joined Waldorf and used wavetables from the PPG Wave 2.3.

WEM NIGHTSHADE *1975*

Analogue
Mono / 2 VCOs

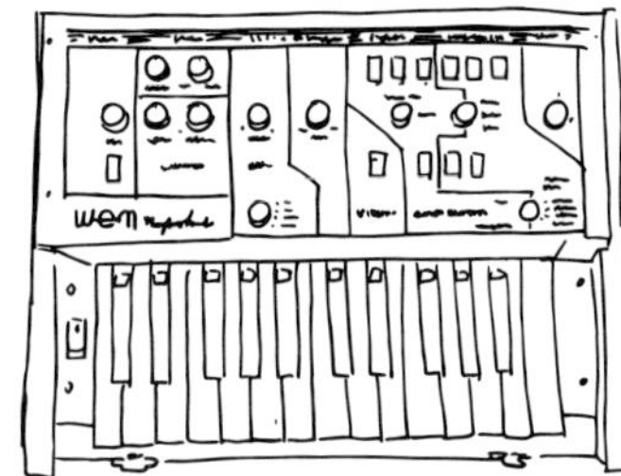

WALDORF THE WAVE *1993*

Wavetable
16 note polyphony / 2 DOs per voice
An epic culmination of wavetable synthesis.

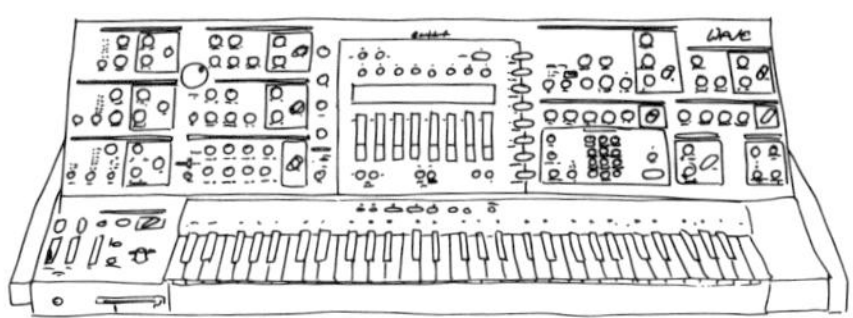

WELSON SYNTEX *1974*

Analogue / 15 Presets
Mono / 2 DCOs
Early Italian mono-synth for use with home organs.

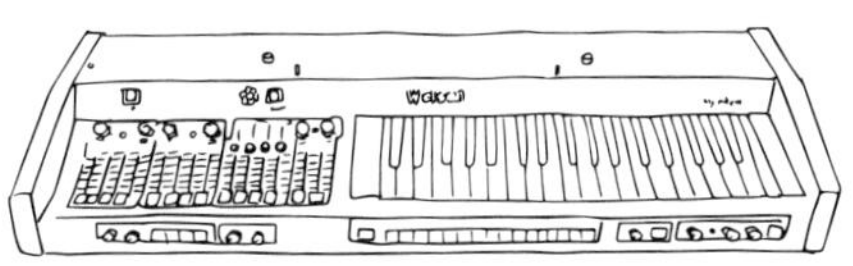

WEM (WATKINS ELECTRIC MUSIC) (UK)

WEM was founded by Charlie Watkins in 1949 and were famous for their PA systems used by rock groups in the late 1960s and 1970s. Their PA stacks can be seen in footage of Miles Davis at the Isle of Wight Festival 1970, Led Zeppelin's Supershow in 1969 and Pink Floyd's concert film 'Live at Pompeii' (1972). They also made tape-echo devices, power mixers … and an oddity of a synthesizer, the 'Nightshade'.

WERSI (GERMANY)

Wersi was founded in 1969 by brothers Wilhelm-Erich and Reinhard Franz. The name is either a combination of the towns of Werlau and Simmern or the first initials of the brothers' names and Simmern. They made a small number of analogue synthesizers in the 1970s and subsequently moved into organs and digital pianos.

WERSI BASS SYNTHESIZER *1977*

Analogue
Mono / 1 master VCO
The master oscillator could generate simultaneous square, sawtooth and sine waves using waveshaping and divide-down technology.

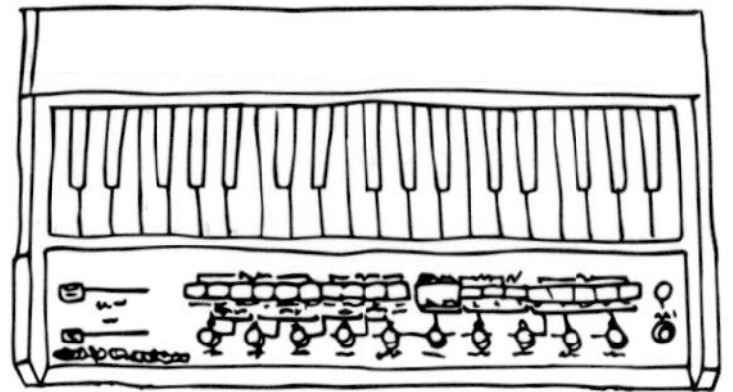

WERSI DX100 CONDOR *1984*

Digital
16 note polyphony / 2 DOs per voice
Digital synthesizer with 40 built-in presets and the ability to load more from cassette tapes.

WERSI STAGE SYNTHESIZER MK1 *1986*

Additive
8, 12 or 20 note polyphony / 4 DOs per voice
The rackmount was the EX-20.

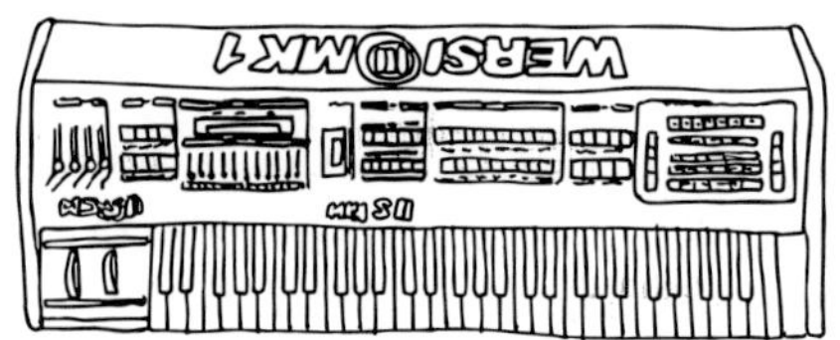

WILL SYSTEMS MAB-303 *1996*

Analogue
Mono / 1 VCO
Distributed by Electric Music of Hannover, Germany, Will System's only product was the MAB-303, a TB-303 clone.

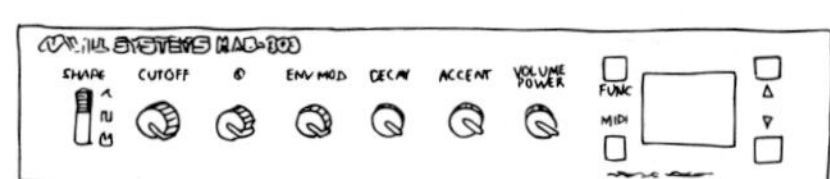

YAMAHA CORPORATION (JAPAN)

Nippon Gakki Company was founded by Torakusu Yamaha in 1887. His first instruments were reed organs and by the early 20th century the company were manufacturing pianos. After Yamaha's death in 1916 at the age of 65 the company was renamed Yamaha in his honour.

The latter part of the 20th century saw Yamaha diversify into motorcycles, sporting goods, semiconductors and even metallic alloys. They also made a wide range of acoustic instruments, and started producing synthesizers in the early 1970s.

Seeing the opportunity for digital synthesis Yamaha licenced FM technology from John Chowning of Stanford University in the early 1970s. This eventually led to the DX7 becoming the first affordable FM digital synthesizer which was an immediate success on its launch in 1983. After releasing a number of synthesizers derived from the same FM technology, Yamaha released the AN1x in 1997, which was one of the first generation of analogue modelling synths.

YAMAHA GX-1 *1973*

Analogue
8 note polyphony / 2 VCOs per voice
Huge £50,000 polyphonic triple keyboard synth and precursor to the CS-80.

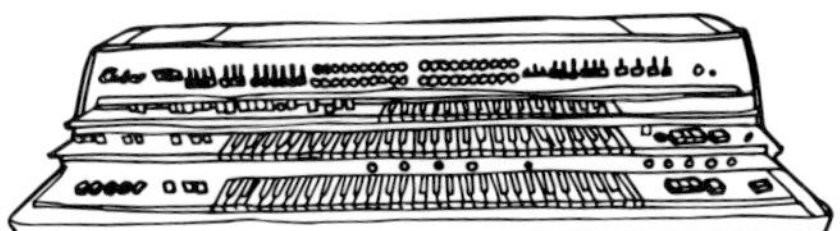

YAMAHA SS-30 *1977*

Analogue / 2 VCOs
Full polyphony (divide-down)
A string synthesizer.

YAMAHA SY-1 *1974*

Analogue
Mono / 1 VCO
A more modest 28-preset analogue synth.

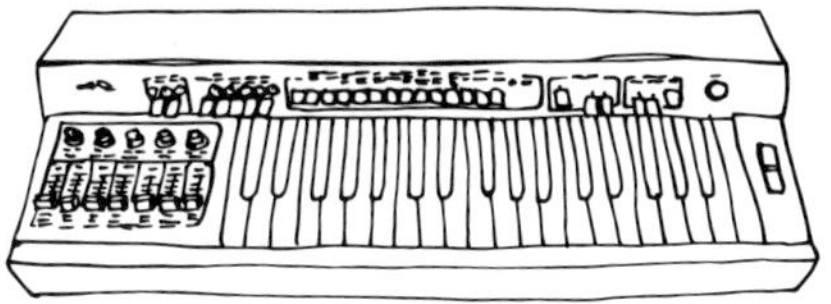

YAMAHA CS-10 *1977*

Analogue
Mono / 1 VCO
The CS series were analogue synths with increasing polyphony, presets and storable memory locations.

YAMAHA SY-2 *1975*

Analogue
Mono / 1 VCO
28 presets and more complex envelope generators.

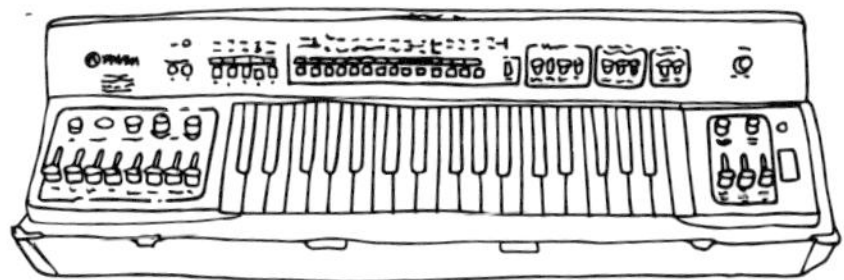

YAMAHA CS-30 *1977*

Analogue
Mono / 2 VCOs

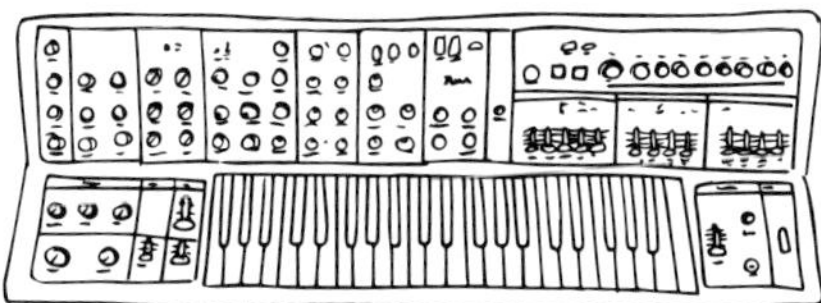

YAMAHA CS-30L *1977*

Analogue
Mono / 2 VCOs
A CS-30 with legs, instead of being designed for the top of a home organ.

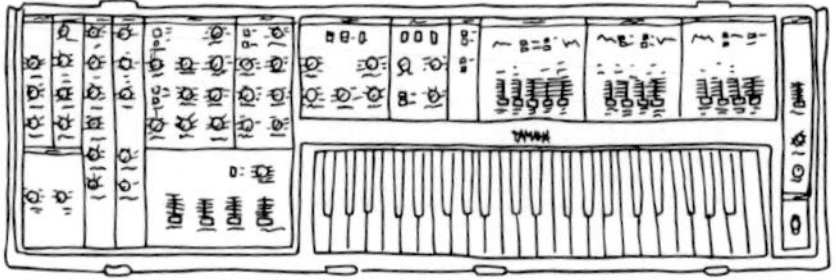

YAMAHA CS-80 *1977*

Analogue
8 note polyphony / 2 VCOs per voice
The classic polyphonic synth with polyphonic after-touch, synonymous with Vangelis and his soundtrack for 'Bladerunner' (1982). The CS-80 weighed 100kg.

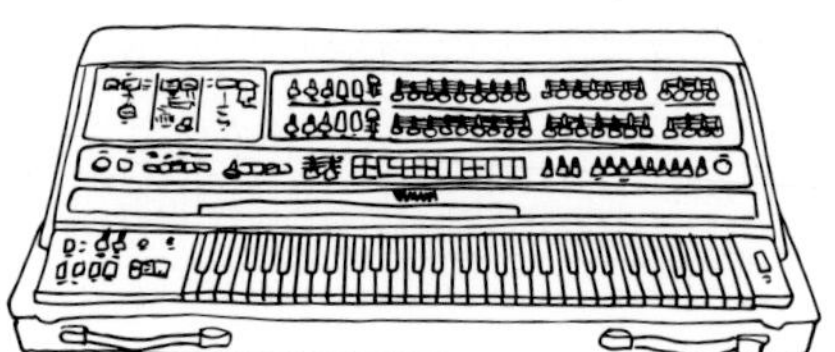

YAMAHA CS-50 *1977*

Analogue
4 note polyphony / 1 VCO per voice

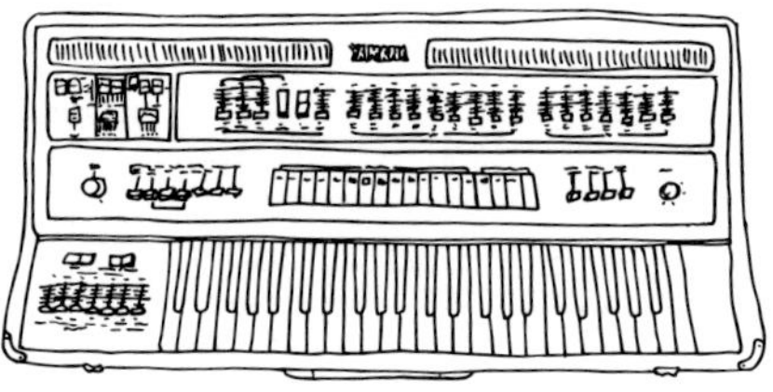

YAMAHA CS-5 *1978*

Analogue
Mono / 1 VCO
Martin Gore's first Depeche Mode synth.

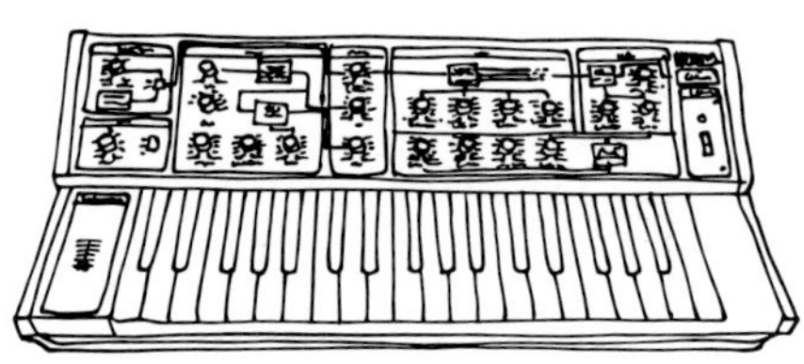

YAMAHA CS-60 *1977*

Analogue
8 note polyphony / 1 VCO per voice

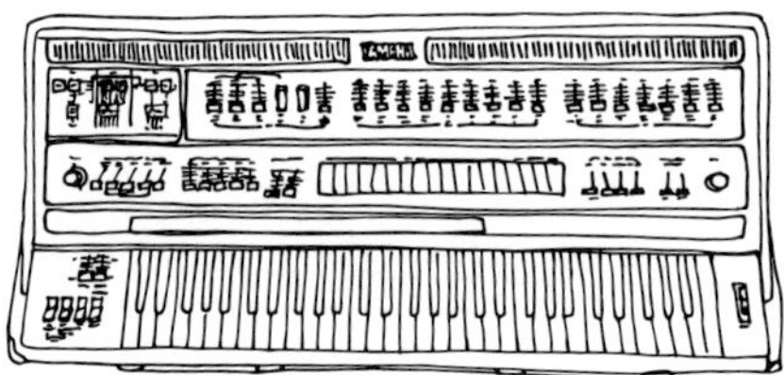

YAMAHA CS-15 *1978*

Analogue
Mono/Duo / 2 VCOs
A two VCO version of the CS-5.

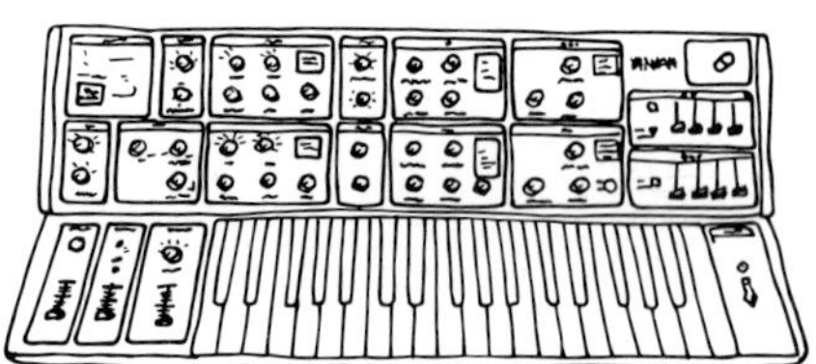

YAMAHA CS-15D *1979*

Analogue
Mono / 2 VCO
Preset monosynth.

YAMAHA SK10 *1979*

Ensemble preset synth: organ, string, brass
7 note polyphony
The SK ensemble range includes the SK15, SK20, SK30, SK50D (dual manual).

YAMAHA CS-20M *1979*

Analogue
Mono / 2 VCOs
The 'M' series CS synths had programmable memory locations (though some without 'M' also had memory locations).

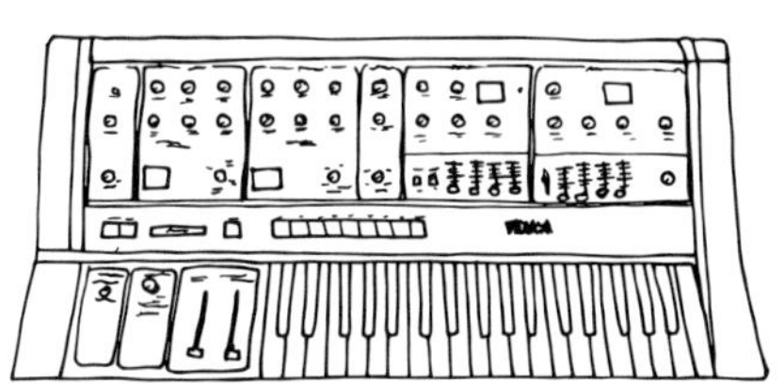

YAMAHA CS-70M *1981*

Analogue
6 note polyphony / 2 VCOs per voice

YAMAHA CS-40M *1979*

Analogue
Mono/Duo / 4 VCOs
Double the VCOs of the CS-20M.

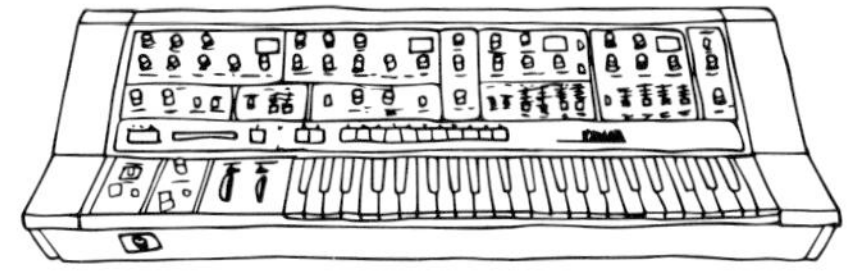

YAMAHA GS1 *1981*

FM / 16 note polyphony / 8-operator
Yamaha's first FM synthesizer, not editable beyond vibrato and tuning. Paving the way for the DX range, it proved the concept introduced by John M. Chowning's paper, 'The Synthesis of Complex Audio Spectra by Means of Frequency Modulation' (1973).

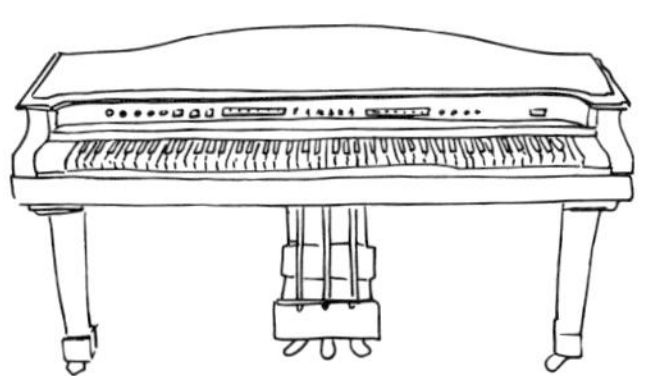

YAMAHA GS2 *1981*

FM
16 note polyphony / 4-operator
A simpler GS1.

YAMAHA SY-20 *1982*

Analogue
Mono / 1 VCO
The last of the Yamaha analogue synths, available only in Japan.

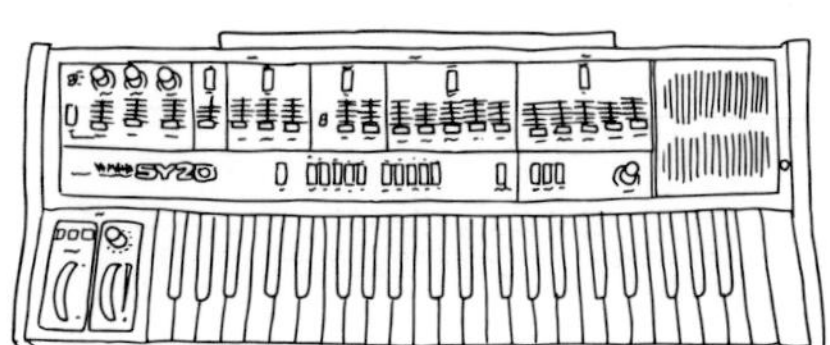

YAMAHA CE20 *1982*

FM
8 note polyphony / 4-operator
A preset FM synth with mono & polyphonic sounds. The CE-25 is a variant with chorus effect.

YAMAHA DX7 *1983*

FM
16 note polyphony / 6-operator
The FM synthesizer that changed the soundscape of the 1980s. The TX7 (1985) was the tabletop version. The audio output of both was mono. Famous for its electric piano - Whitney Houston - 'Saving All My Love For You' (1985). Brian Eno was also a champion of the DX7.

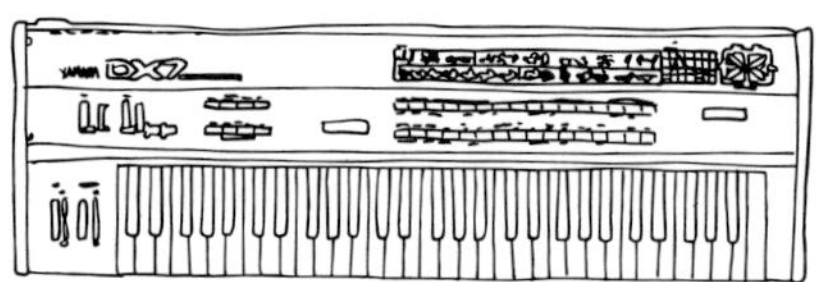

YAMAHA CS01 *1982*

Analogue
Mono / 1 VCO
A simple analogue home keyboard.

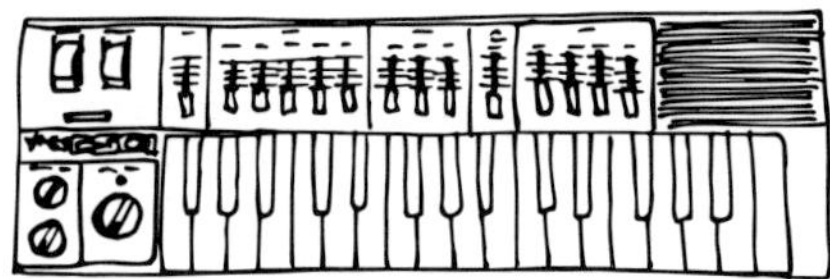

YAMAHA DX9 *1983*

FM
16 note polyphony / 4-operator
A simpler DX7 with fewer operators (4 vs 6) and algorithms (8 vs 32).

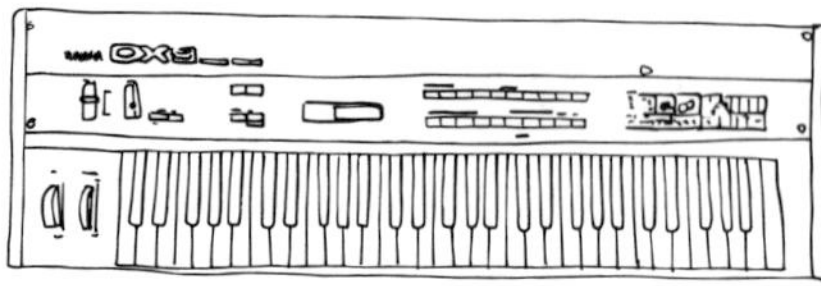

YAMAHA DX1 *1983*

FM
32 note polyphony / 6-operator
The equivalent of two DX7s in one synth.

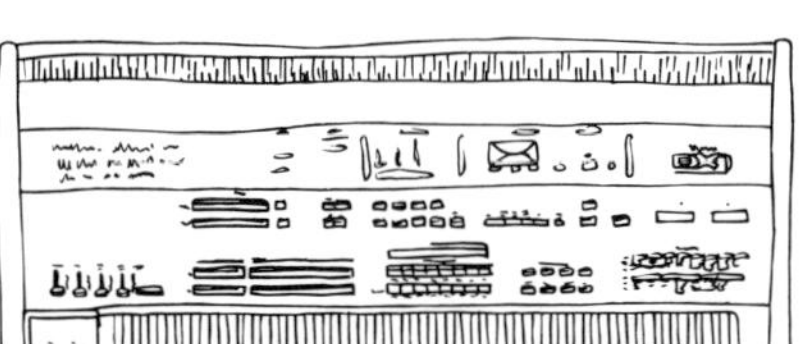

YAMAHA CS01 MK2 *1984*

Analogue
Mono / 1 VCO

YAMAHA TX816 *1984*

FM
128 note polyphony / 6-operator
The polyphony is not a misprint - this was eight DX7 modules (called the TF1) in a rack. The TX116 is the same but was sold with only one module installed.

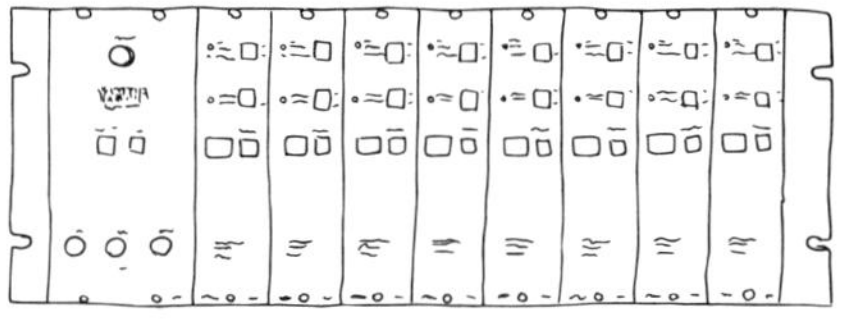

YAMAHA DX21 *1985*

FM
8 note polyphony / 4-operator
A simpler DX synth, derived from the DX9. Madonna – 'Express Yourself' (1989) (bass).

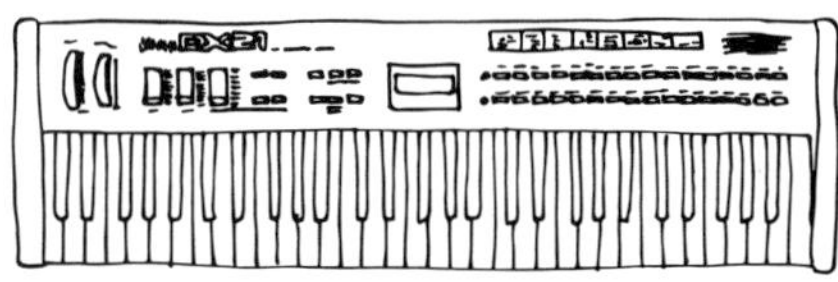

YAMAHA KX1 *1984*

No sound generation - Yamaha's first Keytar-style controller.

YAMAHA DX5 *1985*

FM
32 note polyphony / 6-operator
The power of two DX7s in one. Like the DX1, but missing the polyphonic aftertouch.

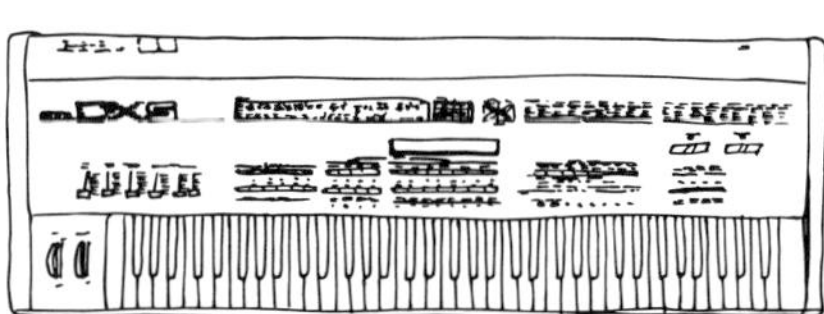

YAMAHA DX27 *1985*

FM
8 note polyphony / 4-operator
The DX27, DX21 and DX100 were a simpler, cheaper range of FM synths. The DX27S had speakers.

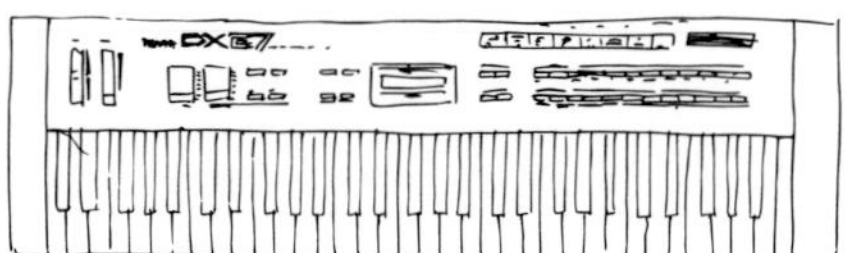

YAMAHA FB-01 *1986*

FM
8 note polyphony / 4-operator
Designed for use with Yamaha's music computer, the CX5M.

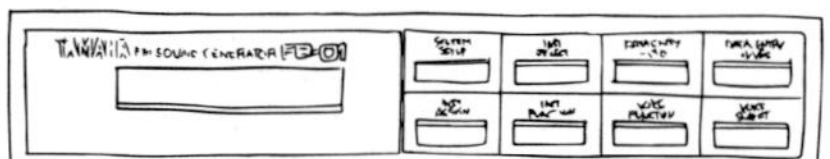

YAMAHA DX100 *1985*

FM
8 note polyphony / 4-operator
Mini-key version of the DX27.

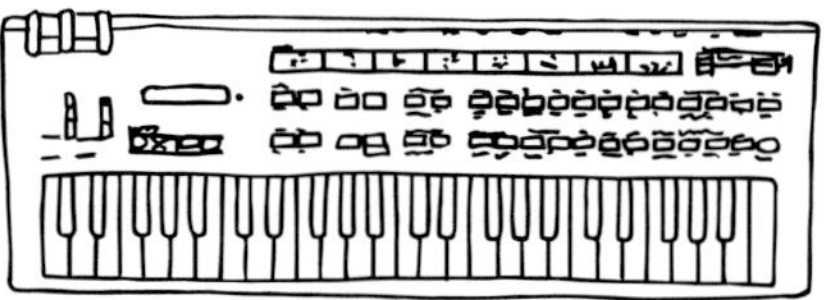

YAMAHA DX7S *1987*

FM
16 note polyphony / 6-operator
No split-mode, which the DX7IID had.

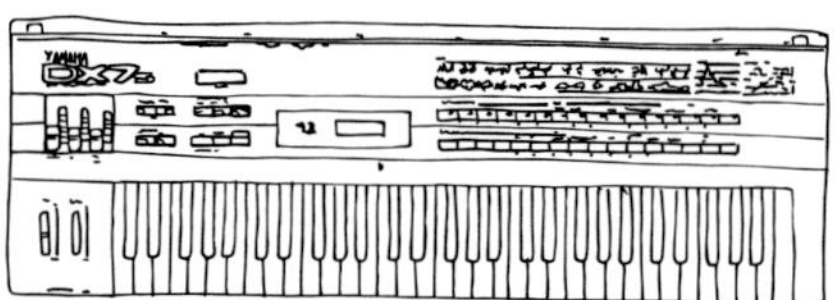

YAMAHA DX7IID *1986*

FM
16 note polyphony / 6-operator
This DX7 upgrade got real buttons and stereo audio output. Also: the TX802 (module); DX7IIFD (Floppy Drive); DX7II Centennial (white rose in colour).

YAMAHA TX81Z *1987*

FM
8 note polyphony / 4-operator
The TX81Z offered a variety of operator waveforms other than the standard sine wave; these are described in terms of having all-odd or all-even partials, or variations thereof. An odd series of partials approximates a square wave tone, for example.

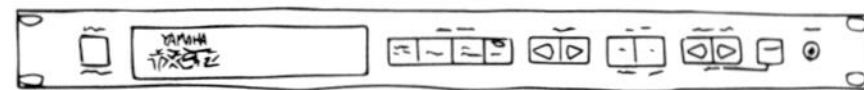

YAMAHA YS-100 *1988*

FM
8 note polyphony / 4-operator
Editing did not include direct access to the operator/carrier algorithms. The YS-200 looked the same but included a sequencer.

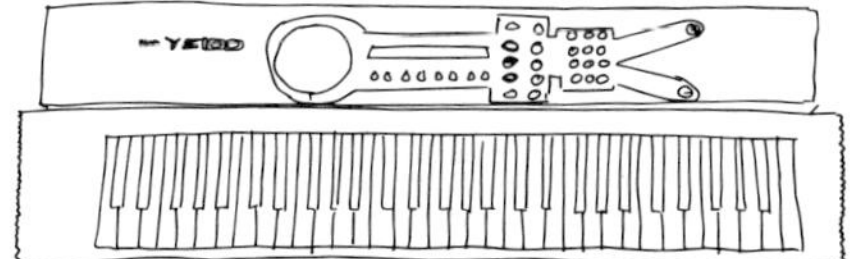

YAMAHA TQ5 *1989*

FM
8 note polyphony / 4-operator
A YS-200 in a box.

YAMAHA B200 *1988*

FM
8 note polyphony / 4-operator
A YS-200 with built-in speakers.

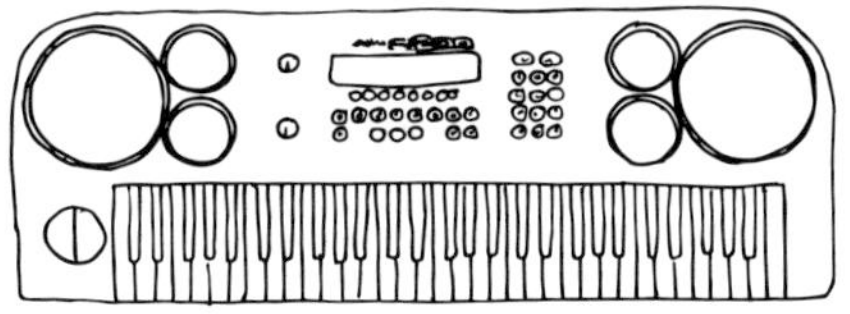

YAMAHA V-50 *1989*

FM
16 note polyphony / 4-operator
Synth, drum machine and sequencer workstation.

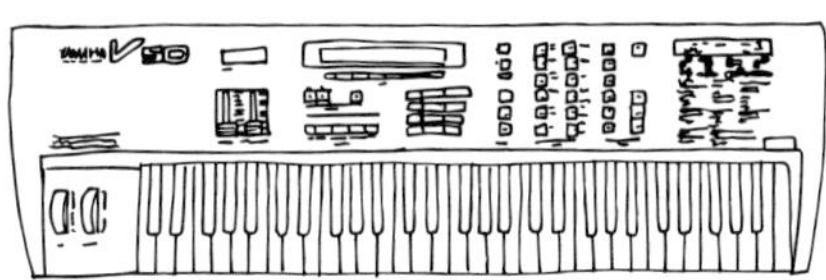

YAMAHA DX11 *1988*

FM
8 note polyphony / 4-operator
The first Yamaha multi-timbral synth and also had the multi-waveforms seen on the TX81Z.

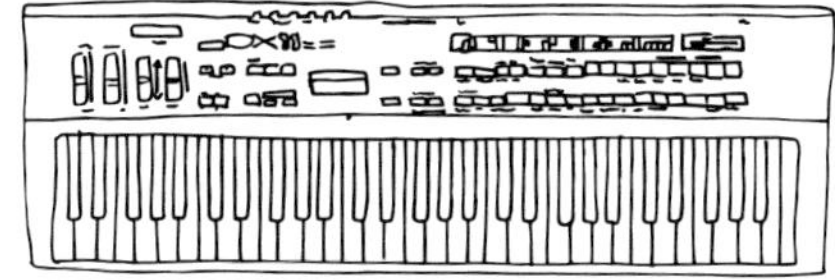

YAMAHA SY-77 *1989*

FM / AWM2 (sample & synthesis)
32 note polyphony / 6-operator
One of the best of the early workstations. The TG77 was the rackmount version, and the SY99 had a longer 76 note keyboard. The SY-22 featured vector synthesis.

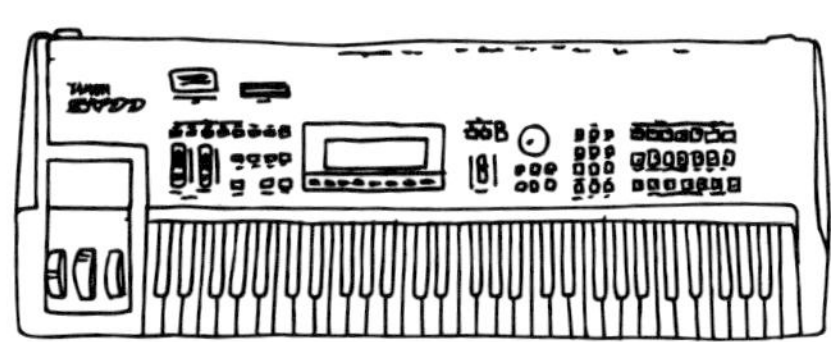

YAMAHA VL1 *1994*

Virtual Acoustic (physical modelling)
Duophonic
The 'Virtual Lead 1' was the first of the physical modelling synths with its acoustic tones generated by digital algorithms. It was capable of highly realistic woodwind, brass and string sounds. The VL1-m is the rackmount version.

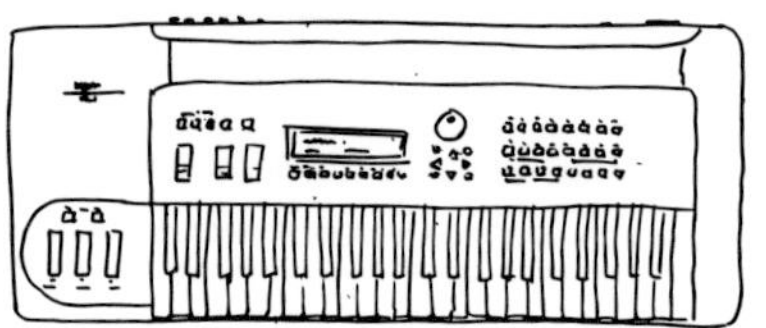

YAMAHA VL7 *1994*

Virtual Acoustic (physical modelling)
Monophonic version of the VL1; the VP1, however, had 16 note polyphony and introduced the concept of F/VA (Free Oscillation / Virtual Acoustic) enabling 'non-real-world' tone generation.

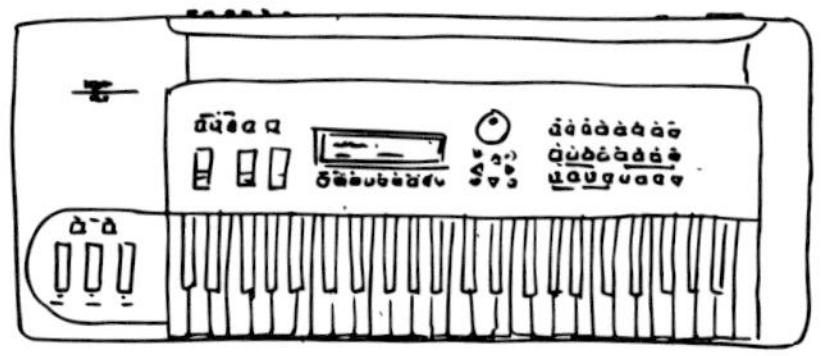

YAMAHA CS1X *1996*

AWM2 (sample & synthesis)
32 / 4 DOs per voice
Using Yamaha's grandly named 'Advance Wave Memory' technology, this 'Control Synthesizer' was a sample-based playback unit, albeit one focused on playability.

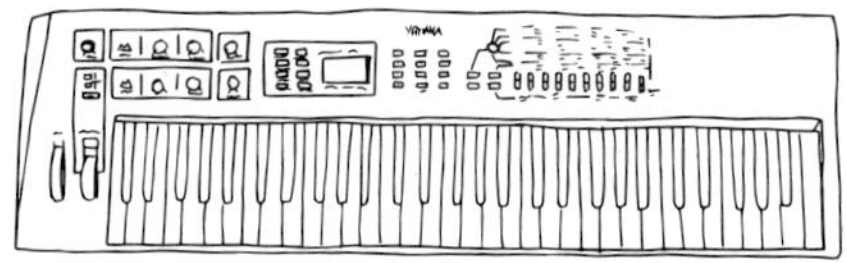

YAMAHA AN1X *1997*

Analogue Modelling / FM
10 note polyphony / 2 modelled VCOs per voice
One of the new crop of virtual analogue synthesizers of the mid/late 1990s.

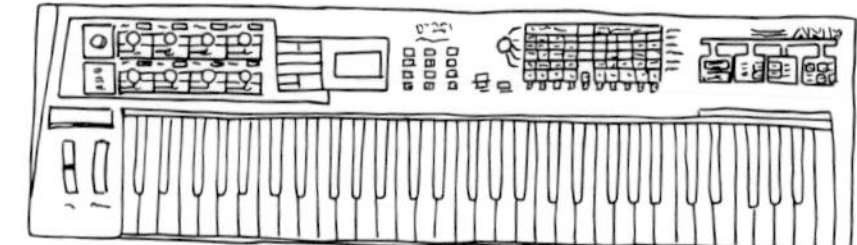

ZILOG Z80 *1976*

The Z80 was an 8-bit microchip commonly used in many electronic devices from the late 1970s, including home computers such as the Sinclair ZX80 which was named after it. The synthesizers that used a Z80 include the E-mu Emulator, SP-1200, Drumulator, Fairlight CMI, Memorymoog, Oberheim OB-8, Roland Jupiter 8, CR-78, Sequential Circuits Prophet 5, 10, 600, and many more.

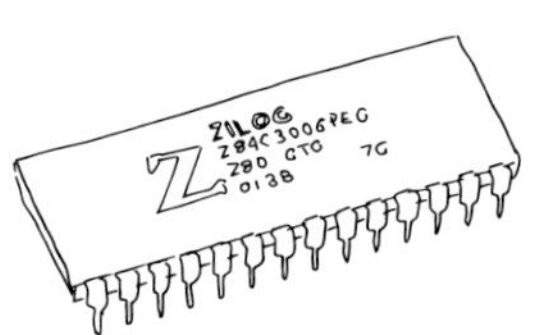

ZW BASSMACHINE *1984*

Analogue
Mono / 2 VCOs
Simple bass machine with 10 presets from Italian firm ZW Electronics.

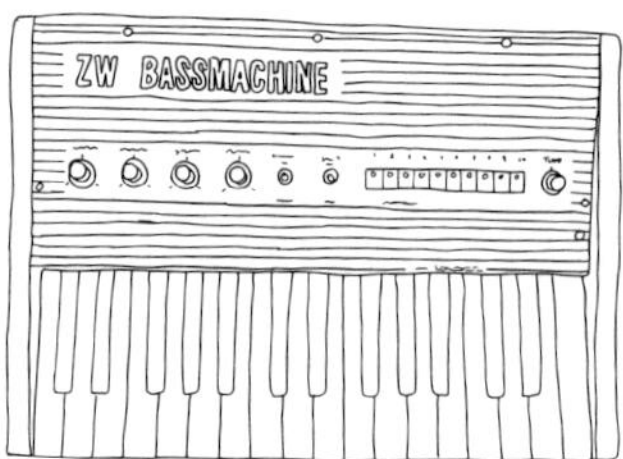

DRUM MACHINES

The goal of the drum machine is to produce more-or-less realistic drum sounds which other musicians can play along with, or that can be used in the making of records and other music productions. It's undergone many evolutionary steps since it was first invented, and that evolution has mostly happened in lockstep with the advances in synthesizer and sampler technology.

The pre-modern drum machines generated simple preset rhythms using a variety of electro-mechanical methods. The Wurlitzer Sideman (1959) and Korg Doncamatic DA-20 (1963) employed a rotating disk with contacts that triggered basic bursts of electronic percussive noise. The Chamberlin Rhythm-mate (1949) replayed tape recordings of drummers on a loop. None of these machines sounded very good, and they were housed in large impractical boxes. In fact, it was the poor sound of the Sideman that led the founders of both Korg and Roland to set up their own companies and invent their own, better, equivalents (though the Korg Doncamatic might not have represented a huge leap forward initially!).

Once the drum machine transitioned into the modern era, thanks to the transistor, the earliest were still basically preset rhythm boxes, albeit now much smaller. They were aimed at the home organ market and featured somewhat basic representations of the waltz, bossa-nova, samba, march and other contemporary dance rhythms. Some, like the Ace Tone FR-1 (1965), offered some flexibility by allowing preset rhythms to be combined and certain groupings of instruments to be muted (or 'cancelled' in the parlance of the day). Ace Tone being notable as the company set up by Ikaturo Kakehashi before he founded Roland in 1972.

Despite the limitations of these early rhythm machines they began to show up on commercial recordings, even though the quality of the sounds was still fairly poor. Sly and the Family Stone became known for their use of the Maestro Rhythm King Mk2 (1971) and they used it so frequently that it eventually became known as the 'funk machine'. It can be heard on recordings such as 'There's a Riot Going On' (1971).

Thanks to microchip technology, the Roland CR-78 (1978) introduced the ability to program custom rhythms, hence the CR - 'CompuRhythm' - moniker. No longer were musicians tied to an unknown technicians' interpretation of the bossa-nova; custom rhythms could now be input directly.

It's fair to say that usage of drum machines in popular recorded music at this point tended to be supplementary rather than the main part of a rhythm section. Despite European musicians like Kraftwerk, Tangerine Dream and Jean-Michel Jarre making fully electronic music which included the percussion parts, this music was still an adjunct to the mainstream.

There was also growing interest in disco music and vinyl-driven rap music in the US during the 1970s, but neither of these styles had latched on to the possibilities offered by their rhythm sections going fully electronic... yet.

The breakthrough record that decisively fused US disco with European electronic music was Donna Summer's 'I Feel Love' (1977), produced by Giorgio Moroder and Pete Bellotte. It was one of the tracks on the concept album 'I Remember Yesterday', each of whose songs were themed to a particular decade. 'I Feel Love' was the 'future decade' song, and so was entirely made on the still-futuristic synthesizers. The Moog modular was used for the famous bassline and lead synths, but also for the crucial bass drum, snare and hi-hats that power the song's relentless and hypnotic groove. (Though, to be fair, the Moog bass drum was overdubbed with another drum sound for added power.)

As well as having a huge influence on the artists of the day - Brian Eno and David Bowie amongst others citing it as the most important record to date - 'I Feel Love' gave the disco sound a whole new direction of machine-driven drums. This ultimately resulted in the somewhat less funky sound of Hi-NRG and Euro-Disco, which focussed on the four-to-the-floor bass drum pattern, off-beat open-hat, and rigid octave-jumping basslines. In any case, these electronic forms of disco turned out to be the genre's last hurrah before suddenly going out of fashion, in no small part due to the thinly disguised homophobic and racist 'Disco Demolition Night' held in Chicago in 1979.

The drum machine, meanwhile, had made some headway in mainstream rock and pop: Phil Collins had popularised the sound of the Roland CR-78 with 'In the Air Tonight' (1981) and the TR-808 with 'One More Night' (1984). Also featuring the CR-78 was Blondie's 'Heart of Glass' (1978). Generally, though, rock bands were not about to ditch their live drummers in favour of the drum machine. Who would be there to be the butt of their drummer jokes if that were to happen?

Towards the end of the 1970s, the subgenre of synth-pop had become increasingly popular in the UK, with Depeche Mode, OMD, The Human League and others going fully electronic. Along with the New Romantics and the more avant-garde of the post-punk bands, such as Devo, popular music was really beginning to reflect the possibilities offered by electronic instruments.

Meeting their needs were the increasingly powerful drum machines of that era. Analogue synthesis was continuing to be miniaturised, and the machines were looking much like the form-factor we most associate with them today - the drum pads, the ability to program grooves and increasing control over tone and pitch.

Even as this range of analogue drum machines evolved, it was beginning to be acknowledged that they were still not that great at producing the realistic drum sounds that could replace an acoustic drum kit in a rock music setting (for those who wanted to do that).

The use of realistic drum samples - to tempt rock bands and pop producers - was pioneered by Roger Linn and his Linn LM-1 in 1980 with the express goal of acoustic realism. Given the high quality of its sampled sounds and being the first to market, it was immediately taken up in pop music production, commencing the 'big snares' phenomenon and the percussion sheen of 1980s pop. The sound of the Linn Drum and its successors, the Linn Drum II (1982) and Linn 9000 (1984) can be found on many of the hits of the 80s: A-ha - 'Take on Me', Frankie Goes To Hollywood - 'Relax', and Harold Faltermeyer - 'Axel F', amongst many, many others.

The Linn Drum also introduced such features as quantize ('fix the timing'), swing ('mess with the timing') and a sequencer that allowed for synchronisation with other electronic instruments.

Pollard launched their SynDrum with its drum-kit like pads in 1977 which enabled a drummer to access its electronic drum sounds by playing in their normal manner with drum sticks. It also gave the world the now-dated sound of the electro-tom fill. Roland launched their Octapad in 1985 which was similar in concept - pads which could be hit with drum sticks - but these were arranged in a neat 2x4 rectangle instead of being distributed in space like an acoustic drum kit (or the Syndrum and the Simmons system).

Given that drum machines containing realistic samples were already available, the release of the Roland TR-808 in 1981 failed to make much of an impression. It still had the 'unconvincing' analogue-generated drum sounds that no longer seemed to cut the mustard. Many of these analogue machines were therefore sold off cheaply once users found they didn't satisfy the wild claims made for them on their advertising literature.

This was seized on by DJs and producers who wanted to make records, but couldn't afford a full band or didn't have the space for recording a full drum-kit - and cared less about realistic drum sounds. These producers went about recreating the sound of disco and post-disco boogie in their new productions. Only now instead of recording live drum kits, they used the newly affordable Roland TR-808, and other similar machines. This was the start of Chicago's house music revolution, spearheaded by Frankie Knuckles and Larry Levan, with many others, who were actually disco DJs just a few years previously. Not only that, it was also the start of the global electronic dance beat that has endured ever since.

Early 1980s hip-hop artists were also producing their own tracks, and instead of recording live drums, they too used drum machines to replicate their favourite funk and soul breaks. And again, typically used the TR-808, and created the whole new genre of electro in doing so. Electro was a relatively short period in the evolution of hip-hop, as producers of that genre had started sampling longer and longer musical phrases and then whole drum breaks from records. The drum machine was still crucial though - particular favourites being the Roland TR-808, E-mu SP-1200 (1985), and Oberheim DMX (1980), the latter of which were both drum machines and samplers, which met producers' needs perfectly.

Another dance scene that must be mentioned in the context of the drum machine is techno. Arising in Detroit in the mid-80s, producers latched onto the available equipment of the time and found that the Roland TR-909 (1984) gave their ultra-futuristic take on Chicago house the exact sound they needed. The 909 has been the staple drum sound of techno ever since.

Sampling too was also becoming integral to hip-hop and the other underground dance genres. Akai astutely released the MPC-60 in 1988, a drum machine with 16 drum pads, the ability to sample, and a sequencer with which to put it all together. J Dilla and DJ Shadow are just two of the innumerable MPC users over the years who forged the new sound with them.

The drum machine continued to be refined throughout the 1980s with newer models adding more sounds at higher quality, offering more polyphony with more multitimbrality, and providing more sequencer memory. The average studio and producer was now expected to be using these as a matter of course in their productions.

And until the 1990s not much changed, except that the increasingly sophisticated synthesizer workstations were also including high quality PCM (sampled) drum sounds in their machines, as they had been doing since the Roland D-50.

It wasn't until 1996 that Novation launched an analogue modelling drum machine, the Drum Station. Like the TB-303 hardware clones popular at the time, the Drum Station aimed to capitalise on the popularity of classic Roland gear by emulating the TR-808 and TR-909 drum machines.

As seen with the invention of analogue modelling which was used in a couple of groundbreaking synthesizers, the significance of this remarkable technology was overlooked somewhat by the rise of the computer and its Digital Audio Workstation (DAW). All these functions - synth, drum machine and sampler could now be carried out 'in the box', and they were! It wasn't until the 2000s and beyond that a resurgence of the analogue drum machine and related analogue gear became a new music production sensation. But that is another story and out of scope for this book!

A word on the selection

Unlike the synthesizer chapter, this drum machine chapter isn't intended to be a comprehensive survey. Instead, the focus is on the more important, interesting or influential drum machines made between 1963-1995. These are the ones that represent the first of their kind, were particularly successful or became embedded in a particular genre.

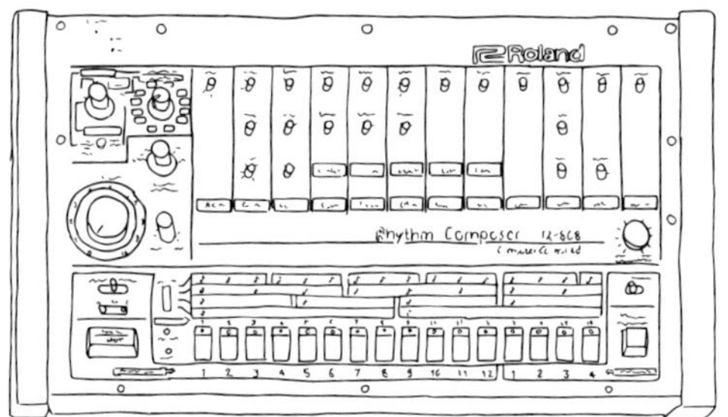

Roland TR-808 1980
16 analogue sounds / 12 note polyphony

DRUM MACHINES

ACE TONE RHYTHM ACE FR1 *1965*

Analogue / 4 note polyphony
16 preset rhythms
Using an innovative 'diode-matrix' for storing its rhythms, it was also incorporated into some Hammond Organs. Sounds included bass drums, snares, hi-hats, shaker, clave, and rimshot.

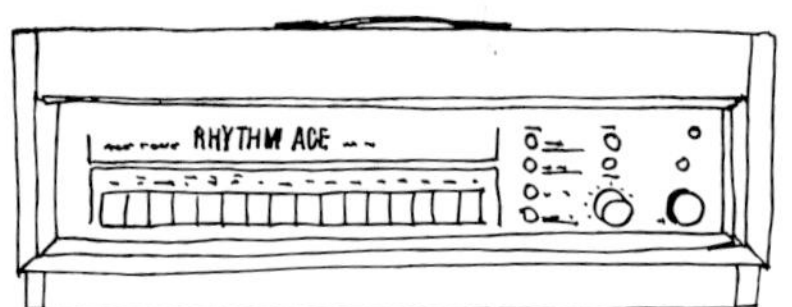

ALESIS D-4 *1991*

501 PCM sounds / 16 note polyphony
The D4 had 12 drum-trigger inputs to enable use as a 'brain' connected to drum pads.

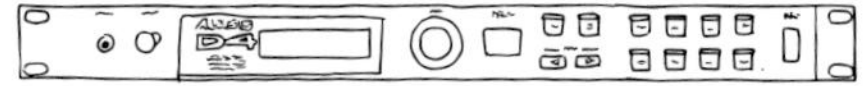

AKAI MPC60 *1988*

32 PCM sounds & 12-bit sampler / 16 note polyphony
Sequencer
The first of the 'MIDI Production Center' workstations - used extensively in hip-hop and other electronic styles, designed by Roger Linn and David Cockerell.

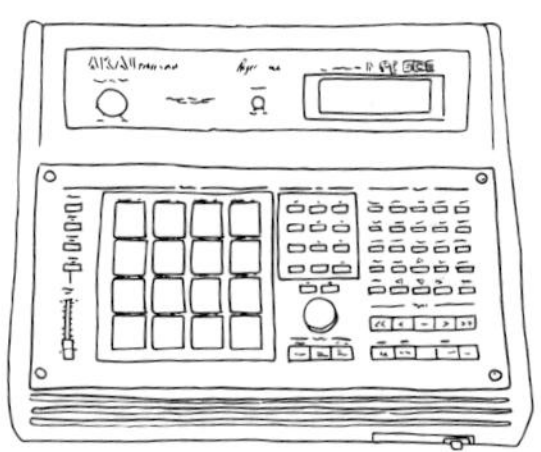

BOSS DR-55 *1980*

4 analogue sounds / kick, snare, rimshot, hi-hat
16-step sequencer
Boss's first Dr. Rhythm drum machine, and the first to offer step sequencing.

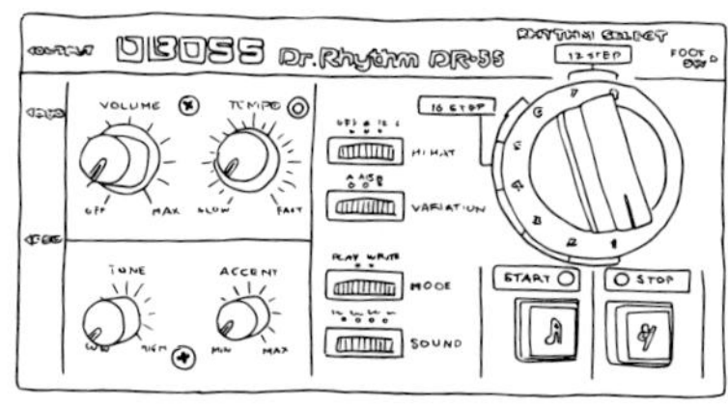

ALESIS SR-16 *1990*

233 PCM sounds / 16 note polyphony
Sequencer
One of the most popular and widely used drum machines of this era.

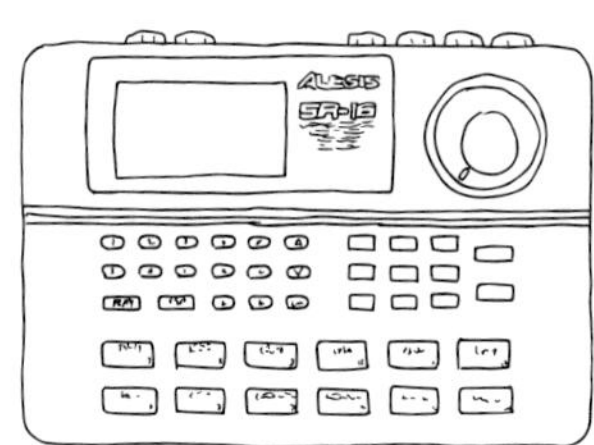

BOSS DR-110 *1983*

6 analogue sounds / full polyphony
Sequencer
Boss's second drum machine.

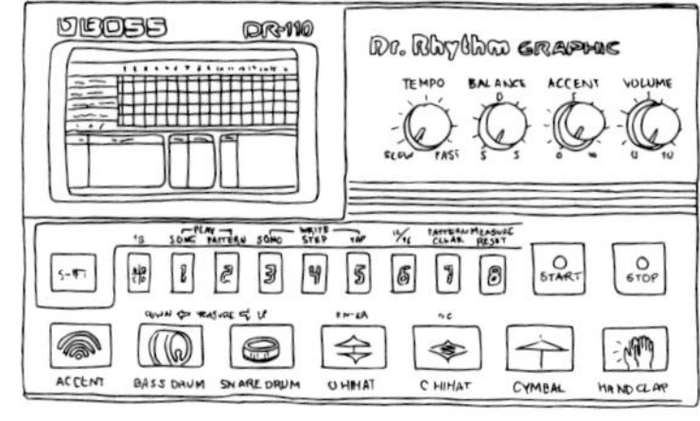

BOSS HC-2 HAND CLAPPER *1984*

1 analogue sound
Adjustable handclap sound with built-in drum pad.

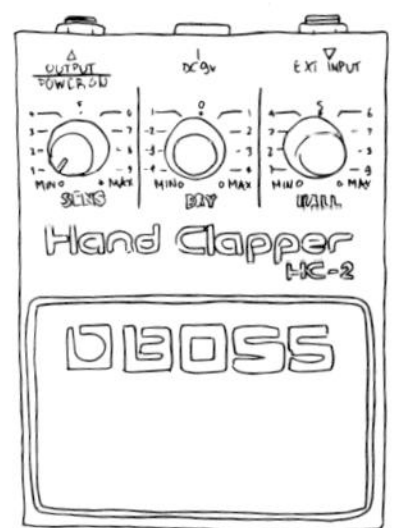

BOSS PC-2 PERCUSSION SYNTHESIZER *1984*

1 analogue sound
Created a range of percussive tones from bass drum to bleeps.

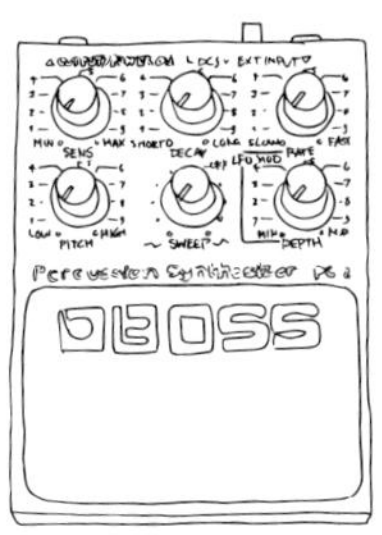

CASIO RZ-1 *1986*

12 PCM sounds / full polyphony
Sequencer
Included the ability to sample four 20kHz sounds for 0.2 seconds, (or one for 0.8 seconds).

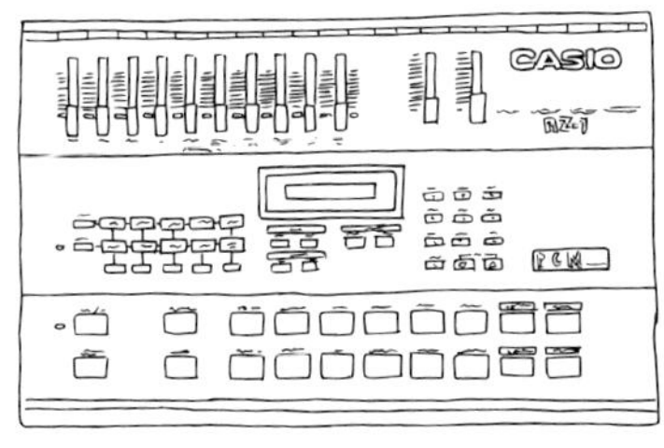

CRUMAR NERVE CENTRE 50 *1981*

16 preset rhythms
Analogue
Came with foot pedals for stop/start and to trigger drum-fills. Also included auto-accompaniment organ/piano/guitar patterns.

EKO COMPUTERHYTHM *1972*

6 analogue sounds
Sequencer
One of the very first programmable drum machines; used by Jarre on 'Oxygene' (1976).

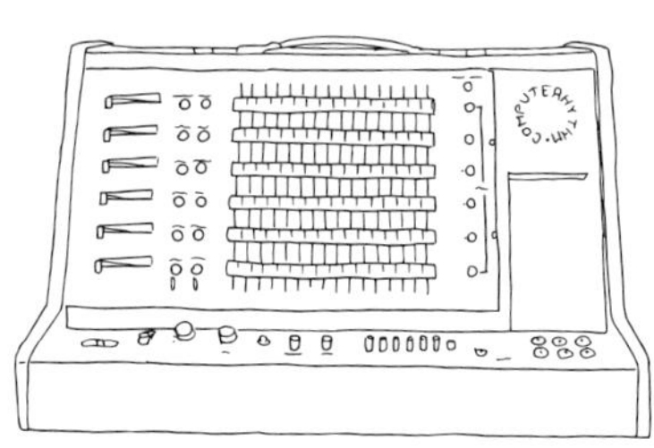

ELKA DRUMMER ONE *1976*

16 presets only
9 analogue sounds / bass drum, conga, toms, cowbell, claves, snare, cymbals
Used by Cluster & Kraftwerk.

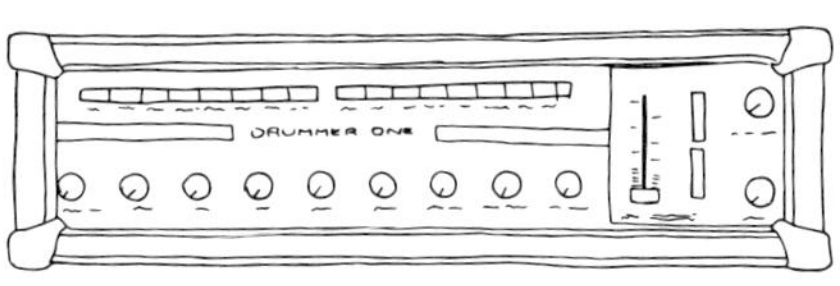

E-MU DRUMULATOR *1983*

12 PCM sounds / full polyphony
Sequencer
Tears for Fears – 'Shout' (1985).

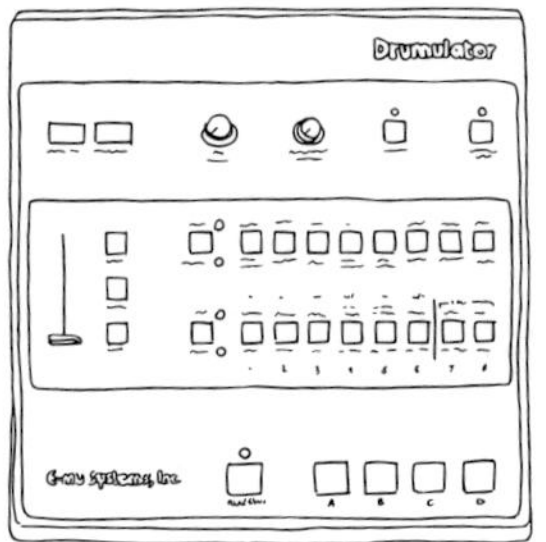

KAWAI R-100 *1987*

24 PCM sounds / 8 note polyphony
Sequencer
Kawai's first digital drum machine.

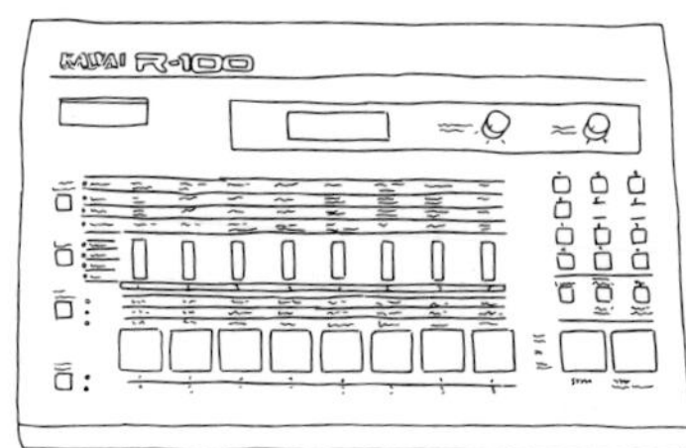

E-MU SP-12 *1985*

8 PCM sounds and sampler (12 bit / 26kHz / 1.2 seconds)
The 'Sample Percussion 12' was popular in hip-hop and dance music production; the subsequent SP-1200 (1987) became a mainstay.

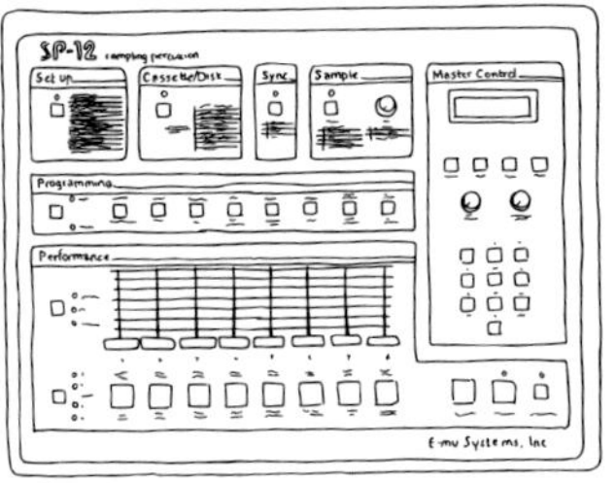

KORG DONCAMATIC DA-20 *1963*

Electro-mechanical
Preset rhythms only
The Doncamatic used a rotary disk triggering sounds with brush contacts.

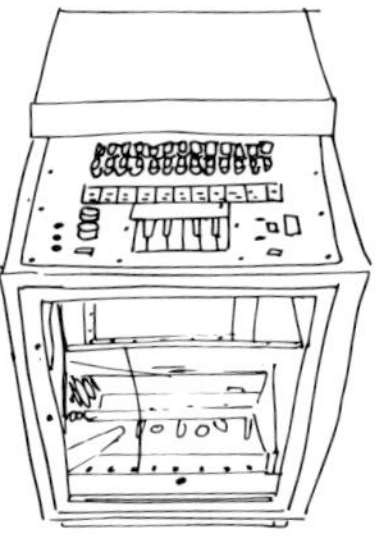

HILLWOOD HR-30 SUPER VARIATION *1977*

10 analogue sounds / full polyphony
Preset rhythms only
Popular in reggae production.

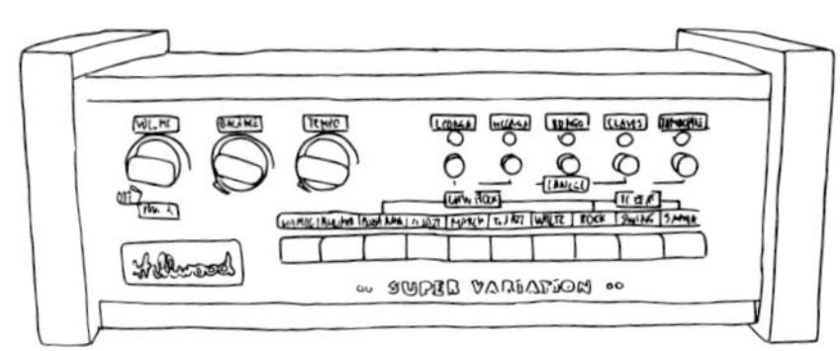

KORG MINIPOPS 7 *1966*

15 analogue sounds
20 presets
The best of the MiniPops range and also used by Jean-Michel Jarre on 'Oxygene'.

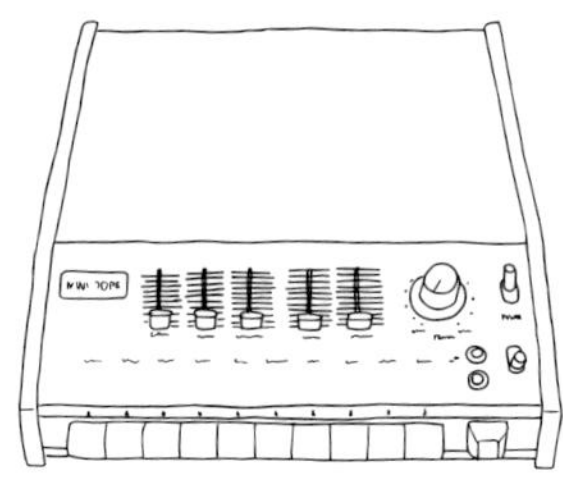

KORG RHYTHM 55 *1979*

12 analogue sounds
48 presets

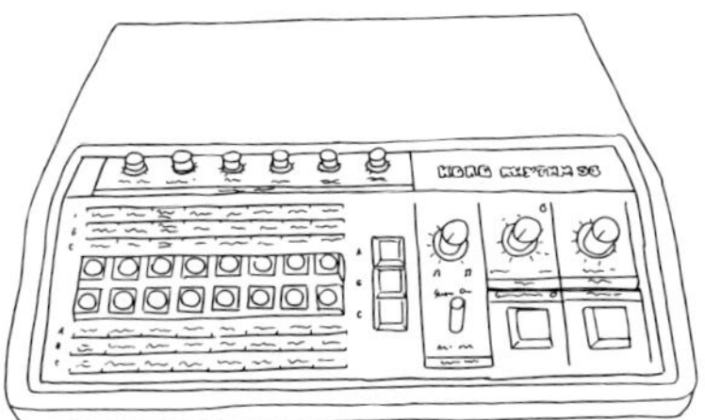

LINN LINNDRUM *1982*

12 PCM sounds / full polyphony
Sequencer
An updated LM-1 with crash, ride and an improved sample rate of up to 35kHz.

KORG DDD-1 *1986*

18 PCM sounds / full polyphony
Sequencer
The 'Digital Dynamic Drums 1' could also sample with the optional DSB-1 board (12-bit / 13.6kHz or 32.1kHz / 3.2s max).

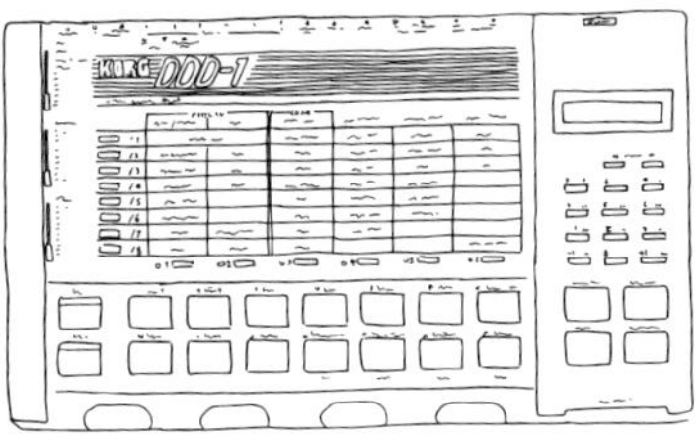

LINN 9000 *1984*

18 PCM sounds and sampler (8-bit / 11kHz - 37kHz)
13 note polyphony
Sequencer
The last of the Linn drum machines - and the prototype for the Akai MPC60.

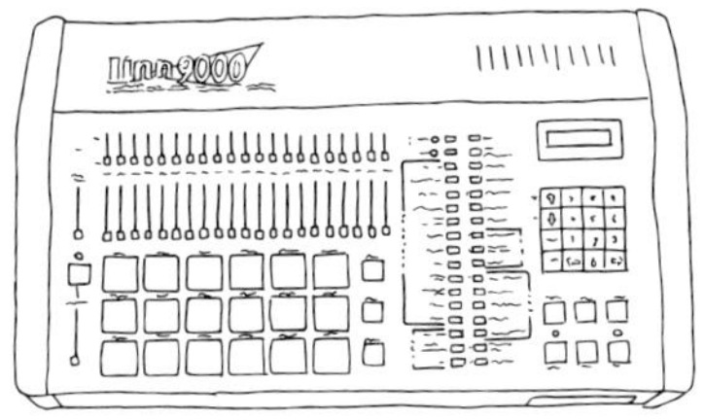

LINN LM-1 DRUM COMPUTER *1980*

12 PCM sounds / full polyphony / sequencer
The first drum machine to use sampled acoustic drum sounds (8-bit at 28kHz). Quantize and Shuffle were also introduced. This, and its sequels, were staples of pop production throughout the 1980s. The Human League - 'Don't You Want Me' (1982).

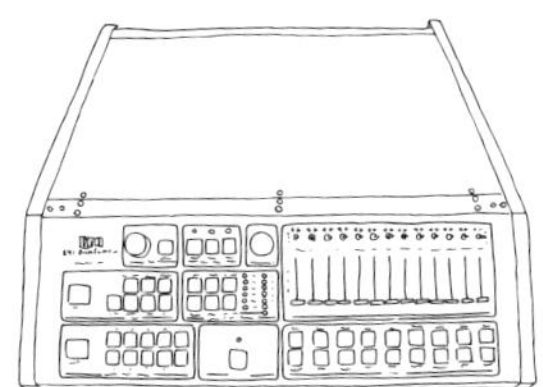

MAESTRO RHYTHM KING MRK-2 *1971*

8 analogue sounds
18 preset rhythms
Used by Sly and the Family Stone – 'There's a Riot Going On' (1971). One of the first commercially successful records using a drum machine, and became known as the 'funk box'.

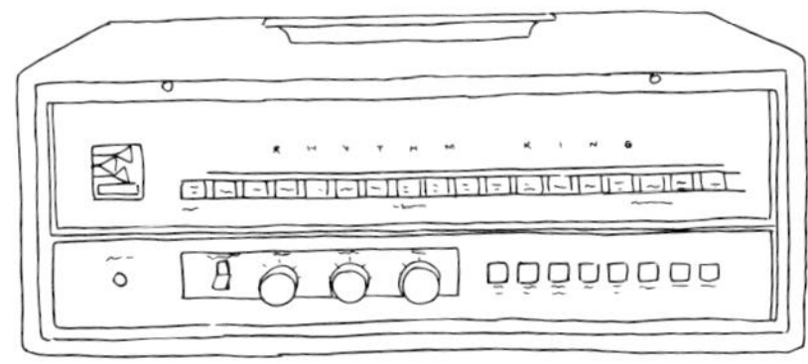

MOOG 701 DRUM MACHINE *1970*

6 analogue sounds, 6 note polyphony (if using the 701 & 702)
Only prototypes were built of this rare Moog drum synth and the 702 Percussion Synthesizer.

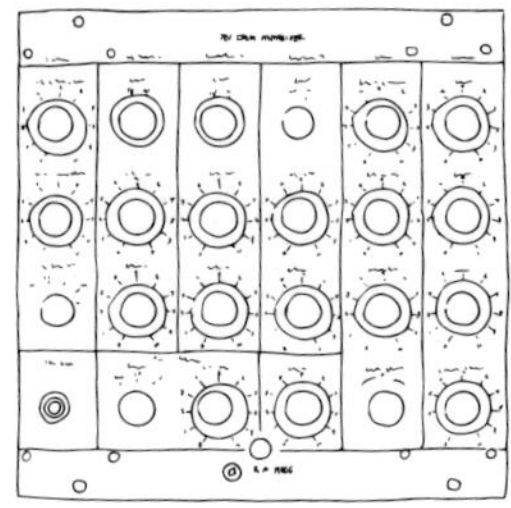

OBERHEIM DMX *1980*

24 PCM sounds / 8 note polyphony / sequencer
Second commercial drum machine to use samples (the Linn LM-1 being the first) and was widely used in hip-hop production during the 1980s. Run DMC - 'Sucker M.C.'s (Krush-Groove 1)' (1983); New Order - 'Blue Monday' (1983).

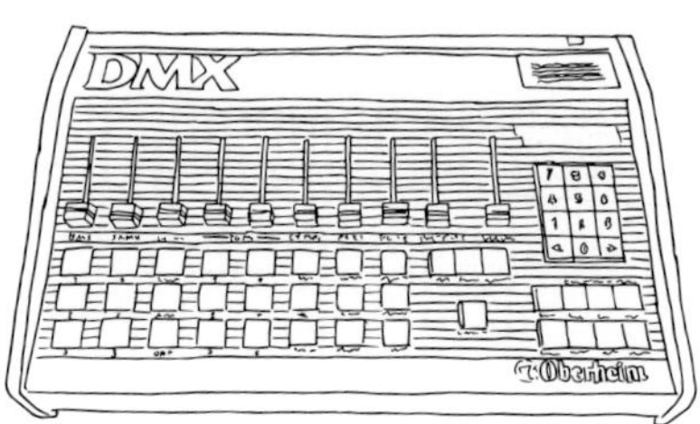

MOVEMENT DRUM COMPUTER MK1 *1981*

14 PCM samples / full polyphony
Sequencer
Rhythms could be programmed, but the 8-bit sounds could not be edited. Eurhythmics - 'Sweet Dreams' (1983).

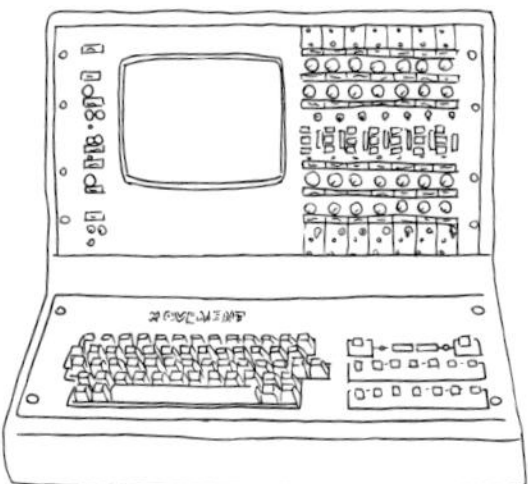

PAIA PROGRAMMABLE DRUM SET *1975*

7 analogue sounds / 5 note polyphonic
Sequencer
One of the earliest electronically programmable drum machines (though not using a microchip).

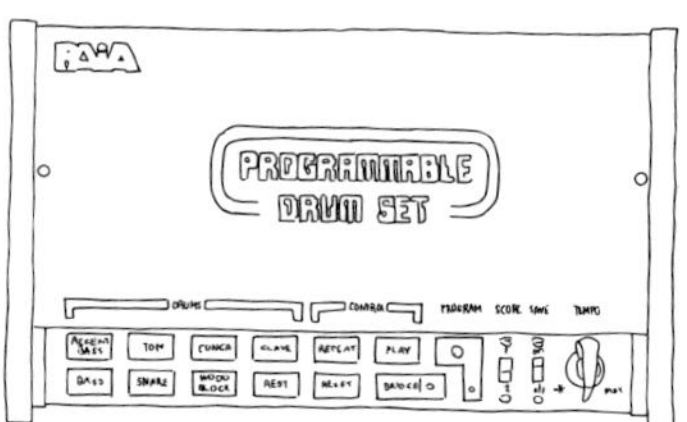

NOVATION DRUM STATION *1996*

17 analogue modelled sounds / 5 note polyphony
A TR-808 & TR-909 clone - but achieved by analogue modelling, not samples.

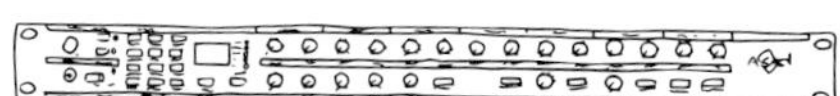

POLLARD SYNDRUM 1 *1977*

1 analogue sound (layered synth tone & 'snare' noise)
The first electronic drumset. Two and four voice versions were also made. The original source of the disco electro-tom dive (Joe Bataan - 'Rap-o, Clap-o' (1979) (intro)).

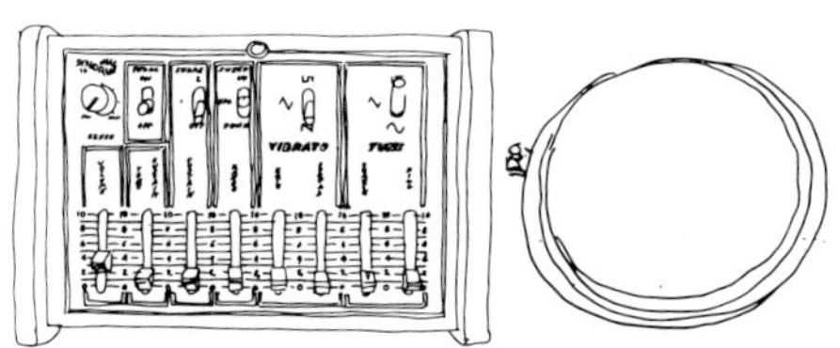

PPG 390 DRUM UNIT *1982*

8 PCM sounds / full polyphony
Sequencer
Only two units made. New sounds could be loaded on ROM cards.

ROLAND TR-33 *1972*

9 analogue sounds
18 preset rhythms
The first 'Transistor Rhythm' units were designed to be used with home organs and were built into some Hammond organs. Similar units were the TR-55 and TR-77 (Ultravox - 'Hiroshima Mon Amour' (1977)).

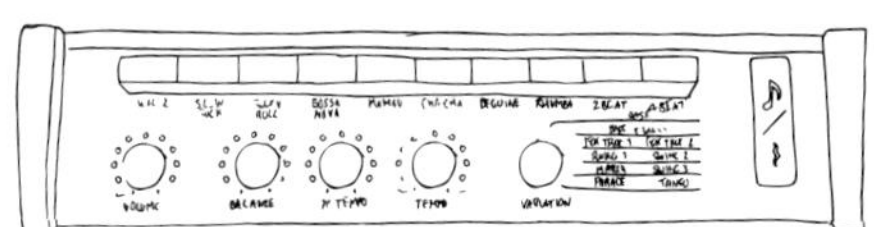

ROLAND CR-68 *1978*

9 analogue sounds
34 rhythm presets
'CR' stands for CompuRhythm. The CR generation used NEC microchips to control the functions. Disco presets were included 'for contemporary sounds'.

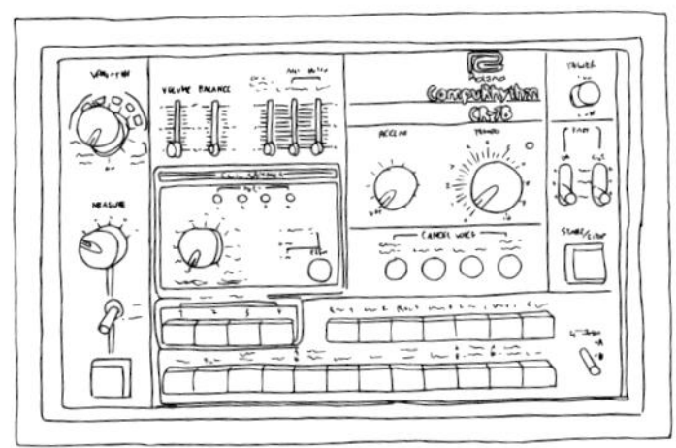

ROLAND CR-78 *1978*

14 analogue sounds / 4 note polyphony
34 presets and step-sequencer
Widely used and popular drum machine. Was the first to offer programmable rhythms alongside the presets, made possible by the Z80 chip. Blondie - 'Heart of Glass' (1978).

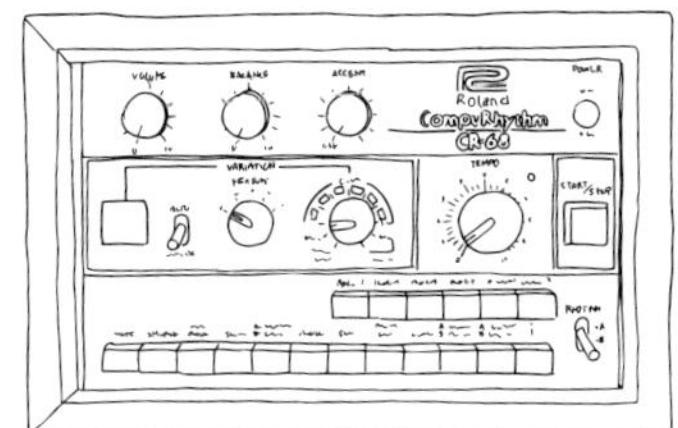

ROLAND TR-808 *1980*

16 analogue sounds / 12 note polyphony
Sequencer
Despite the lack of impact at launch, it's hard to overstate the influence of this drum machine on hip-hop, house and innumerable other electronic music styles over the last 40 years.

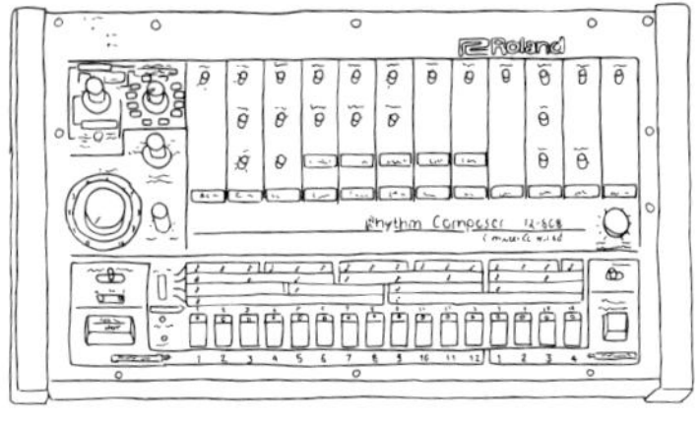

ROLAND TR-606 *1982*

7 analogue sounds / full polyphony
Sequencer
The 'Computer Controlled' Drumatix was designed to partner the TB-303 – note the complimentary design.

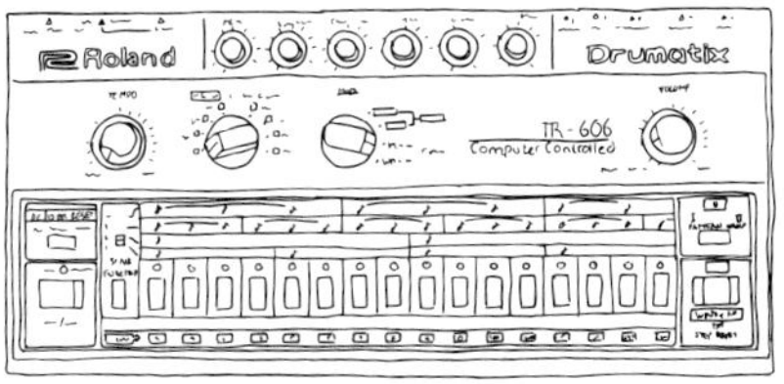

ROLAND TR-909 *1984*

7 analogue & 4 6-bit PCM sounds (crash, ride, hi-hats)
Sequencer
A staple of Detroit techno and many other electronic music styles. Designed by Tadao Kikumoto, who was also involved with TR-808 and TB-303.

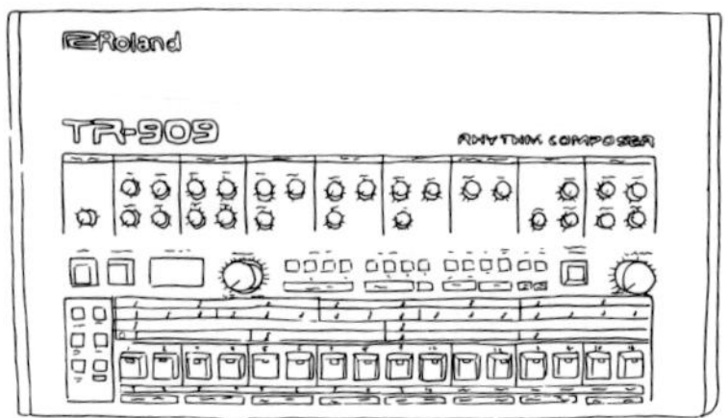

ROLAND TR-707 *1984*

15 PCM sounds / full polyphony
Sequencer
Some sonic similarity to the TR-909.

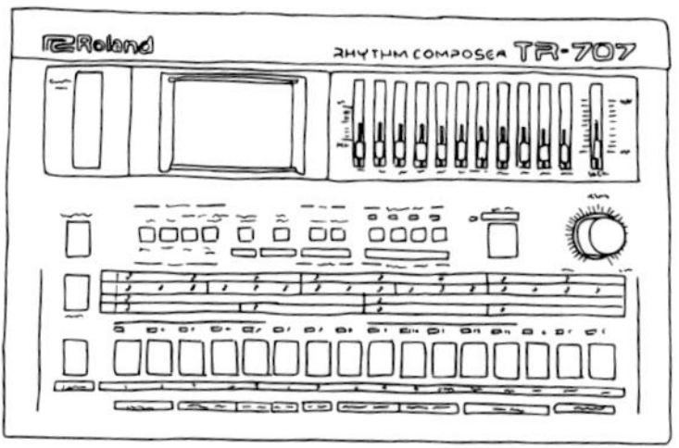

ROLAND TR-727 *1985*

15 PCM sounds / full polyphony
Sequencer
The Latin version of the TR-707 (bongo, conga, timbale, agogo, cabasa, maracas, whistle, quijada, star chime); also widely used in house, tehcno and Latin freestyle.

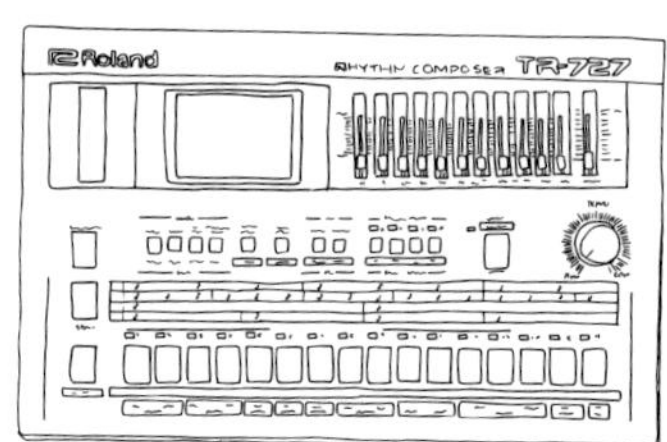

ROLAND PAD-8 OCTAPAD *1985*

Eight pads / no sounds
Drum pad controller.

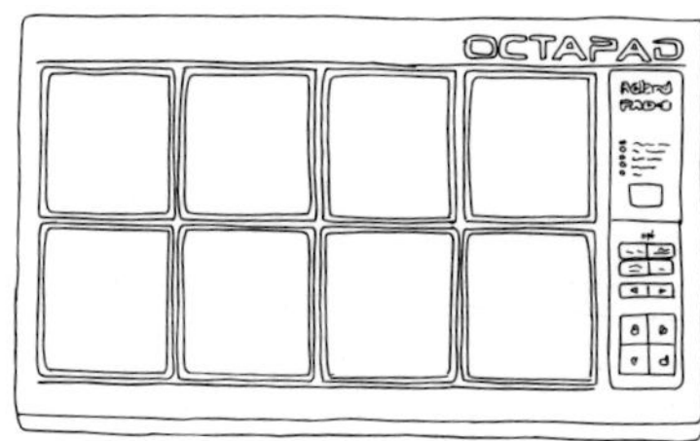

ROLAND R-8 *1989*

68 PCM sounds / 32 note polyphony
Sequencer
There was a MkII in 1992 and a simpler version with fewer sounds, the R-5.

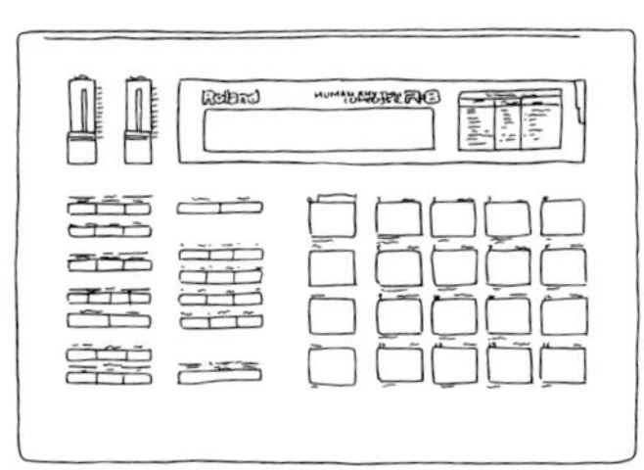

SEQUENTIAL CIRCUITS TOM *1985*

8 PCM sounds / 4 note polyphony

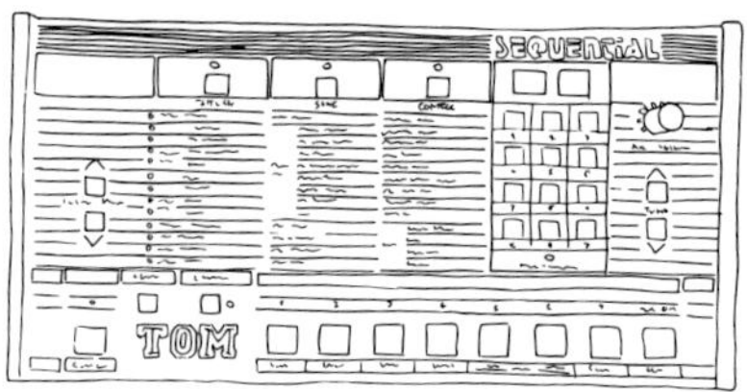

SEQUENTIAL CIRCUITS DRUMTRAKS
1984

13 analogue sounds / 12 note polyphony
Sequencer
First drum machine to have MIDI ports.

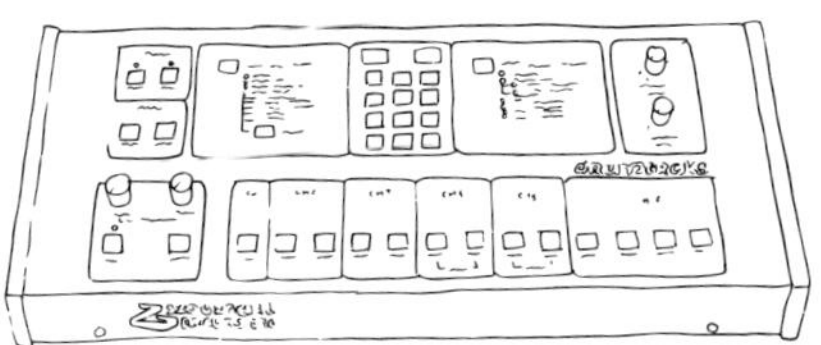

SOUND MASTER MEMORY RHYTHM SR-88 *1981*

4 analogue sounds / full note polyphony
Sequencer
Simple, but programmable, rhythm box.

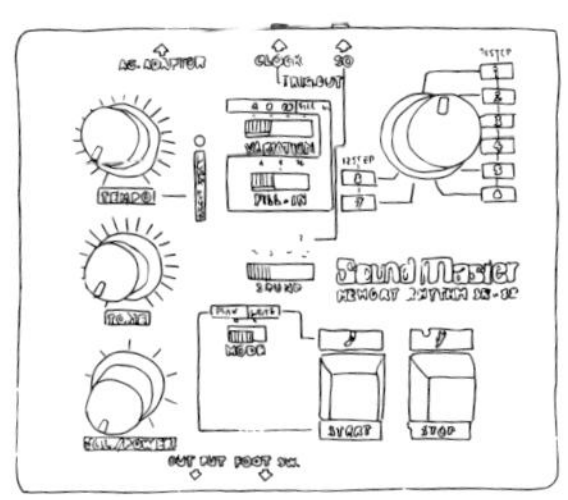

SEQUENTIAL CIRCUITS STUDIO 440
1987

32 PCM sounds and sampler (12-bit at 16kHz - 42kHz)
8 note polyphony / Sequencer
Drum machine sampler with low-pass filters.

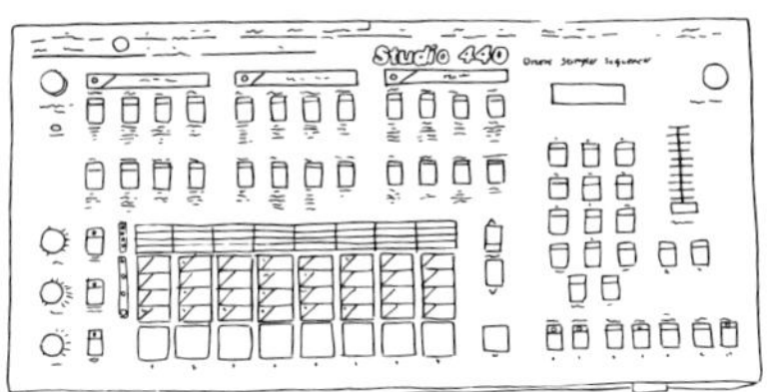

YAMAHA RX-5 *1986*

24 PCM sounds / 16 note polyphony
Sequencer
Sophisticated, but underrated, drum machine.

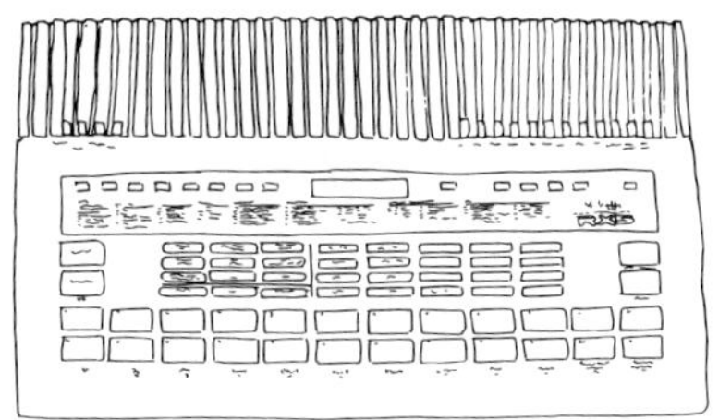

SIMMONS SDS 5 *1981*

5 analogue sounds; bass drum, snare, three toms
Innovative drum pad controllers heard first on Spandau Ballet's 'Chant No.1' (1981).

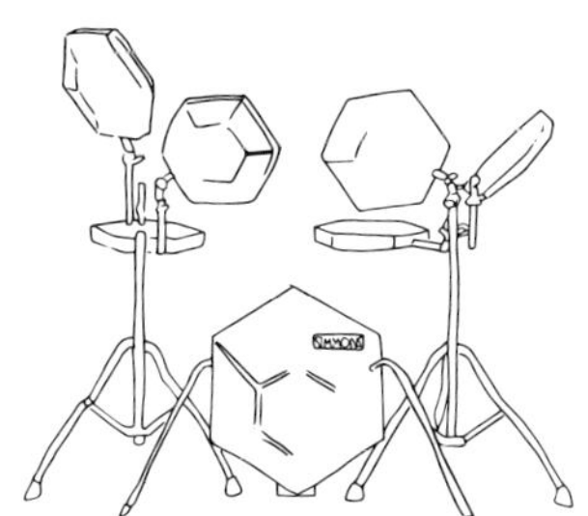

SAMPLERS

Samplers earn a chapter in a book nominally about synthesizers due to their profound impact on music production and musical culture - and because the technology for the 'Sample and Synthesis' synthesizer is derived directly from the technology of sampling.

What is a sampler?

The type of electronic instrument referred to as a 'sampler' records audio into digital memory and then plays it back into the acoustic domain. By playing this audio back at different speeds, it can generate the range of musical pitches required for music composition. For example, playing a sample back at half the speed it was recorded at - thereby halving its frequency - drops the pitch by an octave. All pitches of the musical scale can be achieved by different playback speeds. By this means a 'sampled sound' can be made to play melodies and phrases in a musically useful way.

Tape

The ability to playback and manipulate real-word sounds was previously achieved only by the cumbersome method of recording them on tape and then playing them back at the different speeds required. This meant that each note on a keyboard needed its own tape-recorder with its own specially tuned tape recording. This was the principle behind the Chamberlin (1949), Mellotron (1963), Vako Orchestron (1975), and the Birotron (1976). This last of which used 8-track cartridge tapes and was funded by Rick Wakeman of Yes, but it never saw the light of day due to insurmountable manufacturing challenges.

Creative manipulation of real-world sounds before the advent of digital sampling was also the preserve of tape. Musique concrète was championed by Pierre Schaeffer, Karlheinz Stockhausen and others between the 1940s and 1960s, after which it fell out of favour thanks to the arrival of the synthesizer and other more convenient techniques. Musique concrète involves the intricate and time-consuming process of cutting, splicing and editing fragments of tape to create abstract sounding music. As important a stage in avante-garde electronic music as this undoubtedly was, it can't be said that it ever become particularly popular with either the mainstream or classical music worlds.

Digital sampling

The idea of recording audio digitally was only made possible with the invention of the integrated circuit board and the early microchips, such as the Motorola 6800 (1974). This enabled the type of processing required to record and manipulate digital audio data.

How does a sampler work?

The components that comprise a digital sampler are:

- an analogue-to-digital convertor to record the sounds (the ADC)
- digital storage using memory chips
- digital processing using microprocessors
- digital-to-analogue converter (DAC) to replay the sounds

The ADC turns the continuously varying acoustic wave of sound into a string of digits that describes the sound wave pressure at a series of time slices. (This can be thought of as measuring the 'volume' at each moment). The number of time-slices sampled per second is the *sampling frequency*, and the standard sampling frequency of 44,100 hertz (44.1kHz) means a measure of sound pressure is taken 44,100 times a second. This is sufficient to capture all the sounds the human ear can hear as described by the Nyquist Theorem.

This theorem states that to avoid aliasing effects, the sampling frequency must be twice that of the maximum frequency of the source audio. Given that the upper limit of human hearing is taken to be 20kHz, a sample rate frequency of 44.1kHz (the CD standard), gives the necessary headroom.

The *sample bitrate* describes the numerical resolution with which each of these time-slices can be described. The resolution is the number of discrete volume levels that are available to the system. Sampling is usually only ever done at 8-bit, 12-bit, 16-bit and 24-bit resolutions. (And 24-bit only became common in the late 1990s and is more usually found in a sound-card / computer set-up).

The 'bit' of 'bitrate' refers to the length of the binary number the chip can process. For 8-bit chips, this means the number length is 8 place-values long: in binary this gives the range 0000 0000 to 1111 1111, which is the equivalent of 0 to 255 in decimal. Therefore they have $2^8 = 256$ possible values, or volume levels, available to describe the sound. 12-bit samplers have $2^{12} = 4{,}096$ levels of resolution, and 16-bit samplers have $2^{16} = 65{,}536$ levels.

Clearly, the resolution available in a 16-bit system is far superior to 8-bit, and indeed that is sufficient for 'perfect' reproduction of sound. 8-bit and 12-bit systems, by contrast, have a much grainier, 'inferior', sound.

Early expensive samplers

The first commercial samplers were the notoriously expensive Computer Music Melodian (1976), Fairlight CMI (1979) and NED Synclavier II (1982), each of which could cost as much as a house or two. Despite this, the possibilities afforded to musicians was immediately recognised. Sounds like the 'ORCH5' orchestral stab and the 'ARR1' vocal sound from the Fairlight are still recognisable today, forty years on, and are almost a genre in their own right. Producers like Trevor Horn, Peter Gabriel and Herbie Hancock were immediate converts and the sound of these samplers are heard on many productions throughout the 1980s. For example, Peter Gabriel's 'Sledgehammer' (1986) opens with the Shakhuachi sound from the Synclavier II.

Although the Fairlight CMI launched with 8-bit sound quality, low-frequency sample rates, and very limited storage, its lack of theoretical 'perfection' actually lent these and other early samplers a desirable sound and gave them a character lacking in the later, more 'perfect', samplers. The Synclavier II surpassed the quality of the Fairlight with its 16-bit sampling, and its clean digital reproduction and processing can be heard on Kraftwerk's 1986 album, 'Electric Café' (later re-released as 'Techno Pop').

Trevor Horn set up the record label ZTT specifically to work with Paul Morley, Anne Dudley, J. J. Jeczalik, Gary Langan and a Fairlight CMI on their futurist pop project The Art of Noise in 1983. They explicitly took their inspiration from the Futurist artist Fillipo Marinetti's manifesto 'The Art of Noises' (1913) and the phrase 'Zang Tumb Tumb' from his sound poem about the Battle of Adrianople. Correspondingly their first EP was called 'Into Battle'.

Early 'affordable' samplers

As prices of computer chips and components fell, the next generation of samplers in the early 1980s became (relatively) affordable with machines such as the E-mu Emulator (1981) and Ensoniq Mirage (1984) becoming popular. These were still pretty limited (aka 'characterful') with their 8-bit sampling and perhaps as 'much' as two seconds sampling time. The Emulator can be heard prominently on Depeche Mode's 'Pipeline' (1982).

A next generation with improved 12-bit sampling rates arrived with the introduction of the Sequential Circuits Prophet 2000 (1985), Akai S612 (1986) and E-mu Emax (1986). These all had sampling rates of between 32kHz and 42kHz, and around 10 seconds of sampling time, which was a considerable improvement in sound quality and flexibility.

The Akai S1000 was the true breakthrough instrument in 1988, with its full specification of 16-bit @ 44.1 kHz sampling rate and a luxurious twenty-two second sample time. It soon became ubiquitous in studios and bedrooms worldwide.

Sampler usage

It might perhaps have been expected that producers and musicians would take sampling as a new creative tool to sample any sound from the 'real world' and incorporate it into their electronic opuses in a new burst of 'musique concrète' creativity. However, what actually happened (after everyone had sampled themselves tapping a wine glass) was that it mainly turned into a convenient way of adding realistic instruments and better drum sounds to productions. A sound library industry duly sprung up to service those needs.

More creatively, hip-hop producers realised they could now directly sample drum breaks from their old funk and soul records and work those back into new recordings, thus continuing to innovate a new global style. And of course, beyond just drum breaks, any piece of music was also up for grabs. Though perhaps not quite a musique concrète revival, sampling certainly enabled a new sound collage approach to musical composition, creating new juxtapositions and contexts in which to understand older music. And also creating a new generation of legal headaches as ownership and copyright issues came to the fore.

By the early 1990s, the producers of breakbeat hardcore and rave in the UK and Europe were emulating their hip-hop cousins in the US by sampling older records and manipulating them in ever more imaginative ways. This led to whole new genres such as jungle, drum & bass, ambient dub, trip-hop and many other underground dance music styles which have long since crossed over into the mainstream.
As well as sampling the drum breaks, styles like happy hardcore enjoyed sampling classic records and speeding them up to tempos well beyond what would previously have been considered 'tasteful', creating the frantic chipmunk vocals

associated with that era. An example of creative people responding to cultural needs and using equipment in a way perhaps not fully intended by their makers!

Even with the ability to sample *any* record from the previous century, it's interesting to note that network effects of hierarchy apply even here, leading some sounds to become 'the most famous samples' above all others. Many of these come from 1960s funk records and are now so familiar they are essentially a shared cultural artefact. The 'Amen', 'Apache', and 'Funky Drummer' breaks had already been well used in the disco and hip-hop scenes, being played on vinyl, and inspiring the virtuosic turntablism skills of DJs. But once these breaks made their way into samplers they also became the backbone of breakbeat hardcore, jungle and drum & bass productions.

ROMplers

On the manufacturers' part, they made use of the high-quality acoustic instrument sample libraries as source material for a new range of realistic-sounding synthesizers. This technique became known as 'Sample and Synthesis', and the synths that employed it became known as 'ROMplers', as their sound material was stored in computer ROM.

The end of hardware sampling

The hardware sampler continued to be refined during the late 1980s and early 1990s, with Akai's samplers dominating the market, following on from the previous American pre-eminence of E-mu and Ensoniq. The machines became larger and increased the sample time by making use of hard-drives and increasing the screen sizes for easier editing.

After spurring the creation of so many new music styles, and revolutionising the production of more conventional ones for well over a decade, the hardware sampler underwent a decline towards the end of the 1990s due to the rise of the computer Digital Audio Workstation - as we've seen in the preceding chapters. The computer was able to incorporate both sampling and the ability to record arbitrarily long segments of digital audio, thus rendering the outboard sampling unit with its fiddly interface of buttons and small LCD screens obsolete. The one exception to that decline has been the use of MPC-style drum/sample workstations in dance music production, which is popular still to this day.

Sampling has changed the face of music-making just as fundamentally as any of the analogue and digital synthesis methods, driving new worlds of sound and genres of music, and which are still being explored today.

A note on inclusion

The following selection is not exhaustive. It focuses on the most important, the first, or the most popular of each manufacturer's ranges. Nevertheless, the rapid increase in computing power can be tracked with ease with the rapid increase of sampling bitrates, sample frequencies and sample time over the course of the 1980s.

Sample frequency rates quoted are the input frequencies (the maximum frequency of the resulting sound will be half this). Sample times quoted are for the standard (usually the lowest spec) amount of memory that came with a given sampler.

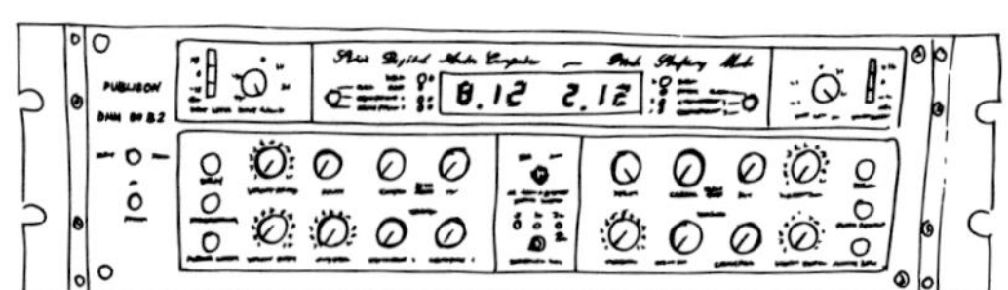

Publison DHM 89 B2 1978
8-bit / 5kHz - 20kHz
0.25s at 20kHz (mono)

SAMPLERS

AKAI S612 *1985*

12-bit / 4kHz - 32kHz / 1s at 32kHz (mono)
6 note polyphony
Designed by David Cockerell - who also designed the EMS VCS3 and went on to work for Electro-Harmonix. Originally conceived as a delay line which used a digital buffer, it evolved into Akai's first samplers.

AKAI S900 *1986*

12-bit / 7.5kHz - 32kHz / 11.7s at 40kHz (mono)
8 note polyphony
The S900 was a significant step up from the S612 in terms of sample quality and memory.

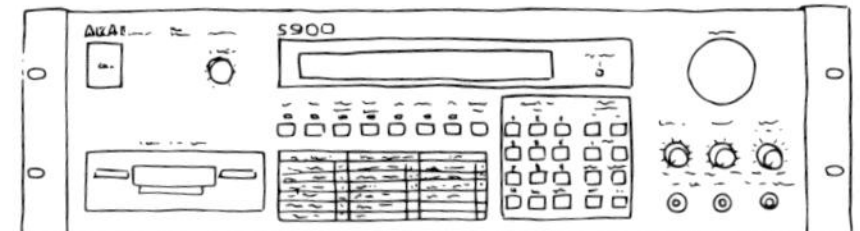

AKAI X7000 *1986*

12-bit / 4kHz - 40kHz / 1s at 40kHz (mono)
6 note polyphony
Building on the S612 with increased maximum sample rate and a 5-octave keyboard. The rackmount was the S700.

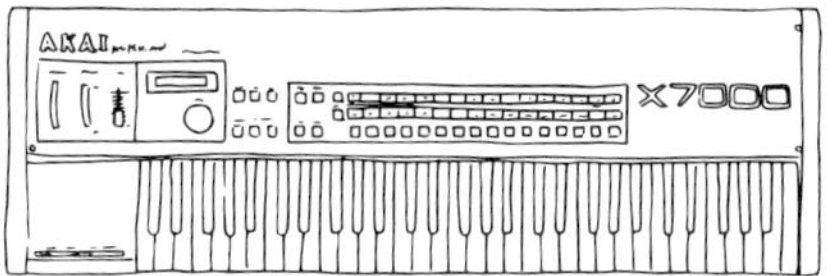

AKAI S950 *1988*

12-bit / 7.5kHz - 48kHz / 9.9s at 48kHz (mono)
8 note polyphony
The S950 saw the introduction of time-stretching and the standard 750KB could be expanded up to 2.2MB.

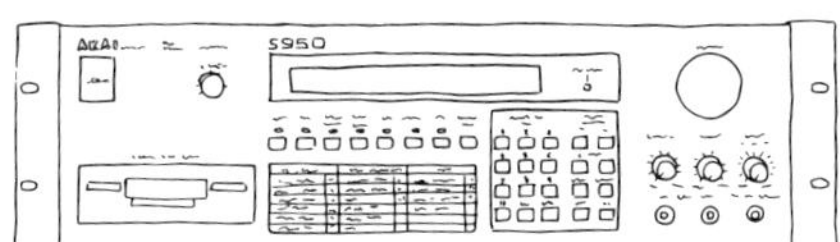

AKAI X3700 *1986*

12-bit / 4kHz - 40kHz / 1s at 32kHz (mono)
4 note polyphony
A simpler X7000.

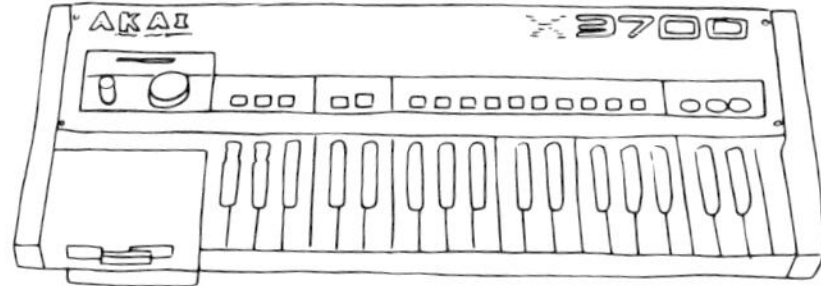

AKAI S1000 *1988*

16-bit / 22.05kHz or 44.1kHz / 12s at 44.1kHz (stereo)
16 note polyphony
The world's most successful sampler. Variants included KB (keyboard), HD (hard-drive), PB (playback only), S1100, and EX(panded).

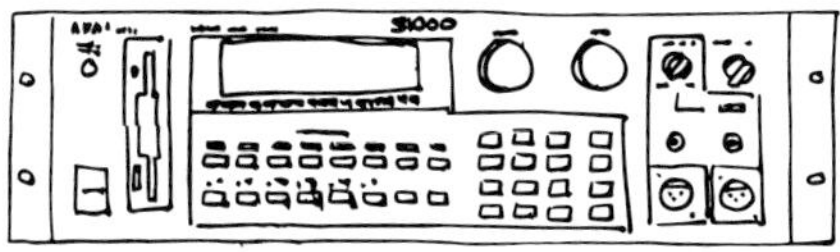

AKAI S3000 *1992*

16-bit / 22.05kHz or 44.1kHz / 12s at 44.1kHz (stereo)
32 note polyphony
Building on the S1000 there were several variants: S2000, S2800 (lower spec); S3000XL - expanded internal drive and memory.

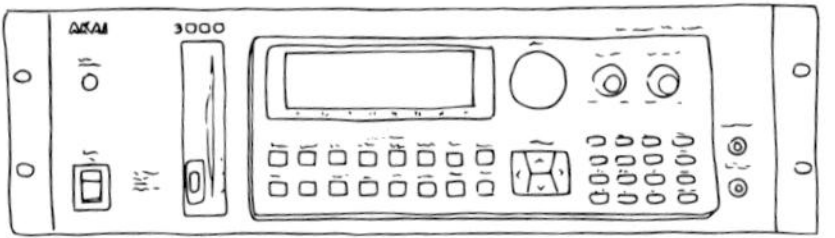

AKAI S01 *1993*

16-bit / 15s at 32kHz (mono)
8 note polyphony
A simplified mono sampler with less than CD-quality sampling.

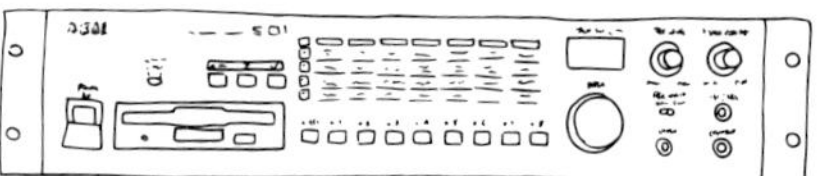

AKAI S5000 / S6000 *1998*

18-bit / 44.1kHz or 48kHz / 46s at 44.1kHz (stereo)
64 / 128 note polyphony
The last of Akai's S-range samplers. Up to 25 minute sample time with the full 256MB installed.

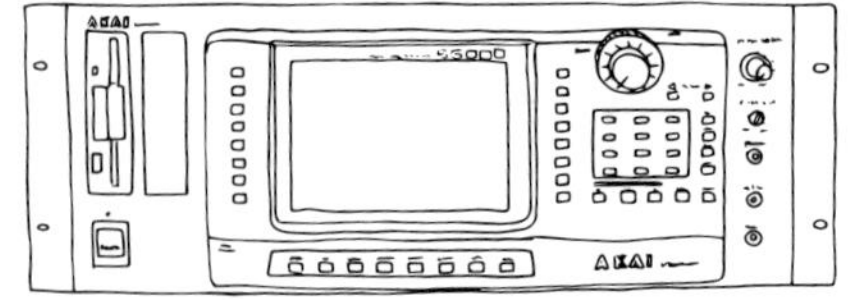

CASIO SK-1 *1985*

8-bit / 1.4s at 9kHz (mono)
4 note polyphony
Although a toy, it samples and even has an additive synth function.

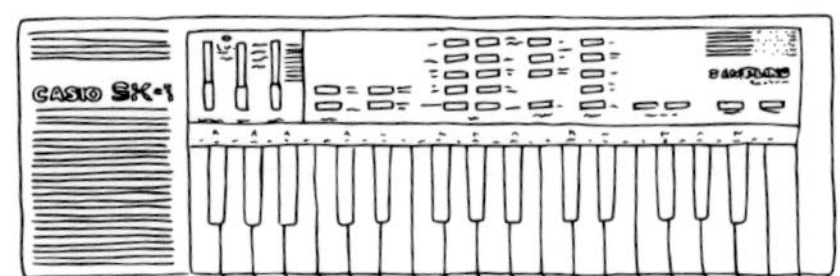

CASIO FZ-1 *1987*

16-bit / 9kHz, 18kHz, 36kHz / 14.5s at 36kHz (mono)
8 note polyphony
Included additive and waveform drawing. Sold as the Hohner HS-1 in Germany.

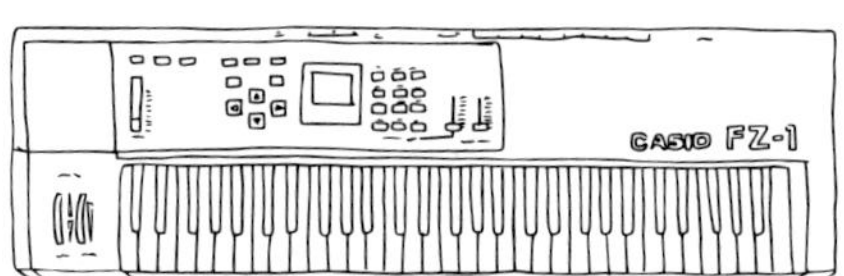

CASIO FZ-10M / FZ-20M *1988*

16-bit / 9kHz, 18kHz, 36kHz / 29.1s at 36kHz (mono)
8 note polyphony
Rackmount versions of the FZ-1 with double the memory (2MB). The FZ-20M had a SCSI port for larger external drives.

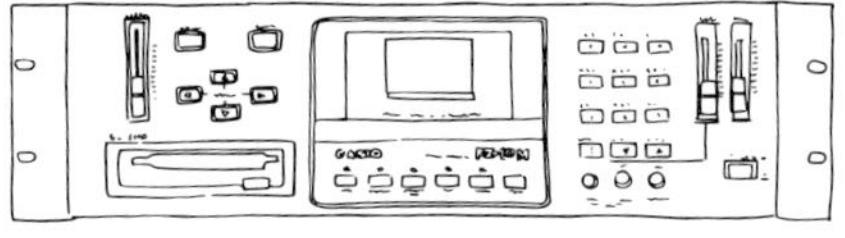

COMPUTER MUSIC MELODIAN *1976*

12-bit / 22kHz / Monophonic
First commercial digital sampler, based on the 12-bit DEC PDP-8/A minicomputer (pictured). It was used by Stevie Wonder on 'Secret Life of Plants' (1979).

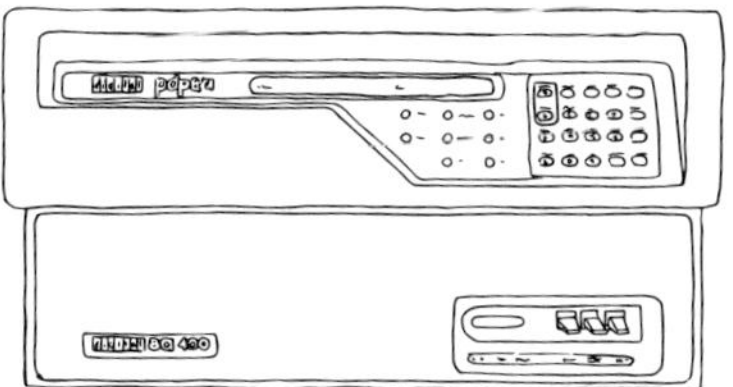

E-MU EMAX *1986*

12-bit / 10kHz - 42 kHz / 12s at 42kHz (mono)
8 note polyphony
Came in keyboard and rack versions; also includes additive synthesizer.

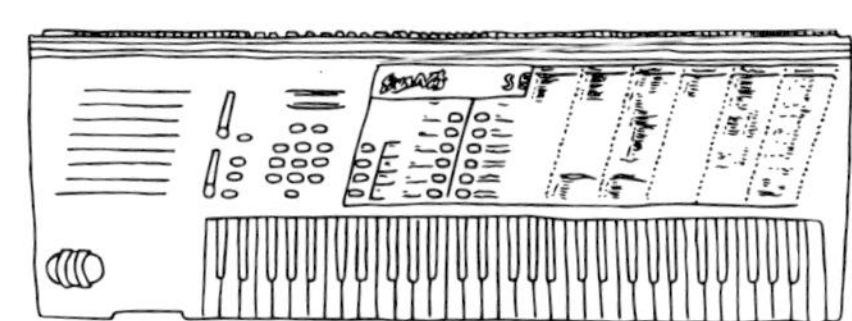

E-MU EMULATOR *1981*

8-bit / 128KB RAM / 2s at 27kHz (mono)
Available in versions with either 4 or 8 note polyphony
Stevie Wonder received Emulator serial number #1.

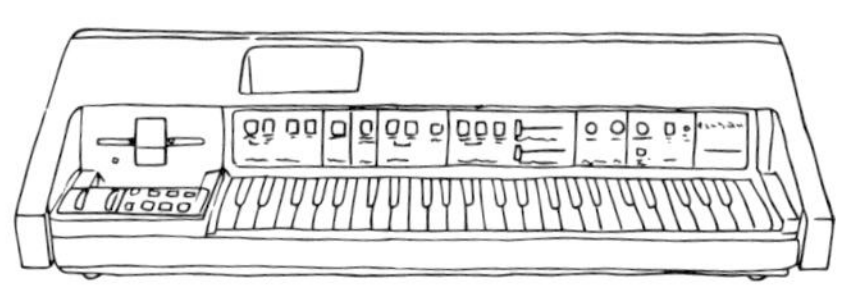

E-MU EMULATOR III *1987*

16-bit / 33.1kHz or 44.1kHz / 67s at 33kHz (stereo)
16 note polyphony

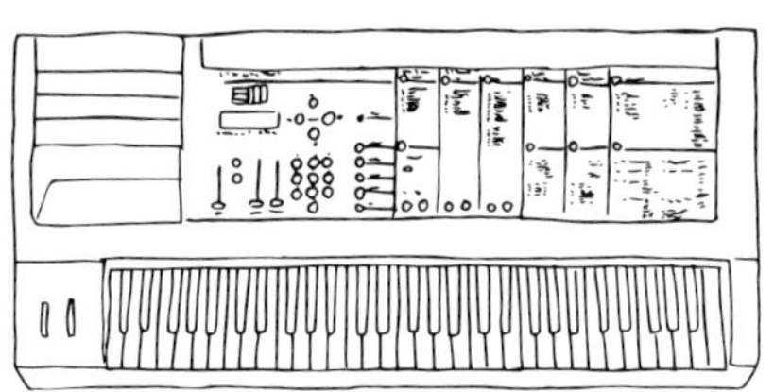

E-MU EMULATOR II *1984*

8-bit / 17.6s at 27kHz (mono)
8 note polyphony
An improved Emulator with 512KB, expandable to 1MB. An Emulator II+ offered 2MB.

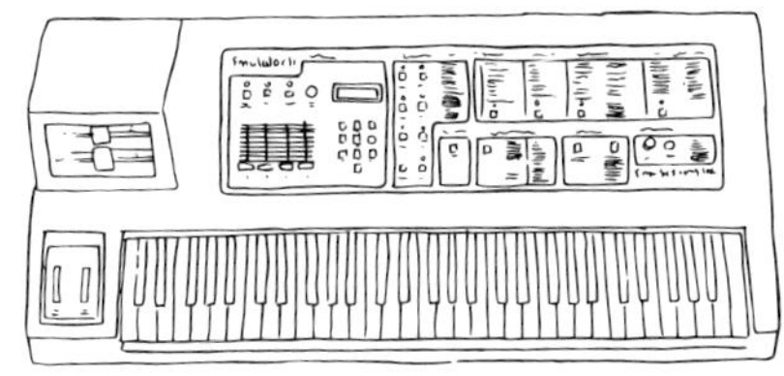

E-MU EMAX II *1989*

16-bit / 20kHz - 39kHz / 6.7s at 39kHz (mono)
16 note polyphony
Later models added stereo sampling.

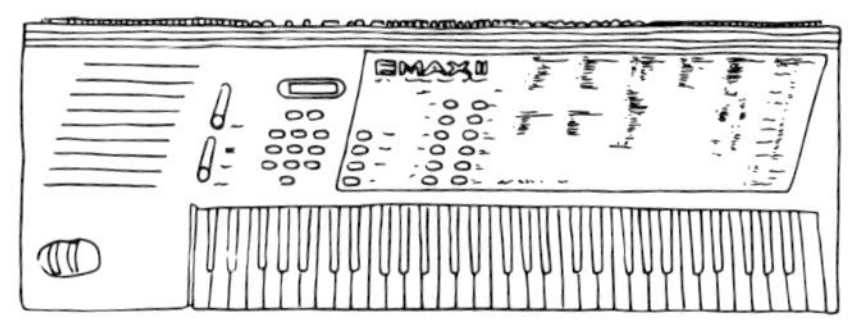

E-MU EMULATOR IV *1994*

16-bit / 22.05kHz - 48kHz / 47s at 48kHz (stereo)
128 note polyphony
Although the top of the range, the last of the Emulators was displaced by cheaper samplers and the rise of increasingly powerful PCs.

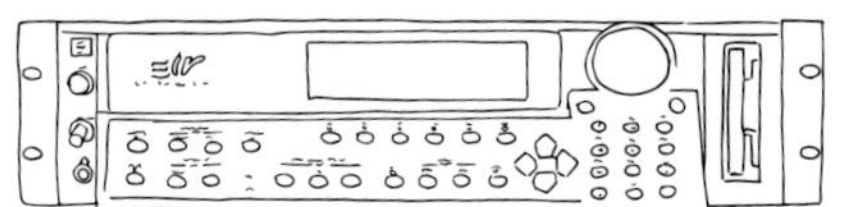

ENSONIQ EPS *1988*

13-bit / 6.25kHz - 52kHz / 5s at 52kHz (mono)
12/16/20 note polyphony at 52/39/31.2kHz
The 1990 version of the 'Ensoniq Performance Sampler', the EPS 16+, offered 16-bit sampling.

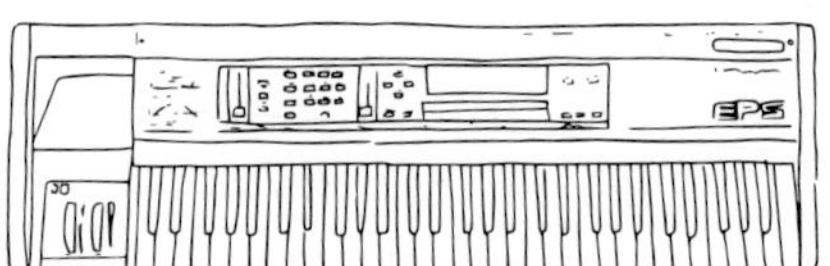

E-MU ESI-32 *1994*

16-bit / 22kHz - 44.1KHz / 11s at 44.1kHz (stereo)
32 note polyphony
E-mu's new generation of samplers following the Emulator series.

ENSONIQ ASR-10 *1992*

16-bit / 29.8kHz or 44.1kHz / 15s at 29.8kHz (stereo)
23/31 note polyphony at 44.1/29.8kHz
Music production workstation.

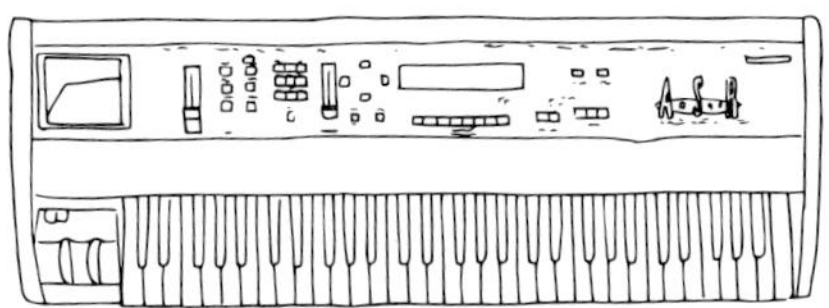

ENSONIQ MIRAGE DSK-8 *1984*

8-bit / 10kHz - 33kHz / 2s at 33kHz (mono)
8 note polyphony
One of the first affordable samplers; the Mirage DMS-8 was the rack equivalent.

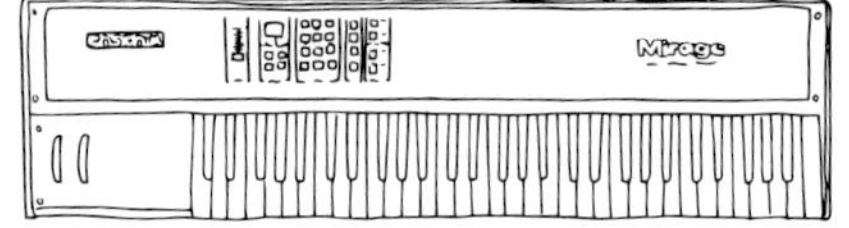

FAIRLIGHT CMI *1979*

8-bit / 0.5s at 24kHz (mono)
8 note polyphony (each voice card had 16KB of memory)
One of the earliest sampling systems, the Fairlight Computer Music Instrument (CMI) cost £12,000 and upwards at launch. The brainchild of Peter Vogel and classmate Kim Ryrie, it was championed by Peter Gabriel and used by many artists such as Kate Bush, Trevor Horn and Jean-Michel Jarre. Named for the Fairlight hydrofoil that ran in Sydney Harbour, Australia.

FAIRLIGHT CMI II *1982*

8-bit / 32kHz / sample time dependent on disk size
8 note polyphony
The second version introduced the 'R' page sequencer and became famous for its library samples, compiled originally by David Vorhaus. Some of the famous sounds include:
ORCH5 - the definitive orchestral stab:
Afrika Bambaataa - Planet Rock' (1982)
Yes - 'Owner of a Lonely Heart' (1983)
Art of Noise - 'Close to the Edit' (1984)
ARR1 - a breathy 'Ah' vocal sound:
Tears for Fears - 'Shout' (1984)
BEATGONG - bell tone:
Quincy Jones - used for intro of 'Beat It'

KURZWEIL K250 *1984*

16-bit / 5kHz - 50kHz / 10s at 50kHz (mono)
12 note polyphony
Ray Kurzweil worked with Stevie Wonder on the K250 to produce a library of the most realistic emulations of acoustic instruments possible at the time.

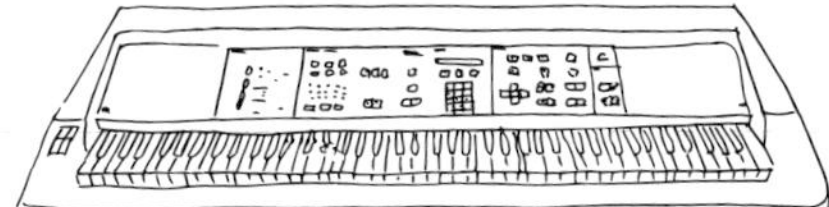

FAIRLIGHT CMI III *1985*

16-bit / 32kHz - 100kHz / >2mins at 48kHz (stereo)
16 note polyphony (expandable up to 32)
Although the first CMI to offer 16-bit / 44.1kHz sampling, it was displaced by the much more affordable samplers becoming available at the time.

NED SYNCLAVIER *1977*

Additive / FM (4 Operators or 'partials')
6 note polyphony
The first New England Digital (NED) Synclavier was 'only' an additive and FM synthesizer, but it paved the way for the more famous sampling Synclavier II.

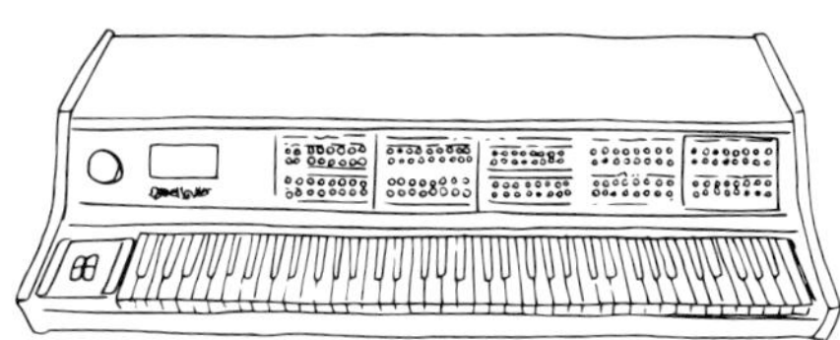

KORG DSS-1 *1986*

12-bit (variable down to 6-bit)
16kHz - 48kHz / 5.5s at 48kHz (mono)
8 note polyphony
The Digital Sampling Synthesizer has the DW8000's synthesizer capabilities (and FX), but uses samples for the source oscillators. Additive synthesis also possible.

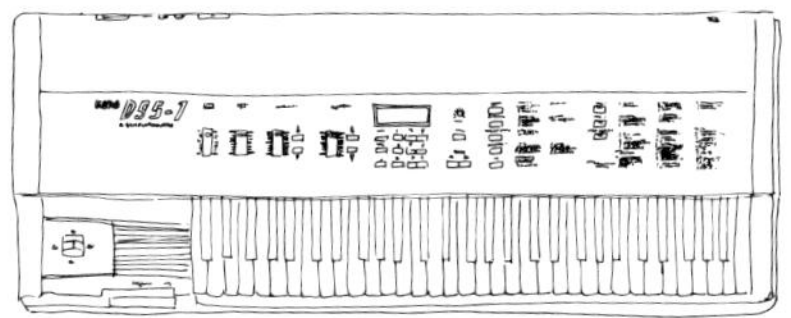

NED SYNCLAVIER II *1980*

16-bit / 1kHz - 100kHz / 32MB expandable to 768MB
4 note polyphony (expandable to 32) (mono)
The Synclavier II included hard-disk audio recording and a full system could cost over £100,000 - even a 16MB RAM card cost £15,000.

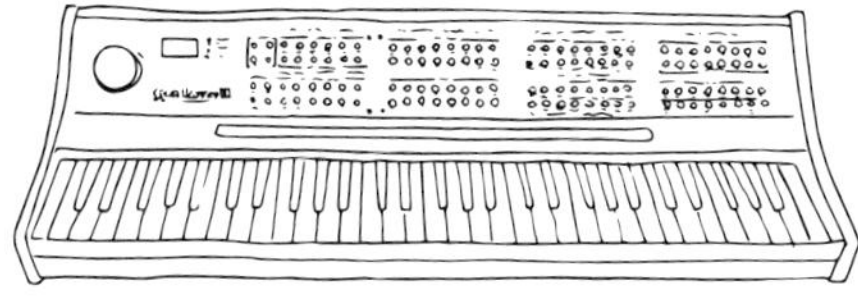

OBERHEIM DPX-1 *1987*

12-bit / 8 note polyphony / sample player only
Could load samples from Akai, Ensoniq, E-mu, and Sequential Circuits. The HDX-20 was an optional 20MB hard drive unit.

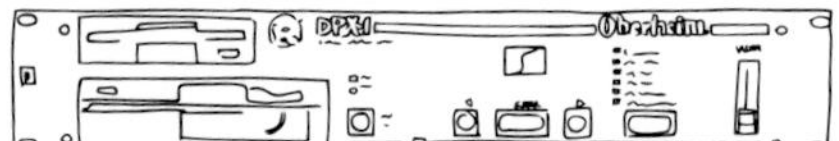

ROLAND S-10 *1986*

12-bit / 4.4s at 30kHz (mono)
8 note polyphony
Limited sampler with only 256KB memory; the MKS-1000 is the rackmount version.

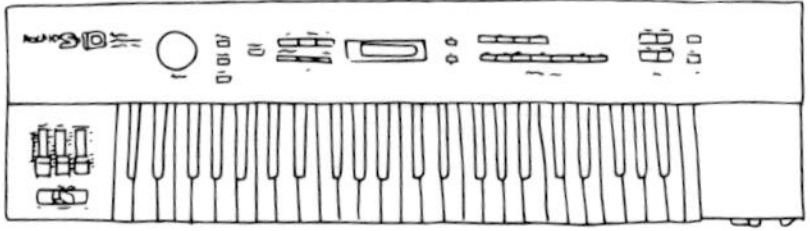

PUBLISON DHM 89 B2 & KB 2000 *1978*

8-bit / 5kHz - 20kHz / 0.25s at 20kHz (mono)
The rackmount is 'just' a digital delay unit, but the addition of the controller keyboard transforms it into a sampler.

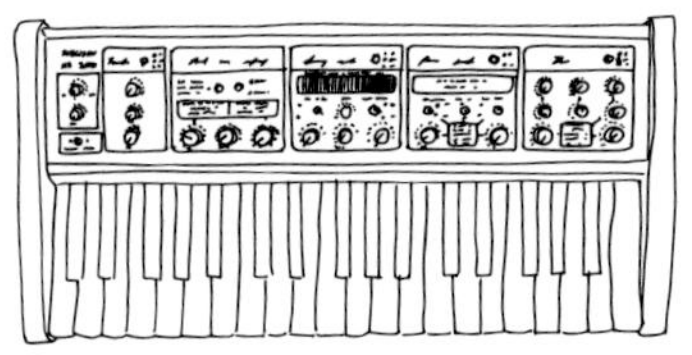

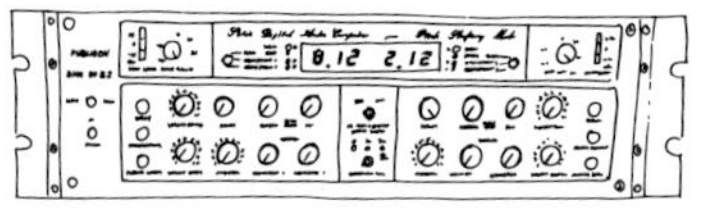

ROLAND S-50 *1986*

12-bit / 15kHz - 30kHz / 14.4s at 30kHz (mono)
16 note polyphony
Rackmount equivalents were the S-550, and the less well-specified S-330.

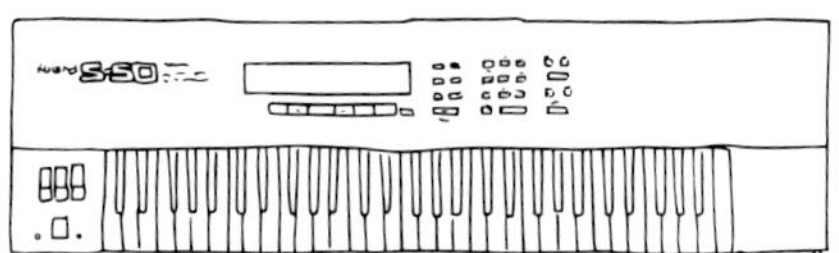

QASAR M8 *1975*

Digital wavetable and additive synthesizer with a mighty 4KB of RAM and a 64KB processor. It was designed by Tony Furze and licenced to Fairlight to form the basis of the Fairlight CMI.

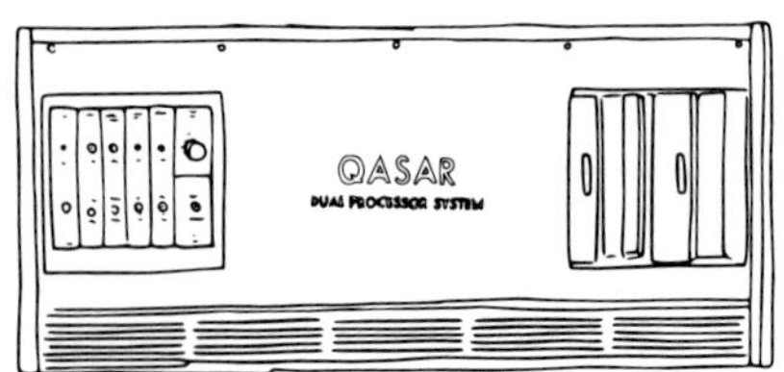

ROLAND S-220 *1987*

12-bit / 15kHz or 30kHz / 4.4s at 30kHz (mono)
16 note polyphony
An upgraded S-10 with double the polyphony.

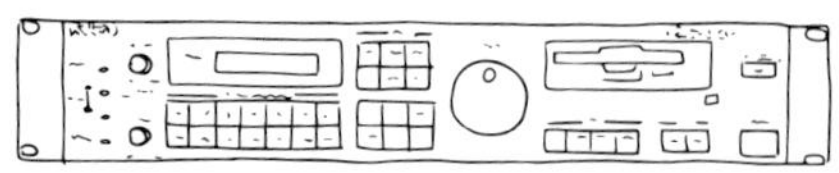

ROLAND W-30 *1989*

12-bit / 15kHz - 30kHz / 14.4s at 30kHz (mono)
16 note polyphony
Music workstation with sampler, keyboard and sequencer. The Roland/Rodgers W-50 was the sample playback version.

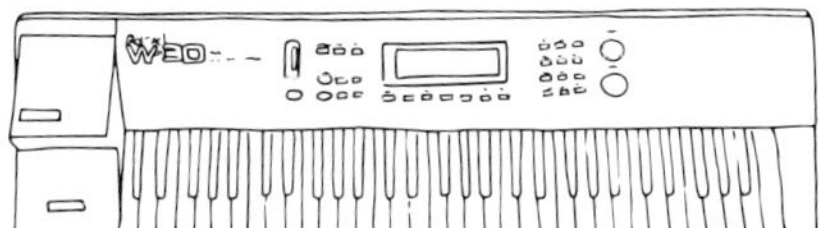

SEQUENTIAL CIRCUITS PROPHET 2000 *1985*

12-bit / 16kHz, 32kHz or 42kHz / 3s at 42kHz (mono)
8 note polyphony
An improved version, the 3000, was released in 1988.

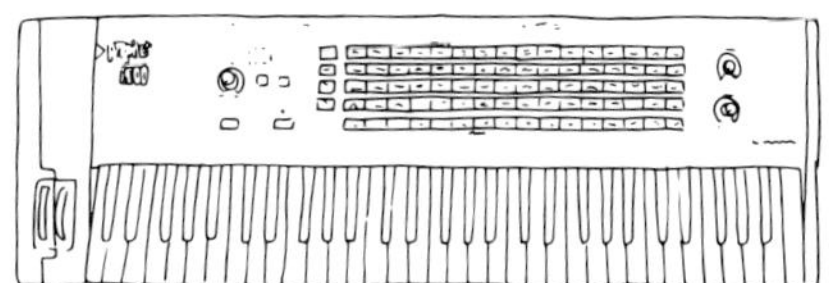

ROLAND S-770 *1990*

16-bit / 22kHz - 48kHz / 22.5s at 44.1kHz (stereo)
24 note polyphony
The new S-770 was a professional 16-bit machine; the S-760 very similar. The SP-700 was a sample playback rackmount.

YAMAHA TX16W *1987*

12-bit / 7.9s at 33.3kHz (stereo)
(Mono - 16.7kHz, 33.3kHz, 50kHz)
16 note polyphony
Yamaha's only sampler until the A3000 in 1997.

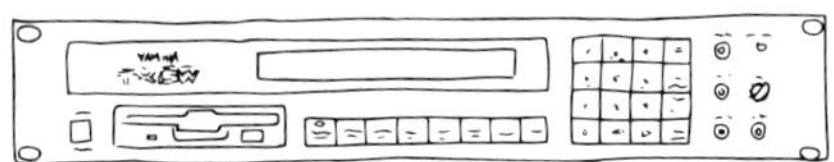

PRE-MODERN INSTRUMENTS

The history of electrical musical instruments that predate the modern era is a rich and varied one. In a sense, once the transistor-based synthesizer was invented the range of instruments quickly narrowed into the synthesizers, samplers and drum machines of the preceding pages. This was evolution finding the best fit for musicians' needs.

These antecedents were arguably more varied in the three centuries preceding transistors, and which the following chapter can't possibly do justice to. It is intended only as a flavour of the various inventions and breakthroughs in the search for usable musical instruments using the newly discovered phenomenon of electricity.

The chronological phases of electrical musical instruments are broadly as follows:

Early electrical experiments

In the 18th century, many experiments were carried out exploring the newly discovered phenomena of electricity and magnetism. These included several trials to create sound, but nothing from this era created a real musical instrument that was worth persisting with and were generally one-offs or novelties.

Electro-mechanical instruments

This is a large category and refers to the type of instrument that uses electricity to drive a mechanism of some sort to create sound, or uses electromagnetic amplification to enhance or extend a physically generated sound. Examples include:

- The electric piano, in which a physically struck tine or wire creates a vibration in an electromagnetic field. The resulting electric signal is then amplified. The Rhodes electric piano is perhaps the most famous of the type, but the first electric piano was invented by the Neo-Bechstein company in 1929.
- The electric organ. The first upgrade was to add an electric motor to drive the air through an acoustic pipe organ in a church. More, ahem, revolutionary is the tonewheel organ. This more portable alternative rotates disks with 'bumps' around the edge that create audio-frequency oscillations in the magnetic field of a static pick-up. The tonewheel organ was invented by Laurens Hammond in 1935, and the Hammond B3 is the byword for this type of electric organ.
- Recording sounds on tape for further manipulation was pioneered by Pierre Schaeffer in the 1940s, and this type of music was explored for some decades by composers such as Karlheinz Stockhausen. Unlike the prior two instrument types, this ushered in a whole new approach to music, called musique concrète, and it was a serious examination of sound and how it worked. It was a radical break with the classical music tradition and not even accepted as music by some.
- Tape was also used to replay pre-recorded instruments in more conventional music styles. Pressing a note on a keyboard would trigger a tape-recording of an instrument playing that note. It's a basic technique, but it worked and was made popular by the Mellotron (1963).
- Photoelectric tone generators - light falling on certain materials can create an electric charge, and this was used to create 'sound from light'. These machines would convert drawn patterns on transparent films to sound using a variety of systems. Notable examples include Daphne Oram's 'Oramics' machine and the Russian ANS synthesizer.

Electronic instruments

Instruments that use electronic components are the direct ancesters of the modern synthesizer and of all subsequent digital instruments. Apart from the mechanical keyboard, knobs, sliders and buttons, these require no moving parts for the actual sound generation:

- Vacuum-tubes - heterodyne effect. Vacuum-tubes are the earliest electronic components; the first being the De Forest audion tube invented in 1913. These were almost immediately used by De Forest himself to create sound exploiting the heterodyne effect - creating beat-frequencies in the audio range by combining the outputs of much higher frequency tubes. The best-known instruments of this type are the Theremin (1922) and ondes Martenot (1928), though De Forest invented his own 'audion piano' (1915).
- Vacuum-tubes - oscillators. Using vacuum-tubes as the direct source of audio signals (rather than relying on the 'beating effect' of ultra-high frequency tubes), these are the direct precursors of the modern analogue synthesizer. The downside of tubes is that they are large (compared to transistors and integrated circuits) and that a large number are needed to make a working instrument. The Hammond Novachord

(1939) required over 160 tubes, thus making such instruments far less portable than the Theremin, and harder to maintain. Many institutions built their earliest synthesizers from such components, such as the RCA Mark I in the following chapter.

Digital computers

The age of the computer began in earnest with the invention of the transistor. Very early digital computers had used electromechanical relays, but vacuum-tubes with arrays of other electronic components were subsequently used for much increased speed - such as the US military's 'ENIAC' computer (which was also the first programmable electronic computer). The ability to manipulate digital information that represented sound was soon seized upon once the miniaturisation and affordability of transistors became a reality in the early 1960s. The earliest digital systems could be as large as a room due to the relatively large size of the components of the time and the exploratory nature of the work. The EMS MUSYS system, built by David Cockerell and Peter Zinovieff in the late 1960s was one such large, room-sized computer/synthesizer.

The early computer chips were used to explore additive synthesis, sound sampling, resynthesis and algorithmic composition as early as the 1960s. Still, they only became more widely available from the mid-1970s, when affordable integrated circuit microchips made their way into the nascent synthesizer industry's products.

Experimental music

Approaching the music made by the vast majority of these experimental and groundbreaking instruments can be challenging. Aside from the electrification of pianos and organs, which had no trouble slotting into the music traditions of the day, most of the music made on such instruments were built from sounds that no one had ever heard before. They may not have had anything to do with equal temperament or western harmonic structures and might be composed according to musical structures that were as far from a verse-chorus structure or sonata form as was possible.

Some of it still sounds very alien (some not unlike dubstep!). I find this early experimental electronic music to be fascinating and highly involving, knowing that it was often the answer to the question, 'what happens if we try making music like this?' Recommended is the album 'OHM: The Early Gurus of Electronic Music 1948-1980' (Ellipsis Arts, 2000), which is a compelling compilation featuring some of the machines in this chapter and many, many more besides.

It all represents the human need to explore, invent, to create and, certainly for these premodern instruments, laid the groundwork necessary for the incredible sound and music-making options we enjoy today.

RCA Sound Synthesizer 1951

PRE-MODERN INSTRUMENTS

CLAVECIN ELECTRIQUE *1759*

Although it translates as 'electric harpsichord', it was actually an 'electric carillon', which is to say, an electrical bell ringer. It used a static charge held in a 'Leiden jar' (a primitive capacitor) to drive the clappers of the bells when a circuit was closed.

THE TELHARMONIUM *1897*

The Telharmonium was a vast instrument (the MkII weighed over 200 tons), which broadcast its music over the telephone, as well as giving performances in the 'Telharmonic Hall' in New York. It was invented by Taddeus Cahill and generated sound using tone-wheels (see patent illustration of these below), which could be adapted to alter the harmonic content allowing for the emulation of some instruments such as woodwind.

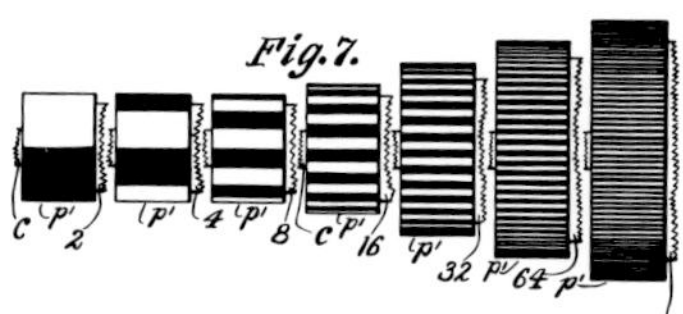

THE MIGHTY WURLITZER *1914*

Although a pipe organ, the theatre Wurlitzer was intended as a full orchestra of sound for the accompaniment of silent film and theatre. Some instruments included percussive and other effects to add to the dramatic presentation.

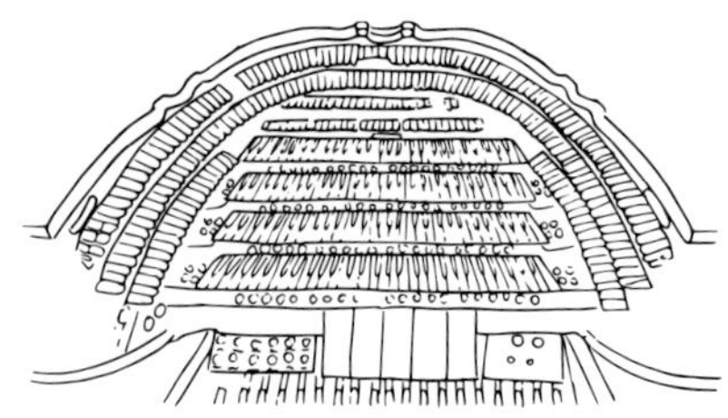

AUDION PIANO *1915*

The audion was a type of vacuum tube - a triode electron tube to be precise - which was invented by Lee de Forest in 1906. He also discovered that audio tones could be generated by exploiting the 'heterodyne effect', in which two detuned high frequency radio waves emitted from the audion would 'beat' in the audio range. A prolific inventor, De Forest built the 'audion piano' using this effect.

THEREMIN *1922*

Also exploiting the heterodyne effect, the Russian inventor Lev Termen (anglicised as Leon Theremin), further used the capacitance effect of the performer's hand coming in close proximity to the terminals to control pitch and volume. Robert Moog got his start in the electronic music industry by selling Theremin kits in his teens, and he modified a Theremin with a fretboard controller for the Beach Boys to use on 'Good Vibrations' (1966).

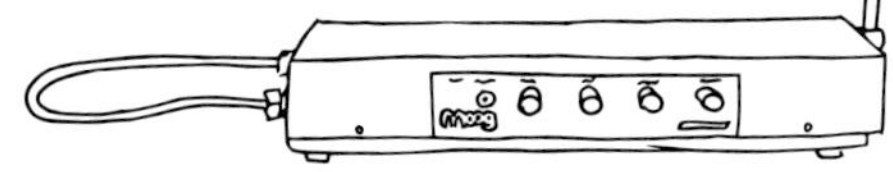

ONDES MARTENOT *1928*

The ondes Martenot ('Martenot waves') is another early 20th century instrument to make use of the heterodyne effect. Control by a keyboard gave it more familiarity to players and composers and is a rare electronic instrument to find success in both serious and popular music alike. Olivier Messiaen used it for his 'Turangalîla-Symphonie' (1946-8); Varèse updated his 'Ecuatorial' in 1961 to include it. And it is still played to this day by musicians such as Jonny Greenwood of Radiohead.

It had a ring controller, which could add vibrato by virtue of the capacitance effect as seen in the Theremin. The 'palm' diffuser (left of image) has 12 transducer driven strings that resonate with the note played; the middle diffuser is called the 'métallique' and the cabinet contains the 'principal' and 'résonance' diffusers.

LE CROIX SONORE *1929*

Included more for its dramatic appearance, the Croix Sonore ('Sonic Cross') is really just a Theremin-type instrument. Still, its inventor Nicolai Obukov developed a whole range of mystical and occult beliefs about the role of music and sound in human life and invented many other esoteric and unusual instruments to express this.

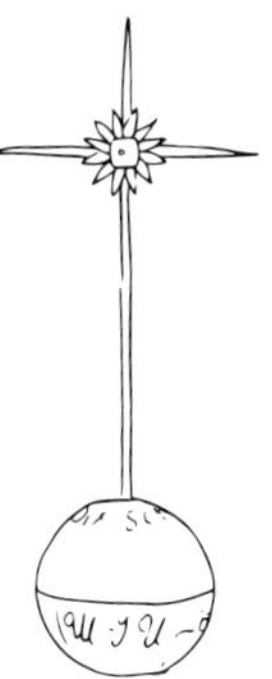

TRAUTONIUM *1929*

Invented by Dr Friedrich Trautwein in Germany, the Trautonium did away with a piano keyboard and introduced a continuously variable metal slider that gave control over both pitch and volume. It used a vacuum tube to generate a tone, and actually had a filter mechanism to modify it further. Distributed by Telefunken in the 1930s it was too expensive and unusual to make much of an impact. A derivative of the Trautonium was the mixturtrautonium which was used by Oskar Sala on his soundtrack for Alfred Hitchcock's 'The Birds' (1963).

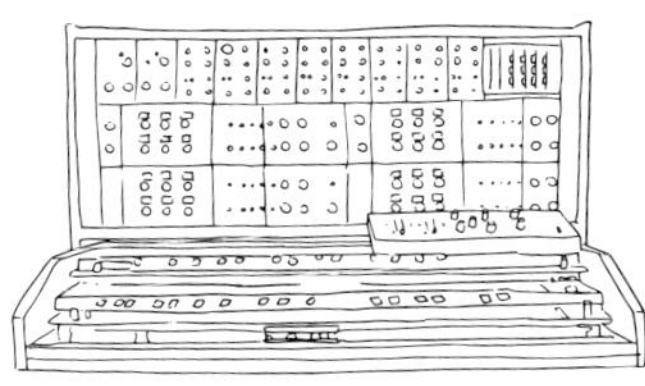

RHYTHMACON *1930*

Lev Termen created this device with composer Henry Cowell. Based, as it was, on mathematical principles, it could have been very interesting - but it's not clear a working prototype was ever managed. The idea was that there were sixteen harmonics to be played: the fundamental harmonic would sound once in a period, the first overtone twice, and the second overtone three times, and so on, each one triggered independently from a keyboard. Thus any combination of rhythmic pulses could be played. It was designed to work using a spinning disk with the necessary number of holes per overtone punched out, through which light would shine and trigger a note using the photoelectric effect.

ANS SYNTHESIZER *1937*

A large and complicated device that generated audio tones from visual images drawn in negative on glass. Tones were created by spinning a disk that could generate 720 discrete pitches, spanning ten octaves in 16 ⅔ cent increments. To prevent them all sounding at once, a sheet of glass with black mastic was placed between the disk and the light source. By etching through the mastic, the corresponding pitches were sounded, enabling a vast array of non-diatonic continuous pitch events to be heard.

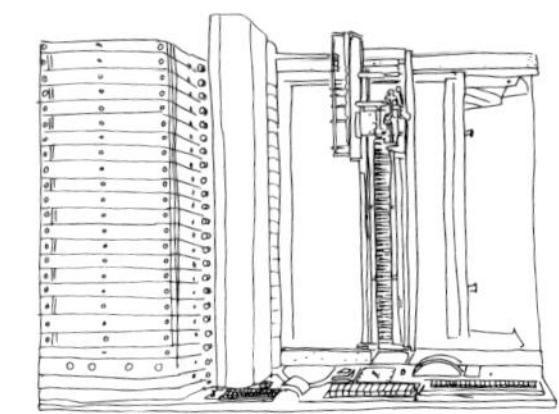

BODE MELOCHORD *1937*

One of Harold Bode's many contributions to the development of electronic instruments was the Melochord, which used vacuum tubes for oscillators. He later wrote a paper in 1961 proposing how a modular synthesizer could be created using the new transistor technology. Robert Moog licenced Bode's designs for ring modulation, vocoding, and more, and used the principles of Bode's proposed modular system in developing his own.

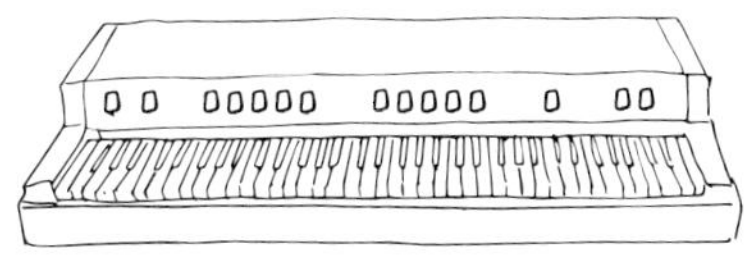

HAMMOND NOVACHORD *1939*

The first subtractive analogue synthesizer ever made, the Novachord had basic tone and envelope control, but was also a complicated beast of over 160 vacuum tubes and 1,000 capacitors.

CHAMBERLIN *1949*

Predating the Mellotron, the Chamberlin played back recordings of real instruments recorded on tape loops and was only distributed in the US. The Rhythm-mate used recordings of real drummers. The Chamberlin's designs were taken to the UK by Bill Fransen and formed the basis of the more widely used and well known Mellotron.

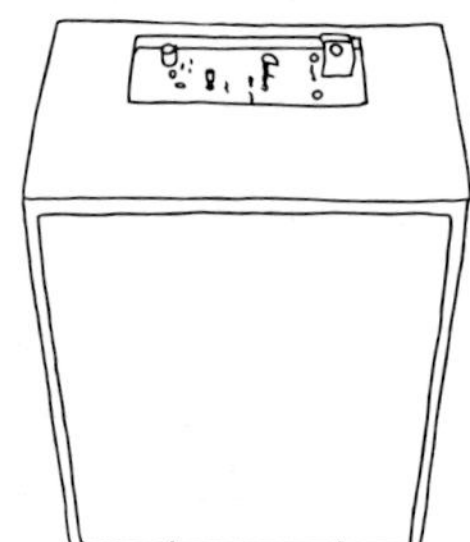

THE VODER *1939*

The human voice has long been a source of fascination with electronic sound engineers. The first artificial voice synthesis was achieved by Homer Dudley in 1938. The voder ('Voice Operating Demonstrator') gave control over the spectral content of vowel sounds, and white noise was used for consonants. It was 'played' in realtime by a skilled operator and could mimic speech and even be made to sing. The illustration shows the Voder being demonstrated at the 1938 World Fair.

LEO COMPUTER *1951*

The LEO was the 'Lyons Electronic Office' and was the mainframe computing system of the UK's Lyons Tea Company. It was discovered by LEO's operators that it could be made to 'play music' by manipulating its software to emit pitched tones, though it was not designed for this purpose. A LEO installed in Melbourne, Australia was made to play Waltzing Matilda at its launch.

CLAVIOLINE *1947*

The Clavioline was a French instrument based on a vacuum tube oscillator, high and low pass filters, and an amplifier. Vibrato was a large part of the sound, and it's been used on many records. A good example is the lead part of The Beatles' 'Baby You're a Rich Man' (1967), which uses the clavioline on its 'oboe' setting.

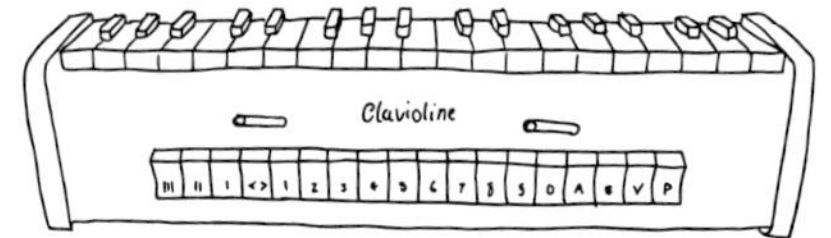

RCA MARK I & II SOUND SYNTHESIZER *1951*

The Radio Corporation of America (RCA) built a mainframe sized programmable synthesizer in 1951. The programming was accomplished by punch card, which was laborious but enabled each note to be defined by pitch, timbre, volume and envelope. The MkII (1959) added filters. Originally intended to generate pop hits automatically, it was actually used by serious composers such as Milton Babbitt and Charles Wuorinen; the latter of whom won a Pulitzer prize in 1970 for his composition 'Time's Encomium' written with the MkII.

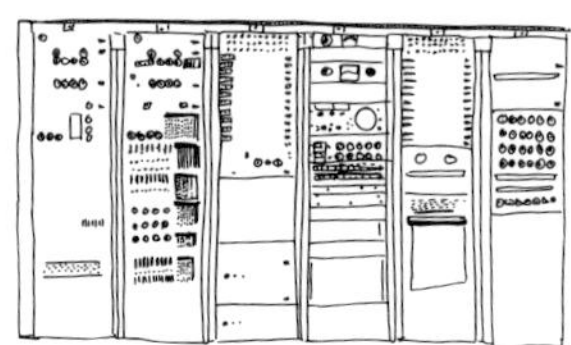

HAMMOND B3 *1954*

The Hammond company launched the B3 church organ in 1954. It used the tone wheel technology that had been around for some decades. With the addition of a percussive click (delayed third order harmonics) and the Leslie speaker it became a perfect fit for the R&B, jazz and rock scenes. One of the most iconic and influential electric organs ever made, it has appeared on thousands of records.

ORAMICS *1960*

Daphne Oram co-founded the BBC Radiophonic Workshop in 1942 and worked there until 1959. Upon leaving she continued to work on a photo-optic synthesizer she had christened 'Oramics'. It was similar in some ways to the ANS Synthesizer, but which used ten parallel 35mm filmstrips on which shapes and lines were drawn. These would be transformed into sound using photoreceptors that generated the tones.

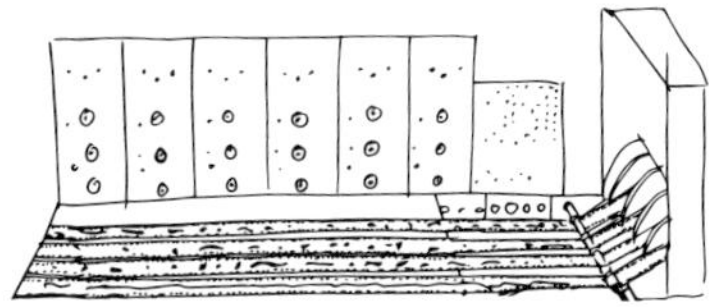

THE CIRCLE MACHINE *1958*

Raymond Scott was a pioneering inventor of electronic instruments and a composer who made use of them. He set up Manhattan Research Inc. in 1946, to exploit his various inventions - waveshapers, ring modulators, envelopers and more. He also worked on an instrument called the Electronium which was never completed – but which led to his employment by Berry Gordy's Motown label as head of operations and chief engineer for six years during the 1970s. Although perhaps not achieving the success he desired, his reputation as an electronic music innovator has more recently been recognised. Samples of his work can be found in contemporary music such as J Dilla's 'Lightworks' (2006).

MELLOTRON *1963*

The Mellotron was an improved Chamberlin and used tape to replay recordings of real instruments such as the violin, cello, voice and more. Its distinctive sound has featured on many pop and rock recordings, for example, the flute introduction to The Beatles' 'Lucy in the Sky With Diamonds' (1967).

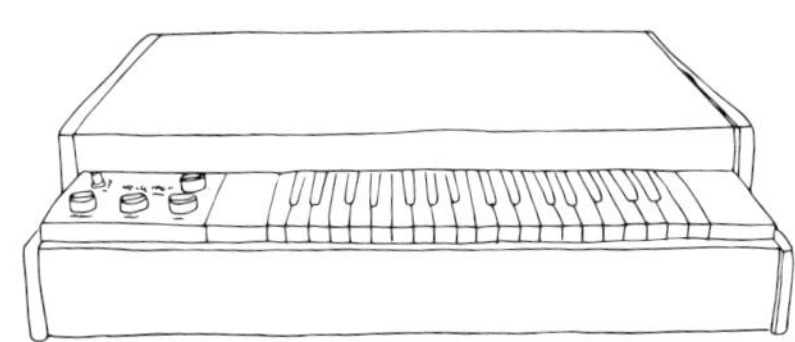

WURLITZER SIDEMAN *1959*

The Wurlitzer Sideman is one of the earliest rhythm machines to generate drum tones and patterns in real time. Its sounds were generated by vacuum-tubes and they were triggered by use of brush-contracts on rotating disks. It didn't impress Ikutaro Kakehashi of Ace Tone (later Roland) and Tadashi Osanai of Korg, who were moved to invent their own superior drum-machines, and led the industry forward with their innovations in doing so.

BIROTRON *1976*

The Birotron was invented by Dave Biro and was a Mellotron-type machine that was to have used 8-track tape cartridges to replay the recorded sounds. Despite being funded by Rick Wakeman and other companies, very few were ever made and the company soon folded. Sampling technology then quickly surpassed any tape-based instrument in terms of sound quality, convenience and cost.

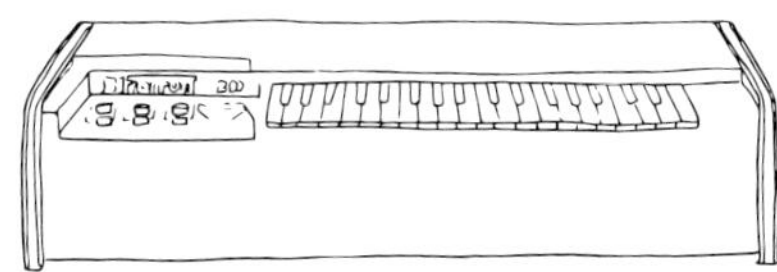

ACKNOWLEDGEMENTS

The biggest acknowledgement must go to the thousands of electronics engineers, the visionaries, the innovators and people with the ability to forge new musical instruments from the fundamental principles of electricity and the material that conducts (or semi-conducts) it. The ability to connect this technical know-how with the needs of musicians who are always on the lookout for new ways to express themselves never ceases to amaze me. Without them, and the support network of marketing departments, distributors, music shops, and more, this would be a very empty book!

This project was initiated by my love of synthesizers and electronic sound, and the desire to tell that story in an illustrative manner to shed new light on some familiar stories and to unearth some unfamiliar ones. The source material has included my experience over the last 25 years in the music industry and working with many of these machines, all the while reading widely on the subject matter, from the originating 'Keyfax' series of Julian Colbeck, 'Vintage Synths' by Mark Vail, 'Analog Days' by Pinch and Trocco, 'A-Z of Synthesisers' by Peter Forrest, and my collections of Sound On Sound, Electronic Sound, Music Technology (now deceased) and many other books and publications.

Online resources are the mainstay of the synth fan, and we are spoilt for choice with comprehensive directories such as Wikipedia, vintagesynth.com, encyclotronic.com, synthmuseum.com, synthark.org, retrosynthads.com and 120years.net being notable. Not to mention the scrupulously maintained blogs such as matrixsynth.com and synthtopia.com, both of whom have kindly helped publicise my previous poster work.

Special thanks to Paul Gilby and Hugh Robjohns at Sound On Sound for their support and to Hugh for his technical notes on the functionality of VCOs. There is now nothing I don't know about astable multivibrators and relaxation oscillators :-) Thanks to Mark Roland at Electronic Sound and vintage synth guru Benge (Expanding Records) for their support of this project. Thanks must also go to my small army of proofreaders – David Freke, Tom Freke, Pat van Kann, and Alice Whitton. Of course, any persisting errors are of my own doing. The patience of my wife, Meg, must also be acknowledged, not just of the time I've spent writing and illustrating, but also the sharing of her life with a certified synth nerd. I know it's tough.

Wikipedia creative commons credits (illustrations adapted from the following photographs): EMS Synthi 100 (Kimi95) and E-mu Modular (Jean Pierre Dalbéra). https://creativecommons.org/licenses/by/4.0/legalcode

synthsounds.net - click a synth and hear its sound!
I believe every synthesizer is unique. Even though they may share commonalities, the unique combination of elements in any particular model make them as different as people.

To demonstrate this, and to enable quick sonic comparisons to be made, I've set up synthsounds.net in order to collect examples of the sounds of every synth ever made. It's a crowd-sourced resource, fully credited. If you have a synth and there isn't a sonic example on the site - get in touch.

synthevolution.net
Please visit the website for posters, mugs and more, all featuring illustrations from the book.

"We have also sound-houses, where we practise and demonstrate all sounds and their generation. We have harmonies which you have not, of quarter-sounds, and lesser slides of sounds; divers instruments of musick likewise to you unknown, some sweeter than any you have, with bells and rings that are dainty and sweet. We represent small sounds as great and deep, likewise great sounds extenuate and sharp. We make divers tremblings and warblings of sounds, which in their original are entire. We represent and imitate all articulate sounds and letters, and the voices and notes of beasts and birds. We have certain helps, which set to the ear, do further the hearing greatly. We have also divers strange and artificial echos reflecting the voice many times, and as it were tossing it, and some that give back the voice louder than it came, some shriller, and some deeper, yea, some rendring the voice differing in the letters or articulate sound from that they receive. We have all means to convey sounds in trunks and pipes in strange lines and distances."

Roger Bacon, 'New Atlantis', 1626

SPECIAL THANKS TO EVERYONE WHO BOUGHT THE BOOK ON PRE-SALE

Guillaume Adam, Robert Adshead, Tom Andersson, Tristan Andreas, Michael Andrews, Borkur Arnarson, Mitch Bacigalupi, Jack Baggott, Chris Barlow, Erik Banhalmi, Robert Bartley, Karl Bernard, Jeremy Bernstein, Michael Beverland, Paul Binning, Frederik Birket-Smith, Kim Bjørn, Michael Bland, Carl Blundell, Vincent Borcard, Urcun Bolkan, Dean Bowley, Duncan Bradshaw, Christopher Brand, Philippe Brodu, Andy Brown, Zach Brown, Alessandro Brunori, Todd Burns, Nigel Butters, Kelly Byrne, Lowell Reagan Call, James Cannings, Andrew Capella, Gianni Cardia, Sergio Cardoso, Enrico Carrer, Francois Cartagenova, Simon Carter, Neal Chant, Owen Charrington, Timothy Child, Simon Chisholm, Sam Chittenden, Paul Chivers, Panagiotis Christelis, Morten Christophersen, Tom Chroscicki-Lee, Pohsun Chung, Falguni Clarkson, Peter Clotworthy, Alexander Coe, Niall Colverd, James Coplin, Pascal Costanza, Paul Cotton, Cedric Coudyser, Matt Cowan, Matthew Craven, Billie Croucher, Craig Czyz, Joe D'Agostino, Li Daniel, Åke Danielsson, Paul Darling, Martin Daubenmerkl, Alan Davis, David Dean, Brian Deitch, Matthew Demanett, Marcin De Rycker, Lilian D'Hondt, Jeremy Dickens, Gerasimos Dionatos, Michael Doherty, Mark Donaghy, Robert Donatiello, Jason Durbin, Mikael Dürrmeier, Daniel Elder, Seth Elgart, Daniel Elton, Krisztina Eory, Michael Feiner, Adam Femia, Luiz Carlos Poppi Ribas Ferreira, Robert Fincher, G Finnegan, Peter Fitzpatrick, Christopher Flett, Stewart Flood, Kevin Ford, Tim Forrester, Robin Fox, David Frangioni, David Freke, Benjamin Gallen, Antoine Gautier, Georgiou Gennimata, Alan H Genzel, Jeremy Gibbard, Mario Glavacic, Mark Gonzales, Ale González, Paul Gorman, Alejandro Sande Guiance, Stephen Hampshire, Philipp Harms, Matthias Gros, Joel Handley, Ky Harcombe, Lasse Harju, Volker Hartmann-Langenfelder, David Havard, Tommy Hazelwood, Christopher Hegstrom, Ulrich Höhne, Matt Horobin, Jonathan Horsfield, William Howard, Chien-Yu Huang, Lucien Hubert, Joel Vila Humet, Michael L Hunter, Ergin Hussein, Carmen Iannacone, Artem Ivanov, Travis A. Jackson, Callum James, Mark Jones, Jennifer Kaefer, Peter Kaminski, Ajai Khattri, Nathan Kellstadt, Jody Kirkpatrick, David Kun, Sandor Lakatos, Brad Lakomy, Michael Lancaster, John Lawter, Alexandre Le Corre, Rosendo Leon, Gabriel Lindeborg, Danielle Lumanta, Xiaoxiao Ma, Robert MacKenzie, Bruce Mackintosh, Sasja Maekelberg, Stephan Alexander Maldener, Dario Mambro, Zahir Manek, Howard Mangrum, Josh Marcy, Florian Markovits-Grella, Matthew Marteinsson, Trevor Martin, David McChesney, Elizabeth McClain, Keelan McMorrow, John McMullan, Andrew Mee, Thomas Meier, Benoit Mercusot, Nuutti-Iivari Merihukka, Robert Merlak, Kris Mets, Andrew Miles, Heather Milligan, Alejandro Monroy, Francesco Mulassano, Peter Nagy, Graeme Neilson, Thomas Nevarez, Rebecca Nolan, Richard Norris, Andrew Oji, Alasdair O'May, Riley O'Keeffe, Greg Okopal, Daen Olson, Mark Orphan, Ole Øverli, Charles Palluau, Matthew Parsons, Marie Patin, Joel Pearson, Rhys Pendred, Christophe Péreuil, Mark Perry, Christopher Petro, Jamila Pierce, Geoff Pinckney, John Place, Jacob Plant, Christophe Polese, Kevin Porter, Ganesh Raj, Paul Reant, Gareth Richards, Jesse Rozof, Mark Ryan, Marcus Sachs, Lars Sandren, Grünig Sandro, Sander Scheerman, Tyler Schoening, Darren Scothern, Byron Scullin, Caroline Selkirk, Matej Šetinc, Tom Shand, Neil Sharkey, Tom Sheader, Jeremy Shervell, Dmitry Shlykov, Andrew Short, Jon Shute, Dylan Singletary, Nikolas Sinkola, Pablo Smet, Stephen Smith, Rick Stoddart, Louis Strydom, Leigh Strydom, Philip Stuart, Jonas Suraninas, Calum Teeson, Stefan Telegdy, Jon Tempest, P-H Texier, Travis Thatcher, Christian Thibault, Dale Thurbon, Michael Tinsley, Filip Tomasetig, Antonio Tomc, Domenico Torti, Charles Trevelyan, Richard Turner, Cory Tyburski, Ty Unwin, Patrick van Kann, Violetta Vaski, Dennis Verhaeg, Alain Viens, Tim Vine, Marjan Vitorijoski, David Waller, Andrew Ward, Paul Watkins, Mathew Watson, Robert Watt, Richard Weeks, Sebastian Weingartshofer, Wes, Joshua Wexler, Michael White, Paul Williams, Rob Williams, Robert Williams, Chris Willis, Timothy Winson, Ian Wood, Tianze Wu, Gleb Zakhodyakin

ALSO ON VELOCITY PRESS

JOIN THE FUTURE: BLEEP TECHNO & THE BIRTH OF BRITISH BASS MUSIC
MATT ANNISS
A mixture of social, cultural, musical and oral history, *Join The Future* reveals the untold stories of bleep's Yorkshire pioneers and those that came in their wake, moving from electro all-dayers and dub soundsystem clashes of the mid-1980s to the birth of hardcore and jungle in London and the South East.

STATE OF BASS: THE ORIGINS OF JUNGLE/DRUM & BASS
MARTIN JAMES
Originally published in 1997, *State of Bass: The Origins of Jungle/Drum & Bass* extends the original text to include the award of the Mercury Prize to Reprazent and brings new perspectives to the story of the UK's most crucial subterranean scene.

FLYER & COVER ART
JUNIOR TOMLIN
Showcasing the mastermind behind some of the most iconic rave flyers and record covers of the late eighties and early nineties, *Flyer & Cover Art* is a comprehensive insight into Junior Tomlin's incredible back catalogue.

BEDROOM BEATS & B-SIDES: INSTRUMENTAL HIP HOP & ELECTRONIC MUSIC AT THE TURN OF THE CENTURY
LAURENT FINTONI
Bedroom Beats & B-sides is the first comprehensive history of the instrumental hip-hop and electronic scenes and a truly global look at a thirty-year period of modern music culture based on a decade of research and travel across Europe, North America, and Japan.

THE SECRET DJ: BOOK TWO
THE SECRET DJ
The Secret DJ returns with the follow-up to their acclaimed debut book. Less a sequel and more a panoramic wide-angle painting of the biggest youth movement in human history, *The Secret DJ: Book Two* charts the rise of dance music over the last 30 years and its connection to western capitalism and culture.

WHO SAY RELOAD: THE STORIES BEHIND THE CLASSIC DRUM & BASS RECORDS OF THE 90S
PAUL TERZULLI & EDDIE OTCHERE
Who Say Reload is a knockout oral history of the records that defined jungle/drum & bass straight from the original sources. The likes of Goldie, DJ Hype, Roni Size, Andy C, 4 Hero and many more talk about the influences, environment, equipment, samples, beats and surprises that went into making each classic record.

LONG RELATIONSHIPS: MY INCREDIBLE JOURNEY FROM UNKNOWN DJ TO SMALL-TIME DJ
HAROLD HEATH
Long Relationships is a love letter to DJing and to every small-town DJ who never made it to the big time but whose life was enriched and improved by DJing anyway. It's packed with tales of gigs, clubs, raves, warehouses, music, record production and record deals, low-rent international travel, shady promoters, dodgy club security, magical dance floor moments and much more.

VELOCITYPRESS.UK/BOOKS